THE GREAT GAME

Story of the First Oil War

Togrul Bagirov

ISBN: 978-0-9851973-1-5 (paperback)
ISBN: 978-0-9851973-2-2 (ebook)

УДК 82-3
ББК: 84

This work of fiction is based on actual historical events. In most cases incidents, characters and timelines have been changed or fictionalized for dramatic purposes. Certain characters may be composites, or entirely fictitious. Any resemblance to actual living persons is purely coincidental.

Published in 2019 by NBP Publishing.

Printed on acid-free paper.
Library of Congress Cataloging in Publication Data
Bagirov, Togrul
THE GREAT GAME: Story of the First Oil War by Togrul Bagirov
HISTORY: Europe / Scandinavia | HISTORY: Russia & the Former Soviet Union | FICTION: Historical / Thrillers
Library of Congress Control Number: 2019916012

NBP Publishing, Washington D.C.
2019

First Edition

"When everyone is dead, the Great Game is finished. Not before."

- Rudyard Kipling

Editorial Introduction – In Memoriam

This novel by Dr. Togrul Bagirov was going through final editing before publication when the author unexpectedly passed away in 2019, without seeing the results of his work as a printed book.

Well-known and recognized as a connoisseur of the Nobel family's history in Sweden, Azerbaijan, the Caucasus and Russia, Togrul Bagirov was knighted with the distinguished award by Carl XVI Gustaf, the king of Sweden – the Royal Order of the Polar Star and the Medal of the Polar Star. As a United Nations expert on global energy security, professor of energy security studies at the Moscow State Institute of International Relations, sponsor and editor of archival research on oil developments in the 19th and 20th centuries, and the founder of the Baku Nobel Heritage Fund (BNHF), Dr. Togrul Bagirov lived and breathed with the history of BraNobel, Villa Petrolea, and the life of the Nobel brothers in Baku and St. Petersburg. It was his genuine lifelong passion.

In 2007, Togrul Bagirov finished the restoration of the Villa Petrolea in Baku – the original mansion of the Nobel family – which served as both office and residence for the first vertically integrated oil company in the world, BraNobel – and founded the Baku Nobel Heritage Fund, in collaboration with several descendants of the Nobel family: Michael Nobel, the late Philip Nobel, Peter Nobel, and others. This was not an easy task – during the Soviet period, Villa Petrolea was completely dilapidated and nearly destroyed, and had ethnic Azerbaijani refugees living in it due to displacement from the war and ongoing occupation of the Karabakh region of Azerbaijan. Togrul Bagirov, himself a native of the Karabakh region of Azerbaijan, gifted a new home to the refugee family, and then the Villa Petrolea and its surrounding park were restored to its former glory by using archival photos and architectural sketches. Today it houses a museum of Nobel family heritage, event venue and conference hall, and welcomed many dignitaries and heads of state, including Haakon, the Crown Prince of Norway, and ministerial delegations from Sweden.

While sponsoring the publication of several academic books and conferences on the history and heritage of the Nobels, Togrul Bagirov decided to popularize this truly incredible history – where household names of the ultra-rich like Nobels, Rothschilds, and Rockefellers, and the Communist revolutionary leaders like Lenin, Stalin, and Beria, are all taking part in the Great Game over Baku's oil; where the first-ever pipelines and oil tankers appear; where empires are falling, revolutions take place and the first-ever predominantly Muslim parliamentary democracy is born. Instead of a dry, heavy on primary archival sources academic manuscript, Togrul Bagirov decided to write this history in a format of a novel, to popularize it globally. The author certainly had to take some literary liberties, such as compressing the historical timeline, creating some composite and fictional characters, and creating dialogues where archives were silent. It is still very much a historical novel – with emphasis being on "historical." It is not often that a native practitioner of energy security and oil diplomacy writes a fascinating novel allowing us to vividly experience how and where it all started.

We are very sad that Togrul Bagirov could not see his work, but know how delighted he would have been to see the publication of his book. All proceeds from this book and its derivatives would go to further Dr. Bagirov's lifelong passion and legacy—the charitable mission of the Baku Nobel Heritage Fund.

PART ONE

Chapter One

Baku, 1876

Emanuel Nobel had never meant to fall in love. In fact, as their ship oozed through the thick haze of oily black smoke from Baku's oil fields, love was the farthest thing from his mind. His mind was still in Stockholm, his heart also. The idea of drilling for oil had worked its way into his father's mind, and because of that Emanuel had been ripped from his friends and his home. Baku, his father had said, was the land of plenty, a wondrous world with endless potential. At this point, Emanuel was finding it very difficult to share his father's enthusiasm. Squinting through burning eyes, he longed for the green grass and snowy forests of home.

Ludvig stood beside his son, a gentle smile of anticipation lifting his beard as their ship travelled the Caspian Sea, coasting toward the crescent-shaped harbor of Baku. Emanuel did not recall having seen that smile back in Stockholm, where the air was clean and the trees were in full flower. His father's inexplicable happiness was both intriguing and infuriating. Crossing his arms over his chest, he lifted his chin and stubbornly refused to enjoy himself. This had not been his choice. For months he had argued about coming here, but Ludvig had only shaken his head.

"Since I am Grandfather's namesake, I deserve to know the details of his failures in Russia. What makes you think we can be successful here when he could not?"

Back in 1837, Emanuel's grandfather, Immanuel, traveled from Sweden to the promising empire of Russia. He had brought with him his wife, Andriette, and their four young sons, Robert, Ludvig, Alfred and Emil (who died when he was only twenty-one, experimenting with nitroglycerin at his father's laboratory in Stockholm). The boys attended both the St. Petersburg Gymnasium and the University, learning that land's languages and customs as well as mathematics and chemistry. After graduation, they went back to Sweden, but eventually returned to St. Petersburg and worked at Nobel's Machine Factory as well as at the rifle factory in Izhevsk.

Ludvig squinted disapprovingly at him. "Your grandfather did not fail."

Cupping his hands around his eyes, Emanuel surveyed the horizon. "How can that be?" He was aware his tone hovered on the edge of belligerence, but it had been a long voyage. His temper was short. "He was bankrupt! You had to pay for him."

"I may have paid your grandfather's debts," Ludvig said levelly, "but he did not fail. You will learn in time. Your grandfather was a hard-working man. Czar Nicholas I believed wholeheartedly in his work. When Nicholas died, Czar Alexander II was determined to start fresh and make his own decisions." He shrugged. "No one is perfect. The fortunate thing, Emanuel, is that you will be wiser as a result of your grandfather's miscalculations."

"When he came home, he was poor."

One bushy black eyebrow lifted in censure. "He was never poor. Besides, that is not what I am talking about. Success is not always about money. The main thing is the work you put into it." He shook his head, forgiving Emanuel's brash comments. "But you are young. It is impossible for you to understand right now. As you mature, you will begin to understand the pleasure one can gain in the victory of enterprise and perseverance of duty, no matter the size of the bank account. Do you remember when you went to work as an apprentice in that factory two years ago? You were only one year older than I was when my father put me to work."

Emanuel barely refrained from rolling his eyes. "Of course I remember it. I worked like a slave there, every day from six in the morning until midnight."

"And you managed to do it for an entire year. Shall I tell you, son, that I was very impressed by your work ethic? And because of that difficult job, you learned early on about the satisfaction that can be derived from hard work."

Emanuel was about to argue, but the ship was swallowed up by a thicker cloud of smoke, and father and son temporarily lost sight of each other. When they eventually emerged into the sunlight, Emanuel was bent over, coughing, his hands over his face.

"So hot!" he choked, laughing at himself.

Ludvig patted his long grey beard. "Good thing this did not light on fire. Ah, but look," he said, holding his hands toward the harbor "Now *that* is a sight to behold!"

*

Emanuel stepped onto the docks of Baku, dumbfounded by the scene. Despite its oil-covered surface and the skunky odor that monopolized the air, the city was mesmerizing. Even the surface of the water was amazing, since every now and then it flared up, burning with actual fires. The air he breathed was both choked with smoke and alive with magic, filled with exotic spices and garbled conversations, blending Azerbaijani, Russian, Arabic, Persian, Turkish, French, English, German and various exotic dialects into a stew that bubbled over with clashing clothes and customs. And just as the variety of people mixed together without hesitation, so too did the mosques, synagogues, churches, and pagan temples. On Emanuel's right the market hummed; weathered, ancient faces sold equally to both rosy cheeked Russians and Mountain Jews while Azerbaijani and Turkish street peddlers strolled through the crowd. On his left, men were loading and unloading ships, moving food, animals, and clothing he had never seen before.

The chaos was invigorating, and as they passed through the ancient walls of Baku, moving further into the city, he felt the exhaustion—and the frustration—from the journey fall off his shoulders. He stepped quickly alongside his father, careful with his footing. The serpentine cobblestone streets were slick with oil, and the stuff became increasingly thick with every step closer to the oil fields. It seemed a feat of great prowess to be able to walk so simply, but he was determined he would master it eventually.

Once he had gotten past his initial bewilderment and the subsequent rush of excitement, he began to notice something else. Hidden behind the colors, quiet beneath the noise, a separate reality sat hunched in the corners while others begged in the street. Desperate eyes blinked in grimy faces, and on some the desperation had melted into an even darker shade of hopelessness. The suffering here was greater than the commerce.

A distant rumble trembled under their feet, distracting Emanuel. No one else seemed to have noticed the noise. Emanuel glanced at his father, wondering if he could have imagined it.

"Just a geyser," Ludvig informed him.

"And that? What is *that?*"

Three hundred yards away, a tower of flames shot into the sky, untamed.

"The Eternal Fires of Zoroaster. Beautiful, is it not?"

"Is it...man-made?"

"No, no. The Fire Temple has burned for three thousand years, maybe longer. That's why they called this land, Azerbaijan, as the Land of Eternal Fire. Look over there. You can see the temple past Balakhani, which is an oil-rich suburb of Baku."

Intrigued, Emanuel followed his father through the gate. The simple, yet impressive architecture of the altar in the center of the courtyard caught his eye, and they wandered closer to watch the Eternal Fires burning within. The ancient walls were broken up by small cells created for pilgrims and monks, and their stone faces were decorated by timeworn inscriptions in Sanskrit and Gurmukhi.

"This temple," his father explained, "was where many people practiced Zoroastrianism, one of the first religions to worship only one god. The mysteries of their god were represented in what they saw as sacred fires, and people from all over the world came to this land to bow before the flames. They believed the fire purified the soul."

"No wonder they came here," Emanuel said, staring at the flames. "It only makes sense that something this magical would be deemed mystical as well."

His father gestured toward the street, and they walked gingerly along the cobblestones, watching the activity. Ludvig squinted ahead at a heavyset, bearded man lumbering in their direction.

"Robert?" Ludvig said.

The man stared at them, confused, then his arms flew apart. "Ludvig! I am so happy to see you! And who is this?"

"Ah, it has been a long time since you've seen my son, Emanuel," Ludvig replied, stepping back. "Emanuel, this is your Uncle Robert."

Fatigue melted temporarily from the older man's eyes. "Ah, Emanuel! I do not believe I've seen you since you began to walk! Time flies so fast... my best years were spent in this 'land of fire'... So, are you ready to take on a new world here in Baku with me?"

"Yes, sir. I am excited to be here."

"Excellent!" Robert put one arm around each man's shoulder. "Let us go, then. I will introduce you to the people of Baku." He scowled at a laborer who had collided inadvertently with Ludvig then kept going. "The first lesson is to be cautious. They're a crafty bunch, and they often regard foreigners as fools rather than friends. We must not allow them to be right!"

Ludvig chuckled. "That is nothing new, is it? Surely that goes for most of the world."

"Always a contrarian your father, Emanuel. Since we were kids, Ludvig had to express at least some opposition to me."

The brothers were similar, of course, but Robert seemed more animated while mildly resentful of constant encroachments and attempts of domination from his brothers. His eyes were forever moving, scanning the crowds.

In the back of his mind, Emanuel heard the echo of his grandfather's words, passed down by his father when he had been in a nostalgic mood: *Robert is predisposed to adventures. Ludvig is a genius. Alfred is a workaholic.* Robert led them through the crowd and into streets which increasingly blackened both in air quality and on the ground. Despite the grime, Emanuel was already relishing this new city. For him, the colors of the people shone through all the filth.

"There is much for you here, Emanuel," Robert said. "And not all will be foreign to you. A lot is influenced by local aristocrats and Europeans."

An Azerbaijani woman strolled by with a couple of friends, their skirts a rainbow of color. She smiled shyly at Emanuel, observing him through a pair of dazzling green eyes, and he was captivated by her exotic beauty.

"I can hardly wait to learn about the customs here," he replied.

"When the work is done," Ludvig said, noting his son's gaze. "When the work is done. Robert will walk us through our oil claim before we settle in at home. We must always remember that no matter how exciting everything else might appear, the oil claim is why we are here."

Emanuel's jaw clenched. He was tired of being treated like a child. After all, he was seventeen, old enough to experience the world like any other young person, and that included laughing, dating, going to parties. One of these days, he promised himself, he would live life the way he wanted.

"This part of Baku is called Black City," Robert informed them. "Oil is so prevalent that everyone has decided to drill wherever there's space, including in their yards. Some of the houses have become refineries of sorts, and the oil turns everything black."

"So we've noticed."

"You'll need separate clothes that you can wear outside," his uncle continued, "and those have to stay outside of the house. It doesn't matter where you go out here, your clothes—

especially your shoes and trousers—will be soaked in the stuff."

The earth rumbled again, closer this time, shifting Emanuel's mind back to the world around him. He tried to keep his expression neutral, as if the sensation did not send a thrill through him. So much was happening all around, but the real story was beneath their feet.

Robert rubbed his hands together. "You must see this."

He led them to the right, down another street, and Emanuel stopped dead at the sight of his first geyser. A velvet black fountain of oil spewed twenty feet above the top of the derrick, and men scurried at its base.

"That one started yesterday," Robert told them.

Emanuel took another step forward, wanting to be closer, but he scampered back when a sturdy, multi-colored cart rattled into the street towards them. Its panicking horse galloped in an arc, following the path of a lost wheel, and its ridiculously tall load of barrels wobbled precariously. When the horse lurched forward again, the barrels tipped onto the street, soaking onlookers from the ankles down. Ludvig scowled, but Emanuel laughed, delighted by the novelty of the moment.

The tense lines of his father's expression eventually relaxed, but he was not amused. "Soon we'll harness our own geyser. Then your energy will be put to better use."

Chapter Two

Their tour led to one derrick in particular. It bore a plain wooden sign marked, "NOBEL". With a sense of awe, Emanuel followed his father and uncle inside, and two laborers stepped back to make room. The door clanged shut, plunging them into a dark, noisy room, completely shut off from the sunshine. The air was so thick he could hardly breathe, and he fought the instinct to escape. Gears screeched continuously, and Emanuel clamped his hands to his ears while he waited for his eyes to adjust. He could not work in this place. He would go deaf.

Beside him, Ludvig was looking disgusted. He stormed over to one of the eight-foot pump wheels and pointed an accusatory finger at the machine. "What kind of fools built this monstrosity?"

"They have used it for the last decade," said his brother.

"It is not good enough! Just look at these jerry-rigged gears. The couplings are designed so badly the rods barely fit, and the belts keep losing their grip. How are the wheels supposed to move if nothing is working the right way?"

"It works," Robert insisted.

"Not well enough. This is ridiculous! Might as well go back to hand digging at this rate. The entire process needs to be redesigned. Let me see about the drill. The bit assembly must..." Ludvig's voice was muffled as he bent over the drill, examining the process. Eventually he straightened and threw his hands in the air. "This is a disgrace to engineering!"

Before anyone could respond, he strode out of the derrick. Emanuel and Robert meekly followed him to the oil well pits, where Ludvig frowned down at the open pools, hands on his hips. Emanuel saw right away what was infuriating his father. As they were now, the pits were accessible by anyone—in fact, he watched a couple of local men scoop up buckets of oil then wander off.

"Unbelievable," Ludvig muttered. At the next drill site, he stretched out one arm in a wide gesture, indicating the field. "Look at this, Robert. You are losing at least twenty percent of your oil here. Since it is not being claimed, it is seeping back into the earth. No other industry on earth is this wasteful." He stooped, picking up a twisted piece of metal. "Look at this. A broken drill bit made from cheap metal." He shook his head, eyes closed. "Take me to the distilling process."

Robert glanced uneasily at Emanuel. Clearly, this was not going to be any better.

The refinery warehouse was a long, crumbling building. Its smokestacks belched thick, continuous columns of black smoke. Inside the building, the oil-smeared workers coughed incessantly.

Robert led Ludvig to a huge metal cooking bowl. "They distill the oil in here, dividing it into black and white. The white is kerosene. After they drain it off, they distill it again."

The fumes were making Emanuel's head swim. How did these men work in here every day? It couldn't possibly be good for their health.

"This operation is so basic!" Ludvig ranted. "I cannot believe it! Hasn't anyone figured out that the refinery machinery and process need to evolve?"

He blustered past them and they burst into the relatively clean air outside, but Emanuel's ears continued to ring.

"The good news," Ludvig declared, "is that this is a huge opportunity for us. Robert, I assume you have drawing papers in your office? Good. I need to draft my plans while they are still fresh in my mind."

Once they reached the office, Ludvig waved them away. "Just leave me here for a couple of hours. I need to concentrate on this by myself. I am sure you can entertain my son in the meantime. Show him the house."

"I can stay, Father."

"Nonsense. Go."

Over the next week, Ludvig buried himself in drawings, and his rough sketches evolved into detailed plans. In the meantime, Emanuel acclimatized himself to the area, buying clothes and food for his father and himself, returning occasionally to offer his help.

The modest two-story house they shared with Robert became an oasis from the noise and dirt. When they changed out of their work clothing at the end of the day, washed, then put on their inside clothes, it was as if they were shedding a grimy second skin. Every evening the three men were met at the door by a servant who relieved them of their coats, and their Azerbaijani cook served them savory, aromatic meals. They marveled at the man's ability to find so many ways to grill fish, lamb, and veal, which was often accompanied by *dogha* soup made from plain yogurt, cucumbers, and spring onions.

Their days were full, but though they were tired, Ludvig insisted they establish a ritual of sorts after the meal, similar to what they had done in Stockholm. The three retired together to the sitting room and made themselves comfortable around the unlit fireplace, where they waited to be served tea. Business was usually the main topic of discussion in the evening, but the mood was more relaxed. The quiet evening conversations helped the men smooth out any ruffled feathers and come to whatever compromises were needed, which was fairly often since Robert was usually uneasy. He was uncomfortable with how the company was being run, and how money seemed to burn as easily as oil. Emanuel fell asleep as soon as his head hit the pillow, but his father stayed awake for hours, envisioning the changes he wanted to incorporate.

As much as Robert liked to argue, Ludvig demanded action. He was impatient for his plans to be put into place. The catalyst happened one morning as a team of workers struggled to drag a broken pump motor from the oily mess of one of the derricks.

"How can this be the way we work?" Ludvig asked, exasperation creasing his brow. "Oil should not be spraying all over the derrick like that. We need to disassemble the apparatus entirely, then replace it stage by stage."

Robert eyed the pit, dubious. "You are talking about an incredible amount of work."

"Of course I am! Think of it this way: if we incorporate a few inventive changes we will dominate the competition. The only wise decision is to push forward. Robert, you are best with the larger moving parts. See what you can do to improve upon the mounts." He turned to his son. "Emanuel, you understand my drawings. Let us put these thoughts into action. But for now, get in there. Get dirty."

That was exactly what Emanuel wanted to do: put his hands in the mess, not just on drawings. As he climbed down toward the pit he heard his father trying to convince his uncle of what must happen next.

"We cannot progress any further until the waste in the drilling, storage, and transportation is corrected."

"Ludvig! It is too much!"

"No, my dear brother. This is just the beginning."

After the broken pump motor and drill were removed, machinists gathered around Ludvig's plans, nodded with comprehension, and made calculations of their own. The finished product fitted exactly into place as it was lowered into the pit. The oil-soaked workers grumbled in a mixture of languages, placing hypothetical bets on how quickly this new machine would fail. The three Nobels and the machinists stood by as well, watching in tense silence, bracing for the inevitable explosion of noise and the rivers of leaking oil. But the engine started up without hesitation, began to purr quietly to itself, and no oil leaked from the well. Ludvig waved the stunned laborers back to work, and they gladly returned. Their jobs had just become a whole lot better.

So began Ludvig's plan to change everything the world had ever known about drilling for oil. Only weeks later, his mind was on the next innovation. Despite his success, Robert was unconvinced. Ludvig was costing them a fortune.

"We cannot keep doing business this way. Spending all we have so we can create a new distilling process is reckless."

"I disagree."

"Of course you do. But look around you. How can we get anything done now that we are taking everything apart? It makes no sense. We are going backward."

Ludvig shook his head. "You are not thinking big enough. Open your mind, Robert. Pumping enough oil will not ever be the problem. Now that we've fixed the drill we are no longer wasting oil. The challenge now is to store it efficiently then ship it." He squinted slightly. "What we need is a pipeline to the port. That will speed up profits."

Robert stopped in his tracks. "A pipeline? This is madness. We have not even proven we have a steady oil flow."

"Madness is using centuries-old methods when we live in the age of modern machinery. Look over there." He pointed toward a camel caravan loping through the field. "Would you rather we be like them? Ladling oil into goat skins?"

"At least that would be less reckless!"

"Just think about the possibilities. A pipeline would be—"

Robert held up his hands. "You do not have to convince me of that. Of *course* it would be ideal. But it is not just about the money. You do not know these people and their customs. I can tell you the clansmen will never allow a pipeline to be built across their land. And you do not want these men rising up against you. Trust me, they can be very dangerous."

Ludvig chuckled. "They did not want a train either, and yet there it is! What about the telegraph and electricity? Times have changed; everything is welcome now. Even the most stubborn people will adapt if we can prove their lives will improve along with our business."

"You are dreaming," Robert grumbled.

"We shall see." He put a sturdy hand on Emanuel's shoulder. "Your uncle raises an excellent point. We need to understand these people better. You will begin research today."

This kind of research required no diagrams or pencils but a lot of walking and listening. Emanuel welcomed the challenge. Instead of concentrating on technical requirements, Emanuel was obliged to open his mind and ears. He engaged the people of Baku in conversation, encouraging them to talk about themselves. In his experience, no one could resist doing that. With practice, Emanuel became adept at rolling up his pant legs and walking as smoothly as the locals, then wandering closer to their conversations. He walked past oil derricks, stopping on the way to listen in on heated discussions among the workers, diggers, camel caravan owners, oil barrel owners, and even *arba* cart drivers. Despite the rich and occasionally unintelligible mix of languages, Emanuel could tell the men were generally unhappy with their jobs. The worst treatment seemed to land on Azeris and Iranians; their discussions always returned to the filthy and unpleasant work conditions. They lived in squalid camps with no toilets, baths, or soap; if they decided to marry, they were usually put out of a job. The few who were married and managed to keep their positions were not allowed to live with their wives at the camp. Some men were paid on average fifty cents a day for twelve- to fourteen-hour days, and they still had to provide meals for their families.

Emanuel returned to the office, satisfied he had the answers his father required. Ludvig barely glanced up as his son wiped off his hands then stood over the drawings, studying them.

"You've had a week," Ludvig said, eyes still on his work. "From what you've learned, where would you suggest we place the pumping stations?"

Emanuel's gaze touched on the now-familiar places. "The high ground mark is here. The next one goes here."

Ludvig placed a pin where his son had indicated. He leaned back in his chair and steepled his fingers, watching Emanuel. "Tell me. What else have you learned?"

"They are talking about your drill. About the new machines. The workers are curious, but most do not believe anything will change. The other owners are envious."

"I did not ask about the other owners."

"No, but I could not help but learn about them when I was meeting people. You should know they are watching. Very closely."

"Of course they are. What else?"

"I am concerned about the distillers. They are not healthy."

"The air is terrible in there. No ventilation, and the process badly needs cleaning up. I have plans for our distillery, and that should alleviate the problem."

Encouraged, Emanuel made a bold suggestion. "Down the line we might want to consider helping with their ailments. Some kind of medical clinic or something. If we are seen to be magnanimous employers, that can only help us."

Ludvig regarded him with interest. "You are seeing something entirely new, son. I like the direction you are taking. Thank you. What else can you tell me from your research?"

"The workers do not like Uncle Robert."

Both men jumped as the door was flung open. Right on cue, Robert stormed into the office.

"Ungrateful muckrakers!" he roared. Robert shook a finger at his brother. "Do not frown at me. I am not overreacting. Just wait until you have to deal with these brutes yourself. The first warning you get is when the workers rebel. The next thing you know your derrick is on fire!"

"I cannot understand why they might feel that way," Ludvig said quietly to Emanuel.

"What way? What are you talking about?" Robert demanded.

"Nothing. Nothing at all. Do not worry," Ludvig replied. "All that nonsense will change when we hit our geyser. With the new machines we'll be able to undercut the competition, and we'll become the workers' best friends."

Robert was not mollified by the promise. "I will believe it when I see it. In the meantime, allow me to be furious at these selfish oafs."

"If that is what you wish, though it will not help your day to stew over it. How about, since you are here, we design a few of these things together? That might help your mood."

Robert scowled then settled at the table. The brothers worked in relative silence while Robert cooled down. His rage at the workers morphed into familiar complaints about Ludvig's constant spending.

"It will be worth it," Ludvig kept saying. "You know I am right."

"I do not. What I know is that I am not making any money right now, and talking with you is like talking to a very expensive wall." He set his hands flat on the desk. "If we are going to continue this expansion, let us ask Alfred for his advice first."

Their brother Alfred, who was in Paris at the time, suggested they form a limited company to help bring in capital. Robert was not convinced, and even went so far as to suggest his brothers were trying to outmaneuver him. Eventually he agreed under duress, and the new company was named Nobel Brothers Oil Production Company, which was shortened to *Brat'yev* Nobel—Russian for 'Brothers Nobel'— then abbreviated to BraNobel. Shares were divided between them as well as between a few other investors, and Ludvig became the largest shareholder.

Chapter Three

Now that Ludvig had reinvented the machinery needed to retrieve the oil, the focus shifted to better moving the product to consumers. Every spare minute was devoted to creating plans for the new pipeline, and dozens of mechanical drawings were spread over the desks. Expanded copies, with details magnified by Emanuel's steady hand, took up an entire wall.

"If my calculations are correct," Ludvig said, handing his son a stack of papers, "we need to raise this amount of capital."

Emanuel flipped through, looking for the bottom line. After a moment he realized he was, in fact, seeing the actual figures. He turned back to the beginning, reading very slowly.

"Uncle Robert is right. This is too much."

"It can be funded privately or through the Russian government."

"But Father ..." He frowned at the paper, incredulous. "You really think you'll be able to raise this kind of money?"

"One never knows. Sometimes it is the most audacious plans which get approved while the meager ones, those with reasonable goals, are passed over. Tell me, if you were an investor, which would you prefer to wager on? Magnificence or mediocrity?"

Emanuel refused to be so easily swayed. "Why should the Czar support us? We are not even from here. We are Swedes, not Russians."

"That does not matter. A few years ago, the Czarist government adopted a resolution encouraging foreign investment in the oil industry. We are exactly what they need.

Everything will be explained at the conference. We have done an excellent job of making our plan irresistible."

He certainly hoped so. Emanuel had no idea what to expect at the Imperial Russian Technical Society conference, but they had been working toward it for the past few weeks. In the morning they would be en route to St. Petersburg, where his father would be speaking.

"Roll those up," Ludvig said, indicating the plans on the wall. "And store each of them in their own separate tube. They must be kept safe. They are irreplaceable."

*

Emanuel and Ludvig leaned back in the comfort of their black and gold landau, drawn by a pair of shining chestnut horses. Their driver sat tall and quiet, his back to the Nobels, and the groom rode along behind. Because of the welcoming sun, the roof of the carriage had been folded down, giving them a view of the elegant yet busy streets of St. Petersburg. The grand imperial buildings stretched for entire city blocks, their marble construction ornamented by stunning façades, boldly declaring to the world that this was a city to be admired.

Eventually the carriage reached the building where the Imperial Russian Technical Society was holding its conference, and Emanuel watched dozens of men make their way inside. The hall itself was like an ornate theatre, filled to capacity with men in suits, their discussions a cloud of French, Swedish, German, Italian, and a great deal of Russian. As Emanuel followed Ludvig toward the stage, a heavily bearded man stood, blocking Emanuel's path. He wore the traditional costume of an Azerbaijan Muslim and a broad, welcoming grin.

"Hello! My name is Zeynalabdin Taghiyev," the man said, holding out a hand. "I have been looking forward to meeting you. You are the gentlemen from Sweden, yes?"

Emanuel had certainly not expected to be recognized. "Yes. Emanuel Nobel. My father is Ludvig."

"You and your father have the derrick with the new engine, am I right?"

"Yes, but we have yet to strike oil."

"It will come. I have been waiting a very long time, but I know it will come."

Zeynalabdin Taghiyev's eyes shone with good sense, but what interested Emanuel even more was his demeanor. A lot of the men he'd met recently reflected Ludvig's serious nature. Taghiyev did not appear to have that sort of sober restraint. Even the slightest smile lifted his cheeks so the same intelligent eyes formed dancing half-moons.

"I believe there is still a half hour before your father's presentation. Let us get to know one another a little."

Emanuel glanced up at his father, who nodded. Ludvig would let him know when his assistance was needed.

"Tell me," Taghiyev said. "How did you end up in the Land of Eternal Fire?"

"Well, it is rather an interesting story. It started with my father and my Uncle Alfred, who are gifted designers and engineers. My father ran a weapons factory, and one day he sent my other uncle, Robert, to Baku. Robert was tasked with buying walnut wood for the factory, but he soon found out there was not enough here for mass weapons production. Nevertheless, my uncle is a chemist with incredible strategic vision, so he understood the petroleum business. He decided to invest the money in our first oil wells. And now my father has brought me here to build an oil company."

"They sound like brilliant men."

"Ah yes. I believe you—and everyone here—will be impressed with my father today. I am fortunate to have so much genius in my family. My Uncle Alfred and I are very close. He is painfully humble despite all he has accomplished, and I have learned a great deal from him. My Uncle Robert is, like I said, a visionary. But the determined one is my father. If anyone can succeed in this new business, it will be him."

"I am looking forward to hearing his presentation. As is my friend, Musa Naghiyev. Let me introduce you to him. Like us, he is in oil in Baku."

Musa was a little shorter than Emanuel and about ten years older, with a similar beard to Zeynalabdin Taghiyev. He peered up at Emanuel through a pair of round spectacles.

"I have heard your name many times, Mr Naghiyev. It is an honor to make your acquaintance."

"And yours," Musa acknowledged. "I look forward to speaking with you after your presentation."

"It would be my pleasure."

At his signal, Emanuel joined his father on stage and helped arrange the presentation. The enormous drawings were affixed to the boards, and a few of the more curious men sidled close to the stage to examine them before the lecture began. When everything had been set up as they wanted, father and son assumed their seats on the side of the stage, waiting for the event's official opening. Emanuel concentrated on holding his hands still, unsure if the shakiness stemmed from being nervous or exhilarated. After all, he was sitting in front of some of the world's greatest thinkers, including his father.

To keep them both occupied, Ludvig quietly described the hall to his son. Specific seats along the main floor, he explained, had been reserved for men of importance. The majority of the attendees would use the theater style seats toward the back of the room. Some in the crowd had arrived too late to claim a chair, and those men stood along the back walls, talking with others.

"Balcony seats are only for the wealthy and most important men. Look over there," Ludvig said, gesturing with his chin toward a decorated balcony box. "That is for the Czar. See? His entourage is already there."

Long, rich green coats hung majestically over his attendants' red waistcoats, all of which were adorned with ornate gold brocade. They were like peacocks among crows.

His father nudged him. "See that man there? That is Dmitri Mendeleev, a good friend of mine. Do you know who he is? That man created the Periodic Table in chemistry."

Emanuel tried very hard not to stare. "He did? Really? That is amazing!"

"He also created the Russian standards for making vodka."

"Ah. A well-rounded man."

Ludvig chuckled. "His thinking is more rational than political; we respect each other's minds. I believe he might be our most likely ally. While I am speaking, I need you to pay attention to his facial expressions."

Emanuel scanned the crowd. "Who is that, do you know? On the right, you see? Waving his hands about something." The black-haired gentleman in question had long, thick sideburns and an intense manner. He spoke in what Emanuel roughly identified as a Scottish accent.

"Ah. That man is very interesting. He is more of a mechanical engineer, I would say, and yet his goals are entirely humanist—"

The man in question barked out some kind of rebuke, apparently disagreeing with something that had been said amongst his peers.

Ludvig chuckled. "And he is a teacher as well, though it does not appear he has a great deal of patience! His name is Alexander Bell. He works with the deaf, even opened a school for the deaf in Boston. I think I heard he moved to Canada recently. Beside him is the promising young American, Thomas Edison. He has done interesting work with improving the telegraph."

His father continued to point out inventors, scientists, and engineers, running the gamut from electrical to mechanical and chemical.

"Look there." He indicated one dour looking, older man standing off to the side. "Louis Pasteur. A chemist. He won the Alhumbert Prize in 1862 for disproving the theory of spontaneous generation." He smiled at Emanuel's blank expression. "He illustrated that microscopic beings need an external influence in order to be produced. They cannot be produced spontaneously. He is also very involved in the science of vaccinations. Quite an interesting field; however, I admit I understand very little of it."

The volume in the room fell, and the crowd parted to make way for Czar Alexander II, wearing a deep, commanding navy and red suit topped with gold epaulettes and brocade. He passed through the outer atrium on his way to the balcony stairs then stepped into the balcony box, greeting his entourage.

"There is much to be learned here today, and most has little to do with science," Ludvig continued, keeping his voice low. "You are perceptive about what drives men, as you have shown with your excellent research around the oil fields. Now I need you to use the better part of your brain to see through the selfish interests and political favoritism which is rife among the men assembled here." His eyes were hard with the sentiment, though that was the only aspect of his expression to change. "A while back you asked about your grandfather. I will tell you right now that your grandfather learned this concept too late. In Russia, the greatest idea of mankind might be refused as the most dimwitted are embraced. It all has to do with politics and ego."

A sharp knock cut through the noise as the Chief Counsel cracked his gavel against the table. He was a stern looking man with short black hair and a thick mustache, wearing a plain but expensive black suit. At the sound, conversations faded away.

"Gentlemen! Please be seated for today's presentation." When they were seated, he spoke again. "It is my great honor to welcome you. Today Mr Ludvig Nobel, having been granted permission by the offices of the State, will present evidence to support oil interests and investments. The diagrams and proposals which will be shared with you today are unique." His brow creased with warning. "They are secrets being revealed to the public for the first time. They should remain so to honor the integrity of this institution."

He scanned the crowd as if to verify all in attendance had been paying attention, then he nodded toward Ludvig. "Mr Nobel?"

"Thank you." His father appeared confident, impatient to speak. "And good day, gentlemen. Welcome to our presentation, entitled, 'Views on the Baku Naphtha Industry and its Future.' I open this presentation with a bold, yet realistic statement." His gaze went to the balcony box from which the Czar and his people were watching. "Russia sits poised to control the world through its growing quest for fuel." He looked back at the men sitting on the main floor. "Oil is the last great resource. It can change the future of a country, which means it can change the future of Russia. In fact, oil can change the future of every man in this room, from citizen to Czar."

He looked speculatively at the drawing, allowing for a dramatic pause. "But to do this," he said slowly, "every aspect of oil production must be improved. By becoming the innovator, the hub of invention, and the model of efficiency, Russia will not only dominate oil production and delivery, it will ultimately win the war which will inevitably be fought over that same oil."

The audience appeared confused for the first time since he'd begun to speak.

Ludvig nodded. "Yes, there will be wars fought over oil, and these wars will make the Spice Wars look ridiculous. The Spice Wars were fought over taste. The oil wars will be fought in a bid for supreme power, independence, and wealth unimaginable."

He held everyone in the palms of his hands, including Emanuel, though he had heard this lecture so many times. With every point, Taghiyev gave a little grunt of approval or acknowledgement, despite the disparaging glances he was getting from men nearby.

"We appreciate and respect our international rivals as much as we need them to propel us to greater economic fortunes," Ludvig continued. "However, it is not an exaggeration for me to say that if Russia were to control the world market for oil via a grand plan, those nations which hound us would be ..." He held out his hands. "Toothless."

His words, actions, and facial expressions—all were perfectly said and beautifully timed. Emanuel laughed along with everyone else. Even the Czar nodded his approval.

"As the innovator and perfectionist in oil, Russia and Russian life will change immediately. Every winter we suffer with the terribly high costs of kerosene and heating. This can be solved through new storage methods, new modes of transport, and improved refining. Through innovations, we will be so far ahead that it will take years before other nations follow suit."

He held up one finger. "And when that happens, they will only do so after buying our Russian patents. Our company will offer the first vertical integration of the 'upstream' and 'downstream' operations. This includes drilling, exploration and development, refining, delivery, and selling of oil. Achieve this, and we as investors will dominate a market that includes Russia, Germany, the Far East, England, France, and beyond. Every nation in the world will become a customer—or rather, *our* customer."

One could have heard a pin drop. Ludvig stood perfectly still, certainty and determination rising from every pore. "And yet," he said, his expression hardening slightly, "the quest for dominance in the future of oil requires more than inventions. The state must focus on countless diplomatic and military concerns. With an abolition of taxes on oil and oil products, privatization will put the financial risks entirely on investors. This allows for unbridled investment without burdening the government."

Prepared for this cue, Emanuel was already on the stage, unveiling maps of the area ranging from Baku to St. Petersburg. As they were being revealed, Emanuel was distracted by movement going on in the back of the room. A man was shuffling from one vantage point to another, pacing erratically in the wings. After a moment, the same man slid out the exit door to the foyer then reappeared upstairs. He handed someone a note, then left the booth and disappeared. Emanuel was frustrated, but he could do nothing to satisfy his curiosity. His place was here, on the stage.

"I shall begin with my analysis of the current methods for extracting the oil," Ludvig was saying.

Emanuel moved to his assigned spot to help with the demonstration. The diagrams were detailed and technical, and listeners hung on every one of Ludvig's words.

"Endorse the future," he urged in his final statement. "Allow Russia to be the innovator in the oil industry. Russia was born for this position."

Ludvig stepped back from the edge of the stage, accepting enthusiastic applause. After this performance, Emanuel could not imagine anyone turning down the opportunity. All their work was about to come to fruition, he was sure.

The audience members rose from their seats and grouped together, discussing the ideas, and Emanuel got to work organizing the mechanical drawings and maps. As he rolled them into their tubes, he shuffled closer to the people gathered near his father, eavesdropping. The crowd shifted, making room for the Czar and his three advisors, and Ludvig bowed his head slightly.

"Your facts and vision of the future inspire me to harness the potential of your discoveries and inventions," declared the Czar.

Emanuel stepped away from the table and to the edge of the stage, needing to hear more.

"I appreciate the fact that my designs fell agreeably upon open ears and a wise mind," Ludvig replied humbly.

The crowd surged forward, wanting to hear more as the Czar's advisor spoke up. "However bold this might seem, I must ask a question."

"Of course," Ludvig said.

The advisor's narrow chin lifted. Had Ludvig been standing on the floor, the man would have been staring down his nose at him.

"A pipeline dedicated to a fuel that can explode," the advisor mused, "running unprotected through cities and mountains? This seems like a monumental danger. To risk this, oil would have to become more critical than all the trade of war supplies and gold combined."

A lesser man might have cowered under the sharp glare. Ludvig accepted the challenge. He nodded at the Czar. "Precisely. That is the very point of my plan, Your Majesty."

"Set up an appointment as soon as possible," the Czar commanded.

Smiling to himself, Emanuel turned back to the table to finish his work. They would be leaving as soon as his father finished up his polite farewells. He reached for the rolled-up maps—and froze. The last map was no longer on the table. He squatted, checking underneath in case it had fallen, but it was gone. Emanuel scanned the audience, and his eyes landed on a man walking with his head down and his entire body curled inward, as if he were holding something inside his coat. Emanuel was staring directly at him when the man glanced back toward the stage. Their eyes locked, and the scoundrel's face burned a guilty red. He turned, hurrying for the door, and all Emanuel could do was watch. If only he could signal someone to stop him, but he did not know anyone. Thinking fast, he reached for a young scribe standing nearby.

"See that man?" he whispered in the boy's ear. "Over there. He has a tube sticking out of the bottom of his coat."

"In the blue coat?"

"Yes. By the gentleman in red." Emanuel dropped a handful of coins into the startled boy's hand. "Follow him. Call the police to help when you can. That man is a thief."

The messenger was gone in a flash. Emanuel moved to the window to watch for him. After a moment, the boy emerged, running through the street after the thief. Emanuel watched until both were lost in the bustle of people and a variety of carriages—along with the pipeline map.

On the ride back to their hotel, Emanuel confessed to losing the map. Ludvig's mouth tightened with disappointment, but he did not appear angry.

"The greatest form of flattery is imitation," he said. "It seems our competition is already nervous. Ah well. They would have learned of our plans eventually. Now they will have more time to stew over it, that is all."

Chapter Four

Czar's Palace, St. Petersburg

At the front of the room stood the Czar's advisor, his lean face set in its usual scowl. Three sober-faced government experts sat in front of him, flanked by four bankers. Ludvig waited before them all, and Emanuel sat on his hands behind him.

"Being neither scientists nor engineers," the advisor declared, pacing, "we were swayed by your passionate presentation." He spread his long fingers. "How could we not be? You offered the best possible scenario."

Emanuel could not see Ludvig's expression, but his posture showed no reaction. He stood very still, hands linked behind his back.

"However—"

Emanuel's stomach clenched.

"—our experts have reviewed the information, and they have decided your plan requires far more time in order to prove itself."

Ludvig's fingers tightened fractionally, but only Emanuel saw.

A stout, balding man at the desk leaned forward, peering dubiously over his spectacles. "There are too many unknown elements to your plan, sir. The success of this pipeline depends upon the success of storage, which depends upon an increase in oil production, which is only possible with new machines. And all of these things are subject to sabotage."

The banker beside him nodded enthusiastically. "Yes. Your plans demonstrate ambition beyond reason, Mr Nobel. What bank could possibly consider underwriting such a system? Especially since the system you described means credit would be exchanged for kerosene, stabilizing supply and demand!"

One of the government experts rolled his eyes up at Ludvig. His expression was friendlier than that of the others. "Our duties require more prudence than do those of private investors. Do keep the Czar's advisors informed of your progress, however. The door remains open."

Ludvig bowed his head slightly. "I am certain His Imperial Majesty sought only the wisest of counsel on this. Please thank His Majesty for his time."

Emanuel left the room in a fog. "This makes no sense," he fumed quietly, holding the door open for his father. "What could they not understand? The truth of the matter is that oil will move the world's armies. That's all there is to it. Why would anyone turn down this plan? It makes no sense."

Incredibly, Ludvig looked satisfied. "'The door remains open'," he repeated quietly.

"I do not understand, Father. Since the Czar rejected our proposal, we have little hope for private investors."

Ludvig shook his head, completely unconcerned. "I am not surprised by today. My experiences with your grandfather taught me to expect exactly that sort of response. In fact, what we just suffered was worth every second. The lesson you just learned on Russian financial governance is more valuable than their loans could ever be."

"What are you talking about? All they did was tell us they did not understand."

Ludvig stopped in place. "No, son. Their decision was based on emotions. More often than not, they fund out of fear of what might lurk within the empire rather than out of awe for what could make Russia stronger." He held out a hand, as if he were indicating the panel. "Look who was judging us. The banks of England and France fear Russia, so they could not possibly endorse a financial deal that could put so much stock in a Russian monopoly. Think of the leverage that would give the Czar!" He shook his head, looking rueful. "And the review by the industrial experts? Rubbish. The last thing they want is reform, for that would require actual intelligence from them. Also, the last of them—if they have not already been bought out by our competitors—do not believe in property rights in Russia."

They walked a few more paces, then Ludvig threw his arms into the air. "This is what makes my plan so revolutionary!" Startled pedestrians scattered before them, staying a safe distance from the ranting gentleman in the long black coat. "It challenges every one of these principles. They know very well that it would work. They know it, and they fear it."

"So what do we do now? Without the Czar's approval, no one will believe strongly enough in us to invest."

Ludvig ground to a sudden halt and stared at Emanuel. "These people will be so united in mocking us, they will not put in any effort to stop us. Remember, we spoke not just to Czar Alexander II, but to the spies who work for our competition, including the one who stole our map. You need to understand something. This plan *will* work, and it *will* change everything. I believe so completely in it that I will borrow from every bank and relative who might be willing. I will appeal to the king of Sweden in person if I must. But Emanuel, I can only do this if you run the factory while I am away."

"What? I cannot—"

"There is nothing you *cannot* do, Emanuel Nobel. Besides, your Uncle Alfred is more than just a very important investor and shareholder." The eager shine returned to his eyes. "Alfred has a legendary history of inventing the unimaginable, and he is extremely intrigued by our discoveries. He will be your most valuable source of advice and guidance while I am away. Write to him daily. Send him our diagrams and keep him up to date on our research and accomplishments."

Even if Emanuel had not believed his father, he could not have resisted his enthusiasm. With reluctance, he agreed.

Ludvig left the following morning, intent on his hunt for funding.

Once he was in Baku, Emanuel gathered the tubes of blueprints and plans that detailed the pipeline and the necessary machinery, then he redrew the missing plan and sent a copy to his uncle along with notes on their progress. Included in the margins were rough drawings of what Emanuel imagined as a Nobel family crest: their name combined with an image of the Temple of Eternal Fires. The ancient site had fascinated him from the beginning and it still did.

Over the next weeks he heard often from his father, who had eventually travelled to Sweden to visit Alfred in person. Convinced of the brilliance of the plan, Alfred loaned Ludvig the money, then the brothers visited all the most important bankers together. Through Alfred's influence they put together a number of lucrative deals. Emanuel was able to purchase the pipes, deliver them to a ship, and sail them down the Volga to Russia.

In the meantime, Emanuel received a package from Alfred. His uncle had approved Emanuel's earlier suggestion that an official crest be made for BraNobel, and when Emanuel opened the box, he pulled a neatly folded square of material. In his hands he held the new BraNobel company flag, embroidered with the crest Emanuel had designed. He set out immediately to find a suitable flagpole.

BraNobel was now in need of a much greater workforce. When Ludvig returned to Baku, he and Emanuel announced they were seeking workers. Hundreds of men were eager to apply. That morning, they ordered planks to be set over barrels to create tables. These they stocked with loaves of bread, legs of lamb, figs, eggplants, baskets of fresh eggs, and much more. On these tables the workers saw more food than they had ever seen before. Once they had applied for the work, they could take as much food home as they could carry.

The translator stared at him, his mouth hanging open. "All of this?"

"Of course."

At the unexpected announcement, the astounded locals bowed in gratitude then moved rapidly into line.

Taghiyev was watching from the side, obviously impressed. "My friend, you are a truly virtuous man. It is unheard of for foreigners—for anyone, really—to come to Baku and treat my friends and our people with so much respect."

"Why shouldn't we?" Ludvig asked. "We are men of common sense."

"What has this to do with common sense?"

"If the men are happy, they will be loyal. If they are loyal, our business will prosper."

Taghiyev shook his head. "If you wish me to keep your secret, my friend, I shall. If you do not want the world to know you are more a man of heart and honor than a regular businessman, I shall keep my mouth closed." He cast an eye over the excited throngs of workers helping themselves at the tables. "But you cannot fool them all!"

*

Emanuel and Ludvig knew they were being observed by corporate spies. They knew they had to be prepared, but attacks always came as a surprise. One morning, as the BraNobel workers were settling in to toil, clansmen charged toward them on horseback. They galloped in circles around the workers, waving weapons and threatening to kill them all. Legitimately frightened, the men grouped together and began to talk amongst themselves about quitting. The next day Emanuel ordered lumber. From it BraNobel built the first of many houses specifically built for the workers. He also built watchtowers and manned them with Cossacks dedicated to protecting those same workers. Under their watchful eyes, the pipeline drew closer to its goal.

"I like the way you think," Musa Naghiyev said, observing the construction.

"So do they."

Ludvig and Emanuel began to work on replacing the old refinery method with a new one which used a series of huge distillery tanks to separate the oil from the kerosene. When everything was ready, they poured the new kerosene into lamps, wanting to test it. Prepared for the typical puff of smoke, they leaned out of the way, but when a worker lit the lamp, the whole room cheered. The line of smoke was thinner than before, meaning the kerosene was cleaner.

Work also began on the construction of an above-ground holding tank for the oil, which would be linked with more pipes to the pumping station derricks. The iron tanks would store oil with no fear of evaporation or leakage.

Robert shook his head. "That's never been done before."

"Now seems like a good time to start," Ludvig agreed.

At long last the necessary changes were completed. The pumps were installed and connected to the pipeline, and they were turned on with great pomp and circumstance. The workers marveled at the astonishing new process, staring with awe as the oil flowed without mishap, traveling from the derrick to the refinery, then to the tank.

The competition could do nothing to either match or destroy BraNobel. They stood helplessly by as the Nobels moved on with the next development: constructing a twenty-five acre compound for the workers and their families. Soon it was impossible to go anywhere without hearing someone rave about the BraNobel projects.

All the Nobels needed now was to strike more oil.

The days were growing cooler, but the work never slowed. Pulling his coat collar up around his ears, Emanuel turned from the derricks toward the office, meaning to get work done before the end of the day. His step faltered when the ground began to rumble—and kept on rumbling. The crowds around him felt the earth move, and their voices lifted with anticipation. In the instant before everyone began to race toward the source, they saw it: a pure black geyser shooting straight into the air some fifty feet above the ground.

"A giant!" someone yelled over the chaos.

Emanuel raced toward the scene, daring to hope. When he arrived, Ludvig stood in a fountain of oil, his broad grin practically glowing through the fresh black smears on his face. "It is ours!"

The derrick housing had been destroyed, blown apart by the geyser, and men ran in all different directions, collecting what they could of the oil. Robert paced in the middle of it all, waving his arms at the workers, yelling orders, taking charge. Emanuel could barely hear anything over the noise—not even the pumping or drilling could be heard anymore—but he heard his uncle's barking commands.

"Go to the warehouse!" Robert bellowed. "Pull the biggest cap rig they have!"

Emanuel was intrigued to see another oil man, Murtuza Mukhtarov, shove through, shouting in Azerbaijani and directing his best men toward Ludvig. Without a word, Murtuza stripped off his coat and led others into the oil. Over the past few weeks Emanuel had been observing Murtuza with interest. The highly-qualified, self-taught engineer was one of the best boring specialists in Baku, and because he seemed so driven, Emanuel imagined he might be on the cusp of soon having his own oil company.

The oil storm was blinding, the thunderous roar a constant. Practically blinded by the dark, semi-controlled chaos, the men pushed through, running to distant wells for equipment or bringing more tools from the warehouse. Nothing could have prevented Emanuel from running in with the others. The Iranian cappers glanced over, seeming surprised to witness the well owners rolling up their sleeves and getting dirty.

This was only the beginning. In the weeks that followed, a second and a third Nobel geyser hit, and Ludvig was prepared.

Chapter Five

One hot, bright morning, Emanuel climbed out of his sleek black Phaeton and onto the oil fields, pausing to stroke the shining neck of his spirited black mare. He did not often travel through the city in the Phaeton, preferring his more staid Landau when in the public eye, but when he was on his own he let himself feel the speed against his face.

Taghiyev was walking toward him, flanked by two little girls in neat, navy blue dresses, and a woman Emanuel surmised was their nanny.

"Good morning, my friend!" Taghiyev called. "I have someone for you to meet!"

The little girls stopped before Emanuel and blinked up at him, their eyes wide with curiosity.

"Who have we here?" he asked warmly.

Taghiyev's deep brown eyes shone with pride. "These are my daughters, the most beautiful and intelligent girls in all of Baku. This is Leyla, and this is Sara. Gerta, here, is their nanny," he said, indicating a small blonde woman standing behind them. "They have learned to speak German from her. Imagine that! Girls, say hello to my good friend, Mr Emanuel Nobel."

Both girls dipped their heads, and Emanuel bowed formally to them in return. "You make your father proud. I can see it in his smile. You must be very good girls."

Leyla and Sara beamed, glancing between Emanuel and their father.

Taghiyev put one paternal hand on each head. "Yes, they are very good, but I am afraid we cannot stay. We cannot be late for school, can we? What would your teachers say?"

The ground vibrated, and a roaring growl rose from deep in the earth. Gerta's eyes flew open with concern, but both girls gave an excited squeak. They clung to each other for support, and everyone turned expectantly toward the Nobel wells.

"Congratulations, Emanuel. Another geyser! Is that seven now?"

A giant fountain of black shot from the ground, spraying higher and wider than any of the others. Oil showered on the neighboring mosque as well as everything else within a mile and a half.

Emanuel squinted into the distance. "Not this time, my friend. Look closely. It is your derrick."

Taghiyev did not move. His expression had gone blank. "Mine? It cannot be."

"Why not?"

He gaped at the massive black column. "Because ... because ..." All at once he threw back his head, laughing. "Because they said it would never happen! They laughed at me, Emanuel! Do you know, over the past fourteen years, two business partners have pulled out, telling me there was nothing here?" Happiness radiated off him like warmth from the sun, and his eyes sparkled with tears. "If only they could see this today! Yes! Yes! Thank you, God! It *is* mine! Finally! After fourteen years of waiting, I have a geyser!"

"You had better go and tend to it then, Mr Zeynalabdin Taghiyev, oil baron!"

Taghiyev began to run toward the field, then he hesitated, realizing his daughters were on his heels.

"Do not worry," Emanuel assured him. "Gerta and I will take care of them."

His friend's relief was palpable. "Thank you." He patted the girls' heads again. "Be good in school," he said, then he was off, sprinting toward the black fountain.

The girls stood close together, watching their father disappear into the confusion.

"This is a very exciting day for your family. I am very happy for you. Shall we go to school now?"

Sara agreed reluctantly, but Leyla looked crestfallen. "I want to see the geyser."

"I know you do," he replied. "Right now, though, it is a busy place and extremely dirty. You both look very pretty in your school clothes. Let us keep them clean. I am sure your father will show you the geyser later."

"We have to go," Sara reminded her sister.

"We can take my carriage," Emanuel offered, and Gerta nodded, appearing grateful. "I want to tell you something," he said as they climbed in and began to roll toward school. "Do you realize that of all the men in Baku, your father will be the greatest of us all?"

Leyla frowned. "But that is what Father says about you and your father."

Intelligence shone in the earth brown irises. She looked wise, the perception in her gaze well beyond her years. For a moment he stared into them, forgetting she had put forward a challenge.

"Is he wrong?"

He forced his thoughts back into place. "No, no. He is not wrong, but he says that because he is a truly generous, loyal friend. The best of friends."

She nodded, satisfied.

"I hope we will all be good friends, Leyla."

She regarded him with those all-seeing eyes, blinking once more before saying anything. "I hope so too, Mr Nobel."

Chapter Six

The pipeline was not Ludvig's final innovation. Not by a long shot. It had not escaped his notice that a huge volume of oil regularly leaked or spilled onto the decks and holds of the ships, as well as through the docks. He began work on a diagram for a very unique ship, but when he went to place his loan request at various banks, he was turned down.

"You know why we are being rejected?"

Emanuel wasn't sure. "I think so."

"The competition. They own the banks, in a way. And they would love to see us fail."

"I am beginning to understand that."

Ludvig would not be discouraged. Once again he went to Alfred, vacationing in St. Remo.

"Why should I give you more money?" his brother demanded. "I have already given you a fortune. Besides, Robert does not think this would be a worthwhile investment."

"Because in return, you will become the third largest shareholder of BraNobel stock."

Armed with Alfred's money, Ludvig traveled to eastern Sweden, plans in hand. He went directly to the Motala Works' shipyard in Norrköping, by the mouth of the river Motala ström, where he placed an order for the world's first tanker built of steel.

"Steel? Why steel?" Sven Almqvist, the manager, cast an experienced engineer's eye over Ludvig's detailed plans. He was skeptical, but not entirely opposed.

"The trouble with oil," Ludvig said, "is that it explodes. Also, the oak casks used by the Americans tend to fall apart during long Atlantic voyages. Besides, it is too difficult to find enough wood around Baku to build more casks. Steel is better."

Sven leaned against the table, his arms crossed. "It has been tried before, but the rolling oil within the ship makes it impossible to cross the Caspian Sea."

"Yes, yes, but that is when the entire ship is one large container. I do not plan to do that. If we use built-in cisterns as ballasts, then remove them in shallower channels, we can regulate the weight. Several separate compartments will be both fore and aft, and the engine will be amidships. There will also be some changes for safety's sake. For example, these cisterns," he said, indicating a section, "will be sealed off from the boiler. They will expand and contract depending upon the temperature. And the hold will be ventilated to prevent a build-up of gas, avoiding explosions."

The engineer tapped a finger against his chin. "Where did you come up with this idea?"

"A long time ago I worked for the Russian navy, designing steam engines for their vessels. I understand ships. I believe this is possible, and it will make the transport of oil not only safer, but simpler." His finger went back to the plan. "The oil will be pumped directly from the pipeline into the hull. The ship will travel from Baku, across the Caspian, and up the Volga. From there the oil will be distributed across Russia."

"This kind of thing has never been done before."

"Do not worry. I specialize in never-been-done-befores."

*

The *Zoroaster* was one hundred and eighty-four feet long with a breadth of thirty-five feet, and she was made entirely of steel. First of its kind, the double-masted steamship arrived at Baku's main harbor, throngs of people gathered, eager to watch her dock. She was clearly not built for speed nor for beauty, but her black steel sides gleamed with promise. Emanuel stood with Robert and Ludvig, who watched her progress with the pride of a father seeing his baby walk for the first time.

Musa Naghiyev, Murtuza Mukhtarov, and Zeynalabdin Taghiyev had joined them and were eyeing the ship with confusion.

"What is this?" Musa held his arms toward the ship. "Your own cargo ship? I think you might be going too far this time, my friends. What is wrong with sending it as it has always been sent? Do you not have enough to manage already?"

"I believe we do," Robert muttered, but he said nothing more. He had made his displeasure known for a while, but he knew not to share his criticisms within public earshot.

"And why steel?" Murtuza asked.

"Barrels leak."

Leaving Murtuza with his mouth slightly open, Ludvig stepped onto the gangplank and faced the onlookers. "Gentlemen," he announced, "I present to you the world's first tanker specifically built to transport oil. This ship is made entirely of steel; it carries no barrels, only tanks. The *Zoroaster* will deliver ten times more oil in one trip than we have ever done before. And she is the first of many such ships that we will build."

"But in high seas," Taghiyev argued, facing Emanuel, "the oil will move. The ship will capsize!"

"No, it will not. My father has solved that problem. He has even come up with a new kind of mineral oil which will run the engines more efficiently than the regular oil."

He gestured toward the ship, and Zeynalabdin, Musa, Murtuza, and a few of the braver men followed him up the gangplank, wanting to inspect the hold.

"That is the most amazing thing I have ever seen," Murtuza said.

"I know," Emanuel admitted. "I had my doubts at first, but I have learned not to question my father. He has an amazing ability to see what no one has ever seen before. Did you see what we named her?"

"I did. *Zoroaster*. Very nice. In honor of the temple, yes?"

"Yes. And of your people."

Musa shook his head. "With all this, no one will be able to match your prices."

Emanuel's smile grew broader. "No one will be able to match our profits!"

*

Weeks later, Ludvig and Emanuel were discussing the undersea telegraph—which Emanuel understood could allow them to manage overseas shipments even faster—when a deafening crash rattled the office windows.

Dread caught in Emanuel's throat. "The *Zoroaster!*"

In two steps, the men were at the window, hoping not to see what they feared most, but the raging fire by the docks was impossible to ignore. A wall of heat pressed against their skin as soon as they ran outside, and it grew more intense as they approached.

"It is not the *Zoroaster,*" Ludvig shouted as they ran. "It is our newer tanker, *Lumen.* But it's loading our oil!"

The site was a disaster. Injured workers lay still or barely moving, and any who could stumble away were bleeding badly. Soot-smeared men swarmed over the docks, trying to extinguish the flames, to at least keep it from reaching other ships docked nearby.

"What happened?" Emanuel asked the shipyard boss.

The man looked shrunken by remorse. "I do not know," he admitted. "There were so many people near the pumps that we could not see how it started."

"It looks like sabotage to me," Emanuel muttered.

Ludvig sighed. "It doesn't matter. We must publicly take the blame so we can honor the injured." He squinted against the oily smoke. "We need to consider the possibility that this could happen again, but I think we can solve the most pressing issue. Look here, where the oil transfers to the ship. This is the weakest link in the system. We need a flexible coupling." He set his hands on his hips and looked around. "Find out who was hurt and what was lost. Tell them we will replace whatever it was. And assure them this will never happen again."

But Emanuel believed that for once his father might be missing something. The simple act of a ship rolling could not possibly have uncoupled the pump from the ship. Not after so many other successful couplings. As much as he hated to consider it, the game was most definitely afoot, and their competitors were incorporating violence into their technique.

Chapter Seven

Within ten years, the Nobel family had changed the face of Baku. They had also changed Baku for many of the faces who lived there. BraNobel employees became the envy of all other workers. Not only were they well paid, they were the only ones who worked in the dozens of clean-operating oil wells in Baku or in the refineries which no longer belched black smoke.

As Emanuel had once suggested, a hospital was built for the BraNobel workers. It was constructed within walking distance of both the oil fields and the clean, comfortable housing areas also built for them by the Nobels. At the end of every day, the employees donned identical light jackets bearing the BraNobel emblem of the Fire Temple and walked home along gravel roads lined by white-painted rocks. Their children, having just returned home themselves, greeted them gleefully, wearing clean new clothes they had worn to either the boys' school or the girls' school—both of which were also built by BraNobel. On their tables that night were good, nutritious meals the wives and mothers had cooked in their new kitchens.

Not only were their employees happy with their jobs, they were happy with their *lives*.

When Ludvig and his son spoke with their men, they embraced them, kissed their cheeks in the Azerbaijani way. It was as if they were all friends— one family.

As the oil barons had predicted, no one could touch BraNobel's profits. Years before they had moved to a larger, though temporary mansion. Now Ludvig declared his intent to build a permanent one — *Villa Petrolea*.

"It will be as much for the people of Baku as it will be for us," he told Emanuel, his eyes sparkling with anticipation. "You will see what I mean when the plans are done."

All work and no play was Ludvig's usual motto; however, he grudgingly allowed Emanuel to plan a party to celebrate their many triumphs. When Emanuel teased him for stepping out of character, Ludvig could only shrug.

"We are like these men, and they are like us. Everyone wants success, and everyone deserves to celebrate achievements."

Emanuel was saddened to hear his Uncle Robert would not be attending. Over the months, Robert had been seen less and less often in the office, though the three Nobels still enjoyed their evening conversations in the sitting room. Robert grudgingly admitted he had been wrong about a great many things with regard to finances, but he was still uncomfortable with the ongoing, expensive changes. When Ludvig informed him of his plan to hold a celebration, Robert said he would not be attending. In fact, he said he would not be attending *anything* in Baku anymore, and his final departure from the country would coincide with the date of the party. He informed his family he would be returning to Stockholm within the week. Permanently.

The party went on despite Robert's news. Since they obviously could not fit the hundreds of workers into the restaurant, the guest list included the top management and their families, as well as a number of other oil barons. All were invited to the Mugham Club, the poshest restaurant in Baku. The five-hundred-year-old medieval *caravansaray* had originally been lodged within a fortress built in the 6th century on the Great Silk Way from China to Europe, but those walls had been rebuilt three hundred years ago. The building was magnificent, but so was the food and entertainment. The guests feasted on succulent lamb *entrecôte* kebabs, exquisite *dolma*, pumpkin *kutabs*, famous Caspian sturgeon, and Beluga black caviar complimented with *pilaf* and made with saffron-covered rice, served with various herbs and greens.

The catering to everyone's tastes but no one's religious customs, were locally-produced juices, cold *ayran* and fresh mineral water, to red wine and cognacs produced for centuries in western parts of Azerbaijan, Cristal champagne, and, of course, Russian vodka. The tables were crowded with exquisite vegetables and fruits.

The sunset flooded through the windows, bathing the lounge in a golden glow and touching the heads of the assembled party-goers with haloes. All were dressed casually—though even their casual wear spoke of relative wealth—and all enjoyed the excuse to relax for a change. The atmosphere, the food, the drinks, and the company were perfect.

"So this is what it is like to sit down without a pencil in my hand," Emanuel said wryly. He raised his glass to Taghiyev, sitting across the table from him. "I had nearly forgotten what that felt like."

Taghiyev laughed, and the hearty sound was contagious. "I think you've forgotten what it feels like to celebrate, my friend. These days I barely even see you smile when your latest conquest is achieved. You and your father are always working. There must be time spent on living as well."

"There is nothing wrong with hard work," Murtuza agreed, "in moderation."

Ludvig gave them a tight smile, but he was clearly uncomfortable in the midst of the lively crowd. His place was at work.

"Everything in moderation," Musa muttered, getting to his feet. "Please excuse me."

Taghiyev chuckled as he walked away. "Remind me to tell you a story about Musa. It will shed light on why he is called 'the stingiest oil baron in Baku'."

"No time like the present," Emanuel suggested.

Ludvig shook his head with disapproval. "We shall not engage in gossip, Zeynalabdin. I am surprised at you."

"No, no, my friend. This is not gossip. It is a well-known story around here, and it involves my wife, so it is all right to share."

"It is a funny story," Murtuza added.

Ludvig relented, leaning slightly forward to hear Taghiyev speak over the noise.

"It was at a charity ball a year or so ago. Musa was standing with another man when my wife, Sona, approached them and asked for a donation for the poor. She is a charming lady and easily convinced the other man to make a generous donation of a hundred rubles. I was watching Musa's face when that happened, and he looked somewhat shocked. He searched his pockets and finally produced three rubles."

"*Three* rubles?" Ludvig demanded, aghast. "What kind of donation is that?"

"That is what my Sona said as well. She reminded him that the other man had offered a hundred rubles. 'What about you?' she asked him."

Murtuza was grinning. "So Musa said—"

Taghiyev held up a hand, one eyebrow raised. "It is my story."

"Of course. I apologize. It is just such an enjoyable punchline."

"It is. My wife asked about his donation compared to the other, and Musa replied, 'But look whose son he is! He is the son of a millionaire! Me? I am the son of a poor peasant!'"

They laughed, and Emanuel's eyes travelled to the people milling behind them. He recognized the men, but the wives and daughters were new to him. One young woman smiled coyly at him, batting long black lashes, so he gave her a nod and a smile, wondering vaguely who she was. Would it be appropriate to ask employees if he could speak with their daughters? The girl's shy expression changed to a scowl when she was nudged to the side by an older woman clearly not her mother. Her disapproval deepened when she spotted yet another young woman pushing in beside her.

Emanuel blinked, noticing suddenly how many young women stood alongside their mothers just a few feet away, looking at him with definite suggestion. It seemed if he showed interest in one, others wanted to be noticed as well. From the way their parents reacted, he was more than welcome to observe their daughters.

At Ludvig's insistence, Emanuel had spent years thinking only of business, but there was more to life. He never wanted to disappoint his father, but he was in his early twenties now, and he craved social interaction. Especially with members of the opposite sex.

"Where is your family today?" Emanuel asked Taghiyev, looking away from his audience. "Your lovely wife and children?"

"Alas, most are at home. The children are too young for such a gathering, and my wife was suffering with a headache. She sends her best wishes to you and your father." He looked beyond Emanuel. "My son, Ilyas, is over there, speaking with the man in the blue coat."

"He looks like you."

"You flatter me," Taghiyev said, clearly pleased. "Where is your Uncle Robert? Should he not be celebrating with us?"

"He is leaving for St. Petersburg tonight, taking the last train." He avoided telling his friend that his uncle had had enough of this country.

"I am sorry I was not able to bid him farewell."

Emanuel smiled. "He would understand. But I am sorry your wife is unwell. I would have liked to have visited with them. I have not seen your family in quite a while. Months. Perhaps a year, actually. Are your daughters still enjoying school?"

Their father's smile was as proud as Emanuel remembered it being before. "Ah yes. My little gems are very smart," he said, "though Leyla is sometimes too smart for her own good!"

"How is that?"

He chuckled. "She is quick to pick out any errors the teacher might make, which is certainly not endearing to the teacher."

"Ha! But it is good to keep the teacher honest, I suppose."

Taghiyev smiled. "Honesty is a very valuable commodity in this world, and sometimes it can be difficult to find. I am very fortunate to have found such a thing with you, my friend."

"I feel the same way about you," Emanuel assured him. "One must know who they can trust when they are in a successful business."

"Life can only be enjoyed if you live it with the right people."

"True. You are a wise man, Taghiyev."

Emanuel's attention was caught by another young woman being jostled to the front of the crowd. He smiled reflexively at her, and the girl's golden complexion darkened with a blush.

"You are also fortunate," he said, his eyes on the beautiful crowd.

"I am. You are right. I am fortunate in many ways. To which are you referring?"

Emanuel regarded him. "You are married to a good woman who loves you, am I right?"

He chuckled. "Yes, for some strange reason, she does love me. In fact, I have been fortunate twice in that department, for Sona is my second wife. My dear Zeynab bore me three children, and I thought I could not bear it when she died so many years ago. Zeynab would have known that, and I am sure she sent Sona to me."

"You have found love at least twice in your life then. Truly fortunate! And yet I am at a loss when it comes to love. I also think you were fortunate to have found love before you made your fortune."

Taghiyev followed Emanuel's wistful gaze. "It is not such a bad thing to have all the young women from Baku dressed in their finest for your benefit."

"No. I cannot complain. But how will I know if a woman loves me for who I am or if it is for how much money I have?"

At this, Taghiyev beamed. "My friend, when a woman loves you, you will know. When you love a woman, you will know. Do not worry. You may have many admirers—and why not, since you are such a handsome devil?—but you will know the difference when you find the right one. Or two, in my case!"

"I hope you are right."

"Besides, there is no rush. You are young, Emanuel. You are doing things an older man might not be able to do because they require so much energy." He leaned back, linking his hands behind his head. "We old men would rather sit back than reinvent the world."

"Now you are joking. For I know you love your business as much as I."

"That is true." He frowned. "I am wondering ... Do you know how much you and your father have done for my people?"

The immediate concerns over finding romance were washed away by a surge of pride. "It has been mostly my father's doing, but yes. I think we know."

Ludvig had been silent throughout their conversation, though he was listening. Now he leaned closer again. "I might have started it, but you are finishing it," he told his son. "I am proud of everything you have done."

Emanuel could not speak. His father rarely gave compliments and kept his emotions hidden behind his greying beard. It was an unaccustomed sight, seeing the blue eyes shine with pride. Inspired, Taghiyev pushed back his chair and got to his feet.

"A toast!" he declared, raising his glass of pomegranate juice. "To Ludvig and Emanuel Nobel!"

Voices were raised in agreement.

"What the Nobels have done with the oil industry here in Baku, here in my country, is nothing short of legendary," Taghiyev proclaimed, and the people cheered. Turning, he addressed both Nobels directly. "Before you came, nothing changed. We were slow, we were dirty, we were inefficient. In just a few years, you have reinvented the drilling process, the refinery, and the shipping. You introduced the world to steel tanker ships, and you are adding tanker cars to railways as well. Baku oil is all over the world because of you."

He waited for the applause to die down, then he continued. "Your vision lived up to the word Emanuel taught me when you first arrived. That word is 'paramount'. For Baku, you have been as paramount to its people as electricity. The homes and schools you built for your workers changed all our lives. People from all over Russia and beyond have come here in search of both employment and happiness.

"And you are not just businessmen. I have found in you the kind of men I would encourage every man to be: honest, generous, and intelligent. I am honored to include you among my close friends." He raised his hand higher. "So I raise my glass to you, Ludvig Nobel and Emanuel Nobel, and I wish you both long futures filled with even more success." He looked to the crowd. "To the Nobels!"

"To the Nobels!"

Emanuel would have liked to say something in return, to tell the crowd how he and his father cherished this land they now called home, how much they had learned from Baku's people, but the crowd surged forward leaving no opportunity to speak. Instead, he stood by his father, humbly accepting handshakes and congratulations, enjoying the swell of pride which had taken up most of his chest.

He looked into the eyes of the man now shaking his hand, vaguely recalling one of the directors of engineering from the derricks. In a friendly gesture, the man held his other hand toward his daughter, apparently in introduction. She grimaced slightly when she was pushed from behind then flashed Emanuel a bright white smile. At least a dozen more young women lined up behind her, all in their finest dresses, their hair and make-up done to perfection. Every one of them was smiling and nodding fondly at him, as were their parents, who seemed intent on moving their daughters to the front of the line.

Could there be love waiting for him in this room? The pretty smiles encouraged him, and his gaze swept over the different faces, feeling as if he had just arrived at a feast. The girl in the blue gown by the post looked sweet, somewhat shy. Shifting in front of her was a taller girl in bold red and yellow. She stretched a broad, somewhat strangled smile his way, revealing an odd dental pattern. Yet another woman wriggled to the front, her dimpled cheeks like apples. Everywhere Emanuel looked he saw color, and while he was somewhat aroused by the potential, he also felt a little uncomfortable at being the center of so much female attention.

Ludvig cleared his throat purposefully, drawing his son's attention. His expression was one of pride, but he was also shaking his head, clearly disapproving of his wandering eye. Emanuel scowled, frustrated by his short leash. Was he a dog? Tethered to his desk all the time? Tied to his father's demands?

The energy in the room was youthful, invigorating, and exactly what Emanuel craved. He needed to let loose, to howl at the moon and celebrate not only his successes, but his sheer existence as a healthy, handsome young man. He laughed when a grinning young man pulled him into a circle where others were attempting to start up a dance, but Ludvig quickly appeared beside him. He gave the other young men a short but direct smile before ushering his son into a small hallway where they would not be interrupted. Emanuel began to object, but Ludvig shook his head.

"Do not lose focus now, son."

"But we—"

"You must understand, Emanuel, that your situation is different from those of the men out there. You are a businessman." Keeping the movement subtle, he jabbed a thumb in the direction of the men carousing on the dance floor. "You wake up with more responsibility than all these youths combined."

"So I can never enjoy myself?"

Ludvig closed his eyes for a second, and Emanuel was reminded of the earlier years, when his father had done the same thing, needing to stay calm and collected. When the blue eyes opened again, their gaze was direct.

"Emanuel, if you walk away tonight and join those men or those women, you will not become the man you could become."

"One night will change me? I do not think so!"

"One night—" A man in the crowd whooped with laughter, and Ludvig's voice was swallowed up by the noise, so he started again. "One night will give you a taste for such things. And that taste might be sweeter and more addictive than your life right now, tempting you to return every night after that. But you must trust me, son, when I tell you that nothing could be as sweet as the joy you will one day experience when you have realized all your dreams and stand on the top of the world."

"My life will be over by the time I realize those dreams, Father. And I will be alone."

Ludvig shook his head, sadness in his eyes. "You will never be alone, Emanuel, and do not think I do not understand your pain. I know how you long for that life. We work hard, you and I, and it is easy to crave something else at times, but I will never apologize for helping you stay on track and for insisting you not be careless. We are Nobels. We are meant for something greater in our lives. We have already done so much, and we both know there is more to be done."

It was impossible to deny his words. What he and his father and uncle were building was a whole new Baku. A new world for all these people and generations to follow. Grudgingly, he swallowed and nodded once.

"Go walk the pump line before you get home," Ludvig suggested. "Maybe Robert is still there. I am sure you can convince him to celebrate with you before he leaves for St. Petersburg."

"He is gone," Emanuel replied stonily. "I am fairly sure he was the first one on the train."

Chapter Eight

There were times when Emanuel agreed entirely with his uncle, wishing he could escape from this land. He imagined his father did as well, but the truth was that they did not have the ability to simply walk away. There was no escape as far as Emanuel could see. With his jaw set, he strode from the hallway, through the Mugham Club's main lounge, and straight to the exit, trying not to dwell on the obvious looks of disappointment on the young women's faces. He kept his eyes on the ground as he headed toward the boardwalk, bundled in his coat.

"I fail to see," he muttered to himself, "how a few hours of social interaction is *careless*. Is it not prudent to plan for a personal life as well as one in business? Careless would be to leave my future unknown for too long. Who knows? Couldn't a courtship lead to more business? Or maybe business could lead to a courtship. Would that be so bad?"

The sunset was melting into a deep orange, its fire dampened by the ever-present haze of smoke. The slippery streets, the smoke, the grime, the heat ... they were all the necessary evils of this life, and he had grown accustomed to them. But the sky was a reminder that there were beautiful things here as well, and his eye went to the distant Temple of Fire. His pace slowed as he gazed upon its ancient majesty, then his feet turned toward it. If he could not go to parties, at least he could enjoy the evening in other ways.

By the time Emanuel reached the temple, the red sliver of the sun was the only visible remnant of the day. The temple's flames threw shadows against the stark walls, drawing Emanuel upstairs, toward the roof. There he stood in silence, the lone witness to a view of the field and of the derricks, their fires like glowing gems in the dark. It had not always been like this. Since he and his father had first arrived in Baku, more than ten times as many derricks now existed. The reminder made him proud.

Still, the longing in his heart persisted. Must he forever ignore the need pulsing in his veins, the biological desire to find a wife, to start a family? How could Ludvig deny him those things he himself had so obviously enjoyed? After all, Ludvig had married Emanuel's mother—who was also Ludvig's cousin—and she had given birth to Emanuel as well as to his younger siblings, Carl and Anna. After Emanuel's mother had died, Ludvig had married again, producing seven more half-siblings, including his tiny half-brother Gösta, born only one year ago. Just like Taghiyev, Ludvig had known love at least twice in his life. Certainly he understood he was the firstborn, the one expected to eventually take over the Nobel name. Carl was still in St. Petersburg running the Machine-Building Factory Ludvig Nobel, but he had also started a family. Their sister, Anna, was already a mother.

Could it be he saw Emanuel as the only one able to withstand the demands of this business? For despite the occasional bouts of loneliness and self-pity, Emanuel did love what they were doing—everything from the planning to the building, including the times when he got dirty with the workers. He loved the sense of achievement and pride he felt when he saw the contented employees head to the houses built specifically for them, to enjoy the meals made possible by BraNobel. It was a great love, and it came with a passion which stirred his heart every time he thought of it. Even now, thinking of it, he smiled. Was it enough? Should he be satisfied? Could his passion for BraNobel be the only love of his life?

Chapter Nine

Every Nobel success increased the competitors' rage, and news travelled fast across the ocean to both Europe and America.

"Rothschild has agreed to finance the Batumi railway, which will run between Baku and Batumi, in Georgia," Emanuel told his father, joining him at breakfast one morning.

"Of course." Ludvig folded the newspaper and looked up. "They wish to exceed our success by further expanding shipping to all of Europe from within the Russian Empire. It only makes sense that they would approach the largest global banking group in the world."

"What kind of man is Édouard Alphonse James de Rothschild?"

"Cautious, I would say. Wary. Actually, he is similar to his father in many ways. He even dresses like his father. From what I understand, he has exquisite taste in art and has started to collect Islamic paintings of late. Of course he can buy whatever he wants, really."

"The Rothschilds have their money everywhere."

"Oh yes." Ludvig frowned, concentrating. "Their family has been in banking for generations. In fact Édouard's grandfather and the bank's founder, James Mayer de Rothschild, actually stipulated the bank must always be represented by the three branches of the family descended from him. So Édouard works with his cousins, though he is in charge. The Rothschilds finance mining for copper, nickel, silver, and gold, and they financed DeBeer's, so they have diamonds as well. Britain acquired Egypt's shares of the Suez Canal only after they were financed by the Rothschilds. The

Rothschild brothers already have experience with building railways. You know they financed Vanderbilt's railroad interests."

"Yes. I read that. It bodes well for Batumi railway. Even Czar Alexander III has supported the project. Actually, that makes sense, considering the crown will eventually receive tariffs on the railway."

"Think, Emanuel. How can we make this work to our advantage?"

Emanuel frowned. "Rothschild is a visionary. He will be thinking of future investments."

"Go on."

"Well," he said, narrowing his eyes in thought, "let us see if we are in those visions."

Father and son accepted the challenge, wooing Rothschild until they were eventually invited to add BraNobel's tankers to the line. The competition—especially John D. Rockefeller, co-founder of Standard Oil—was not pleased that the Nobels benefited. Unfortunately, the trains left a great deal to be desired. They were constantly behind schedule, often becoming congested in the steep, narrow passes among the Caucasus Mountains. Occasionally they stopped altogether when bad weather struck.

"A pipeline," Ludvig muttered, tapping his fingers together as he imagined the scope of the thing.

Emanuel regarded him with interest. Why should his father look so intrigued by the idea of a pipeline? By this point in time he was on his way to having over three hundred pipelines built across seventy miles. The idea was not new anymore.

"Yes. A pipeline."

"Father?"

Ludvig's piercing blue eyes focused on his son. "It will be the largest, most ambitious one yet. From Baku to Batumi."

"But the train . . ?"

"Is insufficient. Now that we are able to produce so much oil, we must be able to ship it just as quickly. Otherwise, what is the point?"

"How will you raise the money?"

There was a short pause, then Ludvig said, "I have an idea."

*

Édouard Rothschild did not take much convincing. Once he discovered Taghiyev was on board, he added his support to the Baku-Batumi pipeline. Work was soon underway. Using his brother Alfred's invention—dynamite—Ludvig blew the mountains apart to clear the way for the pipes. Piece by piece, the heavy equipment was hauled up the sharp cliff roads in carts, and when the workers paused to look around them and wipe the sweat from their brows, to think about what they were creating with these seemingly endless pipes, they could look down into the Georgia Valley and get a spectacular view of the Black Sea.

Pumping stations were set in place, and the valves were finally turned. As Ludvig had foreseen, the Baku-Batumi pipeline was a huge success.

As BraNobel continued to grow, prosperity expanded Baku. When the Nobels had first arrived, Baku had a population of 45,000. Within five years it had risen to over 300,000, and there was no indication that it might slow. With the increase came greater needs, so the Nobels and the other barons opened the doors to beautiful new mosques, churches, and synagogues near the hospitals, schools, university, and theaters they had already built. That way the people could take care of both their spiritual and physical health.

Chapter Ten

Ludvig saw that Nobel's fortunes were tied to Baku oil, and they needed to build a permanent mansion to accommodate their large family and solidify their status as the first among equals.

Ludvig had big plans for this new mansion.

"And you chose this spot out of all Baku. An interesting choice," Emanuel mused.

"Yes. I am pleased," Ludvig replied. "You see, this is the main drive."

Ludvig had already led his son over half of the property, describing exactly how he envisioned their future home. Dozens of wooden stakes had been hammered into the soil by laborers, framing the site of the massive estate. The two men paused, and Ludvig squatted to hammer in another stake.

"I can see that. Do you have all the plans for the building finalized?"

Ludvig straightened. "Mostly. I want the villa itself to reflect the great estates of Paris, but it should also honor the architecture of the local culture."

"Sounds wise." They walked a few more paces. "What will you do with all this land?"

Ludvig's expression lifted with his enthusiasm. "I have an image in my mind of how this will one day look. I have decided the city which marks the center of oil production for the entire world deserves a grand boulevard and park." His arm swept to the front, indicating the open land. "Green grass, hundreds of trees lining the street, and gas or even electrical lights at night."

He had taken three more steps before he realized his son was no longer beside him. Emanuel had stopped and was staring at Ludvig, confused.

"What is it?"

"You are speaking of the impossible, Father. The winds of Baku blew the topsoil away a century ago."

"The impossible? The *impossible*, Emanuel? How many times have we been told something was impossible, only for us to prove them wrong? No, no, it is not impossible, though it will not be a simple thing. I have in mind a true wonder of landscapes, one which will rival the greatest parks in London—and I have a plan to make the impossible possible."

"You plan to change nature? This will be a good one, even for the Nobels. Tell me, Father, how do you plan to control the wind and the sandstorms?"

"We do not have to," Ludvig replied. "We only need to plant enough, and we need to do it quickly enough that the roots will hold everything in place."

Emanuel walked beside Ludvig, trying to understand what his father saw. The sun was hot, the dirt crumbling beneath their feet, but he tried to convince himself that grass gave way beneath his shoes, that the wind rustled through the leaves which would one day grow here.

"I am all ears, Father. Please illuminate me."

"Every ship will already be carrying a load of oil out and up the Volga," Ludvig explained. "When they arrive, the buyers will fill them back up with the best soil from the river. After three months of shipping soil here, I will bring in three months of fresh water."

"Which will come from ... ?"

"I see it as similar to the oil storage. We will fill massive freshwater reservoirs to contain it. Once that is done, I will contract one of the many great horticulturalists from Europe. How could he resist? He will be hired to convert an entire city center into a park." He sighed. "I have decided to call it *Villa Petrolea*. What do you think?"

Emanuel drew in a long, slow breath. "I think that no matter how old you keep claiming to be, you have the visions and energy of one much younger. Villa Petrolea will be magnificent, I am sure."

Within the next few months, the building began to take shape under the direction of both Swedish and Italian architects, who took their orders from Ludvig. While they did that, he led his contracted French horticulturalist over the plans for the landscaping. Ships returning to port from Lankaran carried loads of prime, fertile soil for the park, and the massive water tanks already installed on the boulevard—each one bearing the Nobel emblem—were filled with fresh water from Astrakhan. Before long the agreed upon trees and shrubs were being shipped from subtropical areas of the Caucasus as well as from Italy and France, and with proper care their roots became firmly established. Within two years of starting the project, they had built an oasis, with the mansion being the center of it all.

When it was done, Zeynalabdin, Musa, and Murtuza came for a tour. All three admired the grounds with open envy.

"My friend, you and your father have created something we could never have imagined. I thought you were doing amazing things before, but this! All this green right here in Baku. It is incredible."

"I told my father it was impossible," Emanuel admitted. "I think that word motivates him more than encouragement."

"I believe you. It ..." Musa shook his head, marveling "I cannot tell you how much I admire it. Tell me, how many plants did you put here? It seems endless."

Emanuel chuckled. "I believe there are over 80,000."

"And every one is a thing of beauty."

When he felt the timing was right, Emanuel had electric lighting installed to illuminate the park in the evening. On the first night, just before the lights were switched on, Emanuel led his father to the road to show him the effect. He had already told his workers it would happen that night, so word had spread quickly and crowds lined the boulevard. In the moment the lights came on, the people burst into cheers. Ludvig only nodded, but the lights caught a rare tear in his eye.

Chapter Eleven

As Vice President of BraNobel, Emanuel Nobel was heir to great wealth, living in a city which had now swelled to over half a million people. With so much already accomplished by his father and himself, he was confident in his abilities, and his mind was always on new ideas. Like Ludvig, he was at his best when he was busy, and that was most of the time. Though he enjoyed his social life, he did not participate all the time. He never forgot his father's warnings about the dangers of being reckless.

He waited in the sitting room for Ludvig, glancing impatiently at his pocket watch. Eventually he called the butler and asked him to see what was delaying Ludvig. There were things to do today. They should already be at their office.

Elbek, Emanuel's butler, returned a few minutes later. "Your father has asked that you go without him."

"Why?"

"He is feeling unwell."

This was odd. Though he was getting older, Ludvig was not habitually ill. He rarely took a day off work. Slightly concerned, Emanuel headed up the stairs to his father's bedroom, where he discovered Ludvig still in bed.

"What is it, Father? Are you ill?"

"It is merely an inconvenience, I am sure," Ludvig assured him. "You do not need me today anyway."

"On the contrary. I wanted to go over some plans."

"I shall feel better tomorrow. This affliction comes only occasionally, and it will not last."

The mattress creaked under Emanuel's weight as he sat on the edge of his father's bed. "This has happened before? What is it, exactly?"

Ludvig grimaced slightly, seeming to react to a spasm of pain. He placed a hand on the center of his chest. "It is a kind of pressure here, as if I am being squeezed from within. The doctor—"

"You have seen a doctor about this? And you have not mentioned it to me?"

"I have, and I did not. There is nothing for you to worry about, and nothing you can do. It will be greatly relieved with bed rest." He frowned at his son. "While it is acceptable for one man to stay away from the office for a day, it makes no sense for us both to remain here. You are in charge while I am incapacitated, and you are already late for work."

Emanuel rose reluctantly. It concerned him that Ludvig's pain seemed to be focused around his heart. With no other choice, he descended the long marble staircase of Villa Petrolea, heading toward his carriage, then paused as he often did to admire the beauty of the gardens. His father's dream had become a healthy, vivid reality despite all the odds, made possible by Ludvig's determination. Emanuel had to believe that his father's stubborn nature would also defend him against this 'angina', whatever that was.

Setting his mind on the day ahead, he climbed into his carriage, admiring Baku as they drove through it. As a result of all its recent growth, the city had become a showpiece, a destination for wealthy travelers. Ancient minarets and Azerbaijani mosques provided a colorful contrast to recent marble buildings constructed with beautiful French and Italian architecture. The carriage rolled smoothly past the recently completed theatre, just down the street and across from several magnificent structures including a library, a museum, a science building, and the palace which Musa Naghiyev had built before donating it to the Muslim Charity Society.

Though the streets still sang with a cornucopia of languages, the people of Baku no longer trudged along the oily streets with little on their minds. Now they had a lift to their steps and a destination for their feet. Happy shrieks of children playing ball or riding on the carousel rang through the park. Even the street carts had been transformed. Once they had been covered with oil, restricted to selling tin pans and shoes. Now they were painted in bright colors, and their wares included the latest in fashion from Paris and London. Everyone, from the locals to the increasing number of tourists, had money to spend. Everyone paused to wave to Emanuel when they saw him. They loved him, and he loved them in return.

They pulled up in front of the Nobel office, and he climbed the stairs to the front door then strolled down to his office. An unexpected stranger sat in the waiting room, a cup of steaming tea in his hand. Intrigued, Emanuel walked in and offered his hand. The gentleman had a striking black widow's peak over a pair of heavy-lidded eyes, giving the impression of a man continuously bored with his circumstances. He rose to his feet, brusquely returning Emanuel's handshake.

"Good morning, Mr. Nobel. I am Jules Aron," he said, his English curled with a cultured French accent. "I represent the Rothschild family and Caspian and Black Sea Oil Production and Trading Company."

"It is good to meet you, Monsieur Aron," Emanuel said, curious but wary.

He led Aron into his office, with its dark cherry leather upholstery and oak paneled walls, then he sat across the desk from him.

"I hope you had a comfortable journey."

"Well enough, thank you," Aron assured him. "Are we not able to meet with your father?"

Was he mistaken, or did the man already sound impatient? He shook his head. "He will not be joining us this morning. Of course we had no notice you were coming in today. Had we known someone representing the Rothschild enterprises had an interest in our company, we would have prepared a more customary welcome for you, Monsieur Aron."

Aron managed a brief smile. "No need for that, thank you."

"Have you specific interest in this region?"

"Yes and no."

The man's tone was antagonistic, but Emanuel would not stoop to that level. "Ah," he said, maintaining his hospitable manners. "Then I shall follow that with an offer to answer any questions regarding the future of oil and technology. Have you visited Mr Taghiyev already?"

The Frenchman frowned. "Why would I want to visit him?"

"My apologies. I had assumed you came to gather information on the oil companies, and my friend Zeynalabdin Taghiyev is an excellent person to speak with on that topic. Am I correct? Is it your goal to learn more about the oil companies?"

"My 'goal' is to get an answer, Mr Nobel."

Emanuel beamed at him, hoping to throw the man off balance. "Well, that is wonderful, for I would be pleased if I could, in some small way, assist in solving a riddle or unravelling a mystery for your company."

Aron's eyes narrowed. "I wish to know why you would put your company in such financial risk, sir. Do you not understand that Rockefeller and Standard Oil could crush you in a single quarter by flooding the market with cheap oil?"

It was a deliberate ploy to throw Emanuel off balance, and it failed. "I see. So you are here on behalf of the Rothschilds, wanting to inspect our financial strength so you might offer a loan on a worldwide level. If so, I can easily present you with the records you need."

The loose grip the visitor had on the arms of the chair tightened. "The Rothschilds do not enter a market to make loans in order to strengthen a competitor's hold." He let out an exasperated sigh. "You should know that already. Seriously, Mr Nobel, you must admit you and your father are outside your specialty. You are completely without a vision when it comes to surviving international forces."

Aron's purpose, Emanuel now understood, was to test him while simultaneously trying to make him feel less powerful than he knew himself to be. The normal response would be for Emanuel to bristle, perhaps demand the man leave. Faced with this sort of antagonism, that would be the simplest reaction. But throughout his life, Emanuel had watched his father handle such ignorant comments with style. Ludvig had never allowed emotion to interfere with either business or personal matters, and he had always come out the victor in discussions such as these. Emanuel gave an inward nod to his father then governed himself accordingly.

He maintained a casual expression. "I defer to your wisdom, Monsieur Aron."

It gave Emanuel a small, private thrill to see the man's nostrils flare and the sallow cheeks darken. Emanuel waited calmly for the next play, since the ball was now in the visitor's court.

"Consider this possible scenario," Aron said evenly. "You awake to news that a battle destroyed every storage tank on the Volga. At the same time, Marcus Samuel and his brother, Samuel Samuel, return to dominating shipping from Indonesia, and they overtake Hong Kong and Japan markets as well. There, your pipelines offer no hedge against competitive prices. Standard Oil will capture the Russian kerosene market, and you do not have the fleet of ships to deliver enough so you can pay off your debts." He raised his narrow chin. "This is a realistic scenario. And you, Mr Nobel, are not prepared."

Emanuel knew all about Marcus Samuel, who had rocketed from running his father's import-export business to running Shell Oil, one of BraNobel's chief competitors. Samuel, he believed, was somewhat of an idealist. He also had an extraordinary amount of nerve.

Having seen the success of BraNobel's *Zoroaster* and the subsequent fleet of oil tankers, Samuel had ordered his own such ships to be built. Using his father's string of international shipping contacts, his new role as Mayor of London, and his own persuasive personality, Marcus had approached the government of Britain, which held the rights to the Suez Canal. Rockefeller had already approached them, requesting access for his ships to pass through the Canal, but they had prohibited him from gaining that access. Based on what the government had said to Rockefeller, Samuel redesigned his own tanker, demonstrated that the ship was clearly safe for the Canal, then pointed out that since he was British, the British would have a stake in the success of the enterprise. The government gave its permission. Subsequently, Samuel's *Murex* had filled up with Rothschild's oil in Batumi, then she had floated directly to the Orient.

Rockefeller had been left in her wake, speechless with fury. Emanuel could not help but admire Samuel for his brilliant move.

Aron's point about Standard Oil's potential to take over Russia's kerosene market was valid; however, he had no idea—no one did, yet—that Emanuel was already in the process of solving that implied threat.

The man sitting before him was being both rude and disrespectful, but Emanuel could not allow derogatory remarks to upset him. All he had to do was keep going as he always had, getting the job done, being the first and the best at what he did.

He blinked slowly, letting his gaze harden to match Aron's, but he kept his voice level. "To a predominant family leading the world for generations, I imagine the Nobel family must appear highly reactionary rather than in total control of all elements. Is that the gist of your hypothetical?"

"No, the *gist* is your use of the word 'hypothetical'."

For almost a full minute, the two men stared at each other in tense silence. The only sound in the room was the rhythmic ticking of the clock at the far end of the room. Emanuel waited. He would not be the first to blink.

Aron stood abruptly and slid a folded piece of paper across the table. "I came to make an offer on behalf of the Rothschilds."

Emanuel reached for the paper and lifted the page deliberately toward his face. Without changing expression, he read the offer then folded it again. He rose and walked around his desk toward a specific shelf. Having found the book he needed, he carried it back to the desk and spun it around so Aron could read the numbers within.

"BraNobel is worth over seven times what you offer," he stated coldly.

The ice was even harder in Aron's voice when he lifted his eyes from the accounting page. "Only if you survive this winter."

Emanuel would not be intimidated, and he would not be insulted; however, this bastard needed to be taught a lesson in manners.

He held out a hand which Aron grudgingly accepted. "Your time and offer have been noted with the utmost respect. Sincerest regards for your personal health." He inclined his head slightly. "Good day, sir."

The moment the handshake ended, Aron strode out of the office. Emanuel stood by the window, hands clasped behind his back, waiting until he saw the Frenchman's disapproving scowl. Then he turned away. That, he thought to himself, had gone rather well.

*

Ludvig did not return to the office the following day, nor the next. When he at last rose from his bed and joined Emanuel at the breakfast table, he was alarmingly pale.

"You must eat, Father. You are skin and bones. Did they not feed you well enough when you were recovering?"

Ludvig waved a hand. "They were excellent. Brought me whatever I requested or required. It was I who could not eat. The pain did not abate as it usually does, and though I am certain having a proper meal would have helped my strength, I simply could not manage."

"At least you are here now. You will not make me eat alone this morning."

"No. I shall eat a little."

A maid brought coffee for them both then returned to the kitchen to fetch breakfast. As she left, Ludvig's gaze landed on him.

"I have made a decision," his father declared.

The sense of finality in his voice chilled Emanuel.

"You are aware that your Uncle Alfred and I have been in a state of conflict for many years over finances, but we are not so divided of late. We have been writing to each other, and I have told him I have had enough of this."

"Of what?"

"This work. While I regret nothing, I feel I have been a slave to this company for too long. I have sacrificed my time, my health, and my tranquility."

Emanuel frowned. "I do not understand, Father. This company has been your life's work. Your passion."

"Agreed. But this difficulty with my health has me thinking about other things. I begin to wonder what my life is missing."

Emanuel knew him too well. There were powerful emotions battling within that brilliant mind. Ludvig had long ago disciplined his facial expressions so his emotions were concealed, and that ability had served him well in business. Very few people had been able to see past that mask, but Emanuel knew. All he had to do was look beyond the shield and see the truth revealed in the sky-blue eyes.

"I have decided to retire to Cannes, Emanuel. The doctor recommends it, and I bow to his expertise. I shall no longer be a member of BraNobel's Board of Directors, but I will continue on as a shareholder. I have transferred half of my shares to you. This means you will be the uncontested head of the company and unquestionably the largest shareholder."

A moment passed before Emanuel could speak. The thrill of officially being handed BraNobel's reins sang in his veins, but it was muted by his deep concern for Ludvig.

"I cannot imagine running this company without you, Father."

"And yet you shall be an exceptional leader. You already are. The years are catching up to me. Like this mansion, BraNobel was born as a vision for the future. It needs a young, fresh face."

That admission, Emanuel knew, had been extremely difficult for his father to make. Ludvig's retirement, his decision to leave the company, hurt him as much or more than it hurt Emanuel. It was time for the son to be strong, to support the father in a painful but necessary decision.

"I will make you proud," Emanuel said quietly.

"You always have." He chuckled lightly, trying not to cough. "Do you remember when we first arrived here in Baku? We were on the ship, and you were so angry. You asked about your grandfather, do you recall?"

"Of course."

"Can you see now that he did not fail? Can you see that what he did here was just the first step we needed to take so we could become what we are now? I am not my father, but I am similar to him in some ways. I have carried his lessons with me my whole life, and I used those lessons to develop my own. You are not me, Emanuel. You have my thoughts, my discipline, my drive, but you have even more. You have the heart of the people. You belong here. And, like me, you will accomplish more in your life than your father ever did."

The room was silent. Emanuel held his father's gaze. His father never cried, so Emanuel would not cry.

"Go now," Ludvig said, waving at the door. "Check on the morning reports."

Without another word, Emanuel stepped outside and climbed into the carriage. He felt empowered by his new role, yet suddenly alone. Could he really do this? Could he fill such big shoes? Of course he had worked on his own for a while anyway, learning from his father then blazing his own trails, but this ... this was permanent.

The wheels of the carriage began to roll, and Emanuel felt a lump in his throat. He had never seen his father surrender to anything before. He had never seen him quite so human.

*

The first telephone in Baku was installed in Villa Petrolea, and the first call Emanuel placed was to his father, who had retired in Cannes.

"How are you, Father?"

"Content. I am learning to enjoy leisure time, which was never in my vocabulary before. I am spoiled by my wife and servants—"

"Have you grown fat yet?"

Ludvig laughed, but Emanuel heard an unfamiliar wheeze in the sound. "No, I am afraid I still do not eat as well as you."

"The doctors?"

"Are excellent here. You need not concern yourself. You have other priorities with which to occupy your time. Never forget, son, that you are no longer responsible only for the fate of the company. You have created a new world for the half million people of Baku. They need you to make their home the best it can possibly be."

His father did not need to remind him of that; he would never forget.

One afternoon, Emanuel received a letter from his Uncle Alfred, sent from Paris. In it he discussed the company, but his final thoughts were of Ludvig's health. More than one doctor, he informed Emanuel, had determined the difficulty was with Ludvig's heart.

Even if the state of your Father's health is better, Alfred wrote, *try in every way to distance him from all the business troubles. The sooner he travels and hears nothing for a long time of kerosene, mazut, and other tormentors from Baku's underworld the better.*

Cordial greetings to all of you from your Uncle Alfred.

PART TWO

Chapter Twelve

The oil fields continued to expand—as did the pressure placed on them by the competition. It was imperative that Emanuel maintain the upper hand. It was time to expand.

"I am ready."

He had put one refinery employee in charge of this particular project, and now Emanuel stood back, anticipation tightening his jaw. The progress reports had been good, but this was the first time the team had been comfortable enough to demonstrate the results for Emanuel. Today, he had been told, he would get what he wanted.

He folded his arms and watched carefully as the team set up kerosene lamps on the table before him. "Tell me everything I am seeing here."

"As you have instructed, Mr Nobel, we have collected kerosene from each of our competitors, and they are in separate lamps." He held out a hand, naming each lamp. "This is the kerosene from Royal Dutch, from the Anglo-Russian Oil Company, and from the Trade House Benkendorf, as well as from Shell. Over here is the Russian Oil General Corporation's kerosene, and this is Standard Oil's."

"Excellent. And this final one is ours?"

"Yes, sir. Our latest formula. Your Uncle Robert has a brilliant chemical mind, as you know. He determined the purification process needed to be updated, and at his suggestion we added caustic soda as the cleaning agent. I think you will see and smell quite a difference."

Emanuel focused on the lamps. "Go ahead."

One by one, the lamps were lit. The air immediately clouded with the acrid stink of kerosene and a puff of heavy black smoke. The employee paused before reaching to light the final lamp, and Emanuel held his breath, all his focus on the match. It seemed to take forever for the wick to taste the flame then approve it, but when the lamp was finally lit, Emanuel rejoiced. Unlike every other kerosene lamp in the world, this one produced no stink. Hardly any black smoke rose from it.

"Outstanding!" he cried, companionably thumping the employee's back. "And now I shall tell you why this was so important. Everyone, please gather around."

Half a dozen employees came closer, listening intently.

"As we all know," he said, "Russia has recently welcomed a new Czar, Alexander III. They call him Alexander the Peacemaker, and his Imperial Majesty will want to be the best leader of Russia there has ever been, of course. Therefore, we must prove that we are the best suppliers he will ever have.

"Before the staged event for the industry which we have been planning toward, we will arrange for a private demonstration for the Czar. Just like today, we will use identical lamps of the most common type found in St. Petersburg, and we will light every lamp before his royal eyes. When we present our latest formula he will expect more of the same. "But we will not give him what he expects." He held one hand toward the BraNobel lamp. "We will give him this.

"The success of these results will force our competitors to beat us on price alone. Do you understand how significant this is on a worldwide commercial scale? My friends, with this demonstration we will win *all of Russia*."

The men returned to their work with a new sense of purpose, and Emanuel left the refinery, pleased. Success with the kerosene lamps was exactly what he needed to keep BraNobel ahead of the competition. He felt like celebrating. Fortunately, he had already arranged a grand social event for that evening, though he would keep the kerosene project secret for now.

Hours later, Villa Petrolea's massive rooms were filled with international guests, their clothing and jewelry sparkling in the brightly lit room. Even among the guests there existed a separation of social levels, and while they were all well to do, the more affluent families and visiting aristocrats congregated in the middle of the ballroom while most of the others bordered the dance floor. When Emanuel strode into the room, every female eye went directly to him. He had become used to the attention and no longer paid much attention to their glances. It was rare when either the girls or their parents approached him directly, and he'd tired of doing it himself. It was a strange dance indeed, since neither partner would ask the other to participate.

Besides, since he had made a conscious decision to dramatically change his life, he was no longer lonely. If he craved female companionship, it was easy for him to find. There were times, though, when Emanuel preferred the simple company of Zeynalabdin and Ilyas.

"The crossroads used to bring the Orient to Europe," Ilyas was saying to a few of the visitors. "Now it brings Europe to the crossroads. The melting pot has boiled over."

Taghiyev agreed. "Everyone in Baku is rich. Even the thieves have money—but they do not share."

"Not everyone is as generous as you," Emanuel said, raising a glass to his friend.

"Not everyone is as rich as you!" his friend replied, laughing.

"And not everyone catches the eye of someone like that," Ilyas said quietly, looking past Emanuel's shoulder. "Who is *she*?"

Slowly, Emanuel turned to greet a pair of impeccably dressed guests. The first was an older gentleman he recalled from earlier. *Miller*, he recalled. William Miller. Beside him stood the most exotic woman he had ever seen. The two were plainly waiting to speak with him alone, so he apologized and turned from his friends.

"William Miller, American Vice Consul," said the man.

"Oh yes," Emanuel replied. "I recall your letter of introduction. A pleasure to meet you."

"This charming lady is the Trade Attaché I mentioned, Miss Julie Gold."

Having been given permission, Emanuel let his eyes go to Miss Gold, but he had to fight the urge to admire her more fully. She was magnificent, and her attention was focused intently on him, making him feel as if she saw no one else in the room. He was instantly charmed by her flashing hazel eyes and the provocative curl of her lips. They practically whispered to him that she was well aware of what she was doing and how she appeared. No expense had been spared on Miss Gold's gown; its emerald green satin was shaped in the latest Parisian fashion, and the color enhanced the smooth olive tone of her skin. A delicate string of white and yellow flowers traced the deeply plunging contours of her bodice then followed the line from her waist to the floor, and a single matching flower had been added to her shining mass of chestnut hair, coiled softly behind her slender neck.

"A pleasure to meet you, Monsieur Nobel," she purred, holding out a hand for a kiss. Her voice was low, confident, and unabashedly sexual, and her wide eyes sparkled with blatant invitation. "This is my new method of greeting people. It is very French," she explained in a cultured English accent. "I hope you do not mind, but I absolutely adore all things French."

He brought her gloved hand to his lips. Before he could kiss it she drew both their hands closer to her chest, giving him an opportunity to admire her well displayed cleavage.

"*Enchanté*," he replied, enjoying the introduction very much.

"I was recently in Paris, and I greatly enjoyed myself. The fashion, the food and wine ... it was all very decadent. You must love Paris, do not you, Monsieur Nobel?"

"But of course. Who could not love Paris? Especially when it is offered so attractively." He glanced at Miller, but the American had left them alone. The move had plainly been choreographed, but Emanuel did not mind. "I gather you speak the language fluently."

"Monsieur, I speak seven languages." The tip of her tongue appeared at the corner of her mouth then disappeared, leaving Emanuel with a fleeting suggestion. "I find it helpful to be able to converse easily with men on many levels."

She was truly delicious. "So you are the Trade Attaché? Dare I ask if you bring any tasty morsels of information related to the rather complex theories on future oil marketing?"

"But of course, Monsieur. I come bearing many gifts. I can tell you that England will be diplomatic and loyal in their pursuit of securing future oil supplies, and they will support stability, of course. That would be beneficial to BraNobel, provided the details align with our trade agreements with other nations."

"And by other nations, you refer to the United States."

Her eyes glittered with flirtation. "*Touché*! Yes, of course our relationship with America carries its weight; however, you should look at our introduction as a way to balance it more in your favor ... which should greatly contribute to your pleasure."

He had never met a woman like this, and he was entirely captivated. He knew what she was—an incurable flirt with designs on him—but he could find no reason why he shouldn't take her up on her offer.

"We should make the most of our options then," he replied.

She giggled behind one gloved hand. "Oh yes. We would never forgive ourselves if we did not, *c'est vrai*?"

"*Ah, oui*," he replied. "*Certainement*." He glanced over as Miller returned, frowning purposefully at Julie. "I believe your escort has returned for you. It has been a pleasure making your acquaintance."

She gazed up at him from under long, thick lashes. "The pleasure, Monsieur, has been mine. I look forward to our next encounter."

He watched the slender line of her back as she was led to the other end of the room, enjoying the heat rushing through his body. The sensation was something he had not felt in a very long time. This could be interesting.

"Mr Nobel."

The short, round man addressing Emanuel did not fit in with the glamorous crowd, but he certainly belonged. His large eyes peered through thick spectacles, and though he was not much older than Emanuel, the beginnings of jowls were forming beneath his cheeks. His eyes were alert, but they lacked the confrontational gleam Emanuel might have expected.

"Mr Samuel," he said through his impressive mustache. "I am pleased to finally make your acquaintance. Your attendance here tonight, in an event which celebrates BraNobel's success, proves you to be a man of virtue."

One corner of Marcus Samuel's mouth lifted in a sardonic smile, and he tugged the bottom of his ill-fitting suit jacket. "We shall leave that topic untested, I believe, though I have come to expect good graces from you. I have looked forward to speaking in person."

"Thank you. Was there something in particular you wished to discuss?"

"Well, I will start by saying how remarkable it is, how much you have caused to change here in Baku. Indeed, in the oil business worldwide. Even as a competitor I can admire that." He used one finger to push his spectacles higher on his nose. "However, you should know that I will go to any length necessary to beat you."

Such straightforward talk was refreshing. "As you should," Emanuel replied. "I would expect nothing less. There are reasons why you are in your position, Mr Samuel, and I applaud you for being there."

"My company has the biggest fleet in the Pacific, as you most likely know," Samuel said. "We move seventy-five percent of all the oil in Indonesia. Nobody in the Pacific has ever undersold us. Not even Standard Oil. Now I walk the docks in Japan and find your ships being loaded rather than my own, and when I ask why, the numbers I am shown are quite inconceivable, to be honest."

"Of course, we knew you dominated the shipping," Emanuel said, "and we could not possibly undercut your rates, so we simply had to invent a better way to deliver."

Samuel chuckled and gave a little bow. "I suppose your appreciation falls short of a royalty payment to me."

Emanuel laughed, but it was not derisive. He had never felt obliged to resort to dirty fighting, though many of the attacks dealt to BraNobel had been ugly. Every business must include competition, and the oil business was the biggest business of all. Until this point, he had only ever shared this kind of friendly, honest banter with Zeynalabdin, Musa, and Murtuza, and occasionally with Shamsi Asadullayev, another Azerbaijani oil baron and philanthropist. It was gratifying to find a similar personality in Marcus Samuel.

"Your candor proves you to be a respectable gentleman," Samuel replied. "And your success proves you to be a worthy rival."

This time it was Emanuel who bowed. "Your compliment is much appreciated, sir; however, do not think I will be fooled into underestimating you."

"Ha! No, no. We shall leave the sin of underestimating the innovators and political masters in oil to the Rockefellers."

Their good-natured banter continued for a few more minutes, and both seem equally pleased with it. Eventually, however, Emanuel noticed others waiting for his attention, and he knew he must move on. Reluctantly, he held out his hand.

"We shall speak again," Emanuel said.

"I am counting on it," Samuel replied.

He passed the next hour or so in pleasant, light conversation, but his mind remained on the two which had preceded those. When the clock chimed, Elbek appeared in the doorway. As usual, the butler was right on time. Emanuel's gaze skimmed over the guests' heads, casually seeking Miss Gold.

Without changing his sober expression, Elbek announced, "At this time we ask all of Mr Nobel's distinguished guests to honor him with their presence in the ballroom."

With voices lifted in curious anticipation, the people in the room poured into the ballroom where Emanuel's arranged entertainment waited. He had wanted to provide exactly the right diversion for tonight, so he had gone to one of his workers, a man with a passion for dance. To his delight, he discovered the man had already assembled his own group of dancers, and Emanuel was quickly assured that the group would be deeply honored to perform for the assembly. Many of the locals had seen this type of thing before, but the international guests would regard it as a truly novel experience. When everyone was ready and waiting expectantly, the lead dancer in the troupe stepped up, bowed crisply, then announced,

"Ladies and gentlemen, we present the Lezginka dance, the traditional dance of the people of Caucasus."

He was joined by five other men, all of whom wore knee-length black coats, shiny black leather boots, and black fur caps. The group had brought their own musicians, who were positioned at the side and awaiting the dancers' cue. One squeezed a *garmon* between his hands, another pulled a bow across the strings of his *kamancha,* and behind them stood a pair of drums called the *gosha nagara*. There was even a *balaban,* and the musician was preparing its reed for a noisy demonstration.

When the dancers all stood ready, the music and the dancing began. Emanuel had seen the performance twice before, so he knew the spectacle the audience was about to experience. The men began with a spinning circle, each one keeping a rapid pace to maintain the space between the man in front of him, then the individual, showy dances began. One by one each man demonstrated his skills, captivating the audience with quick, concise steps, turns, and leaps.

"I am truly impressed."

The sultry voice came from just behind his right shoulder, and Emanuel turned slowly toward Julie Gold. Her reappearance was an unexpected surprise. Apparently the evening's entertainment was about to improve even further.

"I know it is terribly brazen of me, but I must admit," she said quietly, "I find great pleasure in admiring strong men."

The heat radiating from her gaze was enough to practically hypnotize Emanuel. "I am pleased to hear you are enjoying the show. Do you have a good enough view?"

Her eyes never left his. "Oh yes. I have the best view in the house."

The crowd cheered, startling Emanuel from his daze, but he did not glance over. He was watching Julie. Since the music continued, he assumed the dancing did as well.

"You are enjoying the party, then?"

"Very much. Only ... well, I hesitate to ask ..."

He chuckled. "I doubt you hesitate with very much, Ms Gold."

She had the good grace to appear abashed at his comment, but she did not deny his suggestion. "I was wondering if I could be so selfish as to ask for a glimpse of your famous Fabergé egg collection."

"Right now?"

"If it is not too much to ask." One satin-clad finger softly touched her lips then moved away. "You see, I prefer quiet conversations over loud music."

"It would be my pleasure."

She slid her hand onto his extended arm, and they left the gathering, heading down the corridor toward Emanuel's beloved art room. Like his father, he took great pride in displaying his collection. Emanuel had discovered the Fabergé eggs recently in St. Petersburg, and since then he had become one of Fabergé's most valuable customers, purchasing up to forty percent of their annual production. The pieces were particular favorites of his, so it gave him added pleasure that Julie had mentioned those specifically.

The room sparkled with light, reflecting off the glass jewelry cases, illuminating a dozen masterful paintings on the walls. Julie headed unerringly toward the centerpiece of the room, and he watched the outline of her back sliding through the satin as she moved.

"It is stunning," she breathed. "I had heard you were a collector, but I did not know about all this!"

"This clock was one of my first purchases, then the goblets, but I am entranced by the eggs. The craftsmanship and care taken to create these works of perfection is fantastic. And this—" He gestured toward the all-white egg in the middle. Inside the treasure was one of Fabergé's trademark surprises: a miniature platinum watch decorated with rose-cut diamonds and rock crystal.

"The Nobel Ice," she whispered, sounding awed. "The one Fabergé himself made specifically for you. Oh, it is divine. Ethereal, really." She looked around the side of the display case. "And these necklaces! So lovely." She gazed up at him from under her lashes. "I can only imagine how luxurious one of those would feel on my *décolletage*."

He chuckled. "I see it from the other point of view, actually. I imagine anything fortunate enough to rest on such a coveted nest would feel caressed by luxury."

"My, my," she purred, looking delighted. "So the legends are wrong. You are not all business."

"Legends? No, no. Those do not apply to me. Legends, after all, rise from fictional characters you never actually meet."

"But of course." In a calculated, intimate move, she lifted her hand and adjusted the lapel of his coat. "On the other hand, I understand many of the tales are inspired by actual men. I should very much like to know if you are one of those."

Elbek stepped through the doorway. "Sir, forgive my intrusion. You requested I find you for the final passing of champagne."

"So I did."

The long, elegant fingers of her right hand fit perfectly onto his as he lifted them to his lips again.

"Until we meet again," he said gently.

"Which I hope will be very soon," she replied just as softly.

Chapter Thirteen

St. Petersburg

The hotel ballroom tables had been arranged in a half circle, and Emanuel stood behind them, hands behind his back. Like the twenty-four invited guests already sitting as close as possible to the display, he waited for Czar Alexander III to assume his seat along with his two science advisors. As he always did, the Czar tilted his head slightly, self-conscious about the large cyst on the left side of his nose. Like everyone else in the room, Emanuel pretended not to notice.

When they were all in place, Emanuel gave a small bow. "Your Majesty! On behalf of the BraNobel company, I wish to thank you for coming. Today's demonstration is a very exciting one. I am confident it will benefit not only Russia, but the entire world'.

"I chose to conduct this presentation in a hotel rather than in a usual laboratory, because it is in this type of environment that we all use kerosene. We are all well acquainted with standing next to kerosene, and we know what happens when it is lit. Today I would like to demonstrate what that means."

He spread his hands, indicating the lamps on the tables. Each one stood behind its own small white card which marked it as BraNobel, Standard Oil, Shell, Royal Dutch, Benkendorf and Co, Russian Oil General Corp, and Anglo-Russian.

"In these lamps is kerosene from the seven major oil companies in Baku, including BraNobel."

Emanuel stepped up to the middle table. "One of the chief complaints about kerosene," he said, lighting one of the lamps, "is that it does not burn cleanly. It leaves black soot marks on the ceiling and can make people sick with its fumes."

He lit the next two lamps, saving BraNobel's for last. "The reason kerosene does this is because of the impurities it carries. You can see that all of these lamps are doing exactly what kerosene has always done."

Everyone sat silently, staring at the lamps, obviously unimpressed.

Emanuel straightened and indicated the final lamp. "And now, gentlemen, I would like to demonstrate the new BraNobel formula."

He leaned in, lit the lamp, and the audience blinked in disbelief.

"Our goals at BraNobel are worldwide; however, with a discovery so obviously impressive, it is my honor to give Russia first rights to our new kerosene, to impress the visitors from governments of the world, and to remind them that the most brilliant minds and inventions come from Russia." He held out his hand, indicating the cleanly burning lamp. "This will produce justified awe in both social and military arenas. If we can beat the world in heating oil, they will wonder what other new inventions will give Russia an edge when it comes to war!"

The audience's reaction was exactly what he had hoped for. "So if it would please you all, I would like to offer His Majesty Czar Alexander III the first honor."

The Czar seemed not to have any of the reluctance shown by the earlier Czar. He practically jumped to his feet in a rush to light another BraNobel lamp. Out of habit, he leaned back as he held the flame to the wick, but he relaxed when the lamp burned clean. Beside him, the Czar's two advisors lit the other lamps, all of which belched out thick black smoke and the anticipated acrid stink.

"This is marvelous," the Czar said, beaming at Emanuel.

Emanuel gave a little bow of gratitude. "My assistants have prepared several cases of oil for the Czar so he can impress his guests in his palaces."

"Excellent."

Emanuel regarded the others. "Among today's audience," he said, stepping back from the table, "sit the largest distributors of kerosene in our great country. Gentlemen, I invite you to conduct any test you wish. As of right now, you control not only supplies from here to Moscow, you can also export to Eurasia and all other countries within and adjacent to the Russian Empire. I encourage you to seize this opportunity to dominate the industry."

Moments later, Emanuel stood at the side of the tables, accepting accolades.

"Remarkable achievement, Mr Nobel," said one scientist. "Our company controls half the imported kerosene in Moscow, and we will gladly cancel all our outstanding orders with competitors if you can meet our needs."

"Excellent. Then you had better be sure you place your order promptly, to carry you through the winter. BraNobel always wants to serve Russians first."

The next man to approach looked unsure. "Your demonstration convinced me, Mr Nobel, but I am confused." He held up a paper. "This letter I received says your kerosene will be tested against others two days from now at the Imperial Russian Technical Society building. Do I have to view the same test twice?"

A warning bell sounded in Emanuel's head. "May I read the letter?"

The scientist handed it over, and Emanuel read through it carefully.

"I must admit that I, too, am confused," he said. "Normally I would be informed—and invited—to attend tests before state officials. In answer to your question, no. You have already seen the demonstration. You already know BraNobel's quality surpasses Standard Oil and all other kerosene."

"How fortunate. That means I can take my train home tonight."

"You certainly can," Emanuel replied. "Would you mind if I kept your invitation?"

"Not at all. And thank you again, Mr Nobel, for this very impressive demonstration. You are to be congratulated."

Perplexed, Emanuel decided to stay a little longer in the family house Ludvig had built in St. Petersburg. That way he could attend the curious meeting using the scientist's invitation.

In the early evening he decided to visit a local restaurant for supper and was surprised to see the lovely Julie Gold was also there, enjoying a meal with another woman and two gentlemen. He did not recognize the other woman, but one of the men looked slightly familiar, and he tried to recall from where. Julie had not seen him yet, since her back was mostly to him, but there was no mistaking her.

The waiter was at his table within moments. "Good afternoon, sir. How may I help you?"

He kept his eyes on Julie while he ordered, purposefully projecting his voice a little above what it needed to be. Hearing him, she spun around, and he was pleased to see her usual confidence waver, though she quickly masked her startled expression. When he tilted his head in invitation, she leaned forward to speak to her friends then excused herself. He stood and pulled out a chair for her.

"I hope you were not saving this seat for anyone in particular, Monsieur Nobel," she said, eyes twinkling.

"Only for you, Mademoiselle Gold. What an unexpected pleasure."

"It is a wonderful surprise," Julie gushed as he returned to his seat. "I did not know you were here in St. Petersburg."

Two very pleasant hours of conversation passed, during which Emanuel enjoyed a couple of Cuban cigars and Julie lit a cannabis cigarette, which he declined when she offered one to him. Throughout the conversation her confidence never left her, but her showy exterior softened. She was an intelligent woman, without a doubt. Her sense of humor was refreshing, as was her ability to speak openly and easily of both politics and personalities.

"Miss Gold, I must be bold and ask a personal question."

She leaned back in her chair slightly. "Ask away."

"Who is this mysterious enchantress before me? I would not for a moment believe you are a simple Trade Attaché."

A flutter of unease crossed her face. "Whatever do you mean?"

"Where do you come from? What has made you who you are?"

"A personal question indeed, Monsieur Nobel. Everyone comes from somewhere, as you say." She examined her drink while she spoke. "I have been to a lot of places, done a lot of things. I thank you for your compliment on my character, but I can assure you it was not always so strong. What was it the late, great French poet Victor Hugo said? 'Adversity breeds character'." Her eyes lifted to his. "I believe he is right about that. Character is built out of necessity."

She was throwing it back at him, he realized, needing more time to consider what sort of man he was before she shared her story.

"'If we had no winter, the spring would not be so pleasant; if we did not sometimes taste of adversity, prosperity would not be so welcome.'"

Her eyes danced in the candlelight. "Who said that?"

"The American humorist, Josh Billings. Not as succinct as Hugo, but just as insightful."

She sighed, giving in. "My mother was born to an affluent family in Indonesia, and my father is Palestinian. He came from a line of successful jewelry merchants," she said, absently touching the pearls at her throat, "and they have always dealt with various royal courts. It was all very glamorous, but I suppose it got a little dull for me. My father sent my oldest brother and me to London to study, but I left Oxford after a year. I was bored with my studies, too. I needed some kind of adventure in my life."

"Did you ever go back to Indonesia? Perhaps visit your grandparents? I have been to Japan, but not Indonesia. I imagine it would be very exotic. They obviously have the ability to produce the most beautiful women in the world."

His words prompted a small dimple on her cheek which he had not noticed before. "I did, but they had died by that time. I stayed for a little while anyway, and I do love the country. I have travelled to a lot of places, met a lot of interesting people."

"Which explains your talent at languages."

"Yes, this is correct," she said in Russian. "I imagine you speak quite a few as well."

He nodded, but he preferred to hear her voice over his own.

She sipped at her drink. "The world is not always kind, but it does teach a woman many things."

"What would be the most important of those lessons?"

Her eyes narrowed slightly. "To survive however I could. I did not always make the right decisions, but I ended up on my feet eventually." She frowned, considering. "To ensure I did not damage the family name through some of my more questionable adventures, my parents have decided not to speak to me anymore."

"I am sorry."

"I am as well, but I understand. I was not an ideal child." She blinked slowly. "Tell me about you, Emanuel. About Sweden. That is one place where I have never been."

Their conversations became more intimate, and their subtle flirtatious remarks deepened into definite possibilities. By the time they had finished a couple of whiskies each, the possibilities had turned to realities, and they took his carriage to his house on Lesnaya Avenue. Throughout the ten-minute journey they spoke little, but the heat rising between their bodies was intoxicating. From the way she looked at him, the way she sat with her arm slightly against his, the breathy tone of her laughter, he could tell she was as anxious as he was for the welcoming embrace of his bed.

Chapter Fourteen

Emanuel was under no illusions that Miss Gold would be a timid lover. Everything about the woman was smooth, from the soft rolls of hair that tumbled down her back when he pulled out the pins, to the rich gold of her skin, and to the warm lips which parted eagerly for his. She tasted of whisky and spices and promise, and he happily surrendered to her hands and expertise. Her prowess was intoxicating, but when he took the lead she dissolved helplessly in his arms, filling him with a sense of power. Afterward, they lay side by side, catching their breath and enjoying the warm sense of contentment.

Her eyes opened slowly, and he was surprised by the tears he saw in them.

"Of contentment," she assured him, letting out a long, satisfied groan. "That was wonderful."

She closed her eyes and was asleep within seconds, the remnants of a smile lingering at the edges of her lips. Hours later, her features had relaxed, but still she slept. A slow pulse beat silently on the side of her neck, exactly where his lips had been just a few hours before.

In the morning he awoke early, as he always did. She still slept soundly beside him, her hair in shiny tangles over the pillow. Gone was the sensual tigress from the previous evening, replaced by the guileless innocence of a kitten.

As quietly as he could, he dressed and crept from the room, not wanting to wake her. He spoke with the butler who promised to send Emanuel's requested newspapers to the room along with breakfast.

Emanuel hesitated. "Bring it in a half hour. I do not believe Miss Gold is awake yet."

She was still in bed when he returned, but she was awake. "Good morning."

Seeing him there, she stretched luxuriously then sat up, pulling the sheets up out of modesty. She had not yet gathered herself sufficiently to present the confident, sensual woman she had been last night.

"Good morning to you. You are up early."

" 'I never knew a man come to greatness or eminence who lay abed late in the morning.' "

She narrowed her eyes. "Wait. I know that one."

"J—"

"Johnathan Swift," she cried, beaming.

He slid out of his shoes and sat beside her on the bed. "Well done."

"Mmm." Her head rested on his shoulder. "Thank you for a wonderful evening, Emanuel."

"My pleasure. Truly."

"It is hard to imagine getting out of bed, really."

Emanuel was not an impulsive man. Not usually, anyway. Her hair was mussed, her eyes dark with lingering sleep, but he did not think she would mind.

"Then let's not," he murmured, introducing her to the soft white sheets again. "Breakfast will be here in a little while."

When the servant knocked a half hour later, she was curled in his arms, her breath tickling the hair on his chest.

"A moment!" he called. He kissed her brow. "Hungry, my dear?"

"Famished."

She excused herself as Emanuel opened the door. The house servant set the table in their suite then set out two glasses of freshly squeezed orange juice alongside French croissants and black *sevruga* caviar with *blini*. A small jar of honey made from Royal jelly was placed near the croissants.

The door closed behind him just as Julie emerged from the toilet room in a laced white corset and matching short skirt. As usual, she was a vision, and she knew it.

"I smell coffee," she murmured.

He pulled out her chair then sat across the table from her, enjoying his breakfast and her company. The newspapers were there as well, but it would be rude to read them in front of her. He would go through them after she had gone.

At first she spoke very little, but she listened to every word. She had the eyes of a cat, alternating between sensual and alert. When she did speak, she either suggested a slightly different point of view, or she teased him. She never let him off easily, and he enjoyed the challenge.

"Would you be available for dinner this evening?" he asked after she had finished dressing.

The sensual cat was back, and she wore an enticing pout. "I would indeed, sir."

"I shall send my carriage, if you would like."

"That sounds divine. I look forward to it."

Paperwork took up most of his day, and as he worked he thought more about Julie. It had taken him a while, but he finally remembered the identity of the man with whom she had originally been sitting the day before. He also recalled why he knew him—or rather, why he knew *of* him. Why did *she* know him?

When dusk settled, he climbed into his carriage and headed to Julie's hotel, *The Angleterre*. His driver went in and waited for her, then she appeared in the doorway in a burgundy gown with a deliciously low, square neckline. A black velvet cape was layered over her shoulders.

"Where are we going?" she asked, accepting his help into the carriage.

"Do you know the *Chekhov*? It is one of my favorites here."

"I do." Her eyes sparkled with anticipation. "An excellent choice."

At her request, he ordered salmon for her, and he requested veal for himself. She drank white wine, he drank red. From the beginning of the meal to the end, both were aware of the electricity sparking between them. Emanuel decided not to ask about the man he had seen her with before. That could wait.

Despite the delicious food and the restaurant's exquisite musical entertainment, neither wanted to remain there another moment. They barely made it to his bedroom before she was naked once more, taking his breath away. Moments later they lay in a tangle of cool white sheets.

"You are flawless," he marveled, running the palm of his hand from her shoulder, over one breast, then past the soft pillow of her stomach. "Pure loveliness."

"I am far from flawless," she chided him, "but I shall let you believe what you like, for it is to my benefit."

He lowered his lips to her stomach, kissing her there. She wriggled with delight.

"In my opinion, you are flawless," he told her. The kisses continued, making their way progressively lower. "And I should remind you, Miss Gold, that a lot of important men value my opinion."

*

In the morning he leaned over her, watching her eyes. They were closed, but she was smiling, obviously awake. He caressed her soft black hair, looping it around his fingers and hoping his news would not entirely ruin everything.

"Good morning," he said softly.

She smiled, her eyes still closed, and made a quiet sound of pleasure in her throat.

"I hope this won't come as a shock," he murmured, "but I should tell you that I recognized the man with whom you sitting at the restaurant."

She was quick to cover her surprise. "Oh? How interesting. I barely knew him. I had been enjoying supper with my friend when her two friends joined us. Like how I joined you."

"Oh really? What a coincidence."

"It is indeed." Her eyes darkened with meaning. "But let us not speak of strangers. Let us instead enjoy each other ... again."

When he rolled obligingly on top of her, she smiled with invitation. He lowered his lips toward hers, and she closed her eyes, anticipating a kiss, but he stopped an inch away.

"What were you really doing with Colonel James Ray?" he asked calmly. "A spy for the British government."

Her eyes flew open, and for a moment he relished the delightfully vulnerable shock in them. When she opened her lips to speak, he leaned in and kissed her, taking control again. Just as quickly she yielded, melting into his arms.

"Do you have an answer, Miss Gold?"

She settled on feigning offense. "You do not believe that I was with my friend before the gentlemen arrived?"

"Of course not."

She swallowed. "I am insulted, sir. You do not know me well enough to accuse me of—"

"*Au contraire.*" With one thumb he brushed a stray lock of hair from her cheek and tucked it behind her ear. "I would say I know you very well, so you might as well tell me the truth. You may be a Trade Attaché, but that is not all. Are you also a spy?"

It was interesting, watching the thoughts change behind her beautiful eyes. Should she continue the lie? Should she weave it more deeply? Or should she admit the truth? Were there consequences to her doing that—or rather, any she could not handle?

Eventually she sighed with resignation. "No. I am *not* a spy. Technically James is not either."

"No?"

"He is a retired MI-6 officer."

"Who is he to you?"

"My protector and mentor." Her voice was wistful. "He rescued me from a very ugly youth, one that could have destroyed me as well as my family, and he took me under his wing. I did tell you that I made some poor choices in my life.

He was there when I needed help. He has taught me a great deal."

He stopped short of asking if that was the extent of their relationship. That was none of his business. "I imagine he has. Retired MI-6 indeed." He shook his head, disappointed. "Now tell me what you are, Miss Gold. What you really are."

Her expression became defensive, even proud. "You are correct. My business goes beyond the title of Attaché. I call myself an independent information agent, which means I am hired to relay information when it is requested."

"And who is requesting information about me?"

"It is not you, Emanuel. It is BraNobel."

"Of course. Which is one and the same." His jaw tightened. "Am I to understand that you are supplying information about my company to Colonel Ray?"

Her nod was almost imperceptible.

Ever since he'd recalled the man's name, he had known that was most likely the case. Still, he was hurt to discover he had been right. He did not often give himself the liberty of enjoying a life outside of business, and this liaise with Julie had been a sort of gift to himself for a job well done. Fortunately, what they had was not love, so he suffered neither a broken heart nor shattered expectations.

"And what will you tell him about this? About our evening together?"

"Nothing. I would never share that, Emanuel."

"What will you tell him about BraNobel?"

Her expression fell a little. "Actually, you have given me nothing. All I can tell him is that you have exquisite taste in art."

He stared at her a moment, undecided. Should he be more angry at her or at himself for so easily falling for her charms? Without a word he rolled up and sat on the side of the bed, facing away.

"I know this sounds terrible, Emanuel," she said quietly, "but I believe I can help you."

"Now you are a double agent?"

"I work for myself. I choose my clients."

He refused to look at her. "How do you imagine helping me? And what's the catch?"

A tentative finger touched the small of his back and continued to progress slowly up his spine when he did not move away. "I would not ask for money from you. I ... I would like to be with you. I like you very much, Emanuel, and I am on your side, believe it or not. I could help by telling the right people what you want them to hear. Something you *want* them to hear but do not want announced through official channels. And I can listen for what people are saying about you."

He reached for a towel then stood and wrapped it modestly around his waist. She had not moved, so when he finally turned back toward her, she lay as he had left her. It was not her fault, he admitted. She was exquisite in every way, from the perfect curves of her fawn colored body to her beautifully crafted manners and speech. She had learned to use those qualities to provide herself with a glamorous and exciting life, learned—as she had said—how to survive. Not many women he knew—or men, for that matter—were either courageous or intelligent enough to do that.

No. This was *his* fault. By caring about her, he had allowed himself to be human, which had been a mistake.

She leaned on one elbow now, watching him with intelligent eyes, her long, black hair falling over one shoulder. "I ... I was actually going to have to tell you in the morning anyway."

"That does not sound true. Why would you tell me?"

"Because I need to tell you something, and you are a smart man. You would want to know how I had come by this knowledge."

"I am supposed to trust you all of a sudden? Why should I?"

Her gaze dropped. "I want you to trust me, but it would not make sense for me to insist upon it, considering what you have just learned about me. And yet I will still tell you the information I have, for it is important for you to know. It is up to you whether you choose to trust it or not."

Even now he was drawn to her. He wanted to sit back on the bed, run his fingers over the slope of her naked shoulder and watch the goosebumps rise magically along her skin.

He crossed his arms instead. "So tell me then, and let me judge for myself."

"It is with regard to your kerosene demonstration the other day. The one you did for the Czar and his advisors."

His eyes narrowed. She should not have known about that. "What of it?"

"This is not the only kerosene demonstration happening here in St. Petersburg."

He had tucked the scientist's clean white invitation into his briefcase after the initial demonstration, unable to make sense of it, planning to learn more by attending the event himself.

"This is not news to me," he said sharply.

"The other demonstration," she continued, "is this afternoon at the—"

"—Imperial Russian Technical Society building. Yes, I know."

"So you know what Rockefeller's top advisors have planned then, do you?"

"Rockefeller's people? What do they have to do with this?"

One smooth, dark eyebrow lifted. "You know he is determined you will not beat Standard Oil."

"Of course."

She sat up slowly, drawing the sheets against her body as if to keep their personal conversation separate from business. "Might I recommend," she said, "that you ensure you have someone in place behind the scenes before and during the demonstration? In the storage room in particular."

The hair on the back of Emanuel's neck lifted. "What are you saying?"

"I am saying," she replied, matter-of-fact, "there is a plan in place to tamper with BraNobel's kerosene and completely destroy you."

Chapter Fifteen

J.D. Rockefeller had a lot of important contacts—though Emanuel sincerely doubted anyone would say they were the man's friends. Emanuel, on the other hand, had both important contacts and friends. Following Julie's warning, he placed immediate phone calls to the chief of the *okhrana*—the Czar's secret police—who assured him his plain-clothed agents would not allow it.

The scientist's invitation gave him easy access, and he quietly joined the hundred or so people already gathered, keeping his head down so as to avoid being recognized. He found a seat near the back, and a few minutes later he was joined by a man he had never seen before.

"Lovely weather for ducks," the man muttered.

Emanuel agreed with a nod, recognizing the code upon which they had already agreed.

The secret policeman looked particularly pleased, though he did not look at Emanuel directly. "This demonstration promises to be quite entertaining," he said quietly.

Trying to maintain a neutral expression, Emanuel leaned back in his chair and waited while the carts of kerosene samples were wheeled into the room. The scientist in charge of the demonstration began by indicating the more than five kerosene lanterns already burning on the stage's display table. As in the other presentation, each lamp stood behind an identification label. Emanuel spotted BraNobel right away, then he made out the labels of Standard Oil, Shell, Royal Dutch, Benkendorf and Co, Russian Oil General Corp, and Anglo-Russian. The scientist gave an introduction to each lamp before he lit it, and the newspaper reporters leaned forward to watch, paying close attention.

"Our final sample is from BraNobel," announced the scientist. "Under the category of relevant disclosures, it should be stressed that this sample is from a refinery using a new process which increases BraNobel's yield. They hope to flood the market with it."

Though the statement was false, Emanuel bit his tongue.

The scientist leaned down to light the BraNobel lamp, and the kerosene smoked furiously, causing him to take a step back. Gasps of surprise were heard through the room, and reporters scribbled furiously in their notebooks, their faces tight with disapproval. Emanuel stared, aghast. Julie had been right. Now what? He glanced in horror at the policeman beside him, but the man said nothing. He held up one hand, requesting patience, then he slipped out of his seat.

"Let the notes reflect an abnormal amount of soot and particles were released by the BraNobel oil," the scientist continued. "Measurements shall be captured for complete analysis relative to the other samples."

The door to the stage was suddenly flung open, and three men strode to the front. One was a government official, one was a scientist, and the third was wearing handcuffs. They were met onstage by the secret policeman.

"Excuse us for interrupting the presentation before it is properly concluded," he said, "however, if we waited we would allow a criminal to escape and a grave error to go uncorrected." He addressed the audience as a whole. "Gentlemen, I regret to inform you that we have witnessed a fraud here today."

The audience members exchanged startled glances as the handcuffed man was urged forward a step.

"We have evidence which proves this man was paid to sabotage the BraNobel sample, and our own agents witnessed him pouring water into the sample in order to destroy its quality."

The reporters had their heads down and were writing rapidly in their books. Emanuel peered over the heads in front of him and smiled with satisfaction at one darkly sketched headline which read: "BraNobel Kerosene Sabotaged!"

"Fortunately," continued the scientist, "we held a private and official test of the new BraNobel kerosene the other day, presenting it for royalty. The test proved conclusively that the superior quality of BraNobel's new formula is above and beyond comparison. As a result, the Czar will soon be presenting an official award to Emanuel Nobel and BraNobel for the discovery."

Julie met him an hour later at a different restaurant. She showed no hint on her beautiful face, but he could tell she was eager to hear what had transpired. Emanuel took the seat opposite her and turned to the waiter before she could say a word.

"A bottle of your best champagne," he said to the man, then he gave Julie the look she had hoped for. "And two glasses."

Julie's eyes were not on Emanuel, but on the small box he had placed in front of her. At his insistence she opened it, and now she stared with disbelief at the contents. Candlelight lit the Fabergé necklace so that it shone tiny stars on her face as well as on her stunning black suit. Emanuel rose from his seat then went around behind to fasten the treasure around her neck.

"You knew they would want vengeance," Julie said carefully, her fingers on the gems.

He returned to his seat and regarded the gift now that it was displayed properly. "Of course. Go ahead, my little spy, and tell me what you have learned."

She scowled, but her fingers caressed the curves and corners of the jewel around her neck. "I do not like it when you call me that."

"And yet that is exactly what you are, my dear."

They stared at each other, both accepting this development in their relationship. At first, Emanuel had naively thought their connection was simply physical. She, on the other hand, had considered him to be no more than a wealthy and charming source. Both had developed deeper feelings already.

"Well, they did not like their nasty little kerosene trick being ruined, and they do not like that the headlines are convincing people not to buy oil products from a criminal."

"I imagine not."

"So what will Mr Rockefeller's next move be in this great game?" Once upon a time Emanuel and the others had likened the oil business to chess. He still enjoyed the comparison.

"I do not know, but I am working on it. He will use his money, obviously, since he cannot do anything to counter your brilliance."

"It will be interesting, whatever he decides."

After the kerosene demonstrations, orders flooded Emanuel's desk. In fact, the orders were so numerous their production would require more money than Emanuel had, despite his many millions. With scientists' reports and orders in hand, he went to the Russian bank for a loan. The bank president with whom he met was unfamiliar to him, but that was no surprise. These people seemed to change often, while his own workers remained at BraNobel's derricks for years without complaint.

The man across the desk folded his hands together, attempting to hide the trembling fingers. Then he denied Emanuel the loan.

"I do not understand." Emanuel placed his hand firmly on the papers before him. "I have contracts here for *millions* of barrels. This will make a fortune over the year, completely dwarfing the loans I am requesting from your institution."

"I am very sorry, Mr Nobel." He spoke quickly, as if he had rehearsed his lines. "As I am sure you are aware, we must follow a strict formula here, and these loans are too speculative. If your process were to break down in any one of its departments, the entire flow of kerosene would stop. If that happened, you would never be able to pay back a loan of this size."

"It will not break down," Emanuel insisted.

"I am sorry, Mr Nobel."

"Fine. Your competition will welcome my visit."

Over the next two days Emanuel visited other banks, but his requests were met by the same astonishing result. Exhausted and frustrated, he returned to his rooms and sank onto his bed, still in his suit. He lay back, letting the mattress cushion the aches in his bones, and stared at the ceiling. His mind played with the off-white, swirling designs, following their patterns until a shape materialized among them. He saw a face in the random art, he was sure. A ... familiar face. That's when he realized why all this was happening.

Rockefeller had made his move.

In the past, the one person who had always known the answers had been Ludvig. All he had to do was look in his father's face and he would know what to do. But Ludvig was in Cannes, enjoying his retirement. And Alfred had warned him against bringing up business, in the interest of Ludvig's health. The best Emanuel could do was pick up a telephone and hope to somehow come up with an answer.

Ludvig sounded pleased. "I was going to telephone you today," he said. "It is indeed a marvelous thing, this telephone. Do you remember when we saw Alexander Graham Bell at the science conference in St. Petersburg?"

"I do indeed."

"While I still prefer written communication, it does me good to hear your voice."

"I agree wholeheartedly, Father. So tell me, why were you going to telephone me today of all days?"

"Because I had a visitor. A large, impressive man who was not particularly fond of you. It is important that you hear his message." He took a deep, wheezing breath. "He said his name was Libby, and he represented Standard Oil."

Emanuel's lip curled with dislike. William Herbert Libby, the American envoy. Though he had never met him face to face, he knew it was wise to understand his enemy, so he had researched Libby. An intelligent man, he surmised. A lobbyist with a Doctorate of Law from Yale and a rapacious hunger for power. Holding the rank of Ambassador and advisor to several nations, Libby rubbed shoulders with presidents and members of Congress. If there was one man who could outmaneuver governments and coerce corporations while treating Congressional inquiries and subpoenas with contemptuous fun, Libby was that man. An unrivaled strategist. The lethal combination made him the perfect puppet master for Rockefeller, which was how he also became Chief Strategist of Standard Oil and Standard Oil's foreign agent.

"Libby came to your home in Cannes? What kind of disrespect is that?"

"Oh, yes. I was rather glad to see him, actually. My days here are beautiful but dull. I know it is better for me here, but sometimes I do miss the challenges you still face. Anyway, I told him I already knew who he was. Do they think they are so smart we do not know who they are?"

He laughed, but the sound disintegrated into a hacking, heartbreaking cough. When it had calmed, Emanuel heard his father take a sip of something.

"He said my son was about to bankrupt the company, said you were reckless."

"Perhaps I am. What did you say?"

"I played the doddering old fool, listening and nodding. The man seemed certain you would be unable to deliver the ridiculous quantity of kerosene Russia demands for the winter, then he said the Czar would blame you for the deaths of a million Russians."

Emanuel's cheeks burned. Was it true? Somehow it seemed that way when it was delivered in his father's voice. Was he going to ruin everything?

"He even had a list of all the banks which had turned down your loan requests. He obviously had done his work, which is why I was not surprised to hear you say you believed Rockefeller is behind their turning you down." Ludvig sighed. "Then the fool tried to buy all my shares of BraNobel, offering several times the amount you were asking from the banks."

"So I was right about him."

"Of course you were, son. You have been correct all along."

Even now his father's faith in him brought tears to Emanuel's eyes. "What am I to do? He is right. If I cannot produce enough kerosene to fill all the orders, I will ruin the company."

"I am not worried, my son. The hard part was getting the contracts, which you have easily done. You showed the world your superior product, and you earned their trust. This problem is a small one. It will be solved somehow by you."

"But how, Father? Rockefeller is determined."

"He certainly is. Ah, Emanuel. You will be fine. You just need perspective. Your mind was always more creative in the social politics of our business. Engineer your situation from the reverse angle. Your investors would be most pleased to receive a considerably higher return for greater risk, do not you think?"

The clouds vanished from Emanuel's mind, making way for the sun. Under its light, the seed of an idea began to sprout and grow.

"Thank you, Father," he said. "I will look at every equation again. When I have figured it all out the way it needs to go, I will tell you my decision."

Ludvig chuckled, but the coughing fit started up again. "You run the business now, Emanuel," he managed. "Do not worry about me. Let an old man be surprised when he reads it in the papers."

As soon as he hung up the phone, Emanuel was already going over the numbers again. There had to be a way he could make this work. Within an hour, he had the answer. Within two days he had four private investors all to himself within the privacy of his office in St. Petersburg.

"Good afternoon, gentlemen," he said. "I appreciate your coming here in absolute confidentiality. I know you are looking around this room, trying to figure out my plan; however, the fact is that the deal I will put to you today is so simple I do not need charts or accounting statements showing graphs of returns."

He took a deep breath, bolstering himself for the giant leap into thin air he was about to take. "I am sure you have read the news about BraNobel's new kerosene. As a result of its unique quality, we have received an extraordinary number of orders. Of course this will greatly increase our production and shipping costs; however, the kerosene will be delivered to storage tanks from here to Moscow before the winter sets in."

The four men sat silently around the table, considering everything Emanuel said as they puffed on Cuban cigars he had provided. Fragrant clouds hovered over their heads. He could see they were interested, knew they had been following the story in the papers. Now he would see how committed they actually were, and if his father was right about him.

"I shall lock in a price today," he informed them. "After people start using the kerosene next month and discover its superior quality, both the demand and the price will go up. You, however, will pay today's price both today and one month from now. Or six months from now. What I offer is the right to own my delivery in the future, but at today's price. I am talking about kerosene which is not yet in storage. You may accept your own bids from buyers in six months, when they need it most. That future date will be in the middle of winter, when kerosene always rises in price. If, on that future date, the kerosene sells for more, you gentlemen will keep the profit."

He could practically see the numbers working themselves through their heads. Sitting back, he awaited the inevitable questions.

"What if you cannot deliver enough?"

"Then the price rises even more. You can make trades between yourselves if you need to."

One of the men tapped his pencil on the table. "This interests me. What are our risks?"

"The only way you lose money is if the demand for our kerosene drops so much that the price is lower than it is today. You all control enough industries that your added orders are a lever against this happening."

All four men thought it over. Emanuel could see his pitch was gaining their confidence. "In any event," he said, "your investment will never be a total loss, only slightly lower. If you get nervous, you can trade with each other to get out of this position."

An hour later Emanuel strode downstairs, clutching the investors' agreements in his briefcase and battling the urge to cheer aloud. He had done it. He had foiled Rockefeller by employing his mind, and he had not had to resort to the dirty, underhanded techniques so often employed by his competitor. Ludvig had been right, as always.

Chapter Sixteen

Emanuel walked amidst the derricks, collecting data from the men in charge of each well, though his mind was already busy with yet another business interest. He had been approached recently by an eager young engineer named Rudolf Diesel, a student at St. Petersburg's engineering school. The young man had apologized for bothering him with something so trivial, but said he was working on perfecting a new generation of diesel engine specifically for ships and thought Emanuel might be interested in hearing about it. Over an enjoyable meal at Emanuel's St. Petersburg house, Rudolf told him the new engine would guarantee the fastest, smoothest running ship in Europe, if not the world. Emanuel was more than a little intrigued.

A plume of dust caught his eye, and he spotted his house servant, Ramiz, roaring toward him in a carriage. His unaccustomed speed drew the attention of a number of workers, who crowded around with curiosity. Ramiz' expression was sombre, and Emanuel bit back the initial impulse to berate him for his reckless driving. He did not appreciate the horse's labored breathing.

"What is it?" Emanuel asked. "Something wrong at the house? Is someone injured?"

"No, sir. Everyone at the house is fine." Ramiz's brow creased, and Emanuel could see him struggling to maintain a calm exterior. "Mr Nobel, I regret to inform you that your father is with God."

A wave of emotion hit Emanuel, as hard and unforgiving as the sea itself, but he fought back. Everyone here had known and loved Ludvig. Now they would look to Emanuel for leadership—though by that point most already did.

Nevertheless, despite his own sharp grief, it was important that he keep his composure in front of his workers.

The King is dead. Long live the King.

Emanuel slid his hat off and clutched it to his chest, though no one saw how his knuckles whitened. He said nothing, only nodded his silent thanks to Ramiz.

Ramiz did not leave immediately. He stood quietly by the carriage, offering a kind of support, Emanuel realized, in case he was not up to staying here at the derricks.

He had never had a chance to tell his father how he had won the kerosene battle, how he had outsmarted Rockefeller yet again. He had never thanked him for his encouragement, for helping him to see through the clouds of his competitor's smoke. He had never really told him how much he meant to him, or that everything Emanuel had become was because of him.

The paperwork in his hands felt heavier than it had before, and the carefully written numbers swirled together.

"Do not worry about me. Let an old man be surprised when he reads it in the papers."

Emanuel raised his eyes and scanned the derrick field, trying to see everything they had created, wishing so badly that he could send the image to Ludvig, wherever he was. He still remembered how bleak and filthy the derricks had looked when they had first arrived twelve years before, how the noise had deafened them.

You did it, Father. You changed the world.

The knowledge that his father was gone left him feeling oddly displaced, as if the air had changed suddenly around him, as if he saw everything through a tunnel.

Neither he nor Ramiz said a word as they lowered themselves into the carriage and drove back to Villa Petrolea. A servant met him at the entrance and brought him tea, which he carried to his art room. Most of the paintings on the walls he had bought for himself. This afternoon he stood before an artist's bold painting of Stockholm. Ludvig had given it to Emanuel when Villa Petrolea had first opened its doors.

Though Emanuel no longer considered Sweden to be his home, he associated it with his father. He assumed he always would.

Ramiz carried a comfortable armchair to the room and placed it silently behind Emanuel. Then he left, closing the door silently behind him. Emanuel sank onto the chair with relief, suddenly exhausted. He closed his eyes, took a deep breath, then let the tears come.

*

In the morning, Emanuel sat at the dining table, waiting for Ramiz to appear with his breakfast and newspaper. He was unusually slow this morning, but Emanuel assumed it was because of the grief they shared. The whole mansion seemed to move more sluggishly this morning. At last Ramiz appeared with the silver tray, but his expression was bewildered.

"Why is it, my friend," Emanuel asked, "that I do not feel you have entirely good news for me this morning?"

"The news is ... rather strange, sir, and it pains me to have to bring it to you."

"Oh?"

"I think you had better read it for yourself," Ramiz replied. He unfolded a French newspaper then set it on the table in front of Emanuel.

ALFRED NOBEL, DYNAMITE KING, DECEASED, read the bold headline.

Emanuel blinked at the paper then frowned up at Ramiz. "Uncle Alfred? Is this true? Is he dead?"

"No, sir. I spoke with his servant today, and your uncle is fine. Not particularly healthy—"

"—he hasn't been healthy in quite some time. But he is alive?"

"Most certainly, sir."

"Then what ... ?" He shook his head and leaned over the paper, reading carefully.

Dr. Alfred Nobel, who became rich by finding ways to kill more people than ever
before, died yesterday.

He glanced up, incredulous. If Alfred was not dead already, Emanuel feared this horrible and exaggerated narrative might kill him. "Did you read this?"

Ramiz nodded reluctantly.

"'*Le Marchand de la Mort est Mort*'? They're calling him the 'Merchant of Death'? What is going on? This makes no sense. 'His water mines drowning sailors by the hundreds'?" Emanuel's eyes followed the text, but the meaning swam together in his mind. A thought struck him. "I must speak with my uncle."

"Yes, sir. Knowing you would feel this was necessary, I did request it of his servant. I was informed that Mr Nobel is behind closed doors today with his attorney and refuses to speak with anyone. He also said he had never seen his master so angry."

Emanuel imagined the scene. "Oh, I can believe that."

Certainly Alfred would take care of this, pursue the newspapers and have them print a necessary retraction. All the details would be taken care of to his uncle's satisfaction, he was sure. But that was not what concerned Emanuel the most.

The article was vicious. '*The Merchant of Death is Dead*', it proclaimed, accusing Alfred of making it possible to kill more people than ever before. No matter what he did to fix the article, the damage had been done; Alfred now knew what the world thought of him. Or at least what the newspapers wanted the world to think of him. Even if he did not die for another twenty years, this was how he would be remembered.

The way Emanuel saw it, Alfred had two choices. He could let this lie overwhelm him and eventually kill him, or he could do something momentous to counter this notion of him as a despicable human being. If only Emanuel could speak with him, get a sense of his mindset. But Alfred had retreated to make plans. Emanuel, like the rest of the world, would have to wait and see.

*

Zeynalabdin and Ilyas stood by Emanuel's limousine. Beside them stood the entire staff of Villa Petrolea, all of whom were lined up along the stairway, dressed in mourning black. Emanuel walked between them and accepted Taghiyev's warm handshake then his gentle embrace.

"Thank you, my friends," he said, then he climbed into the carriage.

When they reached the docks, Ramiz stood at attention at the gangplank of a private yacht, waiting for Emanuel. Ludvig's coffin had been sent directly from Cannes to St. Petersburg, where it would be buried in the Smolensky Lutheran Cemetery. Emanuel crossed the gangplank and made his way toward the bow. As they cast off, Emanuel felt a pang of loneliness. He longed for one last chance to speak with his father. To thank him for everything he had done and everything he had taught him. When they left the protected waters and entered the open sea, the wind pushed against his face, reminding him of the first time they had entered this harbor together. He had been young and brash, his father humble and wise. Emanuel had dared question both his father and his grandfather, he recalled. *How could I have been so naive?* He stroked the coarse black whiskers on his chin, thinking about how the years had flown, how the silver would soon invade his beard as it had his father's.

How inconceivable, he thought, *that a man so driven, a man with more energy than any other man he had ever known could end up in this box.*

A thought came to him then, like a whisper, and he recalled his father making the same movement he was making in that instant, patting his beard in almost exactly this same location so many years before.

Do not worry, Father, he said to the memory. *I will never forget you.*

Ludvig Nobel received the funeral he deserved; over a hundred of Russia's elite came to pay their last respects. He knew his father would have been pleased to see his old friend, Dmitri Mendeleev in attendance as well. His second wife, Edla, had brought Emanuel's sister, Marta, but Emanuel was disappointed that neither of his uncles had come. At least both Alfred and Robert had visited Ludvig before he died.

The following day, Emanuel met with his family's attorney in the office of the house he had recently purchased in St. Petersburg, needing to go over obligatory paperwork. At first, the estate appeared to be straightforward. Ludvig had left everything to his wife, Edla, and his ten surviving children. Emanuel had been left in charge of the Nobel Brothers Petroleum Company.

Emanuel paused, frowning at one of the documents. "This confuses me," he informed the attorney, tapping the paper with his pen. "A few years ago, the family wrote a letter—which I received—stating they approved of my leadership. What is this all about?"

The attorney shifted on his chair. "Matters change over time. Recently, some family members have disputed your authority to lead the company. I believe they were prompted by outside advisors."

Emanuel blinked, shocked at the man's presumptuous answer. He shook his head slowly and deliberately. "No, sir," he said, nostrils flared. "Nothing changes. My father built the Russian Nobel Oil Empire, and it was his legal request that I continue with his vision. In addition, Alfred sees me as the only capable leader. I do not accept this document."

The attorney's thin lips pursed. "Your relatives believe the burden of running the companies should be open to discussion, that the responsibilities and ownership should be shared." He cleared his throat, clearly uncomfortable. "What about your younger brother or your cousins?"

Emanuel got to his feet and glared down at the cowering attorney, who stood and tugged his grey coat around his body as if to defend himself.

"My father's legal request stands. Good day, sir," Emanuel said, striding to the door and flinging it open. "I trust you can see yourself out."

*

When he died, Ludvig had left one dream unfulfilled. For a long time, he had hoped and planned for a day when Czar Alexander III would visit Baku and see the oil fields he had so enthusiastically supported for so long.

When Emanuel received news that the Czar was planning to come to Baku for exactly such a visit, he was thrilled at the opportunity to follow through with his father's wishes. Of course the visit was planned around visiting other oil fields as well, but Emanuel intended to take up as much of the Czar's time as he could. With great pride he led the tour through fields and refineries, skilfully answering every question he was asked. The Czar's party, including his family, were exceedingly impressed by the demonstration at the docks. They watched, mesmerized, as the tanker *Darwin* was loaded at a rate of a hundred tons per hour without spilling even one drop.

"This is amazing," the Czar said, heartily congratulating Emanuel. "I've never seen anything like it before."

Emanuel accepted his accolades with great humility. When the tour was at its end he left everyone with more than memories by gifting the Czar's children with miniature silver drilling towers, complete with their own pump houses. After the tour, Emanuel exchanged toasts with the Czar, all the time wishing his father could have been there to see his dream carried out so well. Perhaps he was watching still.

"Mr Nobel," the Czar said at one point, "I know you are a Swede by birth, but it seems to me you are another nationality in your heart."

Emanuel put his hand on his chest. "Indeed. I am Russian in my heart."

"In appreciation of everything you have done for our empire, I would like to bestow Russian citizenship upon you."

Emanuel could not have refused even if he had wanted. No one ever really said 'no' to the Czar. But he would not have refused anyway. It was both logical and beneficial to his company that he become a Russian. Besides, it was true: Russia was in his heart.

On the day before the ceremony was to take place, Emanuel walked St. Petersburg, enjoying the scenery. He felt oddly free, wandering the sidewalk without any appointments or pressing deadlines. Tomorrow he would be honored by the Czar himself, but today he would blend in with the ordinary people.

Sunlight shot onto one particular window, and Emanuel crossed the street and headed directly for the familiar sparkling display. Perhaps he would not be the 'common man' today after all, he thought. The stunning Fabergé Egg in the window called to him, and who on this sidewalk but he could afford such luxuries? As he gazed through the window, admiring it, a group of noisy young people paraded past, waving a red poster. One of the protesters approached him directly, pressed a miniature version of the poster into Emanuel's hand, then walked on, similarly coming up to anyone who stood on the sidewalk.

Annoyed by the man's presumptuous manner and the noisy disturbance, Emanuel glanced at the handbill. It announced an impending speech in the park entitled, "Emancipation of the Working Class", and the speaker was a man named Lenin. The name sounded familiar but meant nothing to him. Losing interest, he strode into the Fabergé shop and handed the paper to the familiar clerk, suggesting he dispose of it for him.

"Now let me see that stunning masterpiece from the window," he said.

An hour later, the egg stood on display in Emanuel's window, winking cheerfully at him as he dressed for the Czar's ceremony and awaited his carriage.

A small but official crowd had gathered for the ceremony, and Emanuel stood straight and tall as a ribbon was hung around his neck.

"Emanuel Nobel," declared Czar Alexander III, "it is with pride that I grant you Russian citizenship along with the official title of Excellency, in recognition of your valuable contributions to the great nation of Russia."

Later, on Emanuel's 50th birthday – May 25th 1909 – Alexander's son, Czar Nicholas II, granted him the rank of Actual State Counsellor.

There was nothing His Excellency, Emanuel Nobel, could do in response but bow.

Chapter Seventeen

"Miss Gold. How splendid to see you."

One delicate black eyebrow arched in response. "Your Excellency. What a welcome surprise."

In fact, Julie did not appear even the slightest bit surprised to see him. She gave him the look to which he had become accustomed, the expression of a woman who knew very well that her wiles and secrets would get her anything she wanted.

"Enjoying the day?"

She sighed happily, squinting slightly against the reflection of the sun hitting a store window. "How could one not enjoy the day when it is in Baku, the city you have turned into one of the most entertaining in the world?"

"The sparkle of Baku pales in comparison to your own, Miss Gold."

Her chuckle was light, pleased with his reply. She enjoyed the flattery, he knew.

"It seems like forever since the last time we ... spoke," she said, gazing up from under her lashes. "And how fortuitous it should happen today, for I greatly miss our exchanges."

Emanuel was intrigued but not fooled. The woman had a gift for appearing exactly when and where she needed to be in order to either deliver or receive a message.

"Mr Nobel, I have been thinking of our last conversation," she said, taking his arm. "The last time we met we spoke of a balance of influence, if you'll recall. Considering how much we enjoy each other's company, I believe the topic deserves its own focused discussion, without any outside distraction. Do not you agree?"

"Of course. I do hope you will feel free to visit me at Villa Petrolea whenever it is convenient." He frowned past her, hearing the rising noise of angry male voices. In the next moment he spotted a large number of men rushing up the street toward them. "In the meantime, I sense some unpleasantness in the not so distant future."

Her eyes had widened, but she had not yet seen the group of men. She was looking in the other direction, beyond Emanuel, at a number of uniformed men marching toward the mob. They appeared to make up Baku's entire police force.

"I believe you are right," she murmured.

Emanuel cocked his head to one side, indicating a cafe, then urged her out of the way with slight pressure on her elbow. "Would you join me for a drink?"

They entered the dim room flickering with individual lanterns, then moved toward an empty table by the window. As they did so, the apprehensive owner of the cafe moved toward the door and locked it against any further refuge seekers. The other patrons were already staring nervously out at the street, but other than murmured speculations, no one spoke. Tension built within the room as the space between the street's separate forces shrank, and the patrons pulled reflexively away when the two sides met in an ugly, roaring clash. The police were easily outnumbered, and the furious laborers—of which there had to be over couple hundred—came at them with eager fists.

"It is too much!" a woman cried from the dark room behind them.

Indeed, it was quite a violent scene. Emanuel saw Julie flinch a few times, but he noticed she did not entirely look away despite the amount of blood being spilled.

"They'll never survive!" the other woman cried. "Then what? What will happen to us?"

"Who is that?" Emanuel asked quietly.

Staring out the window, Julie pointed at a young man who appeared to be in charge. "Do you see there, the man yelling and gesturing madly?"

"They're all yelling. Which one?"

She squinted then pointed again. "There. The handsome young man with the short black hair and beard. Do you see him there? He is a student, they say. A poet who has become a revolutionary."

The leader stood out, now that Emanuel saw him. Like the others, he appeared hungry for violence, his eyes alight with determination. Unlike them, his furious gaze was always forward, his orders those of a man in charge.

"Rise up!" they heard him bellow. "Stand up for what is yours! You, the people! Rise up!"

"His name is Josef Vissarionovich Djugashvili," Julie said softly, and Emanuel caught a note of reluctant admiration in her voice. "He calls himself Stalin."

Stalin. Russian for "man of steel".

A shop window shattered across the street, and the group stared in disbelief as a mob climbed through the shards of glass, intent on looting the store. The idea caught on, and soon more doors and windows were crashing open.

"Look," Julie said. "Horses."

All heads swiveled toward the sound of rapidly approaching cavalry, their hooves clacking down the street. A second later, the mounted police were racing toward the battle, but the fighters were not easily intimidated. Shots were fired from a few handguns, and everyone near the horses fled in a noisy, frantic human stampede.

"Shoot the traitors!" Stalin barked.

This was getting out of hand. The street outside the window was in chaos, and inside the cafe people sat frozen at their tables, too afraid to move. Emanuel got to his feet and surveyed the rest of the patrons. Most were men. They looked able enough, just confused.

"The tables!" he ordered. "Turn them on their sides and carry them over against the windows and doors."

They immediately followed his suggestion, and though the sunlight was blocked so was the immediate threat. Still, Emanuel and the cafe owner herded everyone to the back of the room, far from the disturbance, and they relocated silently to empty tables.

"Emanuel," Julie whispered, touching his arm.

She tilted her head slightly, and he followed her through a hallway into a small room on the other side of the building. One small, unblocked window looked out onto an intersecting street, and Julie cupped her hands to the glass so she could see clearly.

Emanuel gave her an amused glance. "You've been here before, I see."

She granted him a coy smile then lifted her chin toward the view. "Come and look. I think the people are listening to young Stalin, but some of them are standing up against him."

The people were still running from the guns, but when they turned the corner it was as Julie had said. A line of cart owners, livid after the mob had destroyed much of their businesses, encircled the thugs and descended upon them with wooden boards and flashing knives. The police, taking advantage of the unexpected wall of merchants, moved in quickly and took control.

Emanuel's eyes went to Stalin, one of the first to be handcuffed. The youth stood tall, hostile and defiant to the end.

"People of Baku! Rise up!" he yelled, but his voice was soon lost within the confines of a police wagon.

After he was gone, the incensed crowd continued to yell, to push and shove. The main agitators were quickly rounded up and bound to prevent them from causing any more trouble.

Emanuel turned to Julie. "I would say this calls for a little champagne, do not you?"

"You read my mind."

Once the cafe's tables were back where they belonged and covered in fresh linen, the guests returned cautiously to their earlier conversations, and a waiter appeared with their order.

"A toast," Emanuel said, raising the golden bubbles toward her.

"What are we toasting?"

"Our impromptu meeting," he said with one sardonic eyebrow lifted, "and our subsequent survival."

She raised the flute to her lips, closing her eyes briefly as the bubbles popped in her mouth. The soft line of her throat moved as she swallowed.

"I learned a lesson today, Miss Gold."

"Did you?"

"One never knows when their life might be suddenly in danger."

"A sobering lesson indeed," she agreed.

"Which suggested to me that we should not delay important matters until it is too late. Please allow me to be blunt. Why were you waiting for me today?"

She laughed. "Oh, Emanuel, you know me so well. Do not you even want to *pretend* to have a normal conversation before I tell you a story?"

"I enjoy your stories." He leaned back in his chair. "Besides, you want to tell me. Why else would you just happen to have been in this exact place, where you knew I would be?"

She breathed in through her long, straight nose, looking thoughtful. "I have not spoken with you in a while," she mused, letting out the breath. "But I remember the last breakfast we shared."

How easily that last morning returned to his mind, the warm memories of her smooth curves barely covered beneath the sumptuous white sheets. Perhaps he should have moved this champagne back to his house, he thought belatedly. But no. That would have only created distraction, and she clearly had something she wished him to know.

"I recall that morning very clearly. And I have been remiss in not thanking you for sharing the information you keep coming up with."

"Of course. Your brief complication with finding financing for the kerosene seemed dire, but you solved that little trouble and your kerosene will soon flood the planet. Congratulations." She pressed the edge of her champagne glass to her lips, leaving a bold red imprint on the crystal, then sipped slowly. Her eyes followed the glass as she placed it back onto the white tablecloth. "Your success was noticed far beyond here, you know."

He chuckled. "You do not have to tell me the walls shook in the Standard Oil offices that day."

"I am sure they did. I was thinking, however, of a different office. One in Paris."

"Oh?"

"From what I hear, the great Monsieur Rothschild and his cohort, Jules Aron, were quite impressed."

"Aron?" His jaw clenched at the memory. "I met with him before. He seemed inclined to believe I was out of my league."

She laughed with a rich abandon that made him wish once again that he had invited her to his room instead of this very public cafe. He was well aware he should never underestimate her, but in that moment he allowed himself to enjoy the fleeting fantasy that she was faithful to him alone in both body and mind.

"He miscalculated apparently," she replied. "Well, he has a new respect for you. He is calling you a master at political motivation, and I must agree." She tasted her champagne again, watching Emanuel the whole time. "The talk is that you have created an entirely new way to fund expansion of business by selling the future product at a price above what is set today."

He hesitated, watching her closely. "Is there nothing you do not know, Miss Gold?"

"Very little, I am afraid." She seemed mildly apologetic. "They're saying your new way of financing allows investors to basically become an oil baron without their ever having to build a well, a ship, or a pipeline."

"That sums it up nicely," he admitted, though he was somewhat shaken at how informed she was. He hated to think how she might have collected such private information.

"What will you say, Emanuel, when Édouard Rothschild approaches you next time?"

"You do not already know that answer? I am surprised."

She chuckled and shifted in her seat, leaning back to observe him. "You are an intriguing man, Emanuel. Unlike any other I know."

He leaned toward her, suddenly alert. "What is that?" he demanded. His eyes had gone to her upper arm now that her coat had fallen away. A cluster of small purple circles marred her perfect golden skin. "Fingerprints? Those are bruises!"

She glanced at her arm, and the smile left her eyes. He saw his first glimpse of her afraid, but she quickly tucked the material back over her arm. "I can explain," she said, "but I do not want you to react in the typical male manner."

He frowned then watched in tight silence as she slid her dark coat all the way off both shoulders then took it off entirely, revealing dark sets of bruises on both upper arms.

Emanuel could not help himself. His fists clenched. "Who did this to you?"

"All in good time," she replied, putting her coat back on. "But before I tell you, I require your promise that you will do nothing to exact revenge on my behalf."

He glared at her.

"Emanuel? Do you promise?"

He dropped his eyes, despising the sense of helplessness. "You are impossible."

"I will take that as a promise." She sighed. "There is a powerful man following you. His name is William Libby, and he is Standard Oil's foreign agent."

He knew very well who Libby was.

"Libby's pet thug is an extremely dangerous man named Ezhov. At least that's what Libby thinks. In reality Ezhov works for some very powerful people. So powerful, in fact, that I venture to say he is actually managing Libby rather than the other way around."

"This Ezhov ...?" He indicated the marks on her arms.

"He wanted me to know that he has observed me with you. He knows what I do—outside of being the Trade Attaché, I mean—and he believes the connection between you and me is strictly business. He threatened to tell you about me, but he has no idea you already know. He also assumes I can be played like a puppet, that I will turn on you for the right price, and out of fear of his tactics. Emanuel," she said earnestly, "I will not."

"I do not want you in danger."

She tried to appear as if it meant nothing at all, which was, of course, untrue. "It is part of the job," she said. "Do not worry. I can handle myself. But you have some very powerful enemies." She glanced at her arm. "This was just a reminder."

Chapter Eighteen

Emanuel was thirty years old. He was handsome and fit and wealthy beyond the imagination. And he was lonely.

It was time, he decided, for a change. He no longer withdrew from the world he and his father had created. His imagination wandered from the oil fields and the workers to his own bare walls, to the quiet echoes of the mansion, and he was determined to fill them. Like his father, he began to purchase rare art, but Ludvig's modest purchases were overshadowed by Emanuel's indulgences.

Once it had been unleashed, Emanuel's enthusiasm knew no bounds. He sought out anything his heart desired. Craving competition with finesse, he learned to fence and spar with a rapier, continuing with lessons until he was the finest fencer around. When he needed solitude, he swam for hours, even in the coldest weather—either that or he bathed in the hot springs at the spas of Baden Baden. At other times he dove off the deck of the yacht he kept moored in the Caspian, often inviting friends to join him for day trips.

And then there were the horses. After attending the races one day, he had declared he must have his own stable full of the magnificent beasts. The collection began with a purchase of three golden Akhalteke horses with long necks, short tails, and the most expressive eyes he had ever seen. Weeks later he brought in three more, but this time they were dark Arabian horses, more spirited but also somewhat more intelligent. His final additions to the stable were four small but strong Karabakh mares. Their stamina and courage amazed him. All three breeds were desert animals, but the Karabakhs were what everyone called Azerbaijani horses. He did not always have the time to ride them, but he admired them from afar.

He often spied his father standing by the fields, quietly watching the animals, a look of peace on his face.

Ludvig had been a thinker, uncomfortable in social situations. At Ludvig's insistence, Emanuel had spent years thinking only of business, but in truth he was a social creature by nature. Laughing with his friends was balm to his soul.

Emanuel organized social events, inviting scores of aristocratic guests to his home. He attended parties as well, often meeting up with women who were only too pleased to spend time and even share a bed with the magnanimous and charming oil baron. He became renowned for his excellent dancing skills, leaving ladies both blushing and dabbing at perspiration. Both women and men were frequently given expensive tokens of his friendship; even his servants were treated to unexpected favors.

When he hosted a party at the Mugham Club, there were many dignitaries, ambassadors, Baku oil barons and their families among the guests. The walls were decorated with splendid Azerbaijani carpets, and a central water fountain had been built around a four-tier display of various local fruits. The ancient fig trees, and their sprawling branches enhanced the charming atmosphere. The guests were met by royal Beluga black caviar, and Nobel champagne from Nobel private vineyards in France.

*

A couple of weeks later, Emanuel decided it was time for a celebration at Villa Petrolea and began flipping through his calendar. When he called, the butler appeared in the doorway.

"Sir?"

"I believe I shall throw the largest party Baku has ever seen."

"Excellent idea."

Elbek was familiar with his master's love of extravagances and knew what was expected. Emanuel trusted the man to reach out to the finest chefs, and they in turn would acquire the most exquisite and rare fruits and meats for the event. The tables would be set with caviar, little square *manti* stuffed with ground lamb, and *shashlik*—a variety of meat cooked over an open grill. Another table would offer sweets, like the crunchy, syrup-covered pie the Azerbaijani called *sheki halva* and Emanuel's favorite, the Turkish *bakhlava*. And if any of his guests were so inclined after the meal, they could enjoy Cuban cigars.

Since some of the more devout Muslims among his guests did not drink alcohol, a full selection of plum, lemon, grape, and pomegranate sorbets would be offered, as well as the usual ayran. Of course Elbek would be sure to order enough fine wine, champagne, and cognac for those who did enjoy that sort of drink.

"It will be crowded, so please ensure there will be enough ice to prevent our guests from boiling in their own skins."

The heat produced by that many bodies had proven to be unacceptable in Emanuel's view, and the inevitable odor only made it worse. Most people in Baku had come to accept that sort of thing, realizing that was part of life in this hot climate. For Emanuel, that had been just one more challenge to overcome. He decided to have huge blocks of ice delivered every week to the mansion, and these served to cool the mansion centrally. No one else in Baku had even considered this innovation before.

"Of course, Mr Nobel," Elbek said.

"I also want to host something for the workers."

"Very generous of you."

"Not at all. It is only right. I would have them in here, but even this ridiculously large building is not large enough," he said apologetically. "Yes. We shall give them a party as well. On the grounds."

The celebration was everything he had hoped for and more. As usual, the evening was warm and clear, the stars shining for all to enjoy. Carriages rolled toward the entrance, treating their passengers to a view of decorations and flowers specifically chosen to line the long driveway. The boulevard park was alive with music; the workers and their families danced to the music of a band which had been hired to entertain them as they enjoyed their own special feast.

Emanuel's staff was out in full force, greeting guests and slipping unobtrusively between them to fetch what was required. Dignitaries in national uniforms mingled with aristocrats in business suits, and the women who accompanied them sparkled in fashionable gowns and hats. Emanuel moved contentedly between the groups, joining various conversations spoken in a number of languages, answering questions or adding his thoughts when appropriate.

Listening to the discussions brought him back in time, to the long-ago day more than ten years before, when he had first arrived at the docks. On that day he had stepped off the ship and almost drowned in an unfamiliar sea of people, but the colors and voices of Baku had kept him afloat. Back then, the many languages had all revolved around the topic of commerce. Tonight Emanuel stood in the ballroom of his father's mansion—which was now his—surrounded by the most influential people of Baku. The spirited conversations were still focused on commerce, but now they either discussed oil or talked about how much the people of Baku had benefited from the influence of the Nobels.

"Emanuel!"

He turned at Taghiyev's familiar voice. "My friend," he said, clasping Taghiyev's hand firmly in his own. "You know I throw these parties simply so you and I can enjoy a night off from work together."

The older man's eyes twinkled with laughter. "I do not believe you. You are like me. You love to work."

A small girl popped up beside Taghiyev, her hand clutching his arm, and Emanuel bowed slightly to her. "I see you have brought someone with you." He frowned. "But no. This cannot be ..." He looked at Taghiyev. "This cannot be little Leyla, can it? All grown up?"

The girl beamed up at him, though she was taller than the last time they had met. "Of course, it is me! I am just taller now."

"You are indeed. You're not a little girl anymore. Now you are a beautiful young lady."

"And you look just the same, Mr Nobel."

"Leyla! Your manners!" her father chided, turning Leyla's cheeks crimson with embarrassment.

"Not at all," Emanuel replied. "At least she did not say I look much older than before, which I am certain is the truth."

Taghiyev pressed his fingers to his brow, looking exasperated.

"You said we would be friends," Leyla continued. "Do you remember that?"

"Of course, I do. I am not so old that I have forgotten. I apologize that it has been so long since I saw you last."

"Tell him about school," Taghiyev urged.

"I imagine you are doing very well. You were only just beginning when I met you. I recall speaking about it on the day we celebrated your father's first geyser."

"What a wonderful day that was! And yes, I am doing very well in school," she said, mirroring her father's straightforward approach. "My sisters and I will soon be going to school in St. Petersburg. Papa said you might be able to help us decide which are the best ones."

"I would be honored to help," he said. "What will you be concentrating on, do you know? What are your favorite classes?"

"Literature and Drama," she said without hesitation. "I believe I would like to be a writer."

"Is that so? A worthy occupation. I look forward to reading your work. Actually, I have a book at my house which you might enjoy reading. I will bring it over sometime when it is not so crowded."

She glowed at the prospect. "I would love that. Thank you so much." Her gaze went to her father. "Sara is in the salon, Papa. May I—"

He leaned down and kissed her brow. "Of course, my sweet girl. Go and enjoy the party. We are only boring men with our boring conversations. Ilyas will go with you."

"Thank you, Papa." She smiled back at Emanuel, and he was captivated by the sincerity in her eyes. "I am so pleased to have seen you again, Mr Nobel. I hope it will not take this long before I see you again."

Then she was gone, her slender little shape squeezing through the fancy dresses and formal suits, her brother like a shield behind her.

Emanuel shook his head. "Hard to believe. How old is she now?"

"Fifteen," her father said warmly. "Going on forty, I believe."

"At least she looks like her mother, not her father."

Taghiyev laughed out loud. "That is true, thank God!"

"She will be a beautiful woman very soon, Taghiyev. You had better post guards around your house."

"Her sister Sara is lovely as well. And you are right. I must protect more than their beauty, for men will want their fortunes as well. My poor little girls have no idea what is in store for them!" He laughed, but the sound was wistful. "If only they did not have to grow up."

"I can see why you would say that," Emanuel agreed, "but you must also be intrigued. With so much obvious intelligence, it will be fascinating to see what kind of person Leyla will become."

"She spends a lot of her time in our library upstairs."

"And I imagine you buy her whatever books you can find."

"Only the best for my children. I am especially pleased to see them all reading so well. I, you might not know, never learned how."

That was not unusual in the area, but it was surprising to Emanuel. His friend had done amazing things despite being illiterate. His respect for the man increased further.

The following week, Emanuel appeared at Taghiyev's door, a book in his hand. He was ushered in and shown hospitality right away, but he was impatient to see Leyla.

At last she skipped down the stairs toward him. "Mr Nobel! You came! Did you bring my book?"

He held it out with both hands. "Of course, Leyla. I said I would."

Her eyes rested hungrily on the cover, then she took it gently from him. "What's it about?"

"It is a very old tale and a very beautiful one."

The corners of her lips curled up, teasing. "And look at the title! *The Legend of Leyla and Majnun.* Is it about me?"

An unexpected bout of something similar to vertigo swept through Emanuel in that moment. It was as if the floor dropped slightly. This time the cause was no geyser, but the simple candid question posed by the girl, as well as the way she had asked it. What was it about her that intrigued him so? It was not her beauty—as promising as it was—since she was only a child. The very thought of anyone experiencing lust around children made him physically ill. No, it was not that. There was something else, as if the air between them was charged with electricity.

She blinked guilelessly at him, awaiting his answer, apparently unaffected by such thoughts.

"Yes," he said slowly. "I think the book might be about you, even though it was written hundreds of years ago. It ... it is a love story."

Her gaze softened. "Oh, I enjoy those."

"This one includes many adventures, but it is not a happy ending, I am afraid."

She frowned at the cover. "Why not?"

"You do not wish me to spoil the ending, do you?"

She considered the idea then shook her head. The book was pressed to her chest in an embrace of sorts, and she gave him a small curtsy. "Thank you very much."

He held out the list he had made. "And here are the school suggestions I have for you and your sisters when you go to St. Petersburg. My personal recommendation is the Smolny Female Institute."

"Thank you! I will tell Father."

"I must say, I will be sorry to see you go. And when you come back you will be all grown up for real."

The same look of anticipation lit her eyes. "But you will be here when I return, and I will know so much more. We can have educated conversations like grown-ups, you and I. Please tell me we can do that."

How could he ever refuse her anything? "Of course, dear Leyla. I look forward to those times very much."

She and her sisters were gone before summer ended, and though he felt a twinge of loss at their departure, he was already back to work when Taghiyev returned from the train station, unusually subdued. Though he would visit them often, he mourned as if they were gone forever.

"I remember them learning to walk," he lamented, his eyes welling with tears. "Their little toes, their little noses. Time rushes by far too quickly. Soon I will be a grandfather."

"Ha! Let us not rush things! You must distract yourself from these dire thoughts. Come. Let us make good use of the time we have and get to work. I always find that is the best way to forget my troubles."

PART THREE

Chapter Nineteen

Emanuel missed the first knock on his office door, but when Elbek knocked a second time he looked up. The butler was a serious man, cognizant of his relatively lofty position among the household staff and determined to earn it every day. His suits were always immaculate, his shoes shining, and he never spoke unless addressed directly.

Today he looked tense, and that concerned Emanuel.

"Sir," Elbek said, lifting his chin, "you have a guest. An attorney from Italy."

From Italy? Emanuel did a quick inventory in his head, trying to think what this meeting might include but came up blank.

"Do I know him?"

Elbek gave an almost imperceptible shake of his head. "I do not believe so, and he would not tell me the purpose of his visit."

That explained his butler's guarded expression. He was loyal and protective, and anyone keeping secrets would be regarded as suspect in his eyes.

"Thank you, Elbek. Show him in, please."

Elbek returned a moment later accompanied by an elderly gentleman in a plain black suit. He carried a letter in one hand.

Emanuel rose to greet him. "Good afternoon, sir. How may I help you?"

"Mr Nobel, thank you for seeing me on such short notice. I am afraid I have come bearing unpleasant news." He peered earnestly at Emanuel from behind thick spectacles. "It is with deep regret that I inform you that your Uncle Alfred has died."

Emanuel felt a twist in his chest, and he recognized it as regret. Despite Alfred's criticism and brusque exterior, he had always been Emanuel's favorite uncle, the one who understood him the best—better even than had Ludvig. Ironically, the last time they had spoken was at Uncle Robert's funeral a few months past.

At age thirty-seven, Emanuel was the last of the Nobels involved with BraNobel. He felt suddenly unsure and exposed, though he had been running the company on his own for many years already.

He looked back at the attorney. "That is sad news for our family. Especially after we so recently lost his brother." It had been eight years since Ludvig's death. Ironically, that meant Alfred had lived eight years past the time the newspapers had erroneously reported him to have passed. That, at least, would have given him satisfaction.

The attorney agreed somberly. "Indeed."

"I appreciate your coming in person to tell me of his passing. Does the family in Sweden know?"

"They will be informed today, but that is why I am here with you right now. Your Uncle Alfred knew his time was near, and he dispatched me to Baku a few weeks ago to await his passing. He wanted you to know before the others." He slid the envelope across the desk to Emanuel. "This is his last official Will. It was changed shortly before he died."

Emanuel reached for his letter opener and slid its edge through the seal. The legal paper was thick and felt oddly impersonal compared to the great many letters sent between him and Alfred in the past. He frowned down at the typed pages, feeling a pang when he saw the bold, capitalized spelling of Alfred Nobel's name, then his eyes moved farther down and his breath caught in his throat.

"Oh, my dear God," he whispered.

"He told me ..." the attorney said, hesitating long enough that Emanuel met his gaze again. "He said he knew his Will would be challenged; however, he knew that in your hands his final wishes would be upheld. The family's copy is still sealed;

none of them will read it until you arrive. That is why Alfred said you needed to see it first."

It was a moment before Emanuel could reply, and when he did he already knew the answer to his question. "Did he say anything about what prompted this decision?"

"I believe, sir, it was prompted eight years ago when the French press published the erroneous news of his death. Your Uncle Alfred did not want to be remembered as the 'merchant of death'."

*

A dozen members of the family gathered in the central room of the Nobel House in Stockholm. Emanuel sat behind a desk, watching their faces, hoping desperately to resurrect the spirit of his calm, cool, collected father. He would need that kind of control in the next few minutes.

The attorney read Alfred's Will without expression and without meeting anyone's eyes.

"The whole of my remaining realizable estate," he read to the group, "shall be dealt with in the following way."

Emanuel noticed tiny beads of sweat gathering at the old man's hairline. "The capital, invested in safe securities by my executors, shall constitute a fund, the interest on which shall be annually distributed in the form of prizes to those who, during the preceding year, shall have conferred the greatest benefit to mankind."

He paused long enough for the cousins to exchange a confused glance between themselves.

Oh yes, dear cousins. That is what it says, Emanuel thought.

One year after his father had passed away, Emanuel had done a similar thing by setting up the Ludvig Nobel Prize Fund, which had been awarded for the first time in 1896, the year of Alfred's death. By doing so, he set in motion the ability for the Nobel family to encourage global scientific advances. He gave the Imperial Russian Technical Society the mandate and the capital to set up the fund, which would bestow an award of 1200 gold rubles on the individual who succeeded in the best investigative work in the field of metallurgy and in the oil industry.

Evidently, Alfred had approved of the initiative, since he had now put together his own Fund. Despite the family dissent which would surely arise as a result of this, it meant the family would continue the proud tradition he had started.

"The said interest shall be divided into five equal parts which shall be apportioned as follows: one part to the person who shall have made the most important discovery or invention within the field of physics; one part to the person who shall have made the most important chemical discovery or improvement; one part to the person who shall have made the most important discovery within the domain of physiology or medicine; one part to the person who shall have produced in the field of literature the most outstanding work in an ideal direction; and one part to the person who shall have done the most or the best work for fraternity between nations, for the abolition or reduction of standing armies and for the holding and promotion of peace congresses. The prizes for physics and chemistry shall be awarded by the Swedish Academy of Sciences; that for physiology or medical works by the Karolinska Institute in Stockholm; that for literature by the Academy in Stockholm, and that for champions of peace by a committee of five persons to be elected by the Norwegian Storting. It is my express wish that in awarding the prizes no consideration be given to the nationality of the candidates, but that the most worthy shall receive the prize, whether he be Scandinavian or not."

The relatives' mouths hung open slightly as the attorney folded the Will back into the envelope and handed it to Emanuel.

Robert's oldest son, Hjalmar, was the first to speak. "This is not philanthropy," he declared. "This is Alfred's egotistical wastefulness."

"It is not a problem," Emanuel assured him. "And you will all receive generous financial compensation as well. We can afford to honor Alfred's dying—"

"Every other year you come begging for money," recalled Hjalmar's sister, Ingeborg. "Now, at last, you have money, but you are going to throw it away?"

Emanuel's sister, Marta frowned at her. "How is it throwing money away when you are awarding it to the most worthy? All this does is reward innovation and make our family look both generous and supportive. This is a good thing, Ingeborg."

Hjalmar shook his head. "If the King is wise, he will declare the Will invalid."

His cousin's decisive words surprised Emanuel. "Why is this the King's business?"

"Because the reputation of the Nobel family is uniquely Swedish."

"Alfred's previous two Wills were written and signed when he was sane," Ingeborg reminded them all. "They were in the proper format and written on Swedish soil, in the kingdom of Sweden. I'm sure those are the only ones the King will recognize."

Emanuel shook his head, frowning at Ingeborg's suggestion. "True, but this Will was written and signed—when he was 'sane'—in the Swedish Norwegian Club in Paris. That is perfectly acceptable, and the King will see it that way as well."

"You are wrong," Ingeborg said.

"I do not understand," Emanuel said. "Why can you not open your minds and see this like I do? This prize is an honor for our family name. It will recognize outstanding achievements which will better mankind, not just Sweden."

Ludvig Jr snorted. "Why cannot we see it like you do? Because we are realists, not dreamers."

Alfred would have been ashamed of most of the family's reaction, and Robert would have been embarrassed. Certainly the family was protective of their money, but their intimations went too far. For them to contest the Will was completely selfish and shortsighted. How could they not see that?

"Alfred did not come to this decision lightly," he said. "If he had wanted you to have the money, he would have willed it to you. He had in mind a bigger purpose."

They glared back, but Emanuel sat taller, a familiar surge of power pouring through his blood. He was in charge of one of the world's greatest companies, and he had played a major role in making it that way. He was not about to allow these people—who had not contributed in the least to their family's success—to harm his reputation, his company's reputation, or that of Alfred Nobel.

His eyes passed critically between the faces before him, but their expressions did not soften. *The Nobels are made of strong stuff,* he thought. Still, these ones were in the wrong.

"You would betray your uncle? Your family name?" he asked, but it was a rhetorical question. "And you think word would not spread about this betrayal?" He shook his head. "The scientists and scholars of the world would accuse me of thievery of funds meant for them, when I am the one fighting for them to receive the prize Alfred has so generously bestowed upon them."

The family members might not have inherited the brilliance of Alfred, Robert, or Ludvig Nobel, but they possessed the same stubborn core. Fortunately, Emanuel was even more bullheaded than they were, and he had his uncle's final wishes to back him up.

"The Will of my uncle will be honored as it stands here," he declared, effectively shutting them down. He got to his feet. "I am ready to pay first money into the special Alfred Nobel Foundation and *increase* the amount he bequeathed. I dedicate a *minimum* of three million Swedish Kronas[1]." He took a moment to savor their stunned expressions, then he strode toward the exit. "Good day, cousins."

---

[1] 2019 value is approximately $200 million U.S. dollars

His next stop was in the court of King Oscar II, King of Sweden. He watched in silence as the King and his Advisors discussed Alfred's Will.

"This is not what we had expected," the King told him, frowning.

"I imagine not," Emanuel replied.

"What are your thoughts?"

If only his cousins had been so open. "Alfred's generous vision and gift to humanity will honor Sweden far more than any money he might have willed to the Crown."

Uncertainty hung in the air.

"Your Royal Highness, I do not want the distinguished scientists in the future to lament about our family usurping monies which rightfully should belong to them."

The King and his advisors regarded each other in silence, pondering what Emanuel had said. After a little more discussion with his advisors, King Oscar II nodded.

"Mr Nobel, we mourn with you the loss of your uncle and one of the world's brightest minds. We also stand with you in defending his magnanimous decision to share his gifts with the rest of the world. In fact, I shall contribute to the prize as well."

Relieved, Emanuel packed his things and departed for Baku. When he got home he would help broker amendments to the Will, making sure the family was satisfied with the arrangements. Each cousin would receive a modest bequest of a few hundred thousand kronas, but he secretly planned to ensure they each received a million more. To make them more comfortable with Alfred's plan, he would include them in the development of the statutes common to all awarding bodies, meaning they would have a say in the standards and execution of the prizes.

He had not expected the rush of gratitude he felt when he drove down the road and saw his staff lined up outside Villa Petrolea, waiting to welcome him home.

"It is good to be home," he said, addressing them all.

Elbek led the way into the house, opening the door for an exhausted Emanuel. Despite his need for sleep, he went directly to his office and sat behind the large desk. Elbek had followed him in and now handed him a telegram.

"This arrived for you yesterday," he said.

The telegram had come from Sweden, he saw, and his stomach clenched as he opened it. Then he saw the words and tears blurred his eyes.

"Sir? Are you all right?"

He beamed up at Elbek, handing him back the telegram. "It is from Marta, my sister. She sent it on behalf of all my brothers and sisters."

THE FAMILY WILL NOT CHALLENGE THE WILL. WE HONOR YOUR DECISION.

"What of Robert's children?" Elbek asked. "Will they not pursue it?"

Emanuel closed his eyes. "No. They will not. I will ensure they receive enough financial compensation that they will not complain."

Chapter Twenty

No one could touch the Nobels, but Taghiyev's geysers were keeping pace. Soon he became a key seller of oil, and construction began on his palatial estate.

"It will take up the entire block," Taghiyev declared, leading Emanuel through the area. "I have employed a very good Polish architect named Joseph Goslavski. Have you heard of him?"

Emanuel had not.

"He is a Polish civil engineer from St. Petersburg, and he has a bright mind. He is responsible for the Alexander Nevsky Cathedral of Baku."

"Ah yes. Well! You have chosen an impressive architect then. Tell me more about this palace."

"Today I can only tell you it will be very beautiful. It will be the most complex building in the city—some parts will have four floors!"

"I am impressed. I hope it is built quickly so we might all be able to celebrate with a grand party."

"Do not worry. You will receive my first invitation."

The construction went on for months, and they were busy months. Before long, Emanuel was handed exactly the invitation he had been promised, and he assured Taghiyev he would not miss the grand affair. On the night of the big event, dozens of carriages blocked the road, their lanterns bobbing cheerfully in the night. Anyone who was anyone in Baku was there, dressed to perfection.

He stepped into the entryway, joining the jubilant crowds, and gazed around in awe. Taghiyev's grand estate, with its gold-plated walls, was just as Taghiyev had boasted it would be, exceeding Emanuel's imagination. It easily surpassed the showy, palatial mansions already constructed by other oil barons. Even Villa Petrolea was slightly smaller, though the vast grounds and elaborate architecture still stood as an example to all. As he wandered in with the rest of the crowd, Emanuel admired the glorious gilded arches framing enormous windows and partitioning the rooms, the elaborate staircases leading to even more abundance. All around him, everything and everyone basked in the light of the most beautiful chandelier they had ever seen.

"Emanuel! Emanuel, my friend!" Taghiyev bustled through the crowd, his arms outstretched. "I am so pleased you are here!"

"How could I miss the party of the century?"

Taghiyev kissed Emanuel on the cheek and held out his arms again. "What do you say?" he asked, dark eyes dancing. "Is it not spectacular?"

"It is indeed! Just as you promised." Curious, he set his hand on the back of one dramatically carved armchair. "Is this walnut?"

He had known Taghiyev would appreciate his noticing the details. "Yes! Yes, strong as iron and brought here from Lenkoran."

"Do you know," Emanuel said, "the original reason my family and I came to Baku was for this tree? When my father was producing rifles in St. Petersburg, he sent my Uncle Robert here to find this exact kind of wood for the weapons." His eyes travelled the room, amused. "Evidently you found more of it than he did."

Taghiyev's expression was rapt. "But what an amazing story! Now that you see it, do you wish he had been more successful at bringing it to your factory?"

"If he had, you and I probably never would have become friends."

The big hands went to Taghiyev's chest in an expression of gratitude. "And I would never have been able to show you my house! And now you can see my family as well. They are all here, of course ..." He glanced around, frowning slightly,

"... though I am not exactly sure where. Here is Ilyas," he said, turning slightly as a handsome young man stepped up beside him.

"Good to see you again," Emanuel said, shaking Ilyas's hand. "You are looking very well. You must be pleased to be living in such a palace."

Ilyas glanced at his father, smiling. "Our family is fortunate indeed."

Emanuel breathed in a delicate fragrance as a tall, slender woman wearing a gold silk veil slipped past him. She stopped at Taghiyev's side, and Emanuel's heart missed a beat.

"I am sure my sisters enjoy this vast display of wealth," Ilyas teased.

The young woman glared gently at him. "It is you, dear brother, who revel in all this."

Emanuel stared, incredulous, at the beauty before him, and he fell in love for the second time in his life. She was dressed in the expected glory of a wealthy, single woman, the obvious daughter of an oil baron, but her light *haute couture* dress paled in contrast to the elegant lines of her face. Beneath the veil, a mane of silky black hair fell loose down her back, and the dark eyes flashing at Ilyas were deep as the sea.

Taghiyev noticed Emanuel's hesitation. "It has been a while, but perhaps you recognize my beautiful Leyla?"

Heat shot into Emanuel's cheeks, but it was at least partially camouflaged by the deep black whiskers of his trim beard. "This cannot be the little girl I knew," he stammered.

Her eyes lit with recognition, and his breath caught.

Partially out of respect but also to hide his confusion, he gave a slight bow. "Miss Leyla. I recall the last time we met. You were on your way to school in St. Petersburg. Can so much time have passed already?"

"Mr Nobel," she said warmly, and even in the grown woman's tone he heard the little girl's enthusiasm. "It warms my heart to see you again, sir, though I am heartbroken at the same time."

"What brings you such pain?"

"You broke a promise to me," she replied soberly, tilting her head. "I am afraid you broke it long ago."

His eyes widened, stunned. What was this? How could he—

"When last we spoke, you promised—if I recall correctly, though I was very young indeed—that we would meet again before too long. Alas, it has been too long."

"Leyla!" Taghiyev exclaimed, shaking his head. "What is this, scolding my friend in such a manner?"

But Emanuel smiled, seeing once again that indescribable glow in the girl's eyes. It did not matter that it had been over five years since he had seen it last, for its brightness was the same as he remembered.

"And for that, dear Leyla, I am deeply sorry. I pledge to you that I shall never break another promise to you."

She beamed, showing perfect white teeth. "With that promise I am only too happy to accept your apology."

"Yes," Taghiyev said ruefully. Though he still shook his head at her teasing words, his chest puffed with pride. "Leyla is all grown and back from school. Do you know, she can speak fluent French now, in addition to the German she and her siblings learned from their nanny when they were young. Such a smart girl. She is also a writer now; her talent is quite beyond me. Can you imagine that, Emanuel? A man like me who cannot read or write, and my daughter will become famous for doing exactly that!"

"Papa, you must not say that. Writers do not easily become famous, you know. And I have barely begun."

"You can say such things, daughter, but I am your father. I know the truth. You will be quite famous, I am sure."

Emanuel hoped his apprehension did not show, for he was suddenly aware of a new, very different complication in his life. He absolutely must not disrespect his friend by being attracted to his daughter. That much was clear. The difficulty sprang from Emanuel's inability to imagine staying away from her.

Taghiyev turned toward another guest, and Emanuel felt a jolt of recognition as he recognized Colonel James Ray, the man he had seen having a meal with Julie so long ago. He was tall but not overly so, which Emanuel imagined gave him the ability to vanish into a crowd if he wanted. On the other hand, he could see how the man attracted the eye of many women in the room. He was attractive, with the comfortable posture of a man confident not only about himself, but about his ability to defend it should the need arise. From the fit of his expensive suit, Emanuel could tell he was strong as well. He might have been older than Emanuel, but his face looked as strong as his body, and stone aged well. Julie had spent a fair amount of time with him, and she had been as open as possible about how she and Ray worked here in Russia and Baku. According to her, the British had installed a consular mission in the center of Baku which they used as a hub for organizing public events. The two "spies"—since Emanuel could not think of them in any other way—spent a lot of their time attending balls and cultural events, socializing with the wealthy, upper level people of Baku, since that was where most valuable information could be found. Emanuel watched Ray carefully, knowing he was a man to be both respected and feared. He was rich with both experience and secrets, having served in spy operations in Egypt and Iran as well as Russia.

Taghiyev turned toward the man as if he was a good friend, but Emanuel noticed a forced smile. "Colonel Ray. I am so pleased to see you tonight ..."

His voice faded into the background, as did all other sound in the room as Emanuel found himself alone with Leyla.

"I look forward to reading some of your work," he managed, feeling unusually awkward.

"And I would love to hear what you think, Mr Nobel. Also, now that I am back, I must be sure to return your book to you," she said. "I apologize for having held onto it for so long, but it has become my most favorite story of all. I will have to purchase my own copy, because I cannot bear to be without it for too long."

"My book?"

"Why, of course!" she replied. *"The Legend of Leyla and Majnun."*

The memory of her shining young face when he had given it to her lit his heart. "There is no need to return it to me. It was a gift."

She smiled prettily. "Then I thank you again, for despite all the riches my father showers upon our family, the ancient legend is still my most treasured possession. Since you are so well acquainted with the story, perhaps we might talk about it sometime. Do you enjoy discussing literature?"

Did she know? Did she understand how her simple suggestion thrilled through him like an electric current?

"I do, though I rarely get the opportunity lately," he said. "It would be my honor and great pleasure to discuss it with you."

She opened her mouth to speak, but before she could say anything her father had returned, laughing loudly at something he had heard.

"These British," he said, chuckling. "They think we do not know of their fascination with us, with our success."

Emanuel's mind went to Julie, and he kept his eyes averted from Leyla's, feeling an unexpected pang of guilt. "They are more than fascinated, my friend," he replied, hoping talk of business would clear his muddled thoughts. "They are envious and wish to sell our secrets to their people."

"What shall we tell them?"

"My advice to them would be to keep their friends close and avoid distractions," Emanuel replied. And now he must try to do exactly that. If he intended to keep his best friend, Leyla was a distraction he could not afford.

Chapter Twenty-One

"I have spent too much time with small-minded people of late. If it were a physical ailment, I am positive my doctor would prescribe more time spent with you," Emanuel said. "Business is foremost in my mind, but you and your family are always in my heart."

"As are you, my friend. I am sorry you have had such a difficult year with your family. Both your uncles, then the disagreements of your cousins."

"That has been solved, thankfully."

The two friends had met up at the oil fields after finishing up the day's demands, then Emanuel had suggested they walk the distance to Taghiyev's home. They had done it twenty years before, and Emanuel easily persuaded him that they were not yet too old to enjoy a good walk.

"Your family was wise not to contest the Will."

Emanuel's pale blue eyes remained on the road ahead. It was busy with progress, and new construction was constantly underway. With the Nobels' help, the rumbling black well beneath the city had turned Baku from a place of grime to one of splendor, with palaces and mansions that rivaled those in Paris, Rome, Warsaw, Istanbul, and Baghdad. Based upon the popular Baroque and Renaissance revival architectural styles of the time, the buildings' artistry had been further enriched by adding Islamic characteristics. Foreigners flocked to Baku. Some came for a holiday, but many decided to stay and seek their fortunes. Restaurant and casinos—in which wealth was both made and lost—popped up everywhere, offering local cuisine and entertainment to the many tourists who now came to stay in Baku's prestigious hotels. Of course, along with such prosperity came the less desirable yet just as predictable underworld of prostitution, con artists, and snake oil sellers. Like Robert Nobel had hinted upon Ludvig's and Emanuel's arrival, a careful man was a wise man.

Not every visitor came to enjoy the beauty of the land or the culture of its people. Oil was now the most important strategic commodity in the world, and 50% of that oil was being produced in Baku. That meant Baku had become the prize sought by every one of the great world powers, and they were more than prepared to send people to battle, to die in their quest for domination. As a result, Russian counter-intelligence fought a constant, covert battle against spies from America, Great Britain, Turkey, Germany, France, Italy, Iran, and more.

"These prizes have affected the world by awarding excellence. Especially your father's. The Ludvig Nobel Prize has tied the world of oil and wealth to the world of minds and talent. A worthy, momentous act of benevolence."

"Yes, but with Uncle Alfred I believe it was also a little personal. You recall the day my father died and the newspapers mistakenly announced Alfred had died? They called him the 'merchant of death', remember?"

"A terrible mistake!"

"If it was a mistake at all. I have always suspected Rockefeller of arranging that false story, trying to turn people against the Nobels. I found it interesting that almost immediately after it was printed, all remaining copies of the newspaper's print run—including those archived at the Bibliothèque Nationale de France—disappeared."

Taghiyev lifted an eyebrow. "I did not know that."

"Yes. An interesting coincidence, wouldn't you say? Ironically, Alfred's benevolence has now far overshadowed Rockefeller's failed attempt to besmirch his character so many years ago."

Taghiyev laughed. "That must really upset him. Perhaps that is the cause of him losing all his hair!"

As far-fetched as that seemed, Emanuel supposed the idea was possible. Rockefeller had appeared in public recently looking as he always had, but those behind the scenes knew he wore various wigs. They varied in length, meant to portray his normal hair either in need of a cut or just after one. The reason for this was that for the past few years J.D. Rockefeller had been fighting a losing battle against alopecia, a disease which had stripped him of every hair on his head and body.

As they approached the expansive estate, Emanuel noticed activity in the yard. Looking closer, he made out about a dozen children seated in the grass.

"Have you added more children to your family?" Emanuel teased.

Taghiyev's whole body seemed to swell with pride. "This is Leyla's doing. She is teaching some of the young Muslim girls from the city."

The mention of her name sent a small, secret thrill through Emanuel's chest. "Oh?"

"Do you know how hard it is for women to get ahead in life? They have no education available to them, which means they are completely ignorant of their rights and of the possibilities they might have in life. Eventually these same uneducated and oppressed women will become mothers, and their daughters will grow up in the same environment. The only way to help them is to educate them." He linked his hands behind his back, fondly watching the children. "Of course enlightenment should happen with both girls *and* boys, but an educated girl means an educated mother, and that will create an educated family in the future."

Leyla was walking amongst the children, leaning down to answer questions or make suggestions. She waved when her father called to her.

"As you know," Taghiyev said, "I believe so strongly in the education of women that I sent my beloved daughters to a school far from me."

That had been difficult for him, Emanuel knew. The two had held many conversations about how families had to eventually pull apart for the good of the individuals.

"But it was worth it in the end, was it not?"

Leyla walked confidently toward them, and Taghiyev beamed. "Every minute. Look at the woman she has become, and look how she is helping those children!"

It was shameful, Emanuel knew, but he was well aware of the woman Leyla had become. Every time he saw her he fell more deeply in love with the light in her eyes, the ripened strawberries of her lips, and the soft, forbidden skin of her cheeks. He secretly delighted in the different views he had of her: whether she was dressed like a goddess at important social gatherings, relaxed in her home, or at their family dinner table. Regardless of the situation, Leyla glowed with an energy that burned from within, and he longed to touch its forbidden source.

"Hello, Papa. Hello, Mr Nobel. Where is your carriage?"

"It was a day for walking and talking," her father replied. "How is Leyla's little school?"

All of the little girls had their heads bowed over books. "We are reading," she said. "They are all quite happy about that. What little girl would not love to read? Am I right, Mr Nobel?"

"Of course you are right," he said, uncomfortably aware of the urge he felt to sweep her into his arms. "And with such a wonderful teacher it can only be enjoyable."

At his response, she smiled at him alone, and his cheeks burned. It seemed her gaze lingered a fraction longer than was necessary, and he grasped at the fantasy that she might feel at least a little of what he felt. Did Zeynalabdin see the desire in his expression? He did not seem to; maybe he was oblivious to the connection which Emanuel imagined buzzed like electricity between them. Leyla still had not looked away, and he wondered ... was there a question in those dark irises? How could he answer?

Eventually she tilted her head and regarded her father. "Have you told Mr Nobel about the letter?"

Taghiyev's brow lifted. "No, not yet. But that is an excellent idea. Thank you, Leyla."

A little girl appeared at Leyla's side, observing the adults. She was thin but her clothing was new, and Emanuel wondered if the Taghiyev family was not only educating these children but dressing them as well. It would not have been a surprise to him.

Leyla squatted so her face was by the little girl's. "What is it, Jeyran?" The child leaned in and whispered something in her teacher's ear. "Of course. I will be right there."

She looked back at Emanuel and her father. "It has been nice to see you again, Mr Nobel. I hope Papa will invite you to our home for dinner sometime soon."

"Of course," Taghiyev said. "Now go. Your class needs you."

As she walked away, bending to speak with her little flock, Emanuel was struck by a poignant thought. Leyla, by taking on the responsibility of a teacher, was changing the people of Baku, giving them self-respect as well as education. Twenty years before, he and Ludvig had done the same with Baku's workers, though they had not gone about it through a scholastic education. They had gotten to know the people, recognized and tended to their needs, creating a strong, loyal workforce. They had built a strong base, and now Leyla was educating Baku's future.

"What is this letter?" he asked.

"Ah yes. Come. I'll show you. It is from the director of the People's School of Baku."

Emanuel frowned, walking slowly beside his friend. "Tkhorevski?"

"The very same. He is interested in founding a school in Baku for Muslim girls. It would teach along the guidelines of the People's Ministry of Education, and it would teach stitch work and housekeeping as well."

This was news to Emanuel, and good news at that. "That is excellent."

"Yes, yes, of course. It would be the only one of its kind in the Empire. He has, of course, applied to me for the means to do it."

"And you plan to give it to him?"

Taghiyev hesitated. "I plan to reply to his letter, saying I want to establish a secular Russian-Muslim school for girls at my own expense, but I will also say that it must be run in such a way that the Muslim families respect it without reservation. They must trust it enough that they are willing to send their daughters to it. I know from personal experience how difficult it is for a father to trust anyone with his daughters, and the people of Baku must have no reason to question my school."

Emanuel stopped walking. "But this is wonderful! I wholeheartedly applaud this plan."

"Yes?"

Emanuel was surprised to see the unexpected look of relief in Taghiyev's eyes, though he knew his friend placed great value in his opinion. He always had.

"Some do not," Taghiyev admitted. "Some of the Muslim leaders are shocked by the idea, but I insist the Koran says nothing about not educating girls. In fact, it says they *should* be educated."

"Good for you. If you persuade some of the wealthy businessmen and perhaps clerics to send their girls, you will lose that opposition, I am sure. It is a wonderful idea."

Taghiyev chuckled. "Alexander III was never a supporter of this idea because I had insisted the girls be taught in Azerbaijani Turkish, their native language. I will admit I did not give Nicholas much of an opportunity to refuse. You see, as soon as he became the Czar, I sent his wife a Rolls Royce."

"What?" Emanuel laughed out loud. "You did what?"

"The way to a man's support is often through his wife's approval, I have found. And she is now quite happy to help me with this project."

"Brilliant."

"Yes." He crossed his arms over his chest, looking pleased. "It is a good plan. I would like to name the school after the Empress Aleksandra Fyodorovna."

"Aha! Very smart."

"This dream of mine is still years away from becoming a reality," Taghiyev said, "but I have promised myself that it will happen."

Emanuel glanced back at Leyla, who was laughing along with the girls, her face lit by the sun. "And you already have the perfect teacher for your school."

Chapter Twenty-Two

By the time construction finally got underway for Taghiyev's school, Russia had overtaken the U.S. in oil production. With 210,000 barrels of oil per day, and almost eleven million tons per year, Russia easily pulled ahead. 95% of that oil came from Baku.

BraNobel was not finished growing. Ten years after he first met Rudolf Diesel, Emanuel went to Berlin to listen to a public lecture describing Diesel's new engine, which sounded perfect for BraNobel's fleet of oil tankers. He told Rudolf exactly that over a satisfying German meal of *rinderrouladen* and steamed potatoes. At the conclusion of their meeting the men shook hands, and Emanuel signed a licensed agreement which allowed him to build the world's first diesel engine plant.

By the following year, BraNobel's only oil production was up to ten million tons of oil annually, accounting for more than ten percent of the world's oil supply.

BraNobel's workers were hardworking but content; however, not every worker in Baku was satisfied. Growing social unrest was becoming more than just a nuisance to employers, and the leaders of the revolution were steadily gaining a sort of celebrity status among the working class. Strikes and demonstrations, though usually peaceful, sparked at various factories and in the oil fields. Gangs of dissatisfied laborers, encouraged by the revolutionaries, set fire to the offending oil barons' holdings, burning almost sixty percent of Baku's oil fields and refineries. Despite Baku's terrible losses, neither the BraNobel fields nor those of Taghiyev suffered as greatly as did the others.

"We are so lucky," Taghiyev said, but his expression said he was trying very hard to persuade himself of that.

Worry seemed to have set his friend's dark eyes even deeper in his face, and the once black beard was streaked with white. He and Emanuel were standing back against the wall of his great ballroom, admiring the brightly dressed dancers at Taghiyev's Viennese Ball and trying not to sink into talk of business. Unfortunately, that was unavoidable.

"Luck has nothing to do with it," Emanuel reminded him. "We were smart all along. We took care of our people. Why would they want to destroy a world created just for them? You just watch. Those who did not treat their workers as we did have been the first to fall."

"I do not know. I really do not. Are we safe? These people are so unpredictable. So many of the others have lost their entire fortunes to these attacks. More burn every day."

"We have to believe we are safe and keep doing what we have always done. There is no other option."

"They want to get rid of capitalists, Emanuel. That's us."

"Perhaps. But let us enjoy tonight and trust in the loyalty of our workers. That's all we can do, my friend."

Taghiyev's eyelids fluttered closed, he inhaled deeply through his nose, then he opened his eyes again. "As you say." He could not hide his unease. Not from Emanuel. "I must seek out my son, make sure he has not charmed all the wrong girls again."

Emanuel watched him walk away, then he scanned the crowd, wondering if he should make the rounds again, see who wanted to talk.

"You and your friends certainly do know how to throw impressive parties," came a familiar voice at his elbow.

Miss Gold's curves were sheathed in a stunning dress, its design and color in the popular Oriental style. To his eyes she presented herself like a gift, and his thoughts went to unwrapping her.

"I am pleased to see you here tonight, my dear Miss Gold. It has been a while."

"Far too long, Your Excellency." Her eyes flashed with meaning.

"Your gown must be from your beloved Paris, am I right? Perhaps from the house of Paul Poiret?"

Her eyes widened, impressed. "Why, Your Excellency, you possess an incredible eye for fashion."

He chuckled. "I must be honest. A spy told me."

Her expression tightened dramatically, affecting displeasure. "Come now. Where is the fun in being totally honest? I have found there are benefits to the opposite as well. For example, I always allow a man his crafty ways when I approve his goal of engaging my attention."

"Ah, you are a gem, Miss Gold." He bowed slightly. "Would you honor me with a dance?"

"I cannot resist a waltz. Especially with you."

He put one hand on her lower back, guiding her toward the dance floor with a warm, suggestive pressure. They waited for the right moment then joined the others, already swirling around the ballroom in a rainbow of colorful silk.

Her smile faded slightly as they danced. "May I make an observation?"

"Of course."

"You have not made friends with Rockefeller."

He replied by saying nothing.

"He is a dangerous enemy."

"You think this is news?" He shook his head. "He has been after me since the beginning. He believes he can buy and bully his way into anything, but he will not intimidate me."

He whirled her around the ballroom, hoping to put her at ease, and sensed the moment when she gave in to the rhythm of the dance, when her body moved with perfect synchronicity with his.

"You are a wonderful dancer, Emanuel," she said, meeting his eyes again.

"'We should consider every day lost on which we have not danced at least once,'" he quoted Nietzsche.

"Ah yes," she said, always up to the challenge. "But that comes from a man who they say went mad from syphilis."

He chuckled. "He had the wrong dancing partners, apparently." He put his cheek against the side of her head and spoke softly into her ear. "What is it that occupies your thoughts tonight?"

She hesitated. "Colonel Ray told me some interesting things in confidence," she said carefully. "Things you need to know. Perhaps we might retire to somewhere a little more private to continue our conversation."

She had helped him before. He would be a fool to ignore the urgency compressed between her lips.

"It would be my pleasure. I have been here long enough and was planning to head home soon. Would you be inclined to join me?"

He was rewarded with a look of blatant sexuality. "I thought you would never ask."

As Emanuel ushered Julie inside Villa Petrolea, his house servants arranged two glasses and a bottle of chilled *Cristal* champagne—the same champagne that was preferred by the Czar—on a silver platter, then carried it to his bedroom. When she emerged from the powder room, she tucked her hand in his elbow and they strolled along the elegant hallway, taking in the art which lined the walls. Eventually they reached his bedroom and he led her inside.

"When I was a child," she mused, eyeing the elaborate room with appreciation, "I was always told a story before bedtime."

"Is that right? I have always been more inclined to listen better after lying down for a bit."

The champagne was the perfect temperature, the crystal flutes fogged from the chill. When her cool fingertips went to the button at his shirt collar, goosebumps rose over his entire body. The blood roaring through his veins was hot, and desire flared in Julie's eyes as well. Words could wait.

Yes, she was a spy. No, she was not to be entirely trusted, and she did not belong to him exclusively. Regardless,

Emanuel could not get enough of her, of her obvious expertise and enthusiasm. He saw no evidence of feigned pleasure on her behalf, no indication that she was not enjoying it as much as he. *Unlike any I know*, she had said about him once. Was it true? Or was that a practiced line she had used time and again to get what she wanted from whomever held the prize?

Did it even matter?

She tasted of champagne, smelled of flowers and musk. As their lovemaking intensified her scent became stronger, more alluring, and he left common sense behind. Her skin was like warm, gold velvet, her hair thick and rich in his hands. An hour before her voice had been quiet and suggestive, rich with innuendo. Now she cried out with pleasure, saying his name over and over again.

"I cannot move," she eventually whispered. "Or perhaps I simply do not wish to."

She lay beneath him, her petite body still trembling with aftershocks, a soft sheen of perspiration dotting her hairline. He bent his head to her neck, kissing below her ear, and she sighed with pleasure.

"Now I am ready for a story," he suggested.

"It is a long one." She sighed again then slid out from under him. "I will need another drink for this conversation."

He sat and reached for the bottle. The bubbles danced in a mist over her glass.

"Now then," he said. "Tell me why you were waiting for me today."

"First I have a question. I have heard rumors."

"Oh yes? I imagine there are plenty of those. To which do you refer?"

"Azerbaijan seems on the verge of declaring its own independent nation," she said. "Would you agree?"

"Yes. The Azerbaijan Democratic Republic—though I believe it will be a decade or so before this actually happens."

"I have even heard talk about taking Baku out of the future Republic. To make it a 'free international town'. What do you think of that?"

Emanuel chuckled. He had heard that rumor as well. "I have no thoughts on it. That will be up to the politicians, not me."

She nodded slowly, thinking over his words. "I am curious," she said, "about how the royal palace is reacting to these rumors. Will they allow it?"

"Does Russia embrace losing sovereign rights to the oil? No, of course not. But the Czar and I have spoken. Nicholas listens when I tell him stability must be the primary objective. And of course there are the proper economic incentives to be considered." He shook his head. "Frankly, I pity the Czar. He has spent all his years in the midst of rebellion and war, besieged on all fronts as well as from within. Russia cannot defend its hold on the region, nor can it protect it from raiding armies sent from England. There are so many internal ongoing battles: the Cossacks, the Turks, the Iranians, the Georgians, the Chechens, the Azerbaijanis, and now the Bolsheviks. They're all fighting for revenge first, control second. This is a battle the Czar cannot afford. And that is why a free democratic state is acceptable."

She considered this as she sipped her champagne.

"Your turn," he said.

"All right." She sat up, leaning against the headboard with the sheet draped over her. "Mine is more urgent, I am afraid. Rockefeller recently held a meeting on Jekyll Island with a number of important international businessmen, including bank representatives, members of the Senate Foreign Affairs Committee, Colonel Ray, J.P. Morgan, Andrew Carnegie, Rich Mellon, and William Libby. Libby, of course, is loyal to Rockefeller. He also invited a representative of Tehran. Oh, and Trotsky and his Bolsheviks."

Emanuel stuck out his lower lip, picturing the group. "And to think I was not invited."

"You were there, though. You were the center of the conversation." She took a deep breath. "They met over a map of Baku and discussed how to take over the world through oil."

"Apparently some men are not good at sharing," he said wryly.

She shook her head. "I do not think you are taking this seriously enough. You have a lot of powerful enemies, Emanuel. Libby told them you are having trouble within your own family, maintaining control."

"How does he know that?"

Her shoulders lifted and fell. "People have ways of finding things out, you know. Is it true?"

"No. Not anymore."

"Good. Because they plan to pit the other Nobel heirs against you, and while your family is battling over the future of BraNobel, the Bolsheviks and Russian Secret Police will sabotage everything you have, from your ships to the derricks and everything in between."

His temples began to throb. "The Czar will not allow—"

"They say the Czar's days are numbered." Her voice had a new edge to it, and he listened closely. "The revolution is growing stronger. The Bolsheviks intend to remove all the bourgeois, and that most definitely includes you."

It was true that the revolts were creating havoc in the oil derricks, but the demonstrations were much worse in Russia. Certainly the threat here was building; however, Emanuel still felt confident they would not harm BraNobel. His workers were loyal and would defend his company. On the other hand, it sounded like Rockefeller had a different kind of attack in mind.

"Tell me more."

"Rockefeller is calling this the First Oil War. His friends are determined to come at you from every angle, and J.P. Morgan has ensured them the financial means, which means they can buy any alliance, hire every soldier, bribe every official. Rockefeller even proposed a special austerity plan enabling him to destroy all their rivals and take over the world market of oil and oil products. First, he will launch a media campaign designed to discredit and compromise the rivals, including you and Rothschild. He is also planning to buy out Samuel's and Rothschild's separate oil interests."

"How much?"

"Forty million. He is convinced—"

"They will not sell."

She frowned. "No? You know this ... how?"

"How did you put it? Sometimes people just know things."

In fact he knew because he had recently heard it from the Lord Mayor of London himself, Marcus Samuel. Julie was not the only person who had an ear to the ground, and his competitors were not deaf either.

"Here's the big one, Emanuel. Big money is going into destroying Rockefeller's competition, and even though local muscle will be used, they all answer to Stalin now."

Every time he heard Stalin's name, his mind returned to the café in Baku where he and Julie had taken refuge from the demonstration. Since then, the young revolutionary had come a long way, rising to the top and being recognized as a bloodthirsty leader.

"Rockefeller plans to secretly provoke a civil war throughout the Russian Empire, with the ultimate objective to ruin the Baku oil industry." Her eyes narrowed. "Emanuel, his men are willing to die for the cause, and they have no idea it is being funded by the exact class of people against whom they are rebelling."

If it was a simple question of business, Emanuel's mind would quickly have reached out, played with the possibilities, and come out the other side, victorious. He was always up to the challenge of a puzzle. But this... While he had outmaneuvered Rockefeller in the past, he had a sinking feeling this great game was spiraling out of control. Out of *his* control.

Chapter Twenty-Three

He was in Taghiyev's dining room the following week, enjoying a light meal with his friend by the roaring fireplace. It was a welcome oasis from the biting chill of January 1905. For this moment in time he allowed himself to feel safe and content.

Julie's warning had not fallen on deaf ears. Despite Emanuel's dislike of both Alfonso Rothschild and Jules Aron, he set up a meeting. He had proposed a deal, suggesting they form a kind of partnership, giving them power against Rockefeller. Rothschild was eager to join him, and he immediately began using his own expertise to advance their oil business and create its own international exploration and production company.

As far as the continuing violence in Baku, Emanuel still felt relatively safe in comparison to those oil barons whose workers had been underpaid, overworked, and treated as nothing less than slave labor over the years. They had survived a few attacks, but on the whole they were faring rather well. Taghiyev, too, had lost some of his derricks, but his workers had done what they could to protect the fields. The BraNobel employees—the number had grown to over 12,000 by this point—did not suffer at all. Still, Emanuel went to the derricks more often, checking for vandalism, ensuring his men were happy.

Leyla burst into the room, her face streaked with tears, and both men jumped to their feet.

"My darling daughter! What is the matter? What has happened?"

Her eyes were red, swollen from too many tears. Emanuel had never witnessed Leyla in such a state of distress, and the impact of seeing her in pain roused a physical ache in Emanuel's chest.

"Papa! It is all so terrible," she managed through her sobs. "I hardly know how to tell you what I've just learned."

"Where is your mother? Is she all right? Your brothers and sisters?"

"All of us are fine, Papa, but—"

"Then what is it?"

She was shaking badly, from her trembling fingers to the dark hair which had fallen from its restraints and now fluttered down her back like a fallen flag. Her hands went to her face, and she curled her nails against her brow in an effort to control her emotions. When she was ready, she dropped her hands and faced the men.

"It happened in St. Petersburg." Her brow creased with renewed grief; she held her breath, fighting back sobs. "At the Winter Palace early this morning. There was a ... a demonstration—a *peaceful* demonstration of workers and their families. Thousands and thousands of people went. They ... they had a petition for the Czar, asking him to help with their pleas for better working conditions, but he was not there. He had gone away the day before."

"Sit," Emanuel insisted, taking her arm and guiding her to a couch. "You are trembling."

"No, I—"

"We can listen better if we know you are comfortable. Please, Leyla. Sit."

She relented, sinking onto the soft cushion then seeming to shrink into herself. Taghiyev and Emanuel sat on either side of her, two pillars of strength on which she needed to rely.

Taghiyev called to his house servant, waiting expectantly in the hallway. "Tea!" He turned back to his daughter, his hand on hers. "Tell us now. We are listening."

Her eyes were liquid black and pleading for him to make some kind of sense out of what she had learned. "Papa, they came to the Czar for his help, singing and praying and hoping he would put an end to their suffering. They did not know he was not at home. I am not sure he would have seen them even had he been there, but he ..."

She seemed to lose focus for a moment, then she looked at Emanuel and a tear trickled down the side of her face, breaking his heart all over again. If only he could wipe it from her cheek, draw her close, comfort her... With reluctance he glanced over her shoulder at her father, his best friend in the world, and reminded himself that could never happen.

"They said that at first the demonstrators put all the women and children in the front," she told him, "wanting everyone to see that these were more than unhappy workers. These were *families*. But then the men came to the front. I do not know why. Maybe the children were too slow." She swallowed hard. "None of them knew that ten thousand of the military had already assembled at the Winter Palace, concerned there might be a protest in the Czar's absence."

Emanuel's stomach rolled, thinking ahead.

"They ... they started to shoot because the people just kept coming. Innocent men were being shot! Then—" Her expression twisted, and blood roared to her cheeks as she imagined the tragedy again. "The guards used their sabers! It did not matter who they ran into, they kept marching. Oh, Papa!" she sobbed. "They t-trampled children!"

The men stared at her, unable to speak. She swallowed then took a deep breath and started up again. "There is more. Later, in the afternoon, families were walking on the Nevsky Prospekt, unaware of what was going on. It is Sunday, after all. Families go for walks. There is no law against going for a walk with your family! I do not know why, but the guards came after them as well!" She looked at Emanuel through bloodshot eyes. "So many people are dead! How can this have happened, Mr Nobel? How can it be real?"

He shook his head slowly, unable to think. Maybe she saw the agony in his eyes, or maybe she saw the longing to hold her, to comfort her. For whatever reason, she flung herself into his arms, sobbing uncontrollably. His nose brushed her hair, and he breathed in. Despite her fear, her scent was balm to his soul.

He had dreamed of this moment, when she finally turned to him and sought his protection, but he could never have imagined it would be prompted by such terrible circumstances. He glanced helplessly at her father, but Taghiyev's expression showed nothing but heartbreak for his daughter, and for the victims of this nightmare. He frowned at Emanuel as if to ask if he would mind holding Leyla for a moment, then he strode quietly from the room. Emanuel imagined he was looking for a telephone to confirm the story.

"Shh, Leyla," he whispered, daring himself to run his hand over the tangles of her hair. He told himself it was an attempt to soothe her, but all the while adrenaline pumped through his veins. "You are safe."

She pulled back, blinking at him. "But they are not! Oh Emanuel! Thousands of people are dead!"

Emanuel. How could he think clearly when she spoke his Christian name out loud with such passion, looked in his eyes with so much trust? His hand went to her cheek, his thumb brushed away a tear that was already getting lost on her wet skin.

"This is a grave, unforgivable thing, Leyla," he said softly. "The world will rise up against the Czar for this."

"He was not even there," she whimpered.

"And that is terrible also. For he will be blamed."

He wanted to hold her there forever, look into those eyes and give her anything she could ever desire, but everything about it was wrong. *This is Zeynalabdin Taghiyev's cherished daughter!* He moved his hand away, prepared to relinquish this precious closeness, but she moved with him again, sheltering her face in his chest, sobbing within the safety of his arms. He closed his eyes, breathed in the awful beauty of the moment, loving her and hating himself at the same time.

*

Two days later Elbek announced that Julie Gold was at his door. She met with him in one of the sitting rooms, wearing a black gown which lacked her customary flair. She was as beautiful as ever, but her eyes looked weary.

"What an unexpected surprise," he said, wondering at the tension in her shoulders.

"I am sorry I did not call first. I ... I needed to speak with you."

"Of course. Please. Have a seat. What can I get you to drink? I am aware of your particular fondness for champagne ..." he suggested, raising an eyebrow.

"If only I could, Emanuel." She sighed heavily. "Coffee, please."

Elbek turned toward the corridor then shut the door quietly behind him, giving them privacy as Emanuel seated himself across from her.

"What is it?" Icicles of concern crawled through his gut. "How can I help?"

"Last Sunday," she said, then she stopped and looked down at her hands.

"A terrible, terrible day for Russia."

Her gaze went to him, and he saw the grief in her eyes. "For the world," she agreed. "And for everyone in it, including you and me. The Czar's official reports declared ninety-six had died, with three hundred and thirty-three injured. Those in opposition claim more than four thousand died. The city has been taken over by looting and violence."

He had read all the reports, every one of them worse than the last. "The newspaper quoted Nicholas as calling the day 'painful and sad'." He shook his head. "Not enough. Not nearly enough."

"The Czar will fall as a result of this tragedy," she agreed, "for the people will revolt. How can they not? These people were not even involved in the recent uprisings. They were simply bringing a petition to the Czar, who should have represented them as he always claimed to do. Nicholas was their hope, and—whether or not it was his fault—his own guards slaughtered them. Even the peasants have turned against him now."

"I agree. The violence is only getting worse. This unimaginable flame has lit the tinder of a true revolution. He is just another part of the uncaring government to them."

"So what will you do, Emanuel? The oil fields of Baku are burning, Lenin's revolutionaries are demanding the end of capitalism ..."

"I will do what I have always done. I will support my workers, do whatever I can to help them."

Looking exasperated, she shook her head. "Emanuel, when will you listen to me? The workers will be fine. No one wants to run *them* out. It is you and people like you who are in danger."

He knew that, and yet his mind refused to consider his own personal safety. The most important thing was that BraNobel survive this dark period. He and his father had laid down a strong foundation, and while there would undoubtedly be some damage done, he needed to know it would all eventually work out.

"I will stay until I can stay no longer. I will not leave my people without a leader. I am responsible for them."

Her gaze went to the dancing flames in the fireplace. "I am afraid for you," she said softly.

"Do not be." She sat far enough away that he could not reach her, and he was sorry for that. He wanted to be able to offer comfort and reassurance, though it would be for both of them. "I am a tricky fellow. Difficult to catch."

When she looked back, the sadness had hardened to something resembling regret. "That is very true. You know, I once thought I had caught you," she mused, then her body seemed to sag, as she dropped her defenses "It ended up that I was caught instead. I have grown surprisingly fond of you, Emanuel."

He said nothing, only nodded with acknowledgement. What they had between them was not love, yet they cared deeply for one another on another level.

"But you never felt as I did," she said.

He frowned, startled by the implication. "How can you say that?"

"I only wish ..."

Emanuel could not pull his gaze from the pain in her eyes. "Tell me, Julie."

"I wish you loved me as you love her," she whispered.

He stared at her, mute. How could she know?

"A woman knows," she replied, reading his expression. "I do not know who she is, but I know she exists." She looked back toward the fireplace, sitting straight again. "Emanuel, the British ambassador has suggested His Majesty's subjects return to Great Britain. I am considering his advice. I have seen too much here, and I have put myself in the middle of too many dangerous situations of late. I no longer feel safe."

"I can keep you safe."

Her gaze was compassionate. "You, of all people, cannot keep me safe." She hesitated, considering, then let out a breath. "Emanuel, I have lived here long enough to have an attachment to this place and its people, but my job demands that I play more than one card at a time. I have told you about Ezhov," she said, and he cringed when she shrugged off her coat, revealing even darker, more invasive bruising. "He requires me to turn my back on this country—on you—and I will not do that. That puts me in a dangerous position. He was only playing rough before; now he is serious. He has thrown some pretty serious threats on the table, and soon he will learn that I have double crossed him all along," she said flatly. "If I am not extremely careful, he will kill me, and he will enjoy doing it. I know that."

She sighed, and one corner of her mouth drew up wryly. "Mark Twain once said that 'If you tell the truth, you do not have to remember anything.' I have told far too many lies, Emanuel, and the truths have tangled into some very sticky webs."

He saw the fear in her eyes, the flush that darkened her neck as she mentioned the lies, and it frightened him as well.

He did not like that she put herself in such danger, and yet it was her love for adventure that had first drawn him to her—that and her physical charms, of course.

She swallowed, staring intently at him. "You need to understand something, Emanuel. These people will not stop until they have killed you and ruined everything you have built. Rockefeller envies you to the point that he will do anything, spend anything to destroy you. The revolutionaries despise anyone with money, and their power is growing exponentially. Your time here is running out."

Elbek arrived with the coffee, and she slipped modestly back into her coat. As the butler left, Emanuel battled to control his emotions. Her bruises had shocked and nauseated him as had the images which had pushed in beside them, suggesting how she had been abused. Her direct declaration that all of their lives were imperiled was chilling.

She got to her feet and Emanuel rose with her, his heart heavy.

"I must go now, and I am not sure when I will see you again." She hesitated. "But I leave you with a parting gift. Rothschild and Samuel have put away their differences. They plan to merge Royal Dutch with Shell."

He had known it was only a matter of time before that happened. In fact, the timing could not be better.

"It is only right that I give you a gift in return," he said. "One you can bring back to England with you."

The corners of her lips curled up. "Oh?"

"How much would it assuage London's concerns over who shall control Russian oil if I tell you that I will be merging with them as well?"

Her eyes were wide. "That will change the oil markets entirely."

"It will indeed," he replied, chuckling. "With that alliance, we will control over seventy percent of the Russian kerosene market—fifty percent of the global market."

She swallowed. "Emanuel, while I am happy for your success, the wealthier you become, the more danger you are in. James will be furious at me for telling you, but Ezhov has been making demands of him recently, insisting on support for Stalin. He wants him freed from prison. He also wants money and arms for when Stalin is released—even specified that the weapons should be modern and unused, either German or British. Artillery. In addition, he requested information on Polish war zones."

This was a new concern indeed. "This is far beyond the ongoing violence. He is planning a war."

"And just so you know, Stalin will soon be walking the streets again."

He gave her a sharp glance, but she did not flinch. By including Colonel Ray in his demands, he was hoping to get the British involved. Certainly Ezhov was acting on his own, but he was also working for Lenin, Trotsky, and Stalin. What was he up to now?

She lifted onto her toes and gave him a kiss. "*Ad Victorum Ire Spolia,*" she whispered into his ear. To the victor go the spoils. As she pulled away, her hand stroked the dark beard on his cheek. "Do not forget, there are always those willing to cheat and lie so they can claim the win. Watch all the players carefully, Emanuel. Even when you think you have your eye on the king, remember it is the pawns who usually run the show."

Chapter Twenty-Four

In Russia, tens of thousands of workers joined strikes across the country, shutting down banks and businesses, pulling trains to a standstill. Workers' councils started up in Moscow and St. Petersburg, calling themselves "Soviets". Even the peasants did their part in fighting the bourgeois by attacking and burning manor houses.

Though he had been exiled to Europe, the revolutionary Lenin was at the forefront of the chaos, constantly writing rousing articles.

Geneva, January 10 (23)

> *The working class, which would seem to have stood aside for a long time from the bourgeois opposition movement, has raised its voice. With incredible speed the broad masses of the workers have caught up with their advanced comrades, the class-conscious Social-Democrats. The workers' movement in St. Petersburg these days has made gigantic strides. Economic demands are giving way to political demands. The strike is turning into a general strike and it has led to an unheard-of colossal demonstration; the prestige of the Czarist name has been ruined for good. The uprising has begun. Force against force. Street fighting is raging, barricades are being thrown up, rifles are crackling, guns are roaring.*

*Rivers of blood are flowing, the civil war
for freedom is blazing up. Moscow and the
South, the Caucasus and Poland are ready
to join the proletariat of St. Petersburg.
The slogan of the workers has become:
Death or freedom! Today and tomorrow a
great deal will be decided. The situation
changes with every hour. The telegraph
brings breath-taking news, and all words
now seem feeble in comparison with the
events we are living through. Everyone
must be ready to do his duty as a
revolutionary and as a Social-Democrat.
Long live the revolution!
Long live the insurgent proletariat!*

But on this one festive day in Baku, the people had chosen to look away from the tragedies. The heavy air lifted with music and laughter, and the songs were accompanied by an erratic but confident pounding of hammers. While most of the workers gorged on free food, others attached wooden signs onto every derrick, pump station, and storage tank owned by either Rothschild or the Nobels.

NOBMAZUT OIL COMPANY, the signs declared. The Russian abbreviation of Batumi Oil and Trade Society with the Nobel family name. The establishment of this joint venture company meant BraNobel would merge its efforts with those of Rothschild, but their companies would remain independent of each other. It had never been Emanuel's intention to form an alliance with any other oil barons, but circumstances had put him in that position, and now that it had happened, he was pleased. He had thought about this arrangement for a long time, trying to decide if his father would have approved. Yes, it was Emanuel's company now, but Ludvig's opinion was still valued. In the end he did as Ludvig would have advised: he went over the numbers again, looked at them from every angle, then signed the contracts.

He was now aligned with men he believed were reputable. All he could do was hope the combination would prevail against Rockefeller's desperate attacks—at least for now.

Emanuel strolled along the edge of a small park overlooking the oil fields, enjoying the ongoing festivities. A fine white tent stood just ahead, shielding Édouard Rothschild and Jules Aron from the baking sun. They stood as Emanuel approached.

"Good afternoon," he said, extending a hand. "Congratulations!"

Rothschild and Aron shook his hand then handed a glass of champagne to Emanuel. "Good afternoon to you as well, Mr Nobel. What a beautiful day to celebrate the creation of our formal alliance."

"This partnership can only mean good things for the people of Baku," Emanuel said, closing his eyes and savoring both the bubbles and the accomplishment they represented. "The more success we see in Azerbaijan, the more hope they have for their own futures."

*

At dinner that evening, Rothschild sat beside Emanuel. When it was over, he stood to make an announcement.

"As an ambassador for the Imperial Russian Technical Society, I would like to announce the founding of the Emanuel Nobel Oil Prize Fund."

Emanuel glanced up in surprise. "The Nobel Prizes are run through the family, not through me."

"Ah yes, but this prize is in addition to the generous Nobel prizes already in place," Rothschild explained. "And it will be presented annually for the best works or inventions in the oil business. The ceremony will be held every year on May 25th, which is not only your birthday, but the anniversary of BraNobel. The winner will receive 1,000 gold rubles."

"I am in full support of this initiative," Taghiyev said. "It is only right that it is so named. I pledge to make a financial contribution equal to Rothschild's, and I hope our fellow oil barons—Naghiyev, Mukhtarov and Assadulayev—will follow my suit. Emanuel, this is a great initiative which will highlight and cement your outstanding contribution to the development of the oil industry worldwide, and in Baku in particular. After all, you have entirely changed the face of Baku's oil industry."

The idea made Emanuel slightly uneasy. "I do not know. While I am flattered, I am not sure it is the right thing for me to do. This was never about me. This was about Baku."

"Nevertheless," Rothschild insisted, "the foundation is already in place under the auspices of the Baku branch of the Imperial Russian Technical Society. And the Mazut company has contributed capital of 10,000 roubles with which to create the prize fund. We've even designed the award statue. The first annual Emanuel Nobel Prize will be awarded on your next birthday."

"Hear! Hear!" Taghiyev cried. "It is done, my humble friend. Now you must accept the accolades."

It was decided, so Emanuel grudgingly agreed to accept the honor. Despite his reticence, he was proud. How could he not be flattered? Rewarding excellence was always a good thing. On his fiftieth birthday, the newspapers would declare the winner of the prize. Would anyone even notice the announcement? Certainly the papers were selling well these days, bringing news from around the world. The war across Europe raged, slaughtering thousands every day, and violence increased voraciously across Russia. Closer to Baku and throughout Azerbaijan, hundreds of villages and towns had been destroyed by the invading mixed British, Russian, and Armenian armed expeditionary forces, adventurers, and gangs. As if those events were not enough news, Josef Stalin had come to Baku in 1907. Through his own broadsheet, the *Baku Proletarian,* he encouraged tens of thousands of oil workers to unionize, advocating violence and solidarity. He was eventually arrested, thrown into the Baku Bailovo prison, and transferred to Solvychegodsk in Russia, but he had escaped. He had hidden in Baku's oilfields until he could once again publish his paper and encourage strikes against the oil barons.

No, Emanuel doubted anyone would even notice the announcement.

Then again, they might. The people here were proud of their home. They were unwilling to simply surrender the lives they now lived. They were not oblivious, but determined. Despite global chaos, the people of Baku still went about their normal activities, attending parties, the theater, and the circus. They worked, they played. When the working day was done they frequented the shops and restaurants, or they strolled hand in hand through the vibrant parks and gardens, and along Baku's magnificent boulevard. For them the sun still shone. All they had to do was turn their faces away from the wall of blackness which was closing in on all sides.

Chapter Twenty-Five

Emanuel's shiny new Mercedes pulled up in front of Taghiyev's mansion, slowed to a chuckling roll, then jolted to a stop. He stared at the mansion, paralyzed with apprehension, his palms slick with nervous sweat. For the first time, Emanuel questioned his ability to walk to the door.

His chauffeur, Fuad, disembarked and went to Emanuel's side, ready to offer assistance. The man was huge, but the muscle he had once flexed so bravely in battle had softened in his middle age. His uniform, carefully fitted to ensure it both looked professional and felt comfortable, always seemed snug, as if the buttons and heavy wool worked hard to restrain whatever force still lurked within. Emanuel knew to expect no conversation from his chauffeur. Once upon a time, Fuad had served as a translator for the Russians during the Russian-Afghan/British War of 1885. As a Turkish Muslim, Fuad knew more than a few local dialects, which had made him extremely valuable to the Russian cause, since they wished to communicate with the Iranic and Turkic populations of Afghanistan. Unfortunately for Fuad, he was eventually captured, and the man who had once spoken so many tongues was suddenly relieved of his own.

Considering Fuad's courage in the past, Emanuel always enjoyed the irony of the man's fear of driving. At first he had regarded the Mercedes with the kind of apprehension one might have with a wild horse. It was only at Emanuel's insistence that he grudgingly committed himself to taming the beast. Soon he became comfortable, and with his master's encouragement he had begun testing the other automobiles as well, since Emanuel had not stopped at a single Mercedes. Along with Emanuel's competitive nature had come a desire for speed, and he had indulged this craving by purchasing the finest, fastest automobiles available. A large garage housed his collection, which included a second Mercedes, a Phaeton, a Packard, a Rambler, and an Oldsmobile. Emanuel even drove himself occasionally just for the thrill of it.

"We made it in one piece," Emanuel joked. "Let's see if you can do it again with another person in the vehicle."

Fuad had no idea that his master was just as nervous as he, though it had nothing to do with the automobile.

Emanuel was the wealthiest man in all of Europe, and yet he could not have the one thing he wanted. The irony was not lost on him. Tonight, though, he dared to challenge the impossible. Taking a deep breath for courage, he stepped out of the vehicle and proceeded to the front door of his best friend's house. When he rang the bell, he was welcomed inside the familiar entry with the same warm hospitality he had come to expect. He greeted the familiar staff and admired the familiar art on the walls—except he felt as if he were a stranger, as if he had never seen any of it before.

Because tonight he was here for Leyla.

Taghiyev had agreed wholeheartedly to Emanuel's suggestion that he accompany her to the Azerbaijani national theater for the premiere performance of the opera, "The Legend of Leyla and Majnun". To her father it was an excellent way to assure his daughter would experience her favorite story brought to life without his having to worry about yet another young suitor. She had many of those, Emanuel knew, and yet she had accepted the proposals of none. Her avoidance of marriage was frustrating for Taghiyev, but he would never push his daughter into something which might make her unhappy.

The irony, of course, was that Emanuel was indeed a suitor—and he was the only one who knew.

"Mr Nobel!" Leyla cried, coming down the stairs to meet him. "I am so excited about this evening!"

Every nerve in his body caught fire at sight of her. If asked, he would have to say her gown was black, but the exquisite needlework of golds, pinks, and oranges brought the darkness to life. Beads and pearls were sewn into the silk in the shapes of birds and flowers, and her hair was pulled back under a gold velvet *chutga* layered over with pink veils.

"As am I," he said. "It will be a wonderful performance. Everyone will be there, I am sure."

"But I will not notice any of them," she assured him. "I am sharing this evening only with you, since you were the one who first introduced the story to me." Her eyes twinkled. "I see it as symbolic between us, you know."

"Is that right?" he managed.

She nodded. "Shall we go?"

He held out his arm and she tucked her hand in his elbow. "I have brought a surprise for you."

"Another one? Mr Nobel, you must stop spoiling me!"

"Well, it is not entirely for you, I will admit. You will see in a moment."

The door opened, they stepped into the early evening, and she stopped short with a gasp.

"We are going in your new Mercedes?" she asked, her voice barely more than a whisper.

"What do you think?"

She could not take her eyes off the gleaming black metal. For a moment Emanuel was not sure if his surprise was welcome or not, since she had not taken another step since she had first seen it. Perhaps she was too timid for such a new experience. Perhaps he should have asked her in advance. Perhaps—

She squeezed his arm. "What a beautiful machine! I am very much looking forward to this ride. My father, as you know, hasn't let me ride in his. I think he is afraid to break me."

"Perhaps we should not tell him."

She threw back her head in a gesture like her father's, laughing with delight. "Oh, Mr Nobel, this is the most exciting evening of my life! Let's go!"

She giggled as Fuad started up the engine, then she smiled the entire drive to the theater, waving at carriages and pedestrians along the way. Over the noise of the wind, he explained to her that tonight was actually the first opera in the entire Middle East, and that the composer, Uzeyir Hajibeyov, was Azerbaijani.

She laughed, teasing him. "I already know all that! I have been learning everything I can about it ever since you invited me."

When they arrived at the theatre, Fuad turned off the engine then went around to open her door.

"If I did not know what we were about to see," she admitted, "I would never get out of the automobile! What a grand adventure this is already." She reached for his hand and squeezed it. "Thank you, Mr Nobel. This will be a night I shall never forget."

He lifted her hand and kissed the soft knuckles. "I hope so, Leyla. And I hope you will do me one favor tonight."

"Anything!"

"Will you call me Emanuel?"

He had not thought her expression could brighten any further, but it did at his request. "Gladly, Emanuel."

They waded through the crowds in the lobby, dutifully greeting others, and Emanuel felt an unexpected rush of anxiety. What if Julie was there as well? What would he do if she approached, boldly taking possession of him as she was often did in front of other females? He was relieved when Leyla looked up at him with a grimace.

"I am sorry, but I am uncomfortable in this crowd. Do you think we could go directly to our seats and wait there?"

"With pleasure." He held out his arm. "Come along. We shall escape the noise right away."

He led the way, smoothly working through the bodies. Eventually they reached the stairway and he led her to his box, which was directly across from the stage, in the center. Six velvet chairs were arranged inside; however, Emanuel had made sure that there would only be two people in attendance that night. Thick curtains draped over either side of the box guaranteed them privacy to a certain extent, though at first he worried she might be frightened by the thought of isolation from the rest of the audience. Certainly she was old enough to go out without a chaperone, and her father had approved of the invitation, but still ... what if she—

"This is wonderful!" she said, loud enough so only he could hear. She lowered herself into her chair and beamed at him. "I was hoping we would have a chance to speak on our own, and I know how people crowd around you whenever they can find you, so this is perfect."

"I am pleased you approve," he said warmly. "What did you want to talk about?"

"The story, of course," she replied, blushing slightly. "And the symbolism I see in it when I think of you, Emanuel. I studied the poem when I was at school, you know."

He did not know that.

She sighed fondly, thinking. "I loved it before we studied it, but I love it all the more now. It is such a tragic story. Like *Romeo and Juliet*—except it is so different, of course. I love both stories, but this one means more to me."

"That makes sense. It is Eastern rather than Western, so it would appeal to you more."

She nodded. "It just seems more like us, doesn't it? Like the Azerbaijanis, I mean. The romance, the drama, the madness of it ... It just seems to me that *Romeo and Juliet* is so much more *proper*, though the story is just as chaotic. If I were to paint the two, I would paint Shakespeare's tale in black and white and grays, but I would paint *Leyla and Majnun* in bright, spinning colors."

"I can see that. *Leyla and Majnun* is more vivid. Perhaps that is because the character of Qays was a poet, flamboyant by nature."

"Poor Qays," she agreed with a sigh. "I never really understood why they called him crazy just because he wrote poems for her. And once he was given the name 'Majnun', which means 'madman', he was not *allowed* to be with her. All so unfair."

"And because he was not allowed to be with her, he *did* go mad."

"My professor called both stories tales of 'virgin love'. Because despite their undying love," she said slowly, looking up at him from under her lashes, "the couple never marries ... or consummates their passion."

She was watching him intently, awaiting his response with her lower lip caught between her teeth.

He stared at her, confused. How should he answer? And why had she said the story was symbolic? Was it just because he had given her the book originally, or ... could he dare to dream that she meant they shared a similar situation with the lovers in the story? He could not possibly ask something so presumptuous. It was a moment before he felt brave enough to open his mouth with an attempt at an answer, but he was rescued in the last instant by the orchestra's opening strains. Distracted, she looked away, blinking rapidly as she stared down at the stage. Feeling his gaze, she gave him a brief, apologetic little smile then gestured with her chin toward the stage.

Emanuel faced the stage and tried to let the opera carry him away. It did not work. He spent most of the evening thinking of what she had said, of how she had said it, and of how he could possibly react. She, on the other hand, was caught up in the music, laughing and crying when the familiar story moved her. Occasionally she turned to him, needing to share the moment, but he could only nod. For the first time in his life he felt absolutely no confidence in his next move.

"Oh, it was *wonderful*," she gushed as the final applause died. She seized his hands in hers. "I was right. I will never forget this night. And I am so glad I spent it with you."

"As am I," he assured her, then he quickly released her hands and gestured toward the exit, needing to escape before he said or did something he might regret.

She hesitated. "What do you think might have happened if they had been allowed to be together? Leyla and Qays, I mean."

"Did you not study that?"

"Yes, but I want to know what you think."

Could she read the agony in his eyes?

He would answer the question, that was all. "If they had been together, I have no doubt they would have been blissfully happy. They could have gone mad with love together. But that was not the story. They were destined for separate lives."

Her eyes suddenly shone with tears, but she would not look away. "I do not think it had to end that way," she said quietly.

He was more than twice her age. He was her father's best friend. It *had* to end this way.

"That is the way it must end, Leyla, whether we like it or not," he said brusquely, needing air. "Come. The Mercedes is waiting."

He took her home, kissed her hand at the door, and thanked her for the charming company. When he stepped back from the entrance, she finally blinked and released her tears, a pair of rivulets trickling down her cheeks.

"Thank you for tonight, Emanuel," she said, not bothering to dry her eyes. "And thank you for being such a patient audience to a spoiled young lady's ramblings."

She shut the door between them, and he stared helplessly at it. For the second time that night, she had left him speechless. Which one of them was the mad poet?

Chapter Twenty-Six

How did this happen? How did I become middle aged?
On the afternoon of his fiftieth birthday, about an hour before Villa Petrolea's doors opened to admit his invited guests, Emanuel stepped onto the balcony and surveyed his massive property. The gardens were a marvel indeed, and every time he admired them he remembered how he had doubted his father's plan. When a hot Baku breeze blew past, he closed his eyes and listened to the dancing of thousands of leaves. Like the trees, Emanuel had grown roots here. He could not imagine living anywhere else.

Because it could do no harm to anyone, he allowed himself to imagine living here—with her.

Her hand had been light and cool, so tiny compared to his. She had wanted him to hold it. If their story could have had a different ending, as she had suggested, they would stand in this place—or any other she wanted—and she would listen to his stories, encouraging him, giggling when he flattered her. Then they would trade roles, and he would listen in fascination to her stories, to her questions. At times it would be difficult for him to determine her exact words, since he would be so mesmerized by the gentle movement of those soft lips, the flash of straight white teeth, but he would be content, knowing she shared those words with him alone.

Evening would come and the lamps would be lit, and Emanuel would stroll with her between the trees. If she shivered he would draw her closer, then she would say she wished there was music so they could dance. *Who needs music?* he would ask. In his fantasy they adjusted the hands held between them, then he swept her against him, leading her in a waltz he heard in his head. Around and around they would dance, her slender form light and eager, and when the music slowed he would not let her go. Her eyes would be warm and inviting, then they would close in expectation. He would lean in and brush her virgin lips with his, trying not to scratch with his beard, not wanting to injure the delicate flower in his arms, but she blinked up at him with disappointment. *More,* she silently pleaded. *More.*

He sighed and opened his eyes, battling the same confusion of desire and regret he always felt when he thought of Leyla. In his world of money and business, with the filth of the oil fields always under his nails, the imaginings he had of her were his escape, his oasis, his fleeting moments of clean, delicious freedom. He relished the dreams at the same time as he accepted the reality: his hunger for her would never be sated. Dreaming was the best he could do.

It had been months since he had seen her last. At the opera. Shortly after, she had gone to St. Petersburg to take more courses at school. It was good that she had gone, he reminded himself.

Beyond the trees, the oil fields burned. BraNobel's derricks were still largely untouched, but most of the surrounding fields had been torched. A continuous stream of black belched into the sky. The strikes and protests had not yet made enough of an impression that visitors avoided the city, and Emanuel hoped it would never come to that. Despite the political turmoil, BraNobel itself was operating at its peak, and its profit distribution among the employees raised envy among every competitor. With their own money, the workers had become consumers as well as producers.

But he could not fool himself forever. Baku was no longer safe. Now that oil had become the highest form of competition on the world stage, Baku was the prize they sought. While he hoped BraNobel would survive the game, he hated the realization that the price would most likely be paid in blood by far too many people.

Emanuel's fiftieth birthday was also the thirtieth anniversary of BraNobel, and both of these events called for celebration. When evening fell, Baku society arrived at his doorstep, dressed in their finest and glowing with anticipation of the night to come. He had balked at the idea of his receiving gifts since he already had everything he could ever desire, and he had made it known that no one should bring anything but themselves. Instead, he had broken with tradition, visiting Fabergé in St. Petersburg. There he had purchased items for the numerous relatives, cousins, and close friends he had invited to the party.

It had been a harrowing shopping trip. On his way to the store he walked by the Angleterre Hotel, where Julie was staying, and became aware of a commotion around him. A mob of grubby looking workers ran from the area, looking back over their shoulders as they fled. Confused, Emanuel reached for one and asked what was happening. The man's eyes had been wide with panic.

"Run!" he cried urgently.

"What? Why?" but the worker had jerked away from his grip.

Emanuel's fingers ripped through his sleeve just as an explosion went off behind them, blowing the front of the hotel apart. It was a few seconds before Emanuel realized he lay on the ground, dazed. His ears rang, sounding as if he was at one end of a very long tunnel, and for a suspended moment in time he could not move. Like him, people lay in the street, bewildered, covered in debris from the explosion. Many were crying, yelling for help. Some weren't moving at all. Flames raged through the opening where the front entrance to the hotel had been, and the fire reached up, through the windows of the second floor as well. *Julie!* Was she in there? He had never been to her room and suddenly feared for the worst.

He should not have doubted her. In the next moment, Julie burst through the fire along with two other men, running into the midst of the punks fleeing the scene. Emanuel's first impulse was to run to her, defend her against the violence; she looked so small, so fragile, an easy target in her fine clothes and upswept hair.

One of the thugs ran at her, his hands grabbing at her neck. Incredibly, Julie stepped toward him and swept her arms up between his, moving as smoothly as a professional dancer. Her skilled movement threw the man off balance, and he practically fell into her just as she struck the hard edges of her hands against his neck. The man dropped like a stone, and she wheeled to face another furious attacker coming toward her from behind. This one carried a knife which he arced over his head. In a movement almost too fast for Emanuel to fathom, she redirected his lunge then drove her flat palm into the man's nose. Blood exploded from his face, splattering her, and he fell backwards.

"Gold!" one of the other men yelled at Julie.

She reacted lightning fast, pulling a small gun from inside her bodice and firing three shots, dropping the next would-be attacker. Once he was down, she ran to her cohort's side and helped rid the area of more threats.

Emanuel was spellbound, watching the hard glint of her eyes, the steel-like set of her lips. She was efficient, effective, and disciplined to the point where he saw absolutely no emotion in her face. It was the most violent yet beautiful thing he had ever seen.

All around him, people rushed in to help the fallen victims, and Emanuel found himself lost in the surge of rescuers. He took account of his arms and legs and discovered only a little blood on his face, so he decided not to add to the long list of casualties. With some effort, he roused himself and began to stagger away from the crowds, glancing back once for Julie. She was gone.

He had read of these uprisings, heard of other attacks, but he had never truly taken them seriously before. From the perspective of his safe, isolated existence, they had seemed relatively minor. Now, as he stood in the rubble with fresh blood trickling down the side of his face, they seemed quite significant indeed.

Deep in thought, he had returned home the next day, the valuable Fabergé gifts packed tightly in his suitcase. The world was changing around him. He had better be wary, as others had advised, be alert. This type of violence would not be limited to St. Petersburg.

Tonight he brought out those gifts and sought the recipients from among the guests assembled in the crowded ballroom.

Taghiyev frowned in confusion. "What is this?" he demanded when Emanuel handed him a box.

"It is my way of having a happy birthday," Emanuel told him. "I hope you like it."

"But you—"

"Just open it," Emanuel replied. "I chose it for you especially, and for your lovely wife."

Shaking his head in mock annoyance, Taghiyev unwrapped the gift. He beamed, admiring the stunning gold-plated, diamond encrusted Fabergé clock, then hugged Emanuel tight. "It is beautiful! And yet I already have you for a friend, which is the best gift I could ever have."

"That is how I feel as well. But I thought this might help you be on time for once," Emanuel teased.

Taghiyev's laughter bounced off the ceiling and fell like rain onto the animated conversations of the other guests. Lured by the sound, Leyla appeared at her father's side. He had hoped with all his heart that she would be there, but he had not been sure if she would be home in time or not. The sight of her took his breath. More beautiful than ever, she was aglow in a beautiful silk gown of turquoise with gold lace patterned throughout. Glossy black hair tumbled down her back, partially covered by a sheer, matching veil, and her eyes sparkled in the light of the chandelier over their heads.

"Happy birthday, Mr Nobel," she said, reaching for a hug.

He leaned in, and her slender arms wrapped around his neck. His hands touched the small of her back, but he resisted the urge to press them against her. Out of habit he inhaled her intoxicating scent, noting a touch of vanilla in her hair tonight. Her pure, inviting essence always reminded him of the Thai spas he enjoyed.

"I have missed you," she whispered into his ear.

"As have I, dear Leyla. Truly," he replied just as softly. They drew apart, then he reached into the bag draped over his shoulder. "I brought you a gift as well."

"A gift? For me? You always spoil me."

"Look at my clock!" her father interrupted. "Is it not the most beautiful thing?"

She admired it closely, running her fingers over the diamonds. "Exquisite, Papa. And maybe it will help you stay on schedule for once."

"Hey! That is what Emanuel said!"

They all laughed this time, and Emanuel was relieved that he sensed no awkwardness between Leyla and him. If he could not have her as his lover, at least he could still be her friend.

He held out a box. "I chose this for you."

The egg was a turquoise blue with a gold lace pattern wrapped around the surface, which was coincidentally very similar to her gown. Diamonds glinted along the peaks of the pattern. Like every Fabergé egg, it opened across the middle, and she stared with delight as her new treasure was revealed. Inside was a small carriage, which he had hoped might remind her of him. The tiny gold wheels spun when she touched them.

"Oh, Mr Nobel," she exclaimed, reverting to the more formal address. "It is absolutely stunning. And the little carriage makes me think of our trip to the opera. Thank you so much!"

"It is my absolute pleasure," he assured her.

He was on the verge of asking more about her memories of that night when Elbek approached. "Sir?" he said.

"Is it time?"

"Yes, sir. All is ready. We await your cue."

"Excellent! Come, everyone!" he called, raising his voice above the din in the room. "Everyone outside to the park, if you please!"

Suspended high overhead, between some of the largest trees, had been stretched a long banner announcing, "BRANOBEL OIL – 30 YEARS". Long tables of food and drink were presented below the banner, and one held a large birthday cake flickering with candles. The guests filled their plates and toasted BraNobel, clapping as Emanuel blew out all the candles.

All at once the black night, already dotted by diamonds, exploded into color as fireworks lit the sky, and everyone cheered with delight. Emanuel stood back, enjoying himself immensely.

"Thank you for the extravagant gift," Leyla said at his elbow. "You certainly did not have to do that."

For the first time, Emanuel let her see the love in his eyes. "If I could, Leyla, I would give you the world."

"Emanuel!" Taghiyev called, approaching from behind.

Startled, Emanuel gave her a sheepish grin. "And here comes the reason why I cannot."

Taghiyev was walking toward them, holding up his new clock, oblivious to the scene he had interrupted. "Look here! My clock says I am having a wonderful ... time! But wait. There is something more to show you, my friend."

"To show me?"

"Come along. I know you said there would be no gifts for you this evening; however, a man like me does not get into a position like mine without bending a few rules, yes?"

He led the way to Villa Petrolea's stables, making Emanuel more than just a little curious. Lately he had not had enough time to enjoy his beautiful Azerbaijani horses, and this seemed like a good excuse to visit them.

"You are surrounded by so much majesty and beauty," Taghiyev said, standing back as the stable doors were opened, "but there is no beauty as great as that which is created by God ... then well-bred by man."

In the middle of the stable, with a groom on either side, stood a magnificent Karabakh stallion, his high-set, chestnut neck arched elegantly, his nostrils flared with curiosity.

"This is Khazar," Taghiyev said proudly. "He is a—"

"Khazar? But I have read of him in the newspapers!" Emanuel declared, holding out a hand for the horse to smell. "He is a purebred champion. Everyone is talking of his great speed and potential."

The soft muzzle filled Emanuel's palm, then Khazar exhaled, a warm, moist puff of acceptance. Khazar was indeed magnificent, and his compact, muscular body gleamed, his natural red color looking almost gold in places.

"Hello, Khazar," he said, addressing the soft brown eyes.

Khazar blinked slowly then gently nudged Emanuel's shoulder.

"He is a bold fellow, and very intelligent," Taghiyev said fondly. "He will be a good friend to you—as you are to me."

Chapter Twenty-Seven

Emanuel was used to being in the midst of important people. He was not, however, used to presenting awards in his name, and the concept made him a little uncomfortable. On the other hand, such a prestigious award could only benefit BraNobel's reputation. Under duress, he had agreed that the Emanuel Nobel Oil Prize would be awarded, and today was the big day. The Baku headquarters of the Imperial Russian Technical Society had filled the room with aristocracy and nobility, including scientists, prominent bankers, certainly oil barons and foreign ambassadors. Emanuel's eyes touched on Rudolf Diesel, then the Russian aviation inventor, Igor Sikorsky. Near him sat his father's old friend Édouard Rothschild and Jules Aron were also in attendance, he noted.

When it was time, one of the scientists, stepped confidently to the front of the stage, drawing everyone's attention. "Gentlemen," he said, "I present to you the first winner of the Emanuel Nobel Prize, Dr Viktor Herr, renowned chemist from Germany."

Viktor Herr climbed the stairs to the stage and awkwardly accepted enthusiastic applause for his work. Emanuel waited behind the scientists, relieved that all he had to do was shake the winner's hand. He had very real doubts that he would be able to recite the man's accomplishment.

When the applause ended, the presenter continued. "Congratulations, Dr Herr, on your work of isolating two main fatty acids of the oxalic acid series through the oxidation of fractions of Baku oil from 500° to 1630°C with 1.4 density nitric acid."

Mr Herr shook the scientist's hand, then Emanuel stepped forward to present him with the prize.

"Congratulations, Dr Herr."

After hanging a gold medal around the man's neck—imprinted with Emanuel's profile—he handed him an envelope containing one thousand golden rubles, which the man accepted with alacrity.

"Thank you very much, Mr Nobel," the prizewinner replied, blinking quickly behind his thick spectacles. His handshake was strong enough, but his palm was damp with sweat.

"The honor is mine, sir," Emanuel replied, then he stepped away and gave the spotlight to the little man.

After the formalities were completed, the crowd stayed to mingle and chat over champagne. Emanuel approached Diesel, intent on speaking with him about his latest idea. By the time Édouard and Aron approached they were well into the topic.

"All of us, all the oil refiners, threw out the byproduct as waste," Emanuel was saying. "I no longer wish to do that. With a new refining process, I plan to turn it into a lubricant I call petroleum jelly, made of Balakhani oil. One density has the proper viscosity to lubricate your engines, and the more purified one can be used on human skin."

"On skin?" Diesel sounded doubtful.

"They're already using it in a spa here, you know. The *Naftalan.*"

"What do you do with it?"

"You bathe in it! Think of that. It is an entirely new market, and it is worth millions."

Édouard chuckled. "Still on your never-ending quest to improve life through BraNobel, Emanuel?"

"But of course. As you say," Emanuel replied, "it is never-ending."

Chapter Twenty-Eight

By 1914 the Russian Empire was made up of over 165,000,000 Slavs, Tatars, Jews, Turks, and other nationalities stretching across Poland, Finland, and most of Transcaucasia. Despite a decade of increasingly popular protests, Czar Nicholas II still ruled as an absolute monarch, though he had established a Russian parliament, which he called the State Duma. The Duma basically altered nothing—other than the name of their capital, which changed from St. Petersburg to Petrograd when the Duma declared the former to be too Germanic. During the first six months of that year, almost half of Russia's workforce took part in strikes.

Germany, Austria-Hungary, and Italy had joined together against both Russia and France seven years earlier, forming the Triple Alliance. Determining Germany to be her greatest threat, Russia had responded by forming the Triple Entente with Britain and France. All of Europe began to bolster their military as tensions rose between the countries. In 1912 Russia established the Russian Army Service. Within two years they owned almost four hundred aircraft and sixteen airships, making them the largest air force in the world. Their Navy boasted four battleships, ten cruisers, twenty-one destroyers, eleven submarines, and fifty torpedo boats.

Russia had the largest army in the world. In the summer of 1914, five million of her soldiers prepared to join the First World War. Unfortunately for them, Russia's crumbling infrastructure severely hampered their ability to move the troops. Emanuel read daily updates in all the newspapers—Russian, French, English and German—and watched with dazed disbelief as Czar Nicholas II attempted to bridge the abyss which had continued to deepen between himself and

Russia's people following Bloody Sunday. In an unexpected declaration, the Czar determined he would lead the army himself, despite his lack of any kind of military experience. He did as he had announced, traveling with the troops to the Eastern Front, leaving his wife, the Czarina Alexandra, in control.

Except she was not in charge at all. Her every move, every word was influenced by a man named Grigory Rasputin whom she believed was a holy man. Rasputin not only had the apparent ability to help her hemophiliac son, Alexis, he also made predictions which turned out to be correct more often than not. It was common knowledge that the man was a compulsive gigolo, and yet Alexandra defended him fiercely against anyone who dared speak badly of him.

To feed the war machine, the economy was funneled away from the Russian people and their infrastructure and into the military. The starving masses began lining up in the frozen streets, hoping to procure a loaf of bread.

Emanuel sighed wearily, turning the pages of the *Izvestiya*. The newspaper carried the usual stories, ranging from revolutionary activities to social events, interrupted occasionally by propaganda images intended to boost morale while downplaying the intimidating legends of invincible Germans. Fortunately, Rasputin's dire prediction that Russia would lose the war had eventually prompted the Czar to return from the Front, where he should have been all along, looking after his starving people instead of his borders.

Emanuel looked up at a knock on his door. "A visitor, sir," said Elbek.

"Oh?"

"Colonel James Ray from Great Britain."

Emanuel's brow lifted. This was interesting. "Colonel," he said, standing and holding out a hand. "What an unexpected surprise. I did not realize you were here in Baku."

It had been a while since he had seen the handsome British spy, and Emanuel had wondered at his absence.

Perhaps he had not come by because he had known Emanuel would see right through him.

Ray's handshake was solid. "I returned a while back and have been meaning to contact you," he said, polite and self-assured. "Miss Gold sends her regards as well."

"Ah. How is she?" He gestured toward an armchair facing his. "Please, have a seat. May I offer you a drink?"

"Thank you. I would not say no to a cognac, if it is available."

Without a word, Elbek went to the bar and poured two cognacs.

"Julie is doing well enough. Thank you," Ray replied, glancing up at Elbek and accepting a glass from a silver tray. "She was reassigned. Clearly she was taking this one too ... personally."

How could he resist? "She was very good at her job."

"Indeed," Ray acknowledged. His grey blue eyes showed a hint of annoyance.

"And how is our friend John?"

"John? Do you refer to J.D. Rockefeller?"

"The one and only."

Ray chuckled. "He truly is that, fortunately. I am not sure the world could stand two of him."

Emanuel could not agree more, though it was odd to hear it from Ray. "I had understood you were on good terms with him."

"It is wise to keep up impressions when they are positive, do you not agree?" Ray tapped a cigar from a gold case in his jacket. "Even," he continued, blowing a fragrant stream of smoke away from Emanuel, "if they are erroneous."

"I am not a fool, Colonel. I know you worked with him behind closed doors."

"Yes, and I still do." His eyes narrowed. "However, I no longer support his ambitions."

"Is that right? What could have changed your mind?"

Ray frowned slightly. "I was put off last year after the Ludlow Massacre, to be honest. I cannot in good conscience back a man who would order the cold blooded murder of two dozen miners, as well as their women and children."

"His involvement was never proven."

"Neither was yours, sir, in the matter of the dismantling of Standard Oil's US monopoly, and yet your name is often mentioned when the topic is discussed."

Emanuel's brow lifted. "I had nothing to do with that. Not directly."

"That was quite a setback for J.D." Ray slowly turned his glass between his fingers. "I imagine that would be slightly gratifying after all he did to you and BraNobel."

He would not give Ray the satisfaction of a full answer; however, the truth was that Emanuel was still quite pleased at how that had turned out. "I did very little. I hired the best Washington lobbyists and consultants who worked their way through to the U.S. Justice Department and President Taft." He sipped at his drink, watching Ray with interest. "But this is nothing like the Ludlow Massacre. My lobbyists' work was based on facts and were fully legal."

"It did not have to be proven," Ray replied. "Blood follows oil business everywhere. Still, he has others who are willing to follow and do as he commands, some of whom are very high on the totem pole. I am still among the group; however, I have not participated recently. I am waiting for him to ask me about my lack of enthusiasm, actually."

Emanuel regarded the colonel closely, trying to figure out why he was sitting there. Incredibly, it appeared the man was holding out an olive branch, and the concept was intriguing. If that were so, the same rules applied to him as had applied to Julie, of course, which meant anything he said was to be considered carefully before it was acted upon. He had no reason to trust Colonel James Ray.

"He was very close with J.P. Morgan, I understand," Emanuel said, testing the waters. "It makes sense, since they both controlled the money. Now that Morgan is dead, Rockefeller is on his own."

Ray chuckled. "And I do not believe he will miss J.D. overmuch. Rockefeller has been quoted as remarking, 'And to think of it, he was not even rich.' In fact, Morgan left a fortune of over \$10 billion[2]. Not exactly a pauper, to my way of thinking."

"It takes a certain type of man to think that way," Emanuel marveled "One with about \$300 billion to his name."

"J.P. was J.D.'s right hand man, really. Though he would never admit that, of course. It might interest you to know that Rockefeller recently had a meeting with none other than the American Commander in Chief, President Woodrow Wilson."

"Is that right?"

"The president agreed with him that oil is the number one commodity in the world."

"Of course it is."

"He also helped the president see how Rothschild's merger with Shell redefines the balance of power, putting America at a distinct disadvantage." He gave Emanuel a sharp look, evaluating him, then made a decision. "Wilson has agreed to follow Rockefeller's wishes in this oil war, though he warned that he did not want to know all the dirty little secrets. He will not work against Congress or international leaders, and he'll never admit his participation, but he did agree."

"I see. So the sabotage against the Baku oil barons is now unofficially backed by the President of the United States."

"Not exactly, but he will not put a stop to it."

Emanuel did not see much added threat there, though he was not as comfortable dealing with politicians as he was with businessmen. He would have to wait and see what Rockefeller had up his sleeve.

"I do see a bigger danger on the horizon," Ray said quietly. "You have, I assume, heard of Leon Trotsky."

---

[2]   Currency values throughout the book have been adjusted to reflect inflation in 2019 U.S. dollars.

"The Marxist revolutionary and poet. Of course. What of him?"

"He has been busy of late. Having been deported from Spain for his radical activities, he was sent to America, where he spent three months writing socialist articles for the newspapers and becoming the toast of New York Socialist events. He was treated like a king by Rockefeller and others, enjoying all the luxuries a man in his position should abhor, from limousines to champagne and jewels."

"The irony is perfect."

"Think, Emanuel," Ray said quietly.

Emanuel stared at him, irritated by the man's deliberate use of his first name. From his expression, however, he had obviously done it on purpose, wanting to emphasize his point.

"Why would Rockefeller align with such a dangerous threat as Trotsky?" Ray asked. "Why would the Bolsheviks be on Rockefeller's social calendar?"

It did seem odd. Rockefeller always chose his cohorts carefully, and they were selected based on how useful they could be to him. How could he use Trotsky? The Bolsheviks had intensified their violence against the Russian elite of late, and the perpetually unhappy working class had begun to make threats against the Czar himself, encouraged by the revolutionaries. Lenin and Trotsky were at the head of that force. If Rockefeller was behind that momentum, it was because he wanted something they could give him.

"They want to control Russia," Emanuel said slowly, feeling cold dread seep into his belly. "And he wants to control Russia's oil. In order to do that, he must destroy Baku."

"And you, sir." Ray narrowed his eyes. "You are the richest man in all of Europe, which is a position in which he would much rather not see you. And the truth is, he is not willing to wait much longer."

Chapter Twenty-Nine

The perfect storm washed over Russia in 1917, and Emanuel could only stand on the rocky shores of Baku and watch helplessly via the newspapers. Bolstered by what he now recognized as the continuing support of the Rockefeller cartel, the Bolshevik revolution escalated, and both winter and the war continued to starve the people of Petrograd. The cold was so severe many of her people were no longer able to line up in streets for food—food which might be gone by the time they made it to the front of the queue. Those who stayed indoors shivered in their homes, weak with hunger, and burned any remaining furniture to stay warm.

All it took was one spark, and the match was lit on one fateful morning. Dozens of starving, freezing citizens standing in a bread-line had rushed a bakery out of desperation, and the Russian police opened fire. Their excessive action spurred on a much worse conflict, since over a hundred thousand people were already on strike, filling the streets with demands and rage. When they heard about the innocent shooting victims, they rallied around them—and were both surprised and delighted when the Russian Army went against orders and joined them, effectively disarming the police. The people stormed the arsenal and flung open prison doors. Twisted lines of smoke rose from burning paintings of the Czar, and marchers yelling for "Revolution!" kicked debris from toppled statues as they went. Demonstrators multiplied exponentially on the streets of the capital, and for almost a week Petrograd seethed like an ice-covered ant hill.

Hundreds of years of Czardom could not stand against tens of thousands of furious protesters. Czar Nicholas II abdicated from the throne in February, ending over three hundred years of the Romanov Dynasty, but it was not enough to satisfy the Bolsheviks. Virtually every member of the royal family was executed.

The Duma, meanwhile, faced ongoing protests and strikes by the working class, who claimed the new government was doing nothing for them. At the same time, the government was pushing their resistant troops, wanting them to keep fighting the losing battle against Germany despite Russia's earlier promise to pull out of the war. When Lenin, now the Marxist leader of the Bolshevik party, arrived in Russia that spring, his popularity spread like oil on water, and the Bolsheviks stepped into power the following October. They established the Russian Soviet Federative Socialist Republic, changing Russia's status from autocratic to communist. The Soviet army became known as the Red Army.

The Bolsheviks would not ignore Baku forever, Emanuel knew, and Rockefeller had too much at stake to wait much longer. After all, because of America's love affair with the automobile, that country's oil consumption had risen ninety percent over the past five years. Rockefeller was losing millions every day.

For a long time, Emanuel had chosen to believe he was safe. He had convinced himself that BraNobel was safe as well, based on the loyalty of their workers and the Czar's support. The Czar was now gone, and it was evident that BraNobel's workers would soon be overwhelmed by the inevitable Soviet attack. As it was, the number of BraNobel employees was dwindling, faltering under the constant pressure of hired thugs bent on destroying the oil fields.

Getting to his feet, Emanuel walked down the wide corridor to the front area where Elbek was speaking with some of the other staff.

"Elbek," he said quietly.

The butler excused himself and turned to Emanuel.

"Do you know the whereabouts of the colonel?"

A slight hesitation while Elbek searched his memory. "I believe so."

"Would you mind arranging a private meeting?"

Elbek bowed slightly. "Of course, Mr Nobel."

Two hours later he returned to Emanuel's office and informed him that Colonel Ray would be coming to Villa Petrolea within the hour.

"How did he seem on the phone?"

"Uneasy, I would say. But he was enthusiastic about seeing you."

When Ray arrived, Emanuel agreed with his assessment. The colonel was looking unusually tense. His business suit was as crisp as ever, his manners impeccable, and yet there was a tightness about his face, as if he were straining to hold his thoughts together.

"Please, Colonel. Have a seat." He looked up. "Elbek?"

"Yes, sir. Two cognacs."

"Thank you." He sat opposite Ray and regarded him warily, just as the retired MI-6 officer was watching him. "So. A great deal has happened since we last spoke, Colonel."

"I would say so, Your Excellency," Ray acknowledged. "It has been at least three years of turmoil since then, to put it mildly."

"I am pleased to see you survived the war."

"As am I," he said wryly. "There were moments I was unsure that would be the case."

"Were you in Europe?"

"Here and there. Recently I have been assigned back here. Congratulations, by the way, on the establishment of the Azerbaijan Democratic Republic. It was a brave move to make in this political climate."

Emanuel was not optimistic about the move. Lenin would not have been amused with the decision to establish a democratic society in opposition to the Bolsheviks, and the minimal forces of the A.D.R. would never be able to stand up to the Red Army.

"Yes, though considering the circumstances, it may be mostly symbolic. Tell me something. I have not been to St. Petersburg since it became Petrograd. How are things there?"

"You might not recognize it. The walls are covered in posters of the plain-faced Lenin and handsome Stalin. Even the citizens themselves are dressed in uniforms of the new ruling party, including arm bands."

Emanuel accepted his drink when Elbek returned. "Ah yes. The Bolsheviks." Taking a slow sip of the warm amber liquid encouraged Ray to do the same. "Colonel Ray, I am but a common businessman, as we both know—"

"Excuse me, Your Excellency, but you are far from common."

The flattery had been expected. Emanuel dipped his head slightly in appreciation. "As a businessman," he continued, "I have kept my head in my work and done what I could to stay out of the conflicts. Anything I know has come from the newspapers or my friends. What I need from you is an overview, if you would. A forecast for what I may face in the near future, so I may be prepared."

It was the truth, and he saw in Ray's eyes that he believed him.

Ray tilted his head, thinking. "You recall when we last spoke, we discussed another 'common' businessman's interest in the Bolshevik movement?"

The image of Rockefeller as 'common' made him smile. "Of course. It was a very illuminating discussion."

"The prize jewel is Baku, of course." He watched Emanuel closely. "Lenin has already ordered an attack. Stalin and his army of Cossacks and revolutionary soldiers are presently proceeding south along the Azerbaijan border, planning to take Baku."

Emanuel blinked, startled. He had not realized it was already happening. The oil fields were already burning, the streets were crowded with protesters ... nothing would be able to stop the Red Army if it came now.

"I see. Do you mind telling me if you have a role in this?"

"Actually, I do have." Ray hesitated, peering carefully at him. "It is quite secret, though. I put my life in your hands if I share it."

Emanuel sighed. "I have lived my whole life around secrets. I will not put you in any jeopardy, sir. This is for my own knowledge. I am a trustworthy man."

"I know. I have felt that way all along, and Julie believed it."

His mind flashed automatically to her full, dark lips and the sensual burn of her eyes. "I hope she is well."

"I spoke with her a while ago. She did ask me to pass on her regards if I saw you."

"Please say hello from me as well. Now, please, continue. Tell me your secret. I believe it will help me decide my next move."

Ray sipped thoughtfully at his drink. "Stalin believes I am with him, that America and Great Britain support his Soviet regime."

"Why would he believe that?"

He frowned. "Did Julie mention a man named Ezhov to you?"

The bruised circles on her arms came immediately to mind. "She did. A violent man."

"That's the one. He is my contact. To gain his trust, my government sent him money for the revolutionaries. In return he told me they have been buying up mercenaries from here to Georgia, and their army is massing in the Caucasus, preparing to invade Baku."

"When?"

"Three days."

It was impossible. How could they defend themselves from that kind of threat in so little time?

"However," Ray said, "Ezhov has not counted on my own principles being as strong as his. The British and Turkish armies are even now closing in on their location. They will not make it through to Baku. Not this time, anyway."

Emanuel let out a long breath. "Not this time," he agreed.

It occurred to Emanuel that Ray had put himself at great risk, playing this game with the Bolsheviks. Lenin and Stalin were not gentlemen. They would not hesitate to wipe their enemies from the earth. By assuming the role of double agent, Ray was quite literally playing Russian roulette.

"When they return they will be even stronger. No one will be able to stop them," Ray said. "When that happens, Stalin plans to remove all the oil families from Baku ... by any permanent means."

Emanuel sighed. "The Cheka."

"Yes. The Soviet security force. Do you recall the first official announcement of the Red Terror? I believe it was published in the *Izvestiya*."

"They publish a lot of things. What was it Stalin wrote? Ah yes. 'Print is the sharpest and the strongest weapon of our party.' That first official announcement was a year or so ago, was it not?" Emanuel asked.

"Makes no difference. The purpose is the same today as it was then. They called it the 'Appeal to the Working Class'."

"I recall. It encouraged massive terror and warned that anyone daring to spread rumors against the Soviet regime would be arrested immediately and sent to a concentration camp. It is difficult to forget that sort of thing."

"It is indeed. The article left out the shooting and hanging, though. Do you know how many thousands of people have been killed by the Chekists over the duration of the civil war? Obviously it is more than just the people spreading rumors. Their main targets are men like you, Emanuel, though thousands of others are dying as well. They call you the 'possessing classes'. Look." He unfolded a piece of paper he had slipped from his pocket. "This is a list of a few of the known executions from Kharkov to Odessa and Kiev and places in between. Approximately ten thousand executions between February 1919 and February 1920. The Soviets take their murdering seriously."

"I hear they have trouble with deserters," Emanuel said, eyeing the shocking numbers. "Millions of them. Perhaps their soldiers are unhappy with their jobs."

"And have you also heard that they are executing those deserters? Tens of thousands of them. Stalin has been quoted as saying, 'In the Soviet army it takes more courage to retreat than advance.' "

The air felt heavy, weighted by the gravity of his words. Emanuel had read of the killings, of course, but the black and white of newspapers seemed somehow less personal. It was more difficult to hear the truth from a British spy.

"Julie and I had an arrangement," Emanuel eventually said. "She shared with me her secrets, I shared mine with her. I will carry that over to you, if you would like."

Ray nodded once in invitation.

"Rothschild will be selling his Baku oil interests to a select group of international buyers. He is done with the great game. I will be sorry to see him leave; he has been both a good adversary and a good partner, but I respect his decision. Now it falls to the new investors to continue driving the wedge between Rockefeller and his bid for the global control of oil. If we do not succeed, the price of energy and oil will skyrocket. The entire world will suffer."

"The 'great game'," Ray mused softly.

The Fabergé clock on the mantle chimed three times then resumed ticking. Both men stared at the drinks in their hands.

After a bit, Ray glanced up. "What will you do, Your Excellency?"

At first he said nothing. What could he possibly say? That he felt the end drawing near, sensed it like a physical being pressing against him? That his whole life was here, and that he could not imagine leaving it? That he loved Baku and everyone in it?

Where is Leyla?

He stood and drained his glass. Ray did the same.

"I do not know, Colonel. I have a lot to think about, and it is clear that my options are becoming more limited by the day." He held out a hand. "I appreciate your coming here today, and I appreciate your honesty. Please take care, sir. Ezhov will not be kind if he catches on to you."

"I am well aware of that," Ray said, shaking his hand. "In fact, I believe my options may be dwindling as well. Thank you for today. If I do not see you again, I wish you all the best."

After he left, Emanuel sank back into his chair, deep in thought. Rothschild was moving on, selling his empire, saving himself. Why could Emanuel not do the same? The violence was escalating, the heat building to an astonishing temperature. Clearly it was not a safe environment for anyone, but especially not for those running successful companies like his. So why was he so set against selling?

He supposed his stubbornness was partially to do with his logical mind, the mindset of his father, which reasoned that the Bolsheviks would not possibly kill the golden goose. BraNobel was efficient and productive and could only help the economy more as time passed. The revolution was based on achieving socialism, and the Nobels themselves had essentially been socialistic all along since over forty percent of their profits had been given to the workers over the years, providing the people of Baku with homes, free healthcare, free education, and so much more. Certainly he was not a pauper by any stretch of the imagination, but could the Bolsheviks really consider him to be an enemy when all he had ever done was give back to the people?

He glanced up, startled, when Elbek appeared once again, his expression tight with concern.

"What is it?"

"The NobMazut office building." He swallowed. "There were two explosions in the last hour. The first destroyed most of the building, I am afraid."

"And the second?"

"It detonated while being carried by one of the office workers."

These were not the last of the explosions. Over the following few weeks, the Azerbaijan Democratic Republic building was bombed, as were oil wells and ships in port. Even Taghiyev's theater erupted in flames. The Russian army marched toward Baku, determined to regain control, but Emanuel was no longer sure which side they were on.

Chapter Thirty

"It seems a very long time since we saw the blue sky," Zeynalabdin Taghiyev said.

The two friends stood on the edge of the hill where they had celebrated the merge with Samuel so long ago. Most of the derricks in view burned out of control.

"Look," Emanuel said, pointing. "It is Musa."

The oil baron stood by his derricks, surrounded by his mercenary guards. While Emanuel watched, a number of thugs approached them, brandishing knives and metal bars.

"He should have paid his workers more," Zeynalabdin said sadly. "His guards will not die for him."

Emanuel fought back rage. "They shouldn't have to die for any of us. None of this should be happening."

"But this is Baku," his friend replied wistfully. "We are forever on fire, never fully burned to dust. Baku always rises like the phoenix."

"Perhaps you should have been a poet," Emanuel suggested. "Like your daughter."

His expression warmed vaguely at the thought. "Yes. Perhaps."

"What plans have you made if you need to escape?"

Taghiyev's gaze was still on the oil fields. He shook his head. "Escape is not an option for me. Like you said so long ago, I believe my people will allow me to run my wells. They have spared them many times already. Even the Soviets must know they need at least some wells flowing with oil."

"The Russian Army demands forty percent of our oil for its war machine," Emanuel said. "It is strangling our growth. Marcus Samuel and Rothschild sold their stakes when the value peaked."

"Are you thinking you should have done the same?"

Emanuel still did not know. "What about your family? Are they safe?"

"Ilyas will be safe at my side. Besides, the workers respect him." The thick white brows drew together. "My wife and children will be sent to our vacation home until it is safer."

"Where is your vacation home? If it is in Russia, it might already be sacked. The Cossacks and Cheka have massacred thousands of people already, and they are especially keen to see the wealthy burn. Send your women west. I have friends in Germany who would take them in."

He felt the tension in the older man, felt the sorrow as well. "Thank you. I may take you up on that offer. My accounts are in Switzerland; I can access them from there." The brown eyes shone. "You know, it is truly an honor to be your friend, Emanuel Nobel."

"The honor has been entirely mine," Emanuel replied, folding his friend into a bear hug. "Promise me," he said as they drew apart, "that you will not wait too long to send your family away."

"I promise."

As his automobile drove back toward home, Emanuel thought about what they had just seen on the oil fields, and about what they had said. He had wanted Taghiyev to make haste with his family, but he still had no idea what he was going to do with himself.

An unexpected vehicle was parked in the driveway of Villa Petrolea, and when Emanuel walked into his house he was surprised to see William Libby there, seated in an armchair and sipping contentedly at a drink as if he were an invited guest. He had never met him before, but he knew who he was. He had seen his photograph in the newspapers often enough.

"He had no appointment," Elbek stated.

"No, he did not," Emanuel replied coolly, staring at Rockefeller's man. He was tall and appeared quite solid, with a well-maintained blond beard.

"Mr Libby. I will admit to being surprised to see you here ... in my home."

Libby got to his feet. "Your Excellency, I was going to try to schedule a meeting at your office; however, when you hear the purpose of my visit, you might understand why I felt you would prefer to meet here."

Not even courtesy could entice a welcoming smile to Emanuel's face. He turned away and strode down the hall.

"Might I suggest," Libby said, following closely, "we sit on the upper balcony, to keep an eye on your holdings?"

Two chairs on the balcony faced the harbor, so Emanuel took one, assuming Libby would do the same. Which he did. Fires burned across the land and water, darkening the sky and Emanuel's heart. He still remembered the sour, fatalistic view he had had of this place so many years ago, sailing through the thick smoke outside Baku's harbor. How he had longed for Stockholm. That had been before he had fallen in love for the first time. Now he could imagine living nowhere but here.

"You can skip the formalities and social chatter," Emanuel informed him, his eyes still on the water. "There is only one reason why you would come here."

"Quite recently, Baku was nearly crushed," Libby started. "The only reason the slaughter was avoided was luck, since the Turks intervened."

Ray had already told Emanuel about the failed attack. He kept his expression level, giving nothing away.

"The Turks probably will not be there next time. Even if they are, Stalin will be ready for them. It may happen this month or it may happen next year, but the revolution will come here. Marxist rhetoric will demand you lose everything without a penny of compensation."

Emanuel slid his gaze toward Libby. He had not needed the reminder. The Soviet regime had already nationalized all private property. Emanuel had received a phone call from his younger half-brother Gosta, saying his wife had been confronted by bandits in their home. She had fled upstairs and hidden the children on the balcony, having no idea what the men could want. When she came back downstairs, they had taken everything they could lay their hands on and were on their way to the bedrooms for more. She grabbed a pearl necklace before they saw it and managed to slide it into her corset. That was all they had left.

"You led a valiant charge, Your Excellency. Your name rose to nearly mythical levels among the citizens of Baku." He smiled with closed lips, but the scheming blue eyes were far from friendly. "Unfortunately for you, it is this very fact that will put your head on the chopping block. Especially considering Stalin's hatred for Baku and anyone ruling within it."

Did he think this was news? When would these people stop treating him as if he had no idea what he was doing? First Aron, now Libby ...

"What is the number?" he asked flatly. A gust of wind pushed past, bringing a fresh burn to his eyes.

"Standard Oil makes a one-time offer to buy your majority interest in BraNobel Oil with current production of fifteen million tonnes per year, and most of its assets for $11.5 billion. Generous royalties will be paid out to you and your partners for your shares for ten years. Patent royalties are not included in this offer."

"It could be sold for 40 billion."

"Your production has peaked," Libby informed him. "The groundbreaking inventions that put you ahead of the competition ended with petroleum jelly. If the state government nationalizes your oil, you will lose forty percent of your entire production, if my information is correct."

The Bolshevik takeover was inevitable, and Emanuel now knew with certainty that BraNobel would not survive it. He would end up losing everything. But he still could not bear the thought of giving up, of giving it all to Rockefeller.

"This is far too complex to rush," he said.

Libby appeared unimpressed. "Agreed." He pointed toward a rioting mob in the distance, shattering windows and lighting more buildings on fire. "Explain it to them."

They were like a wave of lava, destroying everything in its path. They would roll over the oil fields, and they would roll over the mansions of the oil barons. They would take what was left and slaughter anyone they found. When it was all over, the Bolshevik would own Baku, the grand prize. They would nationalize all the assets and Sovietize Baku. The oil would be theirs.

The oil would be theirs.

He paused, stunned by a thought. If that happened—and it certainly would—then Rockefeller could never have what he wanted. J.D. had always seen himself as being in charge, calling all the shots, and he had played hard, believing in his ability to achieve the ultimate goal in the Great Game: to win Baku. Certainly he had helped to finance and encourage the revolution in order to clear the land of its oil barons, and Emanuel could only guess at what else had gone on behind the scenes.

But neither Stalin nor Lenin were ignorant men. They would have welcomed the American's contributions to their cause and let Rockefeller believe he held all the cards. Why not? Except the revolution had swept out of J.D.'s control. The Bolsheviks were running amok, fighting amongst themselves and killing anyone who spoke out of turn. They had tortured and raped and pillaged and murdered with no regard to anyone but themselves, and the horror had not slowed with their progress.

The Bolsheviks were now fully in charge. They no longer needed Rockefeller's millions.

Now Emanuel was being asked to sell 100% of BraNobel to him for $11.5 billion. Except all the oil fields would soon fall to the Bolsheviks. That meant any shares J.D. bought from Emanuel would soon be useless. Had Rockefeller's greed deprived him of forward thought? It seemed out of character for such a scheming man to miss this important fact, and yet that was exactly what was being offered.

For months, Emanuel had been hoping for a sign of some kind, and here it sat.

Libby was staring at him, trying not to appear either impatient or concerned. *Your master has made a vital error,* Emanuel wanted to say, but he did not. Mirth bubbled up his throat.

"You may tell Mr Rockefeller that the terms are favorable. The numbers are not what they should be, but with negotiations we could accept his acquisition. In the meantime I will need the offer in writing from Mr. Rockefeller himself."

Libby tilted his head and sucked in his cheeks, barely able to hide his glee. "A telephone call would speed up the process."

He would be damned if he made any of this any easier for the man. He gave Libby a hard stare. "I will send my brother, Gosta, to New York. He will represent my objectives and the company."

*

As Elbek accompanied Libby to the door, Emanuel remained on the balcony, trying to ignore the sinking feeling in his gut. Had he made the right choice? Had he done the right thing? Had there been any other option?

Ramiz, his loyal servant, appeared at his side, providing welcome companionship. They both stared straight ahead, watching the city burn. How long would it be before the criminals torched his gardens?

"They will not touch the trees," Ramiz murmured, reading his mind.

"No? What makes you so sure?"

"They will keep this masterpiece for themselves."

He hoped so, and yet he hated the idea of these bloodthirsty hoodlums enjoying such splendor. It was not for them.

"I feel as if I am closing a book," Emanuel said. "And it has been such a wonderful story I cannot bear to see it end."

It was April, and Villa Petrolea was alive with spring color. Across the way, the trees and flowers of Boulevard Park rioted in rich greens, rivaling anything in Paris. He could see the ships in harbor, many of them still smoldering, and he remembered the day when the *Zoroaster* had first coasted into its bay, how the other oil barons had stared at the huge ship in disbelief. Soon after that they had filled her hold with oil for the first time, and the people had cheered.

So much had happened both before and after that moment. So many amazing things. The story had been a bold adventure indeed.

"I spoke with my father," Emanuel said quietly, "as he faded into the sunset of his life. He was unafraid, at peace." The memory swelled, blocking his words. He took a deep breath then let it out slowly. "I asked, 'Father, did I please you?'"

The simple question had been so difficult to ask, and the genuine pride in Ludvig's eyes had been answer enough.

The warm wind of Baku touched Emanuel's cheek like a kiss, and he swallowed back emotion. Through blurred vision he scanned the land, the home he had come to love with all his heart, and he held out his hands.

"Did I please *you*?" he asked her.

The burning city said nothing in response, and he could not seek reassurance in the eyes of its people.

"Tell me, Mr Nobel," Ramiz said softly, "who have you *not* pleased? You have lived here almost fifty years, making our city into one of the wealthiest in all the world, feeding and educating our people while giving us both the respect and the self-respect we had never known before. You gave us hope." His expression was thoughtful. "Yes, Mr Nobel. You pleased them all."

PART FOUR

Chapter Thirty-One

Mikhail Vavilov
Russia, 1920

Once upon a time, Mikhail had been strong. He had flexed his muscles and roared Russian slogans along with the others. He was young, he was courageous, he was Russian!

Now he was old and beaten and whimpering with fear. With his arms bound so tightly over his head, he could not see the blood, but he felt it dripping down the pale white skin of his chest, winding around the springy white hairs. From far away he heard his own pitiful voice making sniveling, pleading, sobbing noises that could not save him. He was not proud of the wet patch of heat running down the front of his pants, but he was not overly aware of it either. Fear of what might come next far overwhelmed the ache of humiliation.

One of the soldiers squatted by the small fire, speaking with another one and laughing. A third barked an order and the laughter stopped immediately. Mikhail whimpered again, weak with terror. With the end of laughter, he knew from experience, came more serious business, though he did not understand what it was or why.

His eyes slid sideways through their swollen lids, toward the Cheka Guard now clutching a metal poker he had pulled from the fire. Six solid inches of scorching metal glowed in the dark room. Mikhail shook so hard the beam to which he was attached creaked overhead.

"We asked you a question, old man," the soldier reminded him, walking over. "You should have answered."

Before Mikhail could brace himself, the poker was shoved against his chest. White hot pain flashed through his head, and his agonized shrieks echoed off the walls so that he heard them again and again.

"Enough," barked someone.

The pressure eased but the skin continued to burn after the metal was gone. Tears streamed down his face, and the stench of burning hair and flesh filled his swollen nostrils. Every muscle in Mikhail's body shook, yanking on the rough rope, and his chest bumped with sobs.

The officer in command rose and walked slowly toward him, looking thoughtful. Mikhail stared through the slits of his eyes, wondering vaguely how he recognized him. He was short but stocky, his short black hair swept back in a wave above his brow. A thick mustache dominated his features, and his cheeks and forehead were dotted with pockmarks—though they were partially camouflaged by spatterings of Mikhail's blood.

Mikhail's mind clicked, finally remembering where he had seen this man before. It was the posters. They were everywhere.

Josef Stalin bent down to pick up a handful of gravel.

Mikhail had thought the branding was the worst pain he would ever experience, but he was wrong. When Stalin ground the sand and rocks into the freshly burnt flesh, every muscle quit fighting. His cries turned to howls of anguish, and his legs gave in, forcing his arms to take his full weight. Death would be a mercy; these men were not merciful.

Stalin ignored the sobs. His sunken eyes showed no appreciation for Mikhail's agony. "Where are your leaders?" he bellowed.

Mikhail desperately sought some kind of answer, but his mind was blank. He tried to form his lips around words, but his face felt numb.

Looking slightly intrigued, Stalin twisted more sand into the mess of Mikhail's chest, shooting stars into the old man's fading vision. "The ones telling your guards to fight us. Where are they?" he demanded. He drew closer, and Mikhail saw the light of madness dancing in the man's eyes. "You do not have to die today, old man. It is not too late to join the revolution and save your own life, you know." A quick, feral smile flashed under the mustache, but it never reached Stalin's eyes. "All you have to tell me is where they are. Where are the criminals who are holding out on us?"

"Please!" he sobbed, tasting iron. "I am just an old man."

"You are not. You are more than that," Stalin insisted, lifting his hand again.

"Wait! Wait!" Mikhail screamed. "Yes!" he managed, trying to catch his breath long enough to speak. He would tell whatever truth they wanted if only they would stop, and he grasped the only thing that came to mind. "It is true! I was a counselor to the Russian courts long ago, but they do not trust me anymore. I do not know where they hide, and I am too old to fight. I know nothing. Please! Please believe me. I—"

Another soldier barged into the room. "Koba!" he yelled, his fist pumping with victory.

Stalin spun toward him. "What is it?" he growled.

"We did it! We invaded Azerbaijan!"

"Ha!" Stalin bared his teeth then rubbed his hands together with anticipation. "Yes. Prepare my convoy. We leave in an hour. Oh, and send a message to Lenin. Tell him I spoke with Ezhov. He will prepare everything for the complete burning of Baku in case of intervention, and he will ensure that is declared in print in Baku for all to see. I will personally lead the Creative Destruction against the oil dynasties."

"Yes, Comrade. Right away." He glanced at Mikhail. "And him?"

Stalin's hard hazel eyes slid from the soldier to Mikhail. He hesitated only long enough for Mikhail to realize his life was about to end.

"Death solves all problems: no man, no problem. Torture him to death, then hang him naked in the Square." The leader's genial gaze went back to the soldier. "Then shoot everyone in the family until somebody tells us the truth."

Chapter Thirty-Two

Julie Gold
Baku, 1920

Panic was everywhere, and right now it snapped at Julie's heels like a rabid wolf. All she could hope was that the worst of it had stayed behind, too busy swallowing up the helpless people of Baku to chase her. Behind the desperate screams roared the constant crescendo of the burning derricks, and gunfire grew increasingly close.

She hit the docks at a run and raced past a number of port guards sheltered behind crates, appearing well armed and prepared to defend the dock and its ships. She kept running, trying not to think of the fire in her lungs or the stars flying in her head, trying not to shrink away from the occasional bullet whizzing past. There was no time to be afraid, no time to stop for breath. Julie's goal was to keep up with James, who moved with the ease of a man much younger than his fifty-plus years, despite the heavy suitcase he carried. He sprinted ahead of her as if he were being chased by the devil—which, she supposed, was exactly right. The Bolsheviks would not be stopped; the only option was to outrun them.

The *Princess Fidan* rocked quietly ahead of them, looking as old as the docks to which the passenger ship was tethered. Small black puffs of smoke rose from her engine, suggesting Julie's estimate was not far off. She could see the huddled shapes of families cowering within the old boat, praying for survival.

The captain was at the helm, staring at the dock. "Cast off!" he yelled. "Now! Do it!"

James reached the boat and raced up the gangplank, then he reached back to yank Julie on board behind him. She could not thank him over her labored breathing, but that did not matter. He was already on his way toward the captain, cash in hand.

"Go! Go!" he yelled. "No time to wait for the others! Go now!"

Julie put a hand on the side of the boat and hunched over, wheezing. Then James was at her side, urging her behind him as he shot at anyone breaking past the wall of port guards. She pulled out her own gun, squinting through the stars in her sight, and aimed at one thug swinging a sword at a cornered guard. Her first shot went wild, but the second knocked him to the ground.

"Excellent shot, Miss Gold," James muttered calmly. She glanced at him, admiring the profile of his sweat- and oil-slicked face. Even in the most dire of situations, he was always a perfect gentleman.

"James!" she shrieked, spotting an attacker nearing the gangplank, at the wrong angle for her.

He fired off two quick rounds, and the man wheeled backward, splashing like a boulder into the water.

"Go!" James roared at the captain.

The noise was worsening. Soldiers had been alerted by the gunfire, and now they ran toward the noise, shooting as they came. Bullets ripped up the deck, and the passengers screamed and dropped to the floor, ducking behind whatever cover they could find. The captain had been paying attention; the ship was already chugging into the bay, putting them just out of reach, then well out of range. Though many of the passengers still wept, either with relief or shock, the realization that the soldiers could no longer reach them prompted tentative conversations, even the occasional attempt at a nervous laugh.

Julie found her voice. "That was close."

"It is not over," James said. "Look."

She followed his gaze and spotted the problem just as the captain pointed at the open water and bellowed, "Blockade!"

The hulking profiles of at least twenty large military ships gradually appeared from behind the wall of smoke. The passengers of the *Princess Fidan* watched, beginning to weep again until it became obvious that the blockade was closing in on a different ship—one with clean lines and a freshly painted deck. Even from this distance, they could tell she was loaded with a particular, aristocratic passenger list. She was doing what she could to outrun the force, her engine racing.

"They're going to shoot!"

A number of cannons blasted from the blockade, and water shot from the depths like geysers. The ship's stern was hit, and it began to sink, dragging the screaming passengers toward the water. Those who could clung to posts and ropes, desperate to hold on, but nothing could stop the inevitable. Their pathetic cries for help echoed across the water, and the *Princess Fidan*'s sympathetic passengers wept for them. The last thing they saw was the ship's bow, and on it her name: *Azadlyg*, Julie read. *Freedom*.

She clenched her jaw, biting back grief and focusing on the water around them. She knew the kind of people who had just disappeared beneath the surface. She might have even known some of them. *Emanuel* ...

She hadn't been able to resist one last visit. She had not told Ray; he would have forbidden it. All she had said was that she would be back in an hour, that he should be patient.

It was dusk when she arrived at the front door to Villa Petrolea. Elbek had bowed slightly, startled by her appearance, then stepped back without a word. Emanuel happened to be in the front room as well, standing just behind. He was dressed casually, breaking her heart. In another time, another place, the warm, genuine welcome in his eyes could have felt like home, she thought. Ironic that she saw safety in his expression, when she knew he was the most in danger.

"Miss Gold. An unexpected pleasure."

She walked directly to him, unaffected by propriety for once. "Emanuel. I had to see you one more time."

His face fell, twisting the pain in her heart a little more. He cared. He truly did. She could not say that about many others in her past, or even in her present. Did she feel for any of them what she felt for Emanuel? No.

As Elbek removed himself from the room, Emanuel closed the gap between himself and her. Then she was in his arms, wishing desperately that she could stay there. She did not speak, and he seemed to sense that she needed that quiet moment, for he did not question her until she had drawn away. When that happened, the tears on her cheeks were a surprise to them both. She dabbed them away before he could do it for her.

"I do not like the finality of this," he said. "What is prompting your sudden visit?"

She sniffed. "Ezhov is resolved that both James and I must die, and he and I are just as resolved that we will not be here when that happens. He and his lackeys have come too close already. We are leaving tomorrow."

"How?"

"A ship will be waiting for us. James has already arranged it."

He shook his head. "You should not be here, Julie. You have already reminded me several times about the target on my back, and that makes me a poor hiding place for you."

"I ... I know." Heat rose into her cheeks, and she looked away. "I do not know why I came, to be honest, but I had to."

"Can you stay?"

The question was gently asked, but she shook her head. Instead, her hand went to his cheek, to the smooth, black beard which contrasted so beautifully with his eyes. He had commented on her eyes in the past, on their color, but she had not told him how she loved his. So intelligent, so bold, warmed by a generous heart.

"I want you to be safe, Emanuel. I want you to leave here before they come for you. You are too good a man to be murdered by these creatures."

His kiss lingered on her lips, and she clung to the feel of him for as long as she could.

"I will look for you," he said. "When all this is done, I will find you."

She placed her finger on his lips. "No. I do not want you to find me."

"But—"

"Do not come after me, Emanuel. I do not think clearly when I am with you, and that is not a good thing when you do what I do. It is time to move on. If you love me at all, you will leave here, live a wonderful life somewhere far from this place."

He kissed her again, bringing more tears to her eyes. They clung to his lashes as well. But he did not say he loved her.

"You will not have me seek you out, but you cannot stop me from thinking of you and being concerned for your welfare. I wish I could ask you to live a safe, comfortable life away from all this violence, but I know you are set on doing the opposite, my little spy. At least I can ask you to *try* to be safe. To remember you are fragile, no matter how tough you portray yourself."

For an instant she dreamed again of giving it all up, of staying with him if he would have her. *Safe*, she thought. But no. Even here in the circle of his arms she was not safe. Besides, she was not even sure that being safe was what she wanted.

"I will miss you, Emanuel," she whispered against his lips, biting back the urge to tell him how much she truly loved him.

She had run from the house, holding in the tears until she was far enough that he could not see her weakness. Then she tucked herself into a hidden alley and sobbed until the wave of emotion had passed. This was no time for self-indulgence. She was being hunted, and the night was full of menacing shadows. Moving like one of them, she slipped into the darkness, heading toward her meeting place with Ray. By the time she arrived, the swelling and redness had gone from her eyes. Any evidence of her broken heart was gone.

It seemed like another lifetime, that brief oasis with Emanuel. Now she leaned against James, grieving the drowning passengers of the *Azadlyg*, wondering if she would survive this night.

He had no time for introspection. James was always thinking, always planning—which was what she should have been doing, she knew. He jerked his chin toward a small fishing boat bobbing on the waves, bringing her out of her daze.

"That is what we need," he muttered.

While she waited, he sidled past a small family, making his way back toward the captain, who was engaged in a heated discussion with his crew. The money pushed into his hand got his attention, though he argued at first that the request was simply too dangerous to consider.

"Look at me," James demanded, standing tall and projecting as much sophistication as he could. "Do you really want someone like me on this boat?"

Seeing it in that light, the captain made up his mind. They pulled up beside the little fishing boat, and a man peered up at them from its deck with wide, frightened eyes. It seemed to Julie that everyone wore that expression these days. The craft was small and badly in need of care, with splintered boards and an ancient, greasy engine. Every square inch reeked of fish. A perfect, unassuming getaway vehicle.

James held out a handful of British pounds. "We need a ride."

The fisherman stared longingly at the money then back at him. From his strained expression, he was torn, and she knew exactly why. With this much money to offer, they posed an obvious threat. But bribery was all they had. If it did not work, she and James would die very soon. When he pulled out another couple of bills and waved them at the little man, it put an end to the fisherman's hesitation.

The *Princess Fidan* was already pulling away as Ray dropped into the little boat. He turned back to her, arms out, but the chasm between boats was rapidly growing. She took a deep breath for courage and prepared to jump.

Fire exploded in her chest, searing through her, and the shock of the impact temporarily blinded her. She knew in that instant exactly what it was—she had been shot before, though that bullet had only hit her leg. This one spun her around and drove her backward, extending the moment so that it seemed to stretch for hours, then the agony filled her head with stars. Wheeling her arms in a useless attempt to slow her fall, she tumbled over the edge of the boat and plunged headfirst into the Caspian, vaguely aware of the shower of bullets pelting the surface around her. She could not feel her limbs over the burning pain in her chest, and she no longer had any control. The water opened beneath her, cold and hungry, black and unforgiving. In its rush to swallow her up, it gave her no time at all to say goodbye.

Chapter Thirty-Three

Ramiz Veliyev
Villa Petrolea, 1920

Emanuel Nobel paused at the top of the stairs, gazing across the grounds of his home. Concern had etched deep lines across his brow, but his true feelings went much deeper.

Ramiz was only a house servant. He had no concept of either business or commerce, but he understood the misery in Mr Nobel's eyes. His master was the best of men, and right now he bore the impossible weight of the world on his shoulders—or at least the world of Baku.

The concern stretched across his master's brow was for the people he was leaving behind, as well as for the oil fields he had so reluctantly sold to Standard Oil.

The sadness in his master's eyes was for the waste of it all, for the unthinkable violence and damage the Soviets had wreaked on this land.

The regret which weighted his master's shoulders was like an anchor, and yet he could not stay and fix it all, as he had done in the past.

But he had done all he could.

The XI Red Army was hours away. It would be on the doorstep soon enough. Soviet Russia would not bow to the ultimatum they had been given by the Azerbaijan Democratic Republic. The Bolsheviks would never surrender, and it was folly to even hope for that. Emanuel Nobel had waited until the last possible moment, not wanting to abandon his home or servants, but they had convinced him he could not stay any longer. Of all the capitalists in Baku, Nobel would become the largest jewel in the Soviets' crown if they caught him.

Ramiz would drive them to the train station, then he would travel with his master to Gobustan. He would make sure everything was done safely and efficiently, as he always had. The others would remain here, doing what they could to defend Villa Petrolea and its treasures. Emanuel Nobel had packed as quickly as possible, but because of the rush he could not bring everything. Ramiz had spoken with Elbek of this, and the butler had agreed it was a tragedy for the master not to have those things he loved around him, wherever he ended up. Elbek would do what he could, he promised, after Ramiz and their master were gone.

It was noon already. Ramiz was restless but could not hurry this moment. It was not his place to do so. A house servant bustled by, carrying two of his master's three travel trunks, and the sight of him seemed to remind Emanuel Nobel that he could spare no more time on daydreaming or worrying about something over which he had no control. Looking away from the view of the estate he followed Ramiz toward the delivery truck parked at the base of the stairs, alongside his own shining Mercedes.

When he reached the vehicle, Nobel turned back and looked at his staff. "I apologize to you from the bottom of my heart. I have put you in a terrible situation." He frowned. "I need to hear from each of you that you prefer to stay here in Villa Petrolea."

Arthur Lesner, one of BraNobel's powerful executives, stood by the truck. "Sir, we understand the dangers."

"We are safer without you, Mr Nobel," said another. "We can argue that we are only workers, tell them we want what they want."

Arthur Lesner attempted to appear confident. "You need concern yourself over nothing, sir," he assured him. "You have left the operation in our hands many times. We might lose a few derricks, but that should be the worst of it. And it doesn't even matter anymore, in fact, since they are Standard Oil's derricks now. All we do is manage the oil flow and registers for him. There is nothing we cannot leave behind when necessary."

Nobel's dark look returned to the smudged horizon, judging for himself. "The derricks will either stand or they will burn. No one knows what will happen. What matters is that you are all safe."

"We will be safe, sir," said Lesner. "It is a brief interruption, nothing more, then we will return to normal."

The guard stepped toward the gate, wary of an approaching noise. Time was running out.

"Go. Join the guard," Elbek urged the gardeners. "Keep the grounds safe."

A half dozen men rushed down the drive, keen to be of service. Ramiz watched them go. Emanuel Nobel was staring anxiously at them as well. The gnawing sense of impending trouble built.

"If it gets too dangerous," Emanuel Nobel told Arthur, "you and the rest of the production executives must ride out on the oil tankers with your families. Go west in Azerbaijan, through the Karabakh and Naxcivan regions to Turkey. When you can, get on the Orient Express to Europe."

Lesner was a smart, dependable man, as were most of the men in BraNobel. None of them were as intelligent as Nobel, but Ramiz knew that would have been too much to ask for. Emanuel Nobel was a truly unique man. A truly good man.

"I just spoke with the station master, sir," Ramiz reported as Fuad, the chauffeur, opened the door to the Mercedes. "The route is clear to Gobustan."

"Good. Time to go." Emanuel Nobel bowed his head so he could climb inside then hesitated, startled by the sound of gunfire in the distance.

"Please be careful, sir."

"You are the head of this house now, Elbek," Emanuel told him, leaning closer, "which is why I trusted you with its greatest secret. Spread the word with the others that they should act wisely in the face of danger. Honor the house, but protect yourselves above all else."

He swallowed, and Ramiz saw the earnestness in their master's eyes. Holding Elbek's stare, he nodded slowly, his words thick with meaning.

"I have shown you what to do, and I expect you to do it before it is too late."

A soft light filled Elbek's eyes as he pulled away, and Ramiz felt the butler's pain in his own chest. Nobel had changed both their lives. He had given them everything, including dignity. Though they had never spoken of it, both men would willingly give their lives for Emanuel Nobel.

"Yes, sir, I—"

Angry voices rose in the far end of the park, grabbing everyone's attention. A boisterous mob of laborers had entered the grounds and were now barging through it, their bloated sense of entitlement sucking the warmth from the day. They carried sticks bearing banners, and they used those same sticks to prod at anyone they came across. The alarmed citizens scattered, clearing out of the park and making room for the hoodlums.

Disappointment was clear on Nobel's face. *Too soon,* he was plainly thinking.

"Now, Elbek," Nobel said urgently. "Do it now."

Fear, regret, acceptance ... all of it filled Elbek's expression in that moment. "Thank you, Mr Nobel," he said hoarsely, then he turned swiftly and went inside.

The rioters drew ever closer. One of the men marched toward a statue, which he quickly scaled. "We own nothing while they take everything!" he shouted to the rioters. The declaration was greeted by roars of approval, and the crowd's general volume increased as more voices took up the chant.

"They chose the wrong estate to protest," Lesner noted wryly, shaking his head at the noisy crowd. "Our workers are the envy of laborers from here to St. Petersburg."

Ramiz saw it differently. Yes, what Lesner said was true— their laborers were treated better than any others—but he did not think that fact mattered even a little bit right now.

"Envy masks betrayals," Nobel said quietly, echoing Ramiz' thoughts. "And it justifies the worst in men."

The chauffeur, Fuad, stood by the door, patient and silent as always. The banners in the park bumped up and down with the mob's earnest gestures, and even from this distance Ramiz could see the eagerness on their grimy faces. Sunshine reflected off the Mercedes' roof, and Nobel breathed slowly out through his nose. He did not look afraid; Ramiz had never seen his master appear apprehensive about anything. The expression he saw now retained the disappointment he had seen before. As much as Nobel wished it would, this nightmare was not going to go away.

Just before lowering himself into the seat, Nobel cast one more sober glance at Arthur Lesner. "Be prepared, my friend," he said, then he disappeared inside.

Ramiz climbed into the truck's driver side and led the Mercedes down the lane. Traffic was light, and the station was not far. As they passed the familiar landmarks—the closed stores, the broken windows which once featured shiny displays—the images settled into his brain. He had no idea if he would ever see this place again. He had accompanied the master on various journeys, but he had a discouraging sense this one might not include a return trip.

The stately Baku Railway Station appeared in the distance, its chalky marble spire like the engine of its own stationary train, tugging the smaller domes and cathedral windows behind it. The truck pulled into the station, closely followed by the Mercedes, and both vehicles continued along until they reached the luxury boxcars at the tail of the train. Nobel and Fuad stayed in the vehicle while Ramiz hopped out of the truck and approached the captain, tickets in hand. The train's whistle cut through the chatter on the platform, urging everyone to prepare for departure. Other passengers hustled to board, pushing past slower individuals and bidding hasty farewells. Ramiz glanced back at Nobel's Mercedes, but he was not concerned. The train would wait for important travelers like him. The captain paid the familiar whistle no heed, only read the tickets.

Ramiz was turning back toward Emanuel Nobel when a familiar black Rolls Royce—the first of its kind in the Russian Empire—squealed up alongside the train. Nobel climbed out of his Mercedes, curious.

Taghiyev leaped from the back of his Rolls before it had fully stopped. "They're storming the derricks!" he cried, anguish tearing at his breath. "Can I speak for both of us if I can get the Bolsheviks to agree to spare our wells?"

Zeynalabdin Taghiyev was a rare man, and one Ramiz respected with his whole heart. He had come from nothing, had dared to put everything he had into uncertain oil wells, and when he had finally struck it rich, he had—like Nobel—used it to better all of Baku, not just fill his overflowing bank account. He was, as the Europeans would say, a Cinderella story, and he deserved a happy ending. Seeing such a great man in this position was difficult for Ramiz.

"You would be the only one I would trust in this," Emanuel told his friend.

The two great men stood facing each other, and Ramiz was struck by the poignancy of the scene. It was more than a farewell between the two friends, he thought. It was a goodbye.

"Excellent," Taghiyev replied, his voice hoarse with emotion. "I will send word ahead."

An explosion from the dock area rocked the station, and black smoke billowed into the blue sky. When the echo of the blast had died away, screams filled the void.

Taghiyev's eyes were wide with alarm. "That's close to my field!"

Without another word, the large man threw himself into the back seat of his vehicle, his brightly checked red and white headscarf flying like a banner behind him.

"Is your family safe?" Emanuel shouted after him, but the Rolls Royce had already sped away.

Nobel stared at the receding automobile, paralyzed with helplessness. When he reached for his own vehicle's door as if to get back inside, Ramiz pulled on his master's arm.

"No, sir," he said. "We cannot help him now. We must go."

Chapter Thirty-Four

The train rocked gently as it chugged through the desolate region outside Gobustan. The motion had lulled a few of the passengers into dozing, as had the tedious landscape. Beside the occasional sparse offering of green, the only variety beyond the window was presented by the intermittent appearances of huge broken rocks and caves. Among those bubbled the mud volcanoes and the ancient carvings of long-ago people.

Ramiz was wide awake, watching everything.

The train shuddered against its tracks, slowing as it pulled into the station. Ramiz spread his legs for balance against the moving car and folded Nobel's long black coat over one arm. In his hand he held his master's hat. The train jerked as the conductor applied the brakes, and both men stared though the window at smears of dark shades, the outlines of coats and hats of people on the platform. Their faces became clearer as the train slowed, and Nobel frowned at the crowd. Neither of them had expected there to be so many people here. When they had come to a complete stop, Nobel rose and turned so Ramiz could help him into his coat.

"Emanuel!" they heard as they stepped onto the platform. "Emanuel!"

Ramiz tensed, on guard as he always was around his master. The voice sounded friendly, but he did not want to be careless. At first he could not make out the speaker, then a dark brown, long coat wriggled through the crowd toward them. He relaxed, recognizing Nobel's old friend, Heinz Schumann. A golden-haired young man followed, helping a porter with some bags.

"Heinz. How are you, my friend?"

Nobel's friend was a jolly sort, always welcoming, always charming. Today, however, his features were creased with worry. It was to be expected, considering the danger which closed in around them, but the sight was still unnerving.

Heinz shook his head violently as he approached, then he patted Nobel's arm while they waited for the other man to join them. "Good to see you looking so well, my friend. Especially in such a difficult time."

"And you, Heinz." Nobel smiled at the young man beside him. "And you have brought my handsome young godson, I see. Hello, Johann. You are all grown up. I am very glad to see you."

"As am I, sir. This is a good surprise. Are you stopping here?"

"No. I—"

Heinz gripped his forearm. "Oh, but you must. Emanuel, tell me you are not going on to Germany."

"Well, yes. I—"

Johann frowned, holding his ground when someone bumped into him, obviously in a hurry. The two older men glared at the perpetrator as he disappeared into the crowd, but Johann seemed unconcerned with the encounter.

"You cannot!" he exclaimed. "Blockades are going up all around us. They were setting one up as we were coming here."

Heinz appeared to be near panic. "Everyone riding in private vehicles bound for Baku is being arrested and held on charges of crimes against the workers."

Ramiz glanced around, noting the mounting tension in the air. Violence and rioting had been expected, but everything seemed to be accelerating far more rapidly than Ramiz had imagined it might. If they were arresting people in vehicles, the train would not be safe, either.

"You cannot get back on the train," Heinz repeated. "Pull your bags off before it is too late."

In the next instant, gunfire crackled through the air, and the crowd ducked as one, screaming with panic.

"Get your bags!" Heinz yelled. "Go!"

The train was not far, but the platform was so congested it was difficult to weave through all the people. Rapid gunfire started up again, this time from more than one weapon, but Johann pushed them on. Just as Ramiz touched the side of the train, an explosion rocked the platform, spewing flames, smoke, and victims into the air.

The train captain had tucked himself between the cars. He looked shocked when the men appeared and demanded Emanuel's luggage.

"But I cannot!" he cried. "Come, hide here and stay safe. This is insane! We are all going to die!"

"My bags!" Nobel roared, pushing his face into the other man's. "Now!"

*

Gobustan

"Yes, yes. We are fine."

Ramiz gripped the handset tightly, pressing it against his ear to make sure Elbek could hear him over the apprehensive crowd of neighbors gathered in Heinz's mansion. Most of them were strangers to him, though a few seemed to know Nobel. All were obviously concerned. The atmosphere in the room was tense and unpredictable.

A diminutive woman in a green headscarf peered up at Heinz, concern set in the deep lines between her brows. "The Azerbaijan Democratic Republic will return if we make a deal with the revolutionaries, will not they?"

Before Heinz could respond, another woman stepped in, shaking her head with disapproval. "Bah!" she said, flapping a hand. "You worry too much. These mobs have never overthrown the Russian Imperial Army. They never will."

"There *is* no Imperial Army!" a man retorted. "They all joined the revolution, remember? That's why everything is different this time. No one will be able to stop them."

Ramiz turned his back to them, needing to concentrate on Elbek's information. "What of the other news?" he asked. "Mr Nobel needs to know what is happening."

"It is not good," the butler informed him. "The mobs control the entire city. Anyone who is not part of one is being beaten, and they have cut the phone lines to the port and the docks. Half the large homes have already been ransacked and are on fire." He hesitated. "The good news is that the wells still stand—for now, anyway." He hesitated. "Ramiz, do you recall Murtuza Mukhtarov's pledge?"

Ramiz grunted assent. The madman had raved to them all that if any of the Red Army dared enter his home, he would kill them, then kill himself. Mukhtarov had always been theatrical.

"He did it."

"No."

"Yes. They say two soldiers broke in—on horseback," Elbek said, his voice cracking. "He shot them both then put the gun to his own head."

Ramiz's eyes went to the tall windows, but there were no stars tonight. In contrast, the night sky above Villa Petrolea would be a rich gold, lit by the flickering wall of derrick fires. The roar would be a constant rumble in the thick, smoky air.

"Is Mr Taghiyev safe? Have you seen him?"

"He cannot be far," Elbek replied. "It is impossible for anyone to leave. They've barricaded the driveway. I do not know how he is or if his telephone still works."

Dread coiled in Ramiz's stomach, cold and hard and spreading fast.

"Thank you. I will make sure our master knows all this. Remember what he told you, my friend."

"It is already done," Elbek assured him.

The scene filled Ramiz's head, stealing his words. He shook it loose and said words they both knew were impossible. "Be safe."

He stared at the telephone as he hung up. He and Elbek were not close, but they knew each other well. Ramiz was

249

filled with the terrible suspicion that he would never speak to him again.

A woman appeared holding a cup of tea. The china rattled in her hands. She handed it to Nobel, and he accepted automatically, barely registering the scalding liquid as he sipped. His attention was on Ramiz, who relayed everything Elbek had said. When she disappeared back into the kitchen he set down the tea, reaching for the telephone instead.

"Elbek said he did not know if Mr Taghiyev's telephone was still working, sir."

"We will find out soon enough."

"Good news," Heinz said quietly beside them. "Your brother and his family made it out."

Nobel agreed, waiting for the operator to connect. "When will they arrive?"

"Near dawn. They have a nurse with them as well, and an army captain." He dragged his fingers through his golden hair. "We will go a different route. Your brother Gosta is waiting with our friend, and he'll have passports ready for us in a few hours."

The operator finally connected him to Taghiyev's estate, and Ramiz leaned in, trying to hear.

"Ilyas. Tell me what I need to know. Is it out of control?"

He stared straight ahead, listening, and Ramiz saw the pain in his eyes.

"What can I do?" A very short pause this time. "And Leyla?"

He wished Ilyas well and placed the receiver carefully in its cradle. His eyes went to his servant, and in them Ramiz saw a much older man. Nobel bit his lower lip, holding in emotion, then he told him what Ilyas had said.

"They were at the derricks all day, negotiating, giving away boxes of gold, doing whatever they could to buy peace. Taghiyev has not yet returned home, but Ilyas thought he would be there very soon. So far he says most of our wells still stand, and his as well, but the rest are burning. All of them. His father tried to call the leaders, to talk with him, but no one seems responsible for making decisions." He swallowed. "He said they fear the worst is yet to come. The Red Army is riding down from the north." His hand went to his brow, his eyes closed. "He told us to stay away. He said it is not safe there. Not even for a Nobel."

Ramiz was almost afraid to ask. "And Miss Leyla?"

Nobel's chest rose and fell, looking temporarily relieved. "He said she is fine. Safer than any of us."

Chapter Thirty-Five

Leyla Taghiyev
Azerbaijan/Iran Border area

The vultures knew where to circle. They might have disguised their feathers within the rough woolen uniforms of the revolutionary guard, but the hungry, intrusive stares could not be mistaken. Over a hundred had gathered here, using the remote housing area as a base while they awaited and trapped unwary travelers Now that the revolution was truly underway, the line of wagons, trucks, and automobiles stretched back to the horizon, barely moving. There was no escape.

Dinner was served.

Before the sun had risen that morning, Leyla Taghiyev had plaited her long black hair, pinning it by her ears and tucking it inside her *orpak,* then she had donned eight layers of colorful skirts under her tunic and overshirt, just like all the peasant women. Carrying nothing beyond the old bag slung over her shoulder, she had ridden in the ancient wagon, side by side with the others.

They had seen the trap as they rolled into the valley, but there had been no way to avoid it.

Now Leyla shook so hard she could barely stand. She kept her eyes to the ground, fearful one of her captors would see through her disguise, know her for who and what she really was. For though she dressed like one, even smelled like one now, Leyla was no peasant. Her father was Zeynalabdin Taghiyev, oil tycoon of Baku and a much desired mark for the soldiers. These men were here for the sole purpose of robbing, imprisoning, and murdering aristocrats who dared attempt escape from Baku. She was exactly what they were looking for.

Her wagon train included twenty other people from Baku, all similarly dressed, as well as their drivers. Their wagons were being torn apart, and huddled travelers lined both sides of the road, awaiting the same fate. She knew what these men would do. She had seen it. Flies were already gathering over the bloodied corpses of some of the earlier victims, stacked in small piles by the buildings.

Dusty black boots approached her, but she kept her eyes down.

The woman beside her cried out when she was shoved out of line, and Leyla reflexively grabbed her own bag, clutching it to her chest as if it were a shield.

"What is this?"

The guard had been drawn by her sudden movement, and she silently cursed her own stupidity. *Be invisible, not obvious!* The soldier's boots scuffed in the dirt as he spun toward her and stepped close. She shuddered with disgust when his foul odor invaded her nose. Sweat and drink did not improve the often unpleasant stink of a man. He ripped the bag from Leyla's hands and tore it open, dumping the meager contents onto the dirt. The toe of his boot prodded the bits and pieces, but she knew nothing in there could satisfy his hunger.

The only thing of value was tucked away where he would never find it, deep within the folds of her skirts. Even if he did find it, he would never know its true value.

It felt like a decade ago when her father had called her in and given her his pocket watch. Really, it had been less than a week. In that time, her whole life had changed, along with everyone else's.

"This is my gift to you, darling Leyla," he had said, holding out his gold pocket watch.

"What is that?" She had laughed, certain he was teasing her. "A watch? For a woman? Where am I supposed to wear that?"

"It is more than that," he told her. "It is a key. A code, really." He opened the little treasure and showed her the engraved numbers on the inside of its cover, the fresh lines dazzling with the firelight. "You see these? They are my secret bank account numbers. These are the numbers you must give the bank to get my money."

It had taken a moment before she realized what that meant. "Papa! What are you talking about?"

"Shh. It is to keep you safe. I am sending you ahead of the family. To Geneva."

"No, Papa. I want to be with you."

"This is the way it must be, my dear. We will not argue."

"But ... but where will you be?"

"Ilyas and I will stay here. Your mother will be with the younger children at the lake house."

"I want to stay with you."

He shook his head, allowing no discussion. "You will travel by caravan—"

"What?"

"It is no longer safe, my darling, for anyone with the name Taghiyev of Baku to ride the trains. No, you will dress as a peasant, travel with the peasants, and escape to Switzerland with them as well. When you show the bank the numbers, you will control our family fortune until I join you, or else I will contact you and give you instructions on where to wire the money."

"When?"

"You must leave right away. I will contact you when Ilyas and I are safe."

The room spun, and she grabbed the sides of her chair for stability. How could she do this? How could she go by herself with strangers, leave her family behind? "But Papa, why me?"

"You speak the best French," he teased, but his smile faded when he saw the fear in her eyes. "You will be fine, my darling. No one is as brave as you."

She had forced herself to concentrate when he led her through the map, explaining the route she must take. All the time he was speaking, she wondered how she could possibly do it by herself.

But she had. And now she stood here, shaking, refusing to look into the eyes of her tormentor. People had complimented her eyes throughout her life, saying how beautiful they were. Their flattery had been welcomed back then. Now those eyes were more of a liability than an asset. What if this thug noticed them and decided he wanted something more, beyond the meaningless items in her bag? If she stayed quiet and submissive, would he leave her alone? Could it be that simple?

He yanked at her coat, pulling her sideways. "Take this off. I want to see your pockets."

She did as she was told, saying nothing, keeping her eyes down as she handed it to him. While she tried in vain not to think of the hard gold shell of the pocket watch tied to her thigh, he rooted through every possible pocket then dropped the coat onto the dirt by the bag. In the next instant, his hand was under her chin, jerking her face to his. Following a desperate, last second impulse, she crossed her eyes.

"*Idbar gadın!*" he snorted, taking in her apparent deformity. At least it prompted him to take a step away. "See that?" he shouted, pointing at the bodies. "Look at that, if you can see anything through that hideous face. You know why they are dead? Because they lied to me. So now it is up to you. Tell me the truth. Are you really a peasant? Be careful with your answer, ugly woman, because if you are lying you will die just like them."

"I am nothing," she squeaked, concentrating on keeping her eyes crossed. They kept trying to wander from her control, to see straight ahead, but if that happened now, he would know she was lying about everything. "Only a peasant. Please, sir. I am only a peasant. Please do not hurt me."

He pushed his face closer, until he was only an inch from her nose, and she breathed through her mouth out of necessity. She did not dare lean away. Every muscle of her body was trembling so badly she was not sure she could move even if she wanted.

"I have never seen eyes like that," he muttered grimly, leaving a fog of stink from his breath. "If he had been a wise man, your father would have taken them out when you were first born."

Her gorge rose, but she fought it back down. "Yes, sir," she managed.

She dropped her chin as soon as he released it and her eyes relaxed. The man moved away, and she breathed again, though she did it carefully in case he heard the tremor. She stood that way, listening but not looking as the men turned from the people to the caravan. No one said a word as the guards removed the only crates of food they had, keeping them for themselves, then ordered them to continue on their way.

Chapter Thirty-Six

Zeynalabdin Taghiyev
Baku, 1920

The Red Army was a river of destruction, and it crested just north of Baku. As morning broke, legions of soldiers and Revolutionary Guards swarmed like ants over the insignificant huts outside the simple village, gaining momentum once they reached the village. Men fought desperately, trying to protect their families, to prevent the villains from breaking into their homes, but most were sliced down by the sabers of mounted horsemen. Women and children were trapped in their burning homes or else they were dragged out and slaughtered like cattle. The stink of burning meat curled within the billowing black smoke.

Thinking fast, two of the women escaped through back doors and collected what they could of hysterical children running wild. They threw the children into a wagon piled high with hay, hoping they could hide from the raiders, but they were spotted. In the next instant the wagon had been rammed and overturned, then the hay—and everyone hidden within— burst into flame.

The Red Terror marched on, a vicious wall of mayhem. Behind them lay mass graves. Before them raged the infernos of the Baku derricks.

Leading the charge were the Cheka guards, and an open truck drove behind. Stalin stood in its bed, shouting encouragement, a beacon for his soldiers.

"Kill everyone!" he demanded, sweeping his arms toward the derricks. "Leave no one alive! Rape and carnage will be rewarded!"

Zeynalabdin Taghiyev's Rolls Royce skidded to a halt, almost hitting a fleeing woman as she ran past him, a screaming baby in her arms. All around him people were running and pushing, needing to escape the approaching red tide. The invasion was a mere two hundred yards from Taghiyev's vehicle and rapidly working its way closer. Paralyzed with horror, he watched soldiers storm into a home and drag out every man they found. Before their families could even attempt to rescue them, the men were shot where they stood.

One of the soldiers spotted his Rolls Royce and pointed, catching the attention of a few others. Jerking from his daze, Taghiyev roared at his driver, who slammed the vehicle into reverse. They raced backward down the first alley he could find, speeding through until he could go no farther.

The driver turned around, panic clear on his face. "I do not know where to go! We are trapped!"

Taghiyev had no idea if they were still chasing him. The walls of the alley felt as if they were closing in on him, but— unlike the driver—he knew where he was. He had played here as a boy so many years ago.

"I will go by foot," he informed the driver. "They do not want you, they want me. If you cannot get out, leave the vehicle. Be safe."

He climbed out, barely squeezing between the door and the alley wall, then he shut the door quietly, hoping no one would hear. At first he hesitated, terrified he had forgotten which way to go, then he spotted the shortcut. He had not been here for a very long time, and he silently thanked his boyhood self for being so curious. With his heart in his throat and sweat streaming down his face, he sprinted through the passage toward home.

At last he burst into an open space a block from his house, and he grunted with surprise when someone accidentally bumped into him.

"Hey! Look where you are—" The man's eyes widened when he recognized him. "Oh! I am sorry, Mr Taghiyev. I did not see you there. Pardon my clumsiness."

Taghiyev barely heard him. He staggered toward his house, now just across the street, then paused a moment to catch his breath.

I made it, he thought. *A blessing from—*

The door of the house flew open, revealing his front entryway—and his son. Ilyas was struggling furiously in the grip of two large Russian soldiers who were dragging him through the door. He was dressed traditionally, in a full black robe. A long, curved dagger hung from a sash around his waist. Taghiyev watched with bated breath as Ilyas pulled it from its sheath in one smooth movement then swung the blade at his attackers, slicing one across the upper arm, the other across his chest.

"Ilyas!" he cried, throwing himself into the frenzied crowds. He pushed through the hundreds of people in his path, needing to be with his son, but it was like wading through tar. "I am coming, my son!" he yelled. "Fight, Ilyas!"

The blade swept back and forth, and finally Ilyas jerked free of their grasp. He ran directly toward his father, but he did not see him.

"Here, son! Ilyas!"

In desperation, Taghiyev grabbed the people stalled in front of him, shoving two to the ground in his urgent need to reach his son. In a moment he would be there. He kept his eyes trained on Ilyas, needing to get to him before he was lost in the crowd, had to—

A single shot cut through the chaos, and Ilyas's expression opened wide, as if he had just seen something he could not believe. He staggered a few steps, then rapid gunfire broke out from all around. Through the panicked crowd he watched his beloved son's body jerk with every bullet before collapsing to the ground.

"No!" The ground swooped beneath Taghiyev's feet, and he stumbled forward. "Ilyas! Ilyas! My son!"

Dizzy with grief and confusion, he lost his balance and was tossed helplessly in the sea of people until someone recognized him. The stranger reached out and grabbed his wrist, pulling him to safety.

"Mr Taghiyev!" he said in a hoarse whisper. "You have to get out of here!"

Taghiyev stared blankly at the stranger, not understanding. He tried to twist out of his grip, but the man held on tight.

"My ... my son! I m-must go to him!"

The stranger's gaze was soft with sorrow, but his words were direct. "Ilyas was a great man, Mr Taghiyev, and this is a terrible loss to all of us. But it is too late for him. They will be coming for you next. You must go."

In the place where he had last seen Ilyas there now existed only a blurred rush of strangers. Tears filled Taghiyev's eyes, turning the blurs to stars until he blinked them away.

"But I—"

Another man stopped, recognizing him as well. "Mr Taghiyev! Get out of here! Are you crazy?"

He fought them when they dragged him away, cried out and wept as the space lengthened between him and his eldest son. He knew they were right—Ilyas was gone, and if he did not go now, he would be next—but he could not think straight, could not stop pulling against them. By now a small crowd of men had gathered around him in a protective wall, and through his daze Taghiyev recognized a few of his workers. That man had sent three daughters to the school he had built. The young man to his left was a new father. Near him was a man whose wife had fallen ill and was now being cared for in the hospital Taghiyev had built. All the thoughts washed over him, dreamlike, and his struggles abated.

One of the men stepped forward and stared into his eyes. "Mr Taghiyev, you have saved my life with your generosity, and you have given life to a whole generations of Azerbaijanis.

We grieve with you for your son, but listen to me, old man, and do as I say. That is the only way you will survive this day."

Taghiyev went with him, meek as a lamb, as he was led into a small building nearby. He watched numbly as the man and his family dressed him in the rags of ordinary peasants, and he said nothing as they rushed him out the door again, urging him into a waiting horse cart. It was not until the cart began to move that he found his voice again.

"Where? Where are we going?" His voice cracked.

"Away," the man informed him. "Out of the city and into the hills, just like everyone else."

Their cart became part of a long, snaking caravan, and over the miles he sank into a state of detached calm. His identity had been swallowed by the closeness of others, cushioned by their kindness, and despite his unbearable grief he felt a deep sense of gratitude to these people who could not afford to do what they were doing for him.

When the caravan was far enough away from the city, he looked back over his shoulder one more time, tears streaming down his cheeks.

"Farewell, Ilyas, my brave, brave son," he whispered, unable to speak the words aloud. "I will see you again soon."

Chapter Thirty-Seven

Elbek Kazimov
Villa Petrolea, 1920

The sun beat down on Elbek's throbbing head, relentless and uncaring. Sweat snaked down his brow, stinging as it met with the fresh wounds on his face, dripping off his chin and landing in the sand. His feet were asleep from having knelt in the driveway for so long, but he did not dare adjust them. He kept his eyes down, fearing direct eye contact might anger his tormentors even more. Five other servants knelt on either side of him, shaking and sobbing, pleading for mercy.

There would be none, he knew.

He comforted himself with the knowledge that they might not all die today, and that was partially his doing. Just before Nobel had left Villa Petrolea, he had sent Elbek inside to carry out his final order. Following the plan, Elbek rounded up ten trembling servants and told them of the secret chamber their master had built specifically for them over the past few months, and of the tunnel which would lead them to freedom. He then told them where their master had hidden money for each of them. Enough to provide for themselves and their families for many years.

"And you, Elbek?" only one had asked.

"I must stay."

He could not save them all. If the Cheka had appeared at the mansion and discovered only him, they would have been suspicious and gone in pursuit of any who had fled. That was why the other five knelt here with him. In addition to choosing the ten fortunate servants, it had fallen to him to decide who would stay. He had chosen those who knew the least about their master. Like anyone, they could eventually succumb to the beatings and tell all they knew. Elbek reasoned they could not say anything if they did not know anything.

If all had gone as planned, the ten were well out of danger by now.

More guards were inside, ransacking the mansion for valuables, of which they would find many. Nobel was a benevolent man, but he had also collected a vast array of treasures for himself. He had never denied his fondness for wealth and all the lavishness that came with it. The art collection, the Fabergé eggs ... Elbek flinched as something shattered inside the house. He had loved many of those pieces almost as much as Nobel had, he thought.

There had been very little time to hide anything since the mobs had arrived during the process. He had to make it look as if nothing in the house was missing, otherwise he feared they would get suspicious. They might start digging and come up with the rest. So Elbek had chosen one particular favorite of Nobel's and one particular tree far from the house, hidden in amongst the others. An unremarkable tree which would attract little to no attention.

This had not been a part of Mr Nobel's plan. It had been one of Elbek's own imaginings, a final show of gratitude to the man who had changed his life.

If Elbek died today, only one other person would know the treasure was there. From the ten, he had chosen one. Like the tree, the young man was indistinguishable from the other servants, but a particular loyalty and intelligence shone in his eyes. Once he was given the task, the youthful zeal had hardened to determination. He had sworn to Elbek he would carry through with the plan.

That was all Elbek could do. The rest was out of his hands.

The guards paced in front, behind, and around each of the servants, like tigers trying to decide which trapped animal to eat first. One of the guards slammed the butt of his rifle against a young man's head, knocking him out cold. It sickened Elbek to hear the dull thud of his skull being smashed. At the same time, he could not help but envy him, despite the bright red blood seeping through his scalp. At least they would leave him alone now that he was unconscious.

The guard stormed directly toward him. "What is wrong with you?" he hissed. "Are you truly this stupid?"

Elbek said nothing. He focused on the pebbles in front of his knees.

"Why throw your life away?"

A sense of peace settled over him, a realization that he could do nothing to prevent what would soon happen. The wheels had been set in motion, and these men would do what they had come here to do whether they got what they wanted or not. He considered the guard's question, and he was pleased that his answer was not thickened by regret. No, he had not thrown his life away. He had worked hard for Nobel, as had all the servants. And by doing so, he had lived a life of relative comfort. He had been not only content, but happy. These men knew nothing.

"Why protect the man who made you slaves to his fortune?"

Moving slowly, Elbek lifted his chin so he could look in the guard's eyes. His life was over, he knew. There was no need to cower if he was about to die. He must say what his heart felt before it was too late.

"There are no slaves here," he said carefully. "No one is protecting him. We told you he is not here. He took the train. He is in Germany."

The guard's narrowed eyes flashed, and he gripped Elbek's neck, just under his jaw. His fingers squeezed, closing together like a vice grip. Pain shot through Elbek's ears and behind his eyes, closing his throat until he saw only pure white agony. He could not breathe; there was no air. His body lurched to one side, losing control, but the pain was endless. Tears leaked out both eyes.

"We stopped the train," the guard spat, no more than an inch from his face. "He was not found. You are hiding him."

The sound of tires on gravel prompted the guard to let go of his neck, and Elbek fell face down on the gravel, gasping like fish on dry land. When he could manage, he blinked away his blurred vision and struggled back up to his knees so he could witness the next terrible thing, whatever it was. The other servants glanced at him, sympathy in their eyes, then they stared back at the military truck pulling to a stop before them. Every one of them was mute with dread.

Before it came to a complete stop, the back doors of the truck were flung open. Several Cheka guards jumped out, yelling and dragging a group of badly beaten men. Elbek's heart tripped as he recognized Nobel's trusted executives, badly bruised and covered in blood. That meant the truck had come from the BraNobel derricks. Seeing them here meant their attempts to keep the derricks safe had been defeated.

The last time Elbek had seen Lesner, the confident family man was enthusiastically assuring Nobel that all would be fine. Now he could barely stand. Fresh blood stained the front of his shirt and coat, and his head swayed as the guards shoved him into place. Both eyes had swelled shut.

When the executives had been positioned into a weak, tottering line before the kneeling servants, the guards stepped back, their weapons trained on Lesner and the others.

"You will no longer have to worry about taking orders from these oppressors!" the man in charge declared. His expression was dark with a heavy mixture of victory and malice, and Elbek's heart shot to his throat. He knew what was about to happen, and he was incapable of stopping any of it. He could not have made a sound even if he had dared.

Gunfire shattered the instant of silence, and the staggering men who had stood helplessly before them crumpled to the dirt. The ground was suddenly wet with blood, and flies swarmed in to take advantage.

With terrifying indifference, the Cheka leader turned from the fresh corpses and strode toward Elbek. "You," he shouted, pointing from him to the long marble stairway. "Pick them up and put them there."

Elbek had always admired the elegant stretch of white stone behind him. The palatial entryway had been a bold yet welcoming acknowledgement of BraNobel's success. To leave the bodies here, to let them bleed out on the marble, seemed the cruelest of ironies.

When he hesitated, the guard shoved the still-hot muzzle of his rifle against Elbek's shoulder, making him cry out.

"Get up! Go! Do it now if you want to live!"

Getting to his feet had never seemed impossible before, but the agony of moving now seemed almost beyond his capabilities. The guard came around and shoved his rifle at Elbek's chest, forcing him upward. *Who is the slave driver now?* Elbek thought wryly, finally struggling to his feet.

Because his was the closest body, Elbek started with Lesner. He knelt by the man's elbow, unable to look at the battered face. Out of respect for the man he had known, Elbek pulled the sides of the expensive suit together and buttoned them, covering the ruin of Lesner's chest. When that was done, Elbek slid his arms under the body, then braced himself before lifting it against his own chest. Lesner was not a big man, but his body felt like a gangly boulder in Elbek's arms. The Cheka guard kept prodding him, trying to rush him, but Elbek held his chin high and took his time. A hysterical urge to smile pressed against his lips. *If you kill me now, you'll have to do this dirty work yourself.*

As he carried the body of William Miller, the American Vice Consul, toward the stairs, he remembered the jolly, pompous sort of man he had been, an unabashed lover of women and wine. From the look of his limp, distorted face it became apparent to Elbek that his jaw had most likely been broken before he had been brought here to be shot. He felt an empathetic throbbing in his jaw. The American would not have understood any of this. He had been a logical thinker, never quite understanding the insanity of the revolutionaries. He would have tried to protect the BraNobel derricks and the other men, standing before them in his terrible tan suit, trying to convince the mob they were doing more harm to themselves than good by burning the best producing wells. But of course they had not listened.

Elbek laid Miller beside Lesner, then one by one he carried four more expensively clad men to the marble stairway. The bodies were heavy; sweat rolled down Elbek's neck and down his back. By the end of the morbid chore, he was exhausted and covered in dead men's blood. His heart felt as if it had been ripped from his chest. He returned to his place in the line of servants, sinking back to his knees on the drive.

"Hey!" came a cry from the top of the stairs. "Look what I found!"

Everyone looked up at the Cheka guard who had just exited the house. He was tossing something small into the air and catching it again, as if he were a child playing with a ball. Except this ball was more of an oval, and when he held it up, the sunlight caught diamond studded pink enamel. The small pink egg looked out of place here in the bloody, violent setting. It seemed vulnerable in the savage's hands. Nobel's heart would have been broken, seeing it like this.

At least it was not the "Ice Egg". That, Elbek knew deep in his soul, these creatures would never find.

His mind travelled far beyond the flames of Baku, envisioning Emanuel Nobel. Wherever he was, Elbek hoped the man's generous heart was still beating.

Chapter Thirty-Eight

Ramiz Veliyev
Gobustan, 1920

The trunks would be left behind. Nobel would not need them anymore, just as he would not need the expensive suits and hats neatly packed within.

The farmers and workers had come without being called. Having learned Ramiz's master was trapped there in Gobustan, they had endangered their lives to save his. They had brought with them the sacks of rags he now wore, along with whatever food they could spare, then they had loaded it all into the wagons and left one of those for him as well. These paltry items were all they had, and they had gladly given them to the great and generous Emanuel Nobel, who had changed their lives. They wanted to thank him, to ensure him that he would never be forgotten. In order to demonstrate their deep gratitude, they provided him with a means to escape the very land he had saved.

It was strange for Ramiz, seeing Nobel dressed as a peasant. The old wool overcoat and heavy pants of a worker were torn, stained, and obviously had been worn a great deal. His master's hair was mussed; they had smudged dirt and oil over his cheeks and into his beard. Ramiz was not sure how he felt about seeing him this way, but he knew there had been no other choice.

"Eugenie, you will be Emanuel's second wife." Heinz's eyes darted over the little group assembled by the caravan, examining the details of their disguises. "Ewlanoff is your son."

Gosta's wife, Eugenie, nodded absently, helping her real children dress in the layers of old clothes. "Gunnar, put this coat on. Yes, I know it is torn. Put it on." She turned to check on her other children, Alfred and Nina, who sat quietly by the side, silent with apprehension.

Emanuel Nobel paced between his family and his friends, doing what he could to keep everyone calm. He glanced at Ramiz, standing across the room.

"You are shocked to see me dressed this way, my friend, but to me it is like old times. My father and I wore these clothes when we first came, before BraNobel had even been created."

Ramiz regarded him skeptically. "Too bad you cannot disguise your blue eyes."

Nobel chuckled, then his expression changed swiftly to concern. He had spotted something that alarmed him, and Ramiz could not help backing up a step when the master strode toward him, pulling out his pocket knife as he approached. He said nothing when Nobel grabbed his arm and sawed through the material of his coat. When he was done he held out the piece of sleeve he had removed. The fabric bore the Nobel Coat of Arms.

"What is this, Ramiz? You cannot wear this! It marks you for death." He leaned closer, making sure he was heard. "Look at me and pay attention. You cannot be a Nobelite any longer. Do you understand? You are a worker. A common worker and nothing more."

"Yes, Your Excellency."

The two men regarded each other sadly, both recalling simpler times, when everyone knew their place, when all had been satisfied with their ways of life.

"No, my friend," Nobel said quietly. "Excellency no more." Reaching into his coat, he produced a rough map which he handed to Ramiz. "Take this. It needs to get to Taghiyev."

This was news to Ramiz, but he would not argue. How was he to find Taghiyev if he was on the caravan with his master?

"You'll have to ride back to Baku in a farm truck."

Realization dawned, stealing his breath for a moment. He would not be with Nobel after all. He lifted his chin, swallowing regret and accepting responsibility for this final assignment.

"He'll know how to read it," Nobel was saying, "and it will help him find us in Germany. After that, I want you to get the money. It is hidden in that place I told you about, remember?"

"Of course, Your Ex—" He stopped himself. "I remember."

He might not be able to use his master's title in public, but it was forever seared into his memory. As were his master's blue eyes and his warm, generous heart. The thought that this would most likely be the last time he saw him was banished to the back of Ramiz's mind.

"When you find the money," Nobel said, his eyes glistening, "I want you to divide it among the servants who are still alive."

The look they shared this time spoke of memories, grief, then hard acceptance. Ramiz said nothing, only nodded.

"Good," Emanuel said. He pointed down the road a bit. "That truck is waiting for you." Both hands gripped Ramiz's shoulders. "*Guds hjälp, min vän,*" he whispered, and Ramiz recognized his native Swedish. He had so rarely heard it of late, but Nobel had taught him the important words early on in case they had needed to speak in private. It was difficult, hearing them now. *Go with God, my friend,* he had said.

"*Du också, ers Excellens. Tack,*" he replied. *You as well, Your Excellency. Thank you.*

He left without a backward glance, for he did not want Nobel to see his tears. The driver of the farmer's truck gestured for him to hop in. The engine started up with a noisy roar, then they were on their way, heading toward the fires of Baku.

What will I find in the ashes? he wondered.

Chapter Thirty-Nine

Emanuel Nobel

The caravan of decrepit wagons and carriages rolled stubbornly onward. The people jostling within hunched over themselves, saying little, afraid to create conversation. Emanuel and his group rode in an open wagon, blending with the poor families, and when he looked across at Eugenie she stared silently back. The only sounds in the air were the eternal *clop clop clop* of the horses' hooves and the resultant hissing of gravel under the wheels. Multitudes of vultures circled overhead, black scavengers on silent wings.

Rough side roads wound through woods and cleared land, and the farther they went, the more they saw evidence of the ongoing violence. After a few miles Eugenie no longer looked at Emanuel, for her downcast eyes were glazed with grief and shock. She pulled the children to her, wanting to hide them from the carnage. But they were young. They wanted to see. As soon as they could, they wriggled from her grasp, eyes wide, and she did not stop them. Nor did she make any move to chastise them, for there was nothing she could do. This was the world in which they now lived. After a breathless moment little Nina returned to her embrace, her body trembling with anguish.

Emanuel was silently relieved the children had been struck dumb by what they saw, since he did not want to hear their whispered observations. Unlike Eugenie, he could not look away. Crumpled bodies lay on the side of the road—mothers and daughters, fathers and sons. Age had not mattered to the killers, nor had the fact that these had been peasants, nothing more. The men who had done this had been deep in the throes of blood lust, seized by greed and power. Occasionally the wagons passed thugs still ransacking bodies, and their smoke-reddened eyes scrutinized Emanuel's caravan as it passed. When they determined the wagons carried nothing but huddled workers, they paid them no mind.

Miles away, smoke hovered in a thick, unmoving cloud, marking the ravaged derrick fields. The caravan plodded ever closer to the water, to the docks, and to the land Emanuel knew so well—the land which had made his sudden, immense fortune and now painted such a large target on his back. How long would the devastation stretch? He thought of the map he had passed to Ramiz, saw again the long, forbidding wall of Karabakh mountains through which the caravan must cross, then Naxcivan. If they survived this and made it to Turkey, they would board a train in Igdir. That would take them to Istanbul. From there a ship would carry them across to Bulgaria. Then—at last—they would take a train to Berlin.

Would they survive? The silent faces around him were lined by grief and fear, their bodies worn by exhaustion which had not been there a few months before. They were weak with helplessness, and this was only the beginning of the voyage. How long would they be able to maintain the charade?

Chapter Forty

Édouard Alphonse James de Rothschild
Paris, 1920

Édouard Alphonse James de Rothschild leaned forward and curled his fingers over the rounded back of a red and gold Louis XIV armchair, allowing the three-hundred-year-old furniture to bear his weight. As usual, his mind whirled with information, and today's events were picking up the pace. The business of banking depended heavily upon world events, and the news out of Baku would certainly influence the next little while.

Rothschild lived his life in the spotlight, owing to his family's continued success in the banking world, and that meant it was difficult to maintain privacy at times. Occasionally—such as this moment—that privacy was important. He glanced toward the executives clustered at the other end of the room, all of them hunched intently over a table, and decided they were too far to hear his muted conversation with Marcus Samuel.

"It is really something," Samuel was saying, gazing thoughtfully into his scotch. The Waterford crystal caught the light as he turned the glass, shimmering like a sunrise on the golden liquor. "Every hour brings worse news. They are saying the invasion will eclipse the horrors of Bloody Sunday."

The Rothschilds had not made their huge fortunes by panicking. Instead, they had honed their instincts over the generations so they could see the silver lining of practically every situation. At Samuel's dire prediction, Édouard merely nodded, staring absently at the mirror over the mantle. Its intricate ormolu frame wound in links of golden vines, and he sought a pattern without realizing he was doing so. Then the clock on the desk began to chime, alerting all in the room to the fading of the afternoon.

"You see only the frightening aspects of this," Édouard said, his voice as smooth as the velvet chair back. "Try seeing it a different way. You and I, we are in an interesting position. Certainly it is enviable, and yet it is damned as well."

He turned slowly toward Marcus Samuel, who was fiddling with his Patek Phillipe watch, matching its time with the chiming clock.

"We are the sole survivors," Rothschild said discreetly. "We are the only ones to sell our holdings at precisely the right moment."

"That is true," Marcus admitted carefully, "although there is a delay while we wait. Is there nothing we can do until the violence recedes?"

Rothschild straightened and rolled his shoulders back, then he eased toward the bar. He poured two fingers of Macallan into his glass and added a few drops of water from the crystal pitcher to release the flavor.

"We are already doing it." Tilting his head from one side to the other, he loosened the tired muscles in his neck while he gently swirled the single malt. "Control the currency, you control the people. Control the people, and you control time itself." He lifted his glass in a toast. "This scenario is taking place on many levels, and it has been building for some time. You must realize there have been forces at play far beyond the imagination of even the Nobels."

He took a sip, letting the liquid warm his throat. "Think of Emanuel's surprise, the poor man. He is about to discover that being the single richest man in Europe does not buy him his life. All it does is make him the richest target."

He half turned, eyeing the men around the far table, oblivious to their conversation.

"What you and I must do, Marcus, is keep an eye on the few who deserve to survive."

*

Rockefeller Mansion, New York

Across the sea, John D. Rockefeller sat alone, enjoying his breakfast. Though seven other chairs stood around the dining room table, he was alone, and that was exactly as he liked things to be. Quiet and orderly. His only company was a stack of newspapers collected from around the world. Sunlight flooded through the tall windows, welcomed by elegantly drawn ceiling-to-floor curtains. Besides the crackling of his newspaper and the lazy ticking of a clock, there was no other sound in the enormous room.

He swallowed his last sip of coffee, then folded the newspaper and carefully patted a crisp linen napkin over his upper lip—where his mustache had once grown. When the door flew open, J.D. glanced up, annoyed.

"Telegram, sir," his assistant explained.

He held out a hand, curling his fingers to suggest the man hasten the delivery. Once he had handed over the small paper, the young man stood facing him, hands behind his back, awaiting orders.

J.D. read the telegram, then he read it again. His bony face creased into a broad, satisfied smile.

"Finally," he breathed. "The trophy."

"Sir?"

"Baku," Rockefeller explained.

The assistant regarded him blankly.

J.D. rolled his eyes. "Baku, my dear man. It pumps fifty percent of the oil supply in the world. Perhaps you've heard of it."

"Yes, sir."

Rockefeller doubted the man even knew how to spell the word. Still, nothing could take this moment from him. When he spoke the words out loud, it all became so much more real.

"Well," he said, enunciating carefully simply for the pleasure of watching the man's cheeks flare with embarrassment. "Baku is now mine. Send messages to every participating executive at Standard Oil."

"Yes, sir. Wh-what shall I say in these messages?"

The words had to be exactly right. After all this time, he could hardly allow the declaration to be a disappointment. He steepled his fingers in front of his nose and narrowed his eyes in contemplation.

"Tell them exactly this," he said slowly. "Machiavellian manipulation wins the Great Game. Repeat that back."

The assistant swallowed. "Machiavellian manipulation wins the Great Game."

"Excellent." He waved a hand. "Write that down. There's more."

A pen and paper were instantly produced, and dictation began. "Tell them this as well: In our dreams, people yield themselves with perfect docility to our plans."

He waited, taking another bite of his breakfast while the assistant struggled to get every word. When he was done, he looked up expectantly.

It was with great pleasure that Rockefeller added his final touch. "As a closing remark, add in the ever-important: Competition is a sin. Own nothing. Control everything."

Chapter Forty-One

Leyla Taghiyev
Geneva, Switzerland

If Leyla were to look for the most positive aspect of the journey, it would be that the camp of guards they had met at the border area of Iran was the only one to stop them. They had been lucky. Realistically, they could have been set upon by many such men bent on violence. Perhaps the others had been distracted by the widespread pillaging and murder which had destroyed her homeland and everyone in it.

Every time she thought of Baku she felt ill. Everything had been on fire when she had left a week ago. Would it all be ashes now? And what of her family? What of Sara? Had she and their mother made it safely with the younger ones to the lake house?

The journey through the mountains had been brutal, and they had been constantly on watch for predators both human and beast. Never in her life had she felt so defeated as she had on those endless days. At least the evenings had soothed her fevered thoughts somewhat. When everyone had fallen asleep, she had stared for hours at the millions of blinking stars, praying for some kind of hope.

Now she was in Geneva, and though it was a clean, thriving city, it looked completely different from St. Petersburg. She felt very small. The clothing she had worn through the trip had been old when she had first put it on. Now it was also filthy and pungent from days on the road. When they began to separate into groups, Leyla bid farewell to her fellow travelers, her hand closing habitually over the fold in her skirts where the watch still hid. Then she headed toward the first bank she saw.

The solid oak doors of the grey stone building loomed over her. It reminded her of her father's house—though this building was smaller—which gave her strength. He had sent her on this mission, and she was responsible for collecting and watching over the family's fortune.

She was no peasant, she reminded herself as she pulled open the heavy door. She was Leyla Taghiyev.

A few questions later, she found herself in a quiet room, sitting at a table opposite an elderly banker. He watched with interest as she unwrapped the small gold watch, opened its clasp, then copied the numbers onto a paper he had provided.

"It has been a terrible journey," she said, sliding the paper across the desk to him. "I appreciate your immediate attention to this matter. I would like to close this account with some haste."

He got to his feet. "Of course. We understand. Please wait here a moment while we confirm the account and safety deposit boxes."

"Of course."

With a rising sense of anticipation, she leaned back in the chair and blew out a long breath, trying to leave the journey behind her. When she was done here, the first thing she would do would be to find a nice hotel and take a long bath. Though she wanted to see more of the city, she was beyond exhausted. The grand tour would have to wait.

When the banker did not come back immediately, she closed her eyes and let herself drift into a half sleep. The first face that filled the darkness was kind, and one she had known her entire life. Where was Emanuel? She had been sent away before she could bid him farewell, and it had surprised her how difficult that had been. There had been times when she longed for him, both in soul and in body, and the need had been so intense it brought tears to her eyes. The idea that she might never see him again haunted her.

The minutes ticked by, and still the banker did not return. A woman entered, bearing a cup of tea, which she gave to Leyla. She apologized for the delay, but she could not offer an explanation.

When the tea had been finished and the cup was cold to the touch, the banker finally returned. He was accompanied by another man who carried a safety deposit box in both hands. Both men were frowning.

Leyla got to her feet, relief flooding into her cheeks. "You have been gone a very long time. Was there a problem?"

The men exchanged a glance then took a seat at the table.

"We did find your safety deposit box intact, and we are able to give you access to it as well as the ownership of its contents," said one of the men. He hesitated. "Unfortunately, the accounts—"

"Is there a problem?"

"I am afraid so."

Relief was instantly overwhelmed by anxiety. "I am sorry, I do not understand. What is wrong?"

"There are conflicting instructions ..."

"About my father's accounts? What do you mean? You cannot deny they exist! I have the actual account numbers, after all."

"Oh no, they exist. The trouble is that a wire transfer order arrived last week. We confirmed that the signatures matched, and the money was transferred to St. Petersburg."

The floor dropped beneath her. "What? St. Petersburg? No! There's been a mistake. My father would *never* move his savings to Bolshevik Russia!"

The first banker pulled a form out of a folder. He placed the paper in front of her and pointed at the bottom line. "This is your father's signature, correct?"

She stared at the familiar signature, but her mind was unable to accept it. Furious, she handed it back to the men.

"No," she said, anger rushing through her veins. "Not to Russia. Never. My father cannot go to Russia; they would kill him. Surely you must know this, which means this transfer was invalid. It is just a lie so the money can be put into the wrong hands."

"I am sorry, Miss Taghiyev; however, when we receive proper instructions we are obligated to do as our client instructs. The account has been emptied of all funds."

"No!" She jumped to her feet. "He would not do that!"

The second man spoke in a condescending tone that did not help at all. "He fled a revolution, Miss Taghiyev. Plans change, sometimes dramatically. You do not know for sure. He could be in St. Petersburg."

"No, he could not. This is wrong. You must give me my father's money. I am responsible for it. I demand that you fix what you have done. Immediately."

The safety deposit box was pushed toward her.

"You have a significant amount of jewelry in here which we are pleased to give you." The banker frowned gently. "Do not worry, Miss Taghiyev. Your father will contact us soon, no doubt. Stay in a hotel here in Geneva, or maybe go to Paris. As soon as we hear from him we'll send you a telegram, and you'll know he has received the money. I am afraid that's the best we can do."

She stared at them, incredulous, as her world crumbled around her. "There's *nothing* you can do? It is all gone? You let someone steal all my father's money?"

"It is not like that." His tone had hardened. "You saw the signature. He must have changed his plans." Judgmental eyes passed over her rough clothing. "You have been traveling for a while. Perhaps he could not contact you and inform you of the change."

It was raining when she stepped into the street, but she did not feel it. A vehicle raced past, honking at her, but she did not hear it. She stared straight ahead as she walked, seeing nothing.

Bit by bit, awareness returned, pressing urgently through her stunned thoughts. *What now?* She needed to sit, to think.

To rest. The money was gone. All she had left were the small velvet sacks in her hands, each of them heavy with jewels. The truth came to her then, cold and harsh. Her first stop would have to be a pawn shop.

The hotel she chose was plain, with a bed, a table and chair, an unexceptional watercolor painting, and one small window. The walls were white. It was unlike any other place she had been, but she had chosen it on purpose; she had to be wise in how she spent her meager funds. She had also bought a meal and a set of unremarkable clothing. The only other purchase she had made was a book of blank pages and a pen, which she set on the room's little table. Her new black coat had been folded and placed in the corner of the room.

The mattress was soft when she sank onto its edge. Not like her bed in Baku, but worlds better than the wagon floor where she had tried to sleep so many times. Not bothering to remove her clothing or pull a blanket over her body, she lay back and linked her hands on her stomach, staring at the plain white ceiling. In her mind she had gone over the conversation in the bank a million times, but it still made no sense. Papa would never have sent money to Russia, and yet that *had* been his signature. Maybe they had been right; maybe her father had simply not been able to contact her. Perhaps if the caravan had moved faster, if she had gone ahead of the lumbering wagons, she could have beaten the false wire transfer. Could all this be her fault?

"Papa," she whispered, tears trickling down her face. "Papa. I do not know what to do."

She could not contact him; she had no idea how to find anyone. She was alone in a strange country.

But I am safe, she reminded herself.

Where were the others? Had they gotten out of Baku before it was too late? Where was her dear sister? Was Sara all right? Had they made it safely away? Her heart went to her father and eldest brother, steadfastly remaining in their home, protecting what was theirs. Had they changed their minds, or were they still there?

And what of Emanuel? His eyes, that direct blue that had cut through her mask of indifference, appeared in her mind. He had seen how much she loved him, and her heart had taken flight when he had essentially said he felt the same way. If only she could telephone him, send a telegram, even mail him a letter. He would know what to do. He would help her, she knew. He would do anything for her. But she had been given no contact information.

Yes, I am safe. But I am alone.

A deep need to share her pain, to let it out and maybe ease the pressure, drove her to the desk where she began to write. The pen had a mind of its own, and she let it lead her.

My dear Emanuel ...

That was how it started, though she had not planned it that way. She paused, staring at the words, wondering what she could possibly do with a letter. He was gone. She had no idea where he might be, so she could never send it to him. Besides, he had told her long ago that he could not give her what they both wanted, and she had known all along that he was right. Emanuel and her father loved and respected each other deeply. She could not interfere with that.

But she had to write. Her hand almost vibrated with need.

"I will tell a story. A true and tragic story," she said out loud. Her voice was tentative, and it fell flat on the old wood floor. She looked at the blank pages, experiencing an unexpected sense of loss. Her favorite book, her treasured gift from Emanuel, had been left behind in Baku. She had abandoned it since she had no way of carrying it through the mountains. If she could have, she would have chosen it over all the jewels she had.

She crossed out what she had written and started again.

For my dear Emanuel.

That would work. Every book needed a dedication.

Once the words began, they would not stop. She called upon her memories and spilled them onto the page, going back as far as she could. It charmed her that one of her first thoughts was of Emanuel himself, on that day her father's first geyser had blown. What a day that had been! Her father had not come home all night, though she and the others had stayed up as late as they could, hoping to hear his joyful news. In great detail she described the mansion her father had built, then the theater and all the other buildings he had constructed for the people. She wrote about school in St. Petersburg, about how her new friends and teachers had taught her so much, but also that she had taught them as well. Then she wrote the bittersweet memory she had of finally seeing Emanuel when she returned home from school. By then she was all grown up, and for the first time she saw her forbidden lover with the eyes of a woman.

She hesitated, remembering January 22, 1905. Bloody Sunday, they now called it. Her grief had been something she could not have fathomed, and it had led her to him. He had held her close, smoothed her hair, unknowingly roused her fragile emotions to a place where she forgot for an instant what had so upset her. How she had wanted to kiss him in that moment, to tell him how she truly felt about him, about them. His eyes had been eternally sad, she recalled. Was the sadness for her? Of course not. It had been for those poor, poor people in St. Petersburg. Perhaps, since he seemed always able to see the future before it happened, perhaps he saw the impending destruction of Russia which had sprung from that one horrible day.

For weeks she wrote in her notebook, barely eating, staying in her room unless absolutely necessary. It seemed she had been holding this story inside for so long her seams were beginning to tear, and if she could just let it out the pressure might ease, allowing her to breathe again. She recalled the moments of her life with shocking clarity, and she made sure to add dates whenever she could. Her neat, curling letters covered so many pages, smudged by so many tears, the words bunching up and spreading out depending on the memory, that she soon had to purchase a second blank-paged book, then another.

She reached the day when her dear father had called her to him and had given her the gold watch. That had been the beginning of her journey from Baku. She let her thoughts sink deep into those days on the road, recalling the horrors she had seen and her own continuous sense of terror throughout. At last she wrote about her arrival in Geneva, about how her father's fortune had simply disappeared, leaving her homeless and practically penniless.

When it was done, she set down her pen, took a deep breath, then wrapped the books in a leather bag she had purchased for that purpose. Feeling free for the first time in months, she put on her coat and went out to a restaurant to eat. Surprising herself, she stepped out of her shell and spoke to a waiter, feeling temporarily cleansed of the sorrow which had clung like oil to her heart for so long.

"I am writing a book," she told him in French.

He looked intrigued. "Really? I have always wanted to write a book, but I have no talent with such things. Is it political?"

"No, no," she said. "It is a true story. An adventure."

He beamed. "I love adventure stories," he exclaimed. "Perhaps I have read something of yours before?"

She thought about all the writing she had done in school so long before and shook her head. None of those papers had ever been published. They seemed so unimportant compared to what she had just accomplished. "I do not think so."

"You never know. Tell me your name so I can look for it."

As if someone clapped a hand over her mouth, the words she had been about to say stopped short. She could not say the name Taghiyev. Never again.

"Banu," she blurted. It was the name of a girl she had met long ago. It meant nothing to anyone. She discovered that declaring a false name empowered her. "My name is Banu."

"Well, Banu," he said, "I am honored to make your acquaintance. I will be the first to buy the book when it is in stores."

The idea made goosebumps rise, then a thought bubbled up from within. Writing a book was like writing a long letter, was it not? Maybe, just maybe, if her book made it to bookstores, that letter might someday find itself in the right hands. In Emanuel's hands.

Chapter Forty-Two

Emanuel Nobel
Sweden

It was over. He was safe. The Bolshevik terror was far from here, raging across the sea. And since BraNobel no longer existed, neither did the threat of Rockefeller.

He was a free man, and he was still one of the wealthiest men on the planet. Except in that moment he would trade it all for those he'd left behind. As far as he knew, everyone for whom he had ever cared was still in the clutches of the Red Army. Zeynalabdin and Ilyas had vowed not to leave, banking on the generous spirits of the men they had helped over the years. In the face of such violence, Emanuel could hardly believe their gratitude would be enough. He could only pray they had escaped. What of his servants at Villa Petrolea? And the BraNobel executives? The servants, at least, might survive. After all, they were not the managers, the bosses for whom the Bolshevik hungered. Arthur Lesner and the other executives had been so sure they could manage; they had sent him away with full confidence. The Bolsheviks, they insisted, would need them to properly manage the oil. Emanuel had argued. He did not believe that was true. He thought the Red Army would see replacing his men as a simple thing.

Then there was Leyla. Over the phone in Gobustan, Ilyas had assured Emanuel that she was safe—safer than any of them, he had said. Without any other information, he had to be satisfied. He was not.

He had never been so miserable nor felt so useless in his life.

Upon his arrival in Europe, Emanuel had immediately renounced his Russian citizenship. His next act had been to visit the British embassy.

"I am looking for two people," he told the clerk. "One is a Trade Attaché named Julie Gold. The other is a retired MI-6 officer named Colonel James Ray."

The man behind the desk looked unsure. "I do not know these people," he said.

"Someone will. Please pass along my name and contact information. I must reach at least one of them. Time is of the essence."

He returned to the large office in his new mansion and sat behind the desk, drumming his fingers on the surface, trying to figure out what he could do. After all the chaos, the silence was terrible.

Why had he not planned ahead for this? Certainly he had waited too long to make his exit from Baku. He knew that now. If he had been smart, he would have put plans in place. He would have been able to take others with them and ensure their safety. Thinking back on his mistakes, he accepted that it had been pure folly to believe he could emerge from the nightmare unscathed. Of everyone there, he had been the primary target, yet he had convinced himself he was safe.

At least he had saved a few. He and Elbek. Good, loyal Elbek with the heart of a lion. Since Gobustan, Emanuel had not received word from anyone at the mansion. The servants, he reminded himself, were unimportant in the eyes of the new government. There would be no way to trace any of them through official channels. He hoped they were safe.

When he could not bear to think of his friends, he thought of his company. At first it had hurt, seeing Rockefeller's victory over him plastered throughout the newspapers. Rockefeller and Rothschild had become the uncontested wealthiest industry families in the world— Emanuel had imagined J.D. crowing that perhaps he should feed a revolution every year if it helped his profits in this way. Without BraNobel in the way, Standard Oil became the only vertically-integrated worldwide monopoly on oil. Financially, it became more powerful than any nation on earth. The world had been shocked by the sudden astronomical rise in the global price of oil.

Rockefeller had believed he had won the Great Game, but Emanuel knew better. What J.D. had failed to realize was that the game was not about oil. Not entirely. Certainly money and oil were part of the strategy, but the Game was really about *people*. That fact had eluded Rockefeller, and as a result his gloating had been cut gloriously short. As Emanuel had predicted, Lenin double-crossed Rockefeller by declaring Baku's oil to be state property. True only to themselves, the Bolsheviks had forcibly removed all Standard Oil executives from the offices, even threatened them with execution for their crimes against the people. Once they were gone, the Bolsheviks flooded the market with cheap oil, threatening to bankrupt Rockefeller entirely.

How satisfying it had been to read those stories. And yet even knowing Rockefeller had lost did not completely comfort Emanuel.

It would be a while before anyone would locate either Julie or Ray. There was nothing he could do to find his friends until the spies were found. To distract himself from the helplessness threatening to crush him entirely, he attended more social events than ever before. He no longer wore the heavy mantle of Russian citizenship, and because of that he found a new sense of freedom. He dated more women, and once he settled into his new life he laughed more than he had in years—though it was occasionally forced. He purchased a fleet of automobiles and whatever else he desired. He had it all.

Except no matter how hard he tried, it was impossible not to think of his past and of those people who had shaped it. Every morning he read the international newspapers, searching for familiar names. The First Oil War had come to a conclusion, but he knew very well the Great Game continued—though he now watched the players from afar.

Part of him missed the challenge, but the greater part of him enjoyed the entertainment from the sidelines for a change. He was, after all, sixty. Time to sit back and watch for a change.

Weeks later, during a vacation in the Mediterranean, his friend Rudolf Diesel had come to visit. As a result of their latest contract, Emanuel's St. Petersburg factory was producing fifty diesel engines a year. Soon he would launch the first two diesel-powered oil tankers in the world. On this visit, Rudolf had brought his new engine, and Emanuel had attached it to the boat he purchased in anticipation of his visit. Dozens of interested people had come to the dock to celebrate the maiden voyage and learn about the engine.

Rudolf had offered Emanuel the opportunity to be the first man aboard what he claimed would be the fastest boat on the planet. Emanuel said nothing about the butterflies in his chest, not wanting to be considered 'old'; however, the truth was that his sight was not as good as it once was, nor was his balance. Feigning indifference, he sank into one of the chairs on board and gripped the side of the boat with apprehension.

"Are you ready?" Rudolf asked. "I promise not to kill you."

Emanuel silently chastised himself. He had never been afraid of anything in his life, and he would not allow this boat to frighten him. He gave a confident nod.

"Then let's go!"

They laughed out loud as the boat accelerated, shoving them back in their seats, then it took off across the water, easily passing all the others. When they returned to the dock, their hair tousled and their cheeks reddened from the adventure, tears ran down Emanuel's cheeks because of the wind. He could hardly wait to do it again. The crowd cheered their return as Rudolf carefully docked the boat, and people lined up to shake their hands and to board the amazing craft, to inspect its unique design and engines.

"Now that looked like fun."

Emanuel turned at the familiar British accent, and his fingers self-consciously patted his windblown hair back in place. "Colonel James Ray! What an unexpected pleasure, sir." The men shook hands warmly. "I am extremely pleased to see you."

"As am I, Mr Nobel. You are looking well, I must say. Retirement suits you."

They strolled away from the crowds, and Emanuel felt the usual twinge which came from seeing one of his old contacts, either friend or foe. Yes, he was relieved that hectic life was over, but there were times when he truly missed it.

"I had heard rumors," he admitted, "that you and Miss Gold were missing. That you had been caught and killed escaping Baku."

"I had heard those rumors as well." Ray held out his hands. "I am fine, as you can see."

He did not mention Miss Gold, and Emanuel would not ask again. The truth might be too painful.

"I remember one of our last conversations included mention of a man named Ezhov," Ray said. "I imagine you've seen his name in the newspapers of late."

"Of course. The little man is everywhere."

"He is Stalin's man. Terribly dangerous. He is also a survivor. He has backed the right horse—for now, anyway. We'll see. As long as Stalin's in power, I believe Ezhov will be right there with him." One dark eyebrow lifted. "You most likely know he was behind the BraNobel sabotage attempts all along."

This was news. "What are you talking about?"

"Ezhov works for many masters, but chiefly he works for himself. That being said, I happen to know from my discussions with Rockefeller that he was directly responsible for a certain map which went missing many decades ago." His gaze was intent. "Do you recall? It was at the Imperial Russian Technical Society conference in—"

The memory hit Emanuel just as it had in that moment when he realized the map had been stolen. His father had put him in charge of protecting those plans, and he had failed. He clearly remembered the man in the audience, trying to hide the tube under his coat as he snuck away. Emanuel had seen his face, though it had been on the opposite side of the room. Could that really have been the infamous Ezhov?

"That cannot be. How could he have known of me?"

"Libby knew you had the map, and he needed it for Rockefeller, so Ezhov got it for him."

That had occurred years ago. The map's loss meant nothing to anyone these days, and yet the information shook Emanuel. If Ray was right, that meant Ezhov had been close to him all along. A snake winding through the reeds, observing him while he waded into the pond, planning when and how to strike to cause the most damage.

"He also paid the clansmen to terrorize your workers. And there was an explosion on the docks one time, with one of your tankers. The *Lumen*, I believe it was."

The terror of that devastation had shuddered over the city. "I remember. We were so naive back then. We knew we were being spied upon, but we always assumed the accidents were ... just accidents."

"With J.D. Rockefeller, I do not believe there are any accidents." Ray stopped walking and frowned at the ground. "Actually," he said, looking back at Emanuel, "there is one occasion which strikes me as somewhat of an accident on his part."

"Oh?"

"Then again, it was more of a mistake than an accident." He folded his arms, looking smug. "Something about a poor investment of over eleven billion dollars?"

"That is not altogether fair, is it?" Emanuel asked, feigning innocence. "How was he to know Lenin would nationalize everything, leaving all capitalists with nothing?" He frowned. "Then again, that was the whole point of the revolution, was it not?"

They both laughed and began walking again, and Ray patted Emanuel on the shoulder. "Brilliant," he said.

They reached the end of the path and looked out over the water, then Emanuel turned to him. "I appreciate your coming. I did not know how else to reach you other than through the embassy."

"It was the right thing to do. They found me."

Once again, Emanuel noted sadly there was no mention of Julie. "I require the sort of assistance that only a person with your skills could provide."

"You wish to find your friends."

"More than anything."

Ray blew out a long breath, but his expression was unclear. "Well, Taghiyev is still alive."

"I do not like your tone. Is he all right?"

"Physically he is healthy. Ironically, his kindness was repaid by a number of the Bolsheviks whose university tuitions had been paid years before by Taghiyev. They took care of him, offering him a safe home in any one of over a dozen mansions. He now lives unmolested in his summer house in Mardakan, surrounded by his surviving children and grandchildren."

"I am sorry, but his *surviving* children?"

"His son, Ilyas, was killed," Ray said quietly. "Taghiyev witnessed it."

Pain knifed through Emanuel at the thought. "That young man was his pride and joy."

He swallowed hard, thinking of Ilyas' young sister. *Where are you, Leyla?*

"I wonder, Colonel Ray, if you have heard anything about Taghiyev's daughter, Leyla." He kept his voice level. "I know she escaped with a caravan of Kurdish contrabanders, but I have heard nothing since. I am concerned about her."

Ray frowned. "Haven't heard anything, but then again, I have not been asking. I could, if you would like."

"I would like that very much." He shook his head. "Poor Zeynalabdin. He is a good man. Always has been. I miss him terribly, but I will never go back to Baku. Not even to visit him."

*

Three months later, Emanuel's butler presented him with a large envelope which bore no return address. He reached inside and pulled out a book. A letter was attached to the front cover.

> *Dear Mr Nobel,*
> *I hope this package finds you in good health.*
> *I am sending you a book which I believe will interest you. It is the autobiography of a young aristocratic woman who fled from Baku in 1920. The author's name is Banu. You are not expected to recognize the name; I did not. However, intrigued by the story, I did some sleuthing and came up with an interesting conclusion. "Banu" is actually a pseudonym, used because the author realized her surname was recognizable enough to land her in hot water should she be discovered. On the same grounds, I will not print her name here. What I will say is that I have determined that she is the same young lady you requested I investigate.*
> *The other information I was able to collect was that she arrived safely in Geneva. Unfortunately, she was unable to retrieve any of her family's money, due to circumstances beyond her control. In a state of near poverty, she married an Azerbaijani man named Ali Assadulayev. When they received notice from the Iranian ambassador a few years later, saying that he was to be arrested, they arranged for him to be sent safely to Iran as a result of a bribe. His wife and their three children were not included in this arrangement, but she apparently took the children and loaded them (and her) onto a boat to Iran. After that I lost her trail.*
> *I hope this answers your question.*
> *All my best wishes,*
> *Colonel James Ray*

A surge of heat roared into Emanuel's face. He set Ray's letter aside and laid a trembling hand flat on the plain, off-white cover of the book. He was almost afraid to open it.

My Life In Caucasus
- Banu

She had done it. She had survived the escape despite everything Ray had told him. Near poverty? What could that mean? He blinked the tears from his eyes and read through the letter again. Married with three children. Her entire life had changed.

Many years ago he had made it clear to them both that they could never be with each other. Why, then, did it hurt so much to know she was with another man?

He let out a long breath, bracing himself. It felt almost wrong, reading this, as if he held her private journal, not a published book. And yet the book had come into his hands for a reason. He opened the cover and flipped to the first page.

For my dear Emanuel ...

Tears streamed down his face. He could not place exactly why.

Chapter Forty-Three

She had always been a wonderful writer; her father had raved about her prowess. Now that Emanuel was deep into the story, she held him rapt. It was as if she carried him with her, a small, silent witness to the life she had survived.

I was in the railway station along with many others, and my heart ached, seeing the families bidding each other farewell. When the Red Army soldiers burst into the room we were all startled, and many tried to hide, but there was nowhere to go. I watched in amazement as the soldiers cornered one wealthy family, searching their bags and yelling with frustration when they came up empty handed.

"Where is your father?" one soldier shouted in the young boy's face.

The boy mumbled something unintelligible, making the soldier suspicious. Clamping his hand on the boy's jaw, he forced the little mouth open then crowed with victory when he produced a large diamond ring from within. His mother and siblings were glancing desperately around, seeking escape, for they knew they were next. It was fascinating to see what the family had done in an attempt to deprive the scavengers of their possessions. The woman had filled the children's mouths with more jewelry, sewn some into their hems, even tried to hide diamonds in her hair! As terrifying as the situation was, I could not help seeing the comical side of it. Fortunately, after the family had been relieved of all their treasures, they were released and sent home without further interference.

The situation with the banker in Geneva stunned Emanuel. He wanted to give them the benefit of the doubt, but he had known enough greedy bankers in his time to suspect them. Perhaps they had thought Taghiyev had been killed, and they had felt able to simply take his fortune. Or perhaps Stalin himself had found Taghiyev's account information. Emanuel knew the Red Army had already seized his friend's Rolls Royce, as well as all his other vehicles, artwork, and treasures.

Later on in the book she wrote of her arrival in France.

Ali and I enjoyed the warmest of welcomes when we reached Paris. A few were actually members of the Nobel family, which made me long for my old friend, Emanuel. What would Emanuel think if he knew I'd married the son of a friend of his, fellow oil baron Shamsi Assadulayev?

Life for us was not easy, but Ali found work doing translation and interpretation. I enjoyed the times he was working, for I was not obligated to be with him.

Emanuel would never want Leyla to be unhappy. Even so, he would admit to a smug sense of satisfaction, knowing she was not entirely enamored of her husband.

My greatest joy, she wrote, *is when I receive communications from my father. He can neither read nor write, so his missives are written by another's hand. The words, however, are from his heart—a large, generous, loving heart which has suffered far too many injuries of late. For fear of exposing me, he cannot use my name; however, he sends funds to me when he can find a route through a bank or a traveller. Nothing extravagant, for that would open too many eyes. He sends what he can. He still searches for the fortune lost by the bank. The mystery remains unsolved.*

My greatest sorrow is that I shall never see him again.

*

Several months later, his butler Stefan brought Emanuel a telegram. He reached for his spectacles, settled them on his nose, then held out a hand.

The words before him stole his next heartbeat. He waved a hand, dismissing the messenger. He needed to be alone.

"Zeynalabdin," he whispered, blinking back tears. "Oh, my old friend." *I am so sorry I was not there.*

It did not seem real at first, that such a man as Zeynalabdin Taghiyev could be dead. He had always seemed larger than life, with an uncontainable spirit. How could such a man simply not exist anymore?

PNEUMONIA, the telegram informed him. Further down he saw the words, SUMMER HOUSE CONFISCATED.

The funeral would be soon. "I cannot be there, old friend," he said out loud, recalling what he had said to Ray at their last meeting. "Not in body. But my heart is with you."

Dear Banu had been right. She would never see him again.

Chapter Forty-Four

Vladimir Lenin
Gorki, Russia, 1923

The damn woman had killed him after all. Certainly she had taken her time, doing a fine job of extending his ill-deserved suffering, but the result would be the same.

Vladimir Lenin stared at the ceiling—as he had been doing for months now—unable to do much else. The doctors talked among themselves, but he knew he was done. Death would arrive very soon. He hoped so, at least.

He had been speaking at the *Hammer & Sickle* factory in Moscow that day, he recalled. Six long years ago. Fanya Kaplan, a young, proud, unattractive Socialist revolutionary, had called out to him just as he was about to get into his automobile. He looked up, and she fired three times. The first bullet had missed, but it had come close, cutting through the thick material of his coat. The second and third had made their targets his jaw and neck. The neck injury had been dramatic and bloody, and it had demanded extended bed rest in his living quarters in the Kremlin. That same bullet had also punctured his lung. The jaw injury had been excruciating.

The doctors had been useless. Most likely, they had done their best to kill him when she had failed, then they failed as well. Almost three years later they had finally removed one of the two bullets.

They said Fanya was almost blind, the result of beatings she had received during her years spent in a Siberian prison. That was interesting to Lenin. She had quite good aim for a blind woman, he thought. He was not such an outstanding target, he knew, being short, mostly bald, and as plain looking as so many other Slavs. Of course he had been surrounded by his guards—who had proved themselves to be useless—so finding him would have been simple. The Cheka had interrogated her, following no rules, doing as they would, but she had not surrendered. The ignorant woman had boasted about shooting him, saying it was done of her own volition, never revealing the gutless bastard who had provided her with the revolver. He wondered if she had cried in the end, if she had urinated, shaking with terror as she stood in front of the firing squad three days later.

Of course he could not give her all the credit. As a great leader he had driven his mind and body hard. The revolution then the civil war ... it had all added up. He felt much older than his fifty-four years. Ah, but those had been good, productive years.

These past six had been a waste. Four years after he was shot, he had his first stroke, which had rendered him unable to speak, unable to move. He decided this must be the worst of all tortures. He had been determined to beat the infirmity, though. His work was not done! The Party's Central Committee had needed restructuring, so he had forced his hand to hold the pencil, and he had written his Testament, outlining the necessary changes.

It had been satisfying, putting into writing how disappointed he was at that upstart, Stalin. How he had believed in Josef! How disillusioned he had become. He never should have entrusted him to so much power.

Still, Stalin had been loyal of late. The second stroke had knocked Lenin flat, and he had reluctantly retired, moving south to Gorki. Josef came often to visit and had seemed impressed after Lenin showed him how he had once again regained his voice and the use of his left hand. While Josef watched, Lenin had slowly and deliberately written him a note. The note had forbidden him to bring his pet snake, Ezhov, to anymore visits. The little bald man with the shining spectacles was a disgusting, deranged pervert, more interested in raping young girls than he was in the Party. Lenin would have had him executed years before if he had not been so sneaky. And lucky.

Lenin had managed well enough for another year. In March 1923, the third stroke had taken his speech away permanently, depriving him of the means to complain about the unrelenting, ferocious pain which reigned everywhere in his body. He did not think he could bear it much longer. Forming his letters carefully on a fresh sheet of white paper, he had given Josef his final request, which was for potassium cyanide. That would end it, set him free from the pain and the misery. And since Stalin had never cared for humanity and had no reticence at killing anyone, Lenin knew he would obey.

But Josef had disappointed him once again. The murderous medicine was never produced. Stalin might still have dreams of grandeur, but he was a coward. How would he continue once his mentor was gone? For Lenin knew well that death was close at hand. The stroke had happened ten months ago; he would not survive a year. He imagined Stalin's reaction to the announcement of his death. How he would feign grief but celebrate in private. At last the shadow of Lenin no longer followed him. The pompous ass would declare himself to be the lead pallbearer, he imagined. Perhaps even the chief mourner. What of Trotsky? Would Stalin even inform the man of Lenin's passing? Most likely not. He would leave that in the hands of the media and the gossips.

He let out a slow breath, trying to be careful as always, but the six-year-old scar in his lung caught him, setting off a terrible coughing fit. It exhausted him. The nurse entered, pretending to be doing something. He expected her to leave right away with mumbled apologies. Years ago he might have suspected her of planning his death as well as the doctors, but not anymore. Now he only wished she would, and be quick about it.

"Good afternoon, Mr Lenin," the nurse said.

He did not recognize her voice. All he could move was his eyes, and they slid quickly toward her. She was diminutive, harmless as a sparrow. In the old days it would have been easy to snap that slender neck. She was new here.

She glanced at the chart hanging at the end of his bed. The one in which the doctors marked their secrets. "You seem to be doing well," she told him.

His eyes rolled back under their lids. What he did not need was one more stupid, patronizing woman treating him as if he were a child. If he could speak he would tell her what she could do with her misguided sympathy.

"You do not remember me," she said.

Since she had made her statement so personal, he felt obliged to look. Her eyes were quite startling, their vivid green sharp against the pale tan of her face. She was young and pretty. Gaunt, as so many of them were these days, and he imagined tearing the harsh wool of her nurse's uniform from her body. Some part of his ruined body awoke, though there was nothing it could have done.

"I remember you," she said, moving slowly to the side of the bed.

It was difficult to keep looking at her from this angle. She must have realized that, because she moved back into his view. She folded his sheet back over the blanket, keeping the arrangement neat. A thin line of saliva escaped the corner of his mouth and travelled toward the pillow. She should wipe it off, but she did not.

"You came to my village, you and your men."

That got his attention.

"It was very early. The sun was barely up. We were not yet awake when we heard you arrive." Her gaze dimmed as she remembered. "We woke quickly, though."

She swallowed, but her eyes showed no change in her expression. "You killed my father first. He was at the door. They shot him through the head. The bullet went through him, and his blood hit my mother in the face."

She painted a vivid picture, and Lenin brought it to life in his mind. She was wrong, of course. He did remember—

though it might not have been *her* village, might not have been *her* father. There had been so many.

"We all screamed, and my two younger brothers ran out, thinking they might save us. They were so brave, so determined," she continued. "They were too small to do anything, though. Really, they were a waste of your bullets. You left them in a pile by the door."

Someone walked down the hallway beyond his room, speaking quietly between themselves. The nurse shut the door and pulled a curtain around them for privacy, apologizing for the interruption as she did so. Lenin felt a twinge of alarm at this. Was she here to do him harm? To kill him? Then he wondered at his own reaction, for though the idea struck fear into his heart, an odd sense of anticipation began to buzz through him. He would love to die today.

"I am sorry you did not get a chance to speak with my mother, my sisters, or me before you and your men dragged us from our house, beat us, raped us, then left us for dead. I was the only one of us who survived that morning. I wish I had died with them." She sniffed, but he did not see any sign that she was weakening. "Until you came along, Mr Lenin, I had a wonderful family. They were surprisingly intelligent, considering our poor existence, and had plenty of interesting things to say. My little sister and brothers both had wonderful senses of humor." She sighed. "Ah, but you did not pause to ask, did you?"

He closed his eyes, hoping she would get the message that he did not wish to hear her stories. His interest in her sharp eyes and soft curves had been extinguished with her tale.

"I am pleased to see you looking so healthy," she said, "for I am looking forward to visiting you every day, Mr Lenin. I have stories of my family I wish to share with you, so you can understand how very deeply I miss them."

He did not open his eyes. At least he could do that. Still she did not leave.

"I can see you are tired, Mr Lenin, so I will leave you soon. But I will be back tomorrow. And I will be back the day after that as well. You see, the doctors here believe I am a nurse. As far as they know, I will be your private nurse from now until the day you die—and I will do all I can to ensure that day does not come too soon."

Hoping to chase her away, he made the only sound he could: a raspy, choking kind of growl in his throat.

"You will be pleased to hear I have incorporated a new medicine into your daily routine, sir. It is quite effective, I've found. If I were able, I would take it myself, though I am not sure it would help me. My trouble is that every minute of every day, I see once more your soldiers having their way with my sisters and my mother. I was helpless to stop them, for you, sir, had me occupied. Do you not recall me now? Do you not recall ripping my hair as you dragged me down? Smashing a rock on my brow to keep me quiet? Shredding my tunic with your knife? Sure you remember that, how you let your knife dig deep enough that I now bear a scar the length of my torso?"

The memory was vague, but it slowly came to him. Fascinating. How had the girl not died that day?

She had left a small bag by the edge of the curtain, and now reached for it. "I would love to say I do not remember what happened next, but I do. You used me, hoping to tear me apart from the outside in. I was your slave, Mr Lenin." She stepped closer, her lips tightened to a hard edge. "But you failed. I was not destroyed, though I will never forget. I wish you had a voice today, for I have a question only you could answer. I would like to ask how you dared accuse the wealthy of treating us like slaves. How you thought taking away our lives and our ability to make a living was your right."

Her slender fingers drew a pair of gloves from the bag. Strange. The room was not overly cool. When each finger was neatly wrapped in leather, she pulled out an even smaller bag and stepped directly to him.

"My trouble is I cannot stop seeing what happened," she said. "I would not like anyone to suffer as I have, and so I have come to make sure you do not have to deal with that."

In the next instant, she pried his eyes apart with her thumb and forefinger while her other hand gathered what he belatedly recognized as chili pepper flakes from the bag. Her smile was the last thing he saw before she set his eyes on fire.

"I'll see you tomorrow, Mr Lenin!" she called cheerily, leaving him to his own private hell. "I look forward to that!"

No one would hear. No one would come.

Chapter Forty-Five

Emanuel Nobel
Baden Baden, 1923

"I cannot go to every event," Emanuel snapped, scanning the latest letter from the Nobel Foundation. The constant requests for his presence at public events had finally caught up with him, and he had more important things to which he must attend. "Tell them I am occupied that day."

"Sir, it is for the prize in Literature. You told me to remind you of that a month ago, when you promised you would go."

He glared at the butler from under heavy black brows sprinkled with silver. "You are too efficient for your own good, Stefan."

"Thank you, sir."

He supposed he should go, after all. The Prize presentations were important to the family name. The original, the Ludvig Nobel Prize, had been awarded in 1896 and 1898, and a final award had been given out during the turbulent year of 1905 and then frozen for political reasons. The Alfred Nobel Prize had been an annual event ever since its inception in 1901. After that, Rothschild had started up the Emanuel Nobel Oil Prize, which had been awarded in 1909, 1910, 1911, and 1914. That particular award was no longer a concern. He had sworn long ago that he would not sponsor that award for as long as Baku was occupied by the Bolsheviks. That policy still stood. Sometimes he could almost forget what he'd left behind. Never entirely, though. And sometimes it came back to him like a tidal wave, dwarfing any other concern he might be facing. On those days he did what he could to lift his spirits by reminding himself that he had helped the people of Baku, given them hope and strength before the Bolsheviks had come. Except that by establishing the new world of Baku, by creating the treasure trove to the rest of the world, he and the other oil barons had presented an undeniable temptation which brought out the worst in Man.

He had been there, a player in the opening moves of the great game. He had heard the mutterings of discontent, and though he had done what he could to improve the workers' lives, the voices had grown to misguided battle cries. He had watched the millions of oppressed workers rise up, reaching for freedom, only to be cut down by a newer, shinier sword. The whole world had stood at the sidelines, watching the great game, helpless observers of both the triumphs and the tragedies.

He would never forget. The world would never forget.

"You have a visitor, sir." The butler pursed his lips in a clear sign of disapproval. "He declined to tell me his name. I gather it is a friendly visit."

Emanuel leaned back in his chair, intrigued. "Show him in, please."

Stefan exited the room then returned shortly with a young man Emanuel vaguely recognized.

"Orkhan?"

His former stable-hand bowed low. "Your Excellency. I am honored that you remember me."

Emanuel stared at him, bewildered, though he waved him forward in welcome. "Sit. Please."

"Yes, sir." The young man looked relieved to sit, though he did so awkwardly. In their old life, he never would have sat in Emanuel's presence.

"You must tell me how you come to be here, so far from your home."

Orkhan hesitated.

"Stefan," Emanuel said, glancing up at his butler. "Tea, please." After he left, Emanuel indicated the black patch covering the boy's left eye. "What is this?"

Orkhan's fingers went self-consciously to his face. "A memento from the Bolsheviks."

The guilt, Emanuel supposed, would never fade. He would forever be tortured by the knowledge that it had been his successes, his riches which had subjected his servants to such horrors. Still, they had told him long ago that he must not feel this way. They were grateful, they had said, for everything he had done. He tried to remember that when the memories overwhelmed him.

"I am very pleased to see you."

"I feel the same way, Your Excellency."

He shook his head. "Please do not call me that. I am no longer Russian, and I left the title behind. I am simply me."

"Yes, sir."

So many questions flew through Emanuel's head, but he wondered if he was brave enough to ask any of them. He took a deep breath for courage then leaned forward over his desk, fingers linked before him.

"Tell me all that you know. The house?"

"Gone, sir."

What bothered Emanuel the most was how that simple admission had been delivered without any trace of sentiment. As if all the destruction and horror had become so commonplace it no longer made an impact on people's hearts.

"And ... the servants? Elbek?"

At this, Orkhan weakened slightly. "Elbek set us free. He took us to the shelter you had built, and we ran. This," he said, indicating his eye, "was something I picked up later on. What you did for us, sir ... we will never forget."

"Did Elbek join you?" But he knew the answer already. His butler could not have escaped.

Orkhan shook his head. "I do not believe he survived, sir. But he is the reason I am here." He reached to the floor, to a bag he had left beside him, and pulled out a box which he set on the desk between them. "He asked me to bring this to you, and I swore to him I would. It is the least I could do, sir."

Curious, Emanuel opened the box and pulled out a well wrapped package from within. After the first layer of paper had been removed, he already knew what it contained. His need to see the treasure set his hands shaking so hard he was afraid he would shatter it.

When at last he cradled it in his palm, Emanuel raised his eyes. "You brought me the Ice Egg." He shook his head with wonder. "But how?"

"Elbek said he wanted to thank you. Before the Bolsheviks came, he buried it so I could bring it to you."

All at once Emanuel was in Baku, watching his world burn to ashes. Unable to think, his eyes went to the translucent white egg, to its exquisite snowflake etchings and the perfect line of tiny seed pearls around its middle. He undid its latch, needing to see the tiny platinum watch inside, still sparkling with rose-cut diamonds.

He looked up at Orkhan, his vision blurred by tears. "Thank you." Then he closed his eyes and brought Elbek's image to his mind. "Thank you, my friend," he whispered.

Chapter Forty-Six

Emanuel had not dared to hope he might ever see her again. When Julie Gold stepped into his office a few weeks later, as stunning and vital as she had always been, Emanuel simply stared. The years had very little effect on her. The last time he had seen her had been outside the Angleterre Hotel, killing men with her own hands. The last he had heard ...

"Hello, Emanuel," she purred, walking closer.

"Julie?"

"What is it?" She glanced to either side, but he knew by her smirk that she knew exactly what was happening. "You look like you just saw a ghost."

"Ray said nothing about you when we spoke. I heard you had—"

"Been shot? Would you like to see my scar?"

She eyed him coyly from under her lashes, almost hidden under the negligible brim of her *cloche* hat. She had cut her hair, he saw, shaping it into the popular new bob, and though he knew her appearance reflected the times he thought it unfortunate. Her hair had been deliciously long.

"The rumors were true? Dear God. I thought you were dead!"

From the look in her eyes, so had she. "Ray dove in after me, and they just about got him as well. I still am amazed he was able to find me. The surgeons somehow saved me, and recovery was a long, painful process, I'll admit. The bullet had lodged very close to my heart."

"As you are to mine! Julie, my dear. Come here!"

They embraced, and he almost expected to fall right back into their own pattern, but something had changed. Her gaze was still fond as she drew away, but it was not quite as sultry as before. A veil of sadness had fallen over the captivating hazel eyes. Perhaps the nearness of death had changed her. Or maybe it was simply the reality of the tragic times they had survived.

"Where have you been?"

"Here and there," she said vaguely. "Being a 'spy', as you like to call me."

"Did you know that I saw you in action once?"

"Of course you did, my dear," she said, the sensual flirt all over again.

"Not that kind of action, though I did appreciate your expertise in that as well."

She chuckled. "All right, then. To what are you referring?"

"I saw you outside the Angleterre Hotel that day."

"You were there?"

"Doing a little shopping. You were ..." He hesitated, searching for the right word. "Astounding. Absolutely astounding. I had never seen anything like that."

"I hope I did not shock you."

"You did! But not in a bad way. You were magnificent."

"Thank you," she said, almost shy. "Just doing my job."

"And now? Are you still in the Middle East?"

"It seems I cannot get enough of the oil—or the adventure," she said wryly. "Who knows what may happen next? I would not want to miss it, whatever it is."

"I suppose Baku was a good testing ground for an intelligence operative such as yourself."

"I would say so. If you can survive the workings of Baku, you can handle any intrigue! The Great Game continues, after all."

She was as lovely as ever, strong and brave, but underneath the tough exterior he knew she was vulnerable. He had seen it, and he had held her when she needed his strength.

"Are you happy?"

He was relieved she did not give him the easy answer. They had been honest with each other in the past, and he would have been disappointed if that had changed.

Her expression was wistful. "I am not unhappy. Considering the wildness of my life, I must admit very little ever changes when it comes to my overall happiness. Sometimes I think I might have met my match, but something always happens. I will survive as I always have."

"And you are fulfilled by this path you still follow?"

He was surprised to see a tear skim down her cheek. "I cannot imagine living any other life but this. I suppose that is because I have not known anything else, but even then ... Could I have lived a simple life? Content with a husband, children, and a day to day existence which involved neither clandestine adventures nor bloodshed?" She hesitated. "Perhaps with the right man. Perhaps with you. But no. I am what I am, Emanuel. What about you? Are you happy?"

"I am well." He had no need to share with her the grief he could not shed. She knew it just as well as he did. "I miss our time together. I hope you will visit more often."

She pouted slightly, a poignant reminder of those evenings in Baku and St Petersburg. "I would be insulted if I was not invited."

"Consider it an open invitation."

Her head tilted to one side. "I did some research before I came, and I discovered something I thought you would find more than just a little interesting."

"What is that?"

"James said you were looking for someone: Taghiyev's daughter, Leyla."

Emanuel's pulse jumped. "Yes. I had not heard from her since she left Baku."

"It was her, am I right? It was her all along."

Emanuel had never told anyone about Leyla, about how his heart still ached at the thought of her. Even now he wanted to protect his secret, keep her safe. But Julie was watching him closely. Her life was full of secrets; her livelihood depended upon them. He supposed he should be proud that she had not figured his out until then.

"Only from afar," he admitted. It was a relief to say it out loud. "But yes. I have always loved her."

"I know where she is."

She was married with three sons. He knew that from her book. He was unsure if she was happy in her life or not, for she was unclear. And that was not his business. How was she now? Where did she live? Was she still writing? Did she ever think of him?

Zeynalabdin was gone. There was no longer a reason why he could not declare his love for Leyla. And yet ...

He had asked himself a million times what he would do if he ever found her. Now here stood Julie, holding exactly the information he needed to make it a reality. Had he any right to walk into her life? To rip her from it and bring her here? For he knew she would come if he asked. He remembered the love in her eyes that she did not dare speak aloud, and it had matched his own. But he was no longer a young man, and those memories came from a long time ago. Another lifetime.

"Emanuel?"

He blinked. "I am sorry. I was ... elsewhere."

"Do you want to know where she is?"

So many thoughts swirled through his head, so many regrets tangled in his heart. "I do not know."

Her eyes were sad, but he did not know if the sorrow was for him or her. She leaned forward and put her soft hands against his face, then she pressed a tender kiss to his lips. "If you decide, my dear Emanuel, find me. You know I will help you."

He kissed her back, smiling gently. "I do. And I thank you. Promise me you will take care of yourself, Julie. You mean a great deal to me."

He did not see her again, but Colonel Ray eventually came to see him, bearing news. Julie was living in Iran, he said.

"She cannot seem to leave the intrigue of oil behind."

"It is an interesting business, to be sure. I have no doubt she is doing well." Thinking of Julie brought to mind a quote, for he had enjoyed their little game. This one was from the American poet, Robert Frost. He was sure she would have been able to identify it. " 'In three words'," he quoted, " 'I can sum up everything I've learned about life: it goes on.' "

Ray nodded but did not react to the quote. "It does indeed. And what is next for the great Emanuel Nobel?"

"Well, as I am sure you know, so far I have given up the possibility of enjoying a peaceful retirement."

"I noticed. You have become a ferocious freedom and democracy fighter, countering the Bolsheviks at every turn. I hear about your anti-Bolshevik Committee everywhere I go."

He was glad to hear the news had spread. His anti-Bolshevik force united an army of influential businessmen, scientists, bankers, artists, and other professionals who participated in creating and spreading anti-Soviet propaganda. Stalin and the young Soviet government were constantly being denied banking credits and loans, which effectively blocked their economic and financial endeavors worldwide.

"I do not always win the legal battles against Lenin, Stalin, and the rest of the Bolshevik regime, but I keep them occupied, I like to think. I continue to fight them however I can. How can I not?"

"I wish you all the best with your endeavors. Once again, you fight for the people."

They parted as friends, and Emanuel wondered if it was the last he would see of him. Life had changed dramatically over the years, and so many people were gone from it. In Baku he had been surrounded by people, both friends and enemies. He had been courted by the rich and famous.

It goes on. Emanuel had everything a man could want, and he was still surrounded by friends, though they were not the same people as before. Those days were done, but Emanuel was not. It was a new century, a new world, and

Emanuel was still one of the wealthiest men in the world. He had a lot of living to do and a lot of work to be done.

Chapter Forty-Seven

Helsinki, Finland, 1923

Stalin was shorter than Emanuel had expected. No wonder President Truman called him "little squirt". The youth Emanuel had once witnessed passionately leading a revolution through the streets of Baku had hardened into a cold, ruthless tyrant, and his handsome features had been scarred by smallpox. When they shook hands, Stalin tucked his left arm behind his back, keeping it hidden from view, but Emanuel noticed. At the age of twelve, extensive surgery following an accident involving a horse-drawn carriage had resulted in Stalin's arm becoming permanently short and stiff at the elbow, and he was painfully aware of it. Any portrait artists hoping to render Stalin's image had to be very careful to hide both the scars and the arm. Unflattering depictions occasionally resulted in the artist being shot.

"Emanuel Nobel," Stalin said, the corners of his thick moustache lifting briefly. "We meet at last. I must say that I was surprised to hear from you."

"It seemed appropriate, since we were both here in Finland, a neutral country." The hand he shook was small but the grip was firm. "I thought we might discuss any interest the Soviet Union might have with regard to purchasing BraNobel assets."

"So. You have come to negotiate with the enemy. What a delicious irony. Let us walk."

The Esplanadi Park was in full bloom, its summer gardens rioting around monuments, yet not many people interrupted the area's serenity. This was easily understood, since Stalin's guards walked ahead, behind, and around him at all time. No one would want to be in the wrong place at the wrong time if it meant being near Stalin.

"You think the Soviet Union has riches enough to do such a thing? Mr Nobel, I thought you were better informed." Despite his disparaging words, greed sparkled in Stalin's dark eyes. "War has not been easy on my country's coffers. After all, BraNobel was nationalized, as were all the subsoil resources, and they now belong to us, the Soviet people."

"I am informed enough to know that American and European companies will be settling here within the next decade or so, bringing with them the western technology your country needs in order to rebuild." He shrugged, feigning the same indifference displayed by Stalin. "What better way to entice such wealth than with the even greater riches promised by oil?"

Stalin pressed the line of his moustache with two fingers as if to ensure it stayed in place. "You are correct in that," he said, "and it is good that they are coming here. We are already fifty or a hundred years behind the advanced countries. We must make good this distance in ten years. Either we do it, or they will crush us." He stopped walking and stared out at the trees around them, hands linked behind his back. "It is a shame, really. We did not always need them."

Emanuel stopped a few feet away, listening.

"It was a great time, was it not? I had everyone so confused," Stalin said, smiling wistfully. "The whole world. No one knew what would happen, and they all believed they were in charge." He pointed one thick finger skyward. "But I was always the one holding their strings. I am the puppeteer. The great J.D. Rockefeller believes he is a mastermind, and I will give him credit. He thinks intricately. He is able to make things happen the way he wants, most of the time. Libby as well. Such a smart man. But not smart enough. I outmaneuvered them both, and they never saw it coming. Leaders come and go, but the people remain. Only the people are immortal."

Emanuel was tempted to interrupt the man's reverie, ask him if that immortality included the millions of innocent people he had killed, but he decided to wait for just the right moment.

"All your little spies—like that minx, Julie Gold, and Colonel Ray holding the end of her leash—they were mere pawns. Ah yes, I see you are surprised. You see? I fooled you and them as well. Of course I saw them with you. And what of your pathetic little Azerbaijani Democratic Republic?" The moustache lifted with a sneer. "An insect to me. I crushed it without any effort at all."

"Just you?"

"Eh?"

"Since you have always claimed to care about the working man, I'm certain you would give credit to your Red Army, to your Bolsheviks, not to yourself."

Stalin flicked an eyebrow. "Touché."

Emanuel turned and began to slowly walk away. "You may have done great damage with your revolution, but you did not defeat me. You tried, certainly, but you failed."

It was an invitation too blatant for Stalin to ignore. He blustered up beside Emanuel and kept pace. "How is that? You are no longer the king of Baku with slaves cleaning your garden and shining the stairs of your castle. You no longer sell oil like it is water and use petty cash to buy pretty Fabergé eggs for all your friends."

"No, but I am still very rich. I can do whatever I want. My family is safe, and my life is a good one. I have no regrets." He shot Stalin a sideways glance. "And I have done it all without knowingly causing harm to anyone. You, on the other hand, have killed many, including some of your closest allies and compatriots. I wonder if anyone in the entire world trusts you."

Concern crossed Stalin's brow, to be replaced by a stubborn petulance. "If they do, that is their mistake and they deserve what they get. Everybody has a right to be stupid, but some people abuse the privilege. I trust no one. Not even myself."

There had been many moments in Emanuel's life when he had been unsure, when he had questioned his actions, but he could not say he did not trust himself. That was a dangerous statement, and it came from the dark thoughts of a madman.

And that madman would, most likely, never forgive him what he had just said. From now on, Emanuel's life would be in constant danger. Cheka agents were in abundance in Finland, and every one of them was ready to fulfill the orders of their leader at any time. In an attempt to possibly fix his potentially fatal mistake, he changed his tone slightly.

"Everyone needs modern technologies and investments," he said pragmatically. "My friends at the Committee and I could become partners in the New Economic Policy being carried out by your government."

Stalin said nothing for a few steps. A tiny red squirrel dashed across the path before them, the tufts on the tips of his ears ridiculously long. Emanuel watched it disappear into the trees and was glad the little animal was quick; Stalin would have thought nothing of kicking the squirrel out of his way had it been closer. Especially now that Emanuel had raised his ire.

"You say you are safe and happy. That you are extremely wealthy. And yet you are here with me, peddling your oil once again."

"I am a good businessman, with a heart for people and loyalty towards friends," Emanuel agreed, "and the Soviet Union needs capital. Oil will attract the money you need, and it will always have that power. This is a good investment for you and your country, Mr Stalin. After all, we may have just seen the end of the First Oil War, but the Second Oil War is imminent."

What Emanuel did not mention was that petroleum would be a short-term boon for the region and for the Bolsheviks. In the long term, it would be a curse. One that men would fight over forever.

"So you are still playing your game, Mr Nobel?"

"Oh yes," Emanuel assured him, allowing the slow confidence of his smile to emerge. Through this final conversation, his beliefs had been confirmed. Stalin would never be a good business partner. He was unreliable and unrealistic. Based on today, he would do all he could to strengthen the anti-Bolshevik Committee. "I am not the kind of man to leave in the middle of a match. Like Kipling said, 'When everyone is dead, the Great Game is finished. Not before.' "

Epilogue

<u>*Checkmate:*</u>
Threatening the capture of the enemy king such that it cannot escape. This wins the game for the attacking side.

CPSIA information can be obtained
at www.ICGtesting.com
Printed in the USA
LVHW091537210520
656176LV00003B/739